"Let me explain this licking business, then."

"Never let it be said that Vikings do not make themselves clear. You look good enough to lick, Maire the Fair. All over. Stark naked."

"You are a perverted man, Rurik."

"Yea," he agreed with a half-smile. "That is one of the good things about me. Women love it."

"Never let it be said that you are an excessively modest man." Her upper lip curled back in a snarl. "Well, I am not one of your women, and will not be."

"You were once."

"Never again."

He put up a hand, his eyes sparkling with the love of combat. "Protest all you want, Maire. This is my promise to you. Every day I bear your mark, you will bear mine. On fair days I will work with your men and mine to build up the defenses of your castle against the MacNabs, but I will devote the long nights to you and you alone in your bedchamber. On rainy days, there will be more time to devote to your marking, and we might just spend day *and* night in bed. I have so much to teach you . . . so many ways to mark you."

Romances by Sandra Hill

The Reluctant Viking
The Outlaw Viking
The Tarnished Lady
The Bewitched Viking
The Blue Viking
The Viking's Captive (formerly My Fair Viking)
A Tale of Two Vikings
Viking in Love
The Viking Takes a Knight

The Last Viking
Truly, Madly Viking
The Very Virile Viking
Wet and Wild
Hot and Heavy

Frankly, My Dear
Sweeter Savage Love
Desperado
Love Me Tender

SANDRA HILL

The BLUE VIKING

AVON
An Imprint of HarperCollins*Publishers*

AVON BOOKS
An Imprint of HarperCollins*Publishers*
10 East 53rd Street
New York, New York 10022-5299

ISBN 978-0-06-201901-1
www.avonromance.com

First Avon Books paperback printing: March 2011

Printed in the U.S.A.

10 9 8 7 6 5 4 3 2 1

This book is dedicated to my mother-in-law,
Ann Harper, who was born in Scotland and
whose maiden name was Campbell. She was
as generous and proud and full of wit as the
Campbell clan depicted in this book.
To her, family was so important . . .
just like my Maire Campbell.

"No one can speak with certainty
Of what is possible
For people in love."

"He wins whose wooing is best."

"I realized as I lay amongst the rushes,
Waiting for the girl I loved,
That, although she meant everything to me,
She was no more mine for that."

HÁVÁMÁL, A COLLECTION
OF OLD NORSE POEMS
Pre-11th Century

The BLUE VIKING

PROLOGUE

KAUPANG, THE NORTHLANDS, A.D. 935

Before he was a rogue, he was a rascal . . .

"Pig boy! Pig boy! Runt of the litter!"

Rurik's head jerked up with alarm on recognizing the band of youths in the market square shouting taunts at him. "Thor's toenails!" he muttered, and began to run for his life . . . as fast as his skinny, eight-year-old legs would carry him.

Normally, Rurik would have relished the sounds and aromas of the busy trading town. Roast mutton turning on a spit. Oat cakes dripping with honey. Mulled ale sizzling around a hot poker. The clang, clang, clang of the sword maker's anvil. The brays and bleats and neighs and moos and cackles and quacks of various animals. The importuning pleas of the vendors, cajoling passersby to sample their wares.

The ruffians chased after him, as he knew they would, tossing insults like sharp burrs on a north wind. Some of them stuck . . . if not to his skin, to his oversensitive soul.

"Come back 'ere, you bloody bugger."

"Wha' he needs is a good dunk in an icy fjord to wipe off that hog stink."

"Do ya think the starvling suckles on the sow's teat? Mayhap that's why he's so ugly. Ha, ha, ha!"

"Oink, oink, oink!"

Even as he puffed loudly, his arms pumping wildly to match his strides, Rurik's eyes watered at their biting words.

Why do they hate me so?

It mattered not that they were Norse, as he was.

It mattered not that he had only seen eight winters, and they more than eleven.

It mattered not that he was small and frail of frame, while they were strapping youthlings.

Oh, it was true he smelled, from lack of bathing and from living amongst the pigs, but his pursuers were not so fragrant themselves. For a certainty, none of them, himself included, had bathed since last spring.

But what had he ever done to them that warranted such viciousness? They were as poor and ill-dressed and mistreated as he was.

Could it be that some people enjoy meanness for its own sake?

Mus' be.

The first to catch up with him was Ivar, the blacksmith's son . . . the meanest of the lot. Rurik was just beyond the stall of Gudrod the Tanner. *Phew! Talk about malodors!* Right now, the leather worker was spreading chicken dung on a stretched animal skin—an ancient method for curing hides. Ivar lunged forward, knocking him to the ground.

"Hey, now!" Gudrod yelled. "Get out of here, you scurvy whelps. Ye'll ruin me bizness."

Without a sideways glance at the merchant, Ivar stood and dragged Rurik by the back of his filthy tunic to a nearby wooded area. There, in the ice-crusted snow, he began to pummel Rurik in earnest, marking each of his blows with comments such as, "That'll teach you ta run from yer betters." Alas, Rurik was much smaller, and all that he could do was hold his hands over his face protectively.

Ivar's other friends soon caught up and added their jeers and punches to Rurik's battering. Rolling on the snowy ground, they proceeded to wallop him mercilessly.

Suddenly, another voice was heard. "I thought I told you bloody bastards to leave the halfling alone. Some folks're so thickheaded they don' know when their arses are gonna be kicked from here to Hedeby and back."

An ominous silence followed as Rurik's attackers realized that Stigand had arrived. His "protector." The band of malcontents stood as one and began to back away, but not before Stigand grabbed hold of Ivar, their leader. Stigand was only ten years old, but he was big . . . very big . . . for his age. And stonyhearted. More so even than Ivar and his spiteful friends. With his left hand, Stigand lifted Ivar off the ground by grasping his neck. Then he swung his right fist in a wide arc into Ivar's quaking face. Even before the blood started spurting, there was the sound of crunching bone. Ivar's nose had surely been broken . . . perchance even his jaw, too. Stigand landed several other jabs as well, before releasing the now sobbing Ivar to run off after his cowardly companions.

Stigand held out a hand to help Rurik to his feet. Shaking his head with dismay at Rurik, Stigand remarked, "You are pitiful."

"I know," Rurik said, brushing off his tattered braies which now had a few more rips. But he smiled his thanks at his only friend in the world.

Even little Viking boys can dream . . .

A short time later, he and Stigand sat with their backs propped against the pigsty wall. Stigand was playing with a small pig he had named Thumb-Biter. It was the only time Rurik saw any softness on Stigand's face . . . when he hugged and caressed the undersized piglet that had been rejected by its mother. A true runt of the litter when it had been born, it was now flourishing under Stigand's special care.

Rurik's stomach growled with hunger.

Stigand glanced over at him and grinned. "Best you grab a hunk of manchet bread afore the old hag comes home."

Rurik nodded. "I'm in fer one of her beatin's, fer sure, once she sees I been fightin' again."

"I'd hardly call what you do fightin'," Stigand observed drolly.

"Jus' stayin' alive. Jus' stayin alive," Rurik answered with a sigh. "That's my kind of fightin' . . . fer now, leastways."

"Well, you won't be alive fer long if that bitch Hervor catches you. *Poor little ungrateful orphan boy.*" That last was a mimicking of the phrase the old hag liked to use with them afore their beatings with a birch switch.

Both boys grinned at each other.

Rurik and Stigand were among the dozen "orphans" who had been rescued . . . if it could be called that . . . by Ottar the pig farmsteader. Ottar was not so bad, and his intentions were pure. Unfortunately, his wife, Hervor, was not so good-hearted. Also, unfortunately, Ottar was gone from home much of the time. While he was away, all of the orphan boys were worked nigh to death and whipped for the least infraction.

Stigand had been "rescued" after running away several years ago from his birth-home where he'd suffered horrible abuses from his father and older brothers. Hard to believe that anything could be worse than the beatings that Hervor levied, but even at Rurik's young age, he could see that it was so. The blankness that came into

Stigand's eyes on occasion bespoke some unspeakable pain.

Rurik's story was entirely different. In some of the harsh northern climes, there were still Viking people who abandoned newborn babes deemed too frail to survive . . . like Rurik's father, a noble Norse jarl who demanded perfection in his offspring.

Vikings were not the only ones to practice such cruelty to children. In the Saxon lands, and many other Christian kingdoms, the most socially accepted method for getting rid of unwanted children, whether they were illegitimate or imperfect, was to donate them to a local monastery, where life often became hell for the orphan. On the surface it would appear as if these acts were great sacrifices made by loving parents to God, but, in fact, they were a respectable method of cutting off the weakest limbs of a family tree.

Rurik had been born early, small of size and ailing. After one look at him, his father had forced the midwives to lay his naked body out in the freezing snow. It was there Ottar had found him. His mother had died soon after the birthing of childbed fever.

Sometimes Rurik saw his father in the market town, riding his fine horse, laughing with his comrades. Never did he glance Rurik's way, though he was surely aware of his existence. Once, when Rurik was five and had learned of his birth, he made the trek up the hills to his father's grand stead. What a sight he must have been! Half-frozen, snot-nosed, wearing his beggarly garments. He'd been turned away rudely at the gate by none other than his own father, who told him never to return. "No runtling such as you is a get of my blood," he'd added. As far as his father was concerned, he was dead.

"Someday, I'm gonna be so big and strong that no one

will be able to beat me," Rurik promised himself aloud, wiping at tears that welled in his eyes.

"Could be possible." Stigand was still petting his piglet, which kept nipping at his big thumb, rooting for food. "Some lads do not get their full growth till they are twelve and more. Besides that, you can build muscle with hard work, that I know for certain."

"What? I do not work hard enough here on the pigstead? From dawn till dark?"

Stigand elbowed Rurik playfully, which caused Rurik to wince. Ivar must have bruised a rib or two.

" 'Tis another kind of muscle-building work I speak of," Stigand explained. At Rurik's frown of puzzlement, he added, " 'Tis the kind of exercise fighting men engage in. Never fear. I can teach you."

Rurik blinked at his friend, grateful for that small glimmer of hope . . . which gave him courage to hope for more. "It's not just my size," he went on. "When I am a grown man, no one will be able to mock my looks, either, for I intend to be so handsome all the maids will swoon."

"Tall and strong *and* beauteous?" Stigand began to laugh uproariously, he and Thumb-Biter rolling on the ground with glee. Apparently, some dreams were based in reality, and some dreams were just . . . well, dreams.

But dreams were all that Rurik had.

CHAPTER ONE

SCOTLAND, A.D. 955

Clueless men on a road trip . . . and not a longship in sight . . .

"Do witches fall in love?"

"Aaarrgh!" Rurik groaned at the halfwit query that had just been directed at him. He would have put his face in his hands if they were not so filthy from his having fallen ignominiously into a peat bog a short while ago. Distastefully picking pieces of musty moss from his wet sleeve, he glared at Jostein, who had asked the barmy question, then snarled, "How in bloody hell would I know if witches fall in love? I'm a Viking, not an expert in the dark arts."

"Yea, but you have lain with a witch. One would think you have firsthand knowledge of such things," declared Bolthor the Giant. Bolthor was Rurik's very own personal skald, *for the love of Odin!* He'd been shoved off on him at the inception of this three-year trip to hell . . . Scotland, that is . . . by his good friend, Tykir Thorksson . . . well, mayhap not such a good friend, if he'd tricked him into taking with him the world's worst poet.

Rurik would have glared at Bolthor, too, if he were not the size of a warhorse. Bolthor—a fierce fighting man—did not take kindly to glares. He was oversensitive by half.

Jostein, on the other hand, turned red in the face and neck and ears at having earned Rurik's disfavor, and Rurik immediately regretted his hasty words. It was not Jostein's fault Rurik was in such an ill temper. Rurik was well aware that the boy, who had seen only fifteen winters, thought he walked on water. *Foolish youthling!*

"Well, I was just thinking," Jostein stammered, "that mayhap your problem stems from the witch being in love with you."

The *problem* Jostein referred to was the jagged blue mark running down the center of Rurik's face . . . the selfsame mark that was at the heart of his three-year quest to find the damnable witch who'd put it there. . . . Actually five years if one counted those first two years when he'd only searched half-heartedly and spent the winters in Norway and Iceland.

Just then he noticed the reddish-brown stains on his hands and clothing. 'Twas from the tannin in the bogs. Holy Thor! If he was not careful, he would carry not only the blue mark, but red ones, as well. Could his life get any worse than this? Rubbing his hands briskly on the legs of his braies, he grumbled aloud, "Since when do wenches show their love by marking a man for life?"

"Couldst be that you hurt the witch's feelings?" Bolthor offered. Bolthor thought he knew a lot about feelings . . . being a poet and all. "Mayhap Jostein's thinking is not so lackbrained. Mayhap the witch was in love with you, and you hurt her feelings, and she put the mark on you for revenge. What think you of that notion?"

"A fool's bolt is soon shot," Rurik mumbled under his breath.

"What's that supposed to mean?" Bolthor wanted to know.

"Not a thing," Rurik replied with a sigh. "I was just

thinking about Scotsmen," he lied. But to himself, he translated, *Dumb people don't mind sharing their opinions.* "Besides, methinks it matters not *why* Maire the Witch put the mark on me. I just want it removed so I can resume a normal life."

"But—" Bolthor started.

Rurik put up a hand to halt further words on the subject, but Stigand the Berserk, another of his retainers, was already joining in. "The witch made a laughingstock of you. Everywhere you go, people smirk behind your back and make jokes about you."

Rurik frowned. He did not need to hear this.

And, really, what could Stigand be thinking . . . to risk provoking him so? His trusted friend pushed all bounds by reminding him that people were making jest of him; he knew better than most what a sore point such mockery had always been with Rurik.

"You should let me lop off her head," Stigand suggested gleefully. And he was serious.

Was that not like Stigand . . . ever the protector? Rurik could not help being touched at the fierce soldier's attempt to shield him from pain. But Rurik was quick to state, "You are not lopping off any more heads." The bloodlust was always high in Stigand and had to be reined in constantly. He had a habit of decapitating his enemies with a single blow of his trusty battle-ax, appropriately named Blood-Lover. Throughout their three-year quest, they'd constantly had to restrain Stigand, lest a sheepherder or unwary wayfarer get in his path when he was in a dark mood. So intense were his berserk rages on occasion that Stigand actually growled like an animal and bit his own shield. In fact, just last sennight, he'd almost decapitated a Scottish princeling who'd winked repeatedly at him. Turned out the young nobleman was not a sodomite, but had suffered from a nervous tic since birth. "Leastways, do not think of lopping off Maire's head till she has removed the mark."

"I know, I know—" the twins, Vagn and Toste, said as one. 'Twas eerie the way the two grown men, identical in appearance right down to the clefts in their chins, would come out with the same thought.

Vagn spoke first. "I have an idea. Now, do not be offended when I tell you this, Rurik . . ."

Toste snickered as if he knew what his brother was about to say.

Rurik was sure he was going to be offended.

"You always had a certain word-fame for woman-luck, but perchance you have lost the knack," Vagn elaborated, "and that is what caused the witch to mark you. 'Twas frustration, pure and simple."

"The knack?" Rurik inquired, against his better judgment.

"Yea, the ability to bring a woman to pleasure," Vagn explained. "Wenches like the bedsport, too, you know. I certainly have that knack." Vagn puffed out his chest.

"Me, too," chimed in Toste, Bolthor, Stigand . . . even Jostein in a squeaky, not-quite-man voice.

Rurik suspected that the twins were using his mission as an excuse to sample women all across Scotland. This was new carnal territory to explore.

How did I ever gather such a bizarre retinue? Rurik thought. *Which god did I insult to bring on such misfortune?* But what he said was, "The only thing I know for a certainty is that witch-hunting is becoming one immense pain in the arse." He was not exaggerating when he said that. Truly, a Viking should be on the high seas sailing a longship, not bouncing his rump on the back of a horse for days at a time. Portly Saxons, or dour Scotsmen, might not mind the constant jostling, but Vikings, being physically fitter than the average man and having less fat on those nether regions, were better suited to other modes of transportation, in Rurik's opinion. He had to grin at the egotism of that observation.

Mayhap, he should suggest that Bolthor create a saga about it.

On the other hand, mayhap not.

Based on past experience, it would have a title like "Viking Men With Hard Arses" or some such nonsense.

All five men fixed their gazes on him, and he realized that he had been chuckling to himself witlessly.

With a sigh of despair at his own disintegrating brain, he sank down onto a boulder. Picking up a small knife, he began to scrape peat moss and other slimy substances—like mud mixed with twigs and grass—from his leather half boots, which had been made in Cordoba of the softest skins and cost three gold coins.

"This witch-hunting business is becoming bloody bothersome," Rurik continued in a low grumble, but not before spitting out yet another clump of what tasted like soggy charcoal.

They all nodded vigorously in agreement.

Bolthor lumbered up and loomed over him, adjusting the black eye patch over the socket of one eye that had been lost in the Battle of Brunanburh many years before, when he was hardly older than Jostein. He squinted at him through his good eye, then put a palm over his mouth to hide his smile, as if there was humor in a grown man falling into a peat bog.

"You know, Rurik, the Scots poets have a practice of writing odes, unlike we Norsemen, who prefer a good saga. Dost think I could put together an ode or two just for practice? How about 'Ode to a Peat Bog'?"

Everyone guffawed with mirth, except Rurik.

"How about 'Ode to a One-Eyed Dead Skald'?" Rurik inquired.

"It does not have the same ring to it," Bolthor said.

I would like to give you a ring, you dumb dolt. More like a ringing in the ears from a sound whack aside the head with a broadsword.

Then Bolthor added, more soberly, "Methinks 'tis time to put an end to this fruitless venture and admit defeat."

"A Viking never admits defeat," Rurik reminded him.

Bolthor shook his head in disagreement. "Vikings never admit that they admit defeat." That was the kind of daft logic Bolthor came up with all the time.

"I say we behead every Scotsman and Scotswoman we come across," Stigand interjected. "That will flush the witch out of her lair, I predict."

Everyone looked at Stigand with horror. It was one thing to spill sword-dew in the midst of battle, but to kill innocent people . . . even if they were scurvy Scots? 'Twas unthinkable.

Vikings had their ethics, despite the English monk-historians in their scriptoriums, who liked to picture Norsemen as rapers and pillagers. Hah! Every good Viking knew that the Church amassed gold and silver in its chalices and whatnots just to tempt Norsemen. Besides, it was a well-known fact that Vikings invigorated the races of all those Christian countries they conquered. And didn't they embrace Christianity itself . . . even if it was only a token embrace?

But, back to Stigand. Rurik knew about the horrors that Stigand had suffered in his youth . . . horrors that had caused his mind to split. But what had happened to him over the years to make the adult man so hard?

Fortunately, Rurik did not have to respond to Stigand's suggestion because one of the twins, Toste, spoke up. "I have grown accustomed to the blue mark on your face, Rurik. Really, 'tis not so bad. If that is the only reason for continuing this quest . . . well, perchance you should reconsider."

"The wenches seem to have no problem with it, either," Vagn added. "Yestereve that farmsteader's daughter picked you for swiving above all of us, and I'll have you know that I am renowned for my good looks. Godly handsome is how the wenches describe me."

"I did not swive—" Rurik started to demur, then gave up, throwing his hands in the air with disgust. But then he added drolly, "I thought it was your knack the women coveted."

"That, too," Vagn said with a grin.

"I'm more handsome than you are." Toste challenged his brother.

"Nay, I am more handsome than all of you," Bolthor proclaimed, which was so ridiculous it did not even bear comment.

"I think Rurik is the most handsome," Jostein piped up. Jostein was suffering a severe case of hero worship and had been since Rurik rescued him when he was ten years old from a Saracen slave trader with a proclivity for male children.

"Bugger all of you," Stigand said with a mild roar. "I am the most handsome and anyone who disagrees can taste the flavor of my blade." He rubbed a callused forefinger along the sharp edge of Blood-Lover for emphasis.

No one disagreed with Stigand, though he resembled a wild boar. Mayhap he *was* a handsome fellow, but who could tell how he really looked under his unruly beard and mustache? He had not shaved in the past few years.

"I have three more months left," Rurik told them with a weary sigh. "Theta gave me two years to have the blue mark removed afore she would wed me. And that time does not end till autumn . . . three months from now. I do not intend to give up till then."

"Three months! Twelve more sennights!" Vagn griped. "It might as well be a year. Remember one thing, Rurik. Friends are like lute strings; they must not be strung too tight, and we all in your troop are overstrung, believe you me."

"Lute strings? Lute strings?" Rurik sputtered.

"Precisely," Vagn said. "I am sick to death of moors and Highlands and Lowlands . . . and quarrelsome Scotsmen."

Stigand tilted his head to the side, as if thinking hard. "I rather like the quarrelsome Scotsmen. They give me an excuse to hone my fighting skills." He ducked his head sheepishly and added, "They remind me a bit of us Vikings."

Everyone gawked at him as if he had gone senseless . . . which he probably had, long ago . . . after his first hundred or so kills. Perhaps even long before that.

" 'Tis true," Stigand insisted. "They are proud, and independent, and good fighters. And they hate the Saxons the same as we do. So, we have something in common."

"They hate Vikings, too," Rurik pointed out.

That contradiction went right over Stigand's head. Seeing their lack of accord with him, Stigand continued, "Even their practice of constant reaving—stealing shamelessly from their neighbors—is not unlike us Men of the North who enjoy a-Viking on occasion."

They all shook their heads at Stigand's thinking, even though it had some validity to it.

"What I hate most about Scotland is the haggis," Jostein said, gagging as he spoke. "I swear, 'tis a concoction the Scots devised to poison us Norsemen. 'Tis worse than *gammelost*, and that smelly cheese is very bad."

Rurik nodded in agreement. Once he had been on a sea voyage in which their food stores had been reduced to *gammelost*. By the time their longship had finally arrived back in Norway, all the seamen's breaths reeked like the back end of a goat.

"Well, I for one think Theta was being unfair to give you such an ultimatum. Methinks you should have tossed her into the bed furs then and there," Toste opined. He was tipping a skin of mead to his mouth between words, which probably gave him the courage to speak to his leader so. "Without her maidenhead, her father would have had no choice but to force Theta to exchange vows with you." He belched loudly at the end of his discourse.

"Her father is Anlaf of Lade, a most powerful Norse chieftain," Rurik told Toste, as if he did not already know. "And Theta, even being a fifth daughter, is a most willful wench. She would not come to my bed furs without the vows, and I had no inclination to waste long hours seducing her to change her mind."

In truth, Rurik had been thinking on that very subject of late. Sometimes, he wondered if he really wanted to wed the woman who'd made such demands on him. For a certainty, he was not in love with her . . . nor had he ever been with any woman. At the time, it had seemed the right thing to do. His good friends Eirik and Tykir Thorksson had settled happily into their own marriages. So, he'd purchased a large farmstead on a Norse-inhabited island in the Orkneys. Rurik had never had a real home of his own. He was twenty-eight years old . . . well past the age for settling in and raising a family. What it all boiled down to was that he'd made a decision to wed simply because it had seemed the right thing to do.

After these long intermittent years of scouring the Scottish countryside for an elusive witch, Rurik had changed. For one thing, he'd become a sullen, brooding man. His sense of humor had nigh disappeared. He'd lost his dreams. Bloody hell, he could not even remember what they had been. Too much time for thinking and pondering was causing him to doubt all that he'd thought he wanted. Still, he felt the need to finish what he'd started . . . whether it be the capture of a Scottish witch, or marriage with a Norse princess.

"Actually, 'tis not uncommon for highborn women to make such demands." Bolthor had been speaking while Rurik's mind was wandering. "Remember Gyda, daughter of King Eric of Hordaland. She refused to wed with Harald till he defeated his enemies and united all Norway. And Harald did it, too, but not afore making a vow to never bathe or cut his hair till he completed his mission. Thereafter, he was known as Harald Fairhair."

Everyone knew the story of King Harald, and each sat or stood contemplating Bolthor's words. Moments later, one by one, they turned to gape at Rurik, as if wondering why he had not made such a vow. But then, they knew that Rurik was prideful of his personal appearance, and was known to wear only the best crafted fabrics for his tunics and overmantles, adorned with embroidery and precious brooches of gold or silver. Colored beads were often intertwined in the war braids at the sides of his long hair. Never would he go for an extended period without washing the silky black tresses. They did not call him Rurik the Vain for naught . . . a title he disdained, but had earned.

"Methinks 'tis time for a saga," Bolthor announced.

Everyone groaned . . . softly, so they would not offend the gentle giant.

"What happened to your idea of embarking on odes?" Rurik made the mistake of asking.

Everyone except Bolthor scowled at his lackwittedness, as if they at least knew not to encourage the fellow's less-than-artistic efforts.

"Sagas, odes, poems, eddas, ballads . . . I am willing to try all of them," Bolthor answered optimistically.

Oh, gods!

"This is the saga of Rurik the Great," Bolthor commenced.

"I thought Tykir was the one you called 'great' in your sagas," Rurik said. "You were always saying, 'This is the saga of Tykir the Great.' "

Bolthor waved a hand airily. "There can be more than one great Viking."

Rurik did groan aloud then.

"Well, if you insist." Bolthor apparently decided to change his opening. "This is the saga of Rurik the Greater."

"Greater than what?" someone mumbled sarcastically.

Rurik was about to throw a wad of peat moss at whoever it was who had spoken, but everyone stared at him with seeming innocence.

Bolthor had that dreamy look on his face that he always got when he was inspired to create a new poem. Then he began:

Rurik was a winsome Viking,
Many the maid will attest.
With long black hair
And flashing teeth,
All the wenches were obsessed.
Through many a land
And betwixt many a thigh,
Rurik the Vain Wielded
His seductive moves so spry.
But, lo and behold,

Came a Scottish witch,
Her name was Maire the Fair
Because of her beauty rich,
But also because of her
Fairness pitch.
No mere Viking would use her so,
Boast of his conquest,
Then walk away, no impairment to show.
Thus befell the witch's curse so dark
And the painted face mark.
Now the fierce Norse lackbrain
Is no longer vain.
He is known as Rurik the Blue.
Or sometimes Rurik the Greater . . .
This is true.

Disgusted, Rurik tossed his knife to the ground, giving up on removing the peat sludge from his boots and wool braies. Instead, he stood and stomped off to a nearby lake . . . or what the Scots referred to as a loch. It was a strange land, Scotland. At times, its barren, mountainous landscape could appear soul rendingly bleak, and at others, beautiful, almost in a spiritual sense. Not unlike his own harsh Norway.

The weather was often dreary and dismal. A mist; which the Norse referred to as *haar*, poured from the North Sea, even on warm, clear days, like today.

Hearing a loud screeching noise, Rurik glanced upward to see a large golden eagle soaring lazily over the moors, a young red deer in its powerful talons. No doubt it would make a tasty meal for the birdlings left in some lofty aerie. At times like this, he missed his dog, Beast, a wolfhound that he had left behind at Ravenshire in Northumbria to breed with one of his friend Eirik's bitches.

Yea, there was a beauty of sorts in this stark land he had come to hate so much.

Rurik waded, garments and all, into the icy water. Then, with a teeth-chattering exclamation of "Brrrrr!" and a full-body shiver, he dove underwater and swam till the water cleansed him.

When he finally came up out of the water, he heard Bolthor call out to him, "Dost think it wise to go into the lake without a weapon? The Scottish legends speak of huge monsters that reside in the depths of their lochs . . . monsters that resemble a combination of fish and dragon. Hmmm. I recall one of their epics that relates the story of *Each uisage*, which means something like water horse, and . . ."

Rurik didn't wait for more. He dove underwater once again. He would rather risk fierce water dragons, or freezing some precious body part, than hear another of Bolthor's horrible sagas.

But Rurik did wonder as he swam.

Would his quest ever end?

Was he doomed to wear the blue face mark for life?

Why had the witch cursed him so?

And where was Maire hiding?

Hah! She was no doubt living the soft life in some Highland castle chamber, uncaring of all the havoc she wreaked. And she *was* fully aware of his fruitless search for her, he would warrant, and laughing joyously about the idiocy of it all.

THE SAME DAY, NEARBY AT BEINNE BREIGHA

Like a bird in a not-so-gilded cage . . .

Maire was living in a wooden cage . . . a *cage*, for the love of St. Colomba! And she was so miserable she felt like weeping.

"Puir lassie! The old laird mus' be rolling over in his grave at yer sorry state. Tsk-tsk," Nessa, her maid and companion, said to her.

Sorry state didn't begin to describe Maire's predicament. She was locked inside a wooden cage that hung suspended high in the air from a long plank fixed to the parapet above the courtyard. Far below, a large pit had been dug and filled with snakes, the top covered with a huge woven mat. If she jostled her cage too much, or someone tried to rescue her, there was always the danger of falling into the pit, cage and all.

Thus far, she'd been in the cage for five days, and would remain there till she agreed to betray all that was precious to the Campbell clan . . . something she would never do. All her people—crofters and fighting men alike—had fled to the woods, at her orders, taking her son with them. Other than the MacNab guards stationed about her keep, the only ones left were a few servants and those too old or frail to leave their homes. Duncan MacNab showed up periodically to shout at her and issue threats.

Maire didn't even look up from where she sat now, her back pressed against the wooden bars of her "prison," as Nessa clucked and tutted at her while she leaned out over the parapet, passing her a bowl containing her one meal of the day—boiled neeps and flat bread. By her doleful tone, you'd think that Nessa was an elderly servant and not a young widow a few years older than Maire's twenty-five.

"Well, my father has rolled more than once over my problems these many years he's been gone."

"Doona be disrespectin' the dead. Yer father was a good man, despite the troubles that seem to flock yer way," Nessa chided, the sympathetic tenderness on her face belying her reprimand.

Maire was not in the mood for arguing. In fact, she was not in the mood for anything other than a hot bath and a soft bed. But she had work to do . . . *Magick*, if you will . . . if she was going to reverse the bad luck that had befallen her people.

"What? What are ye about, Maire?" Nessa asked curiously.

Maire was standing in her cage now, facing east, and was preparing to center herself with legs shoulder-width apart and two hands wrapped around one of the wooden bars. She wished she had her staff with her, but the wooden bar would have to do.

"Ooooh! Doona tell me. Yer gonna try the witchly rites again, I wager. One thing is for certain . . . if ye try that whirling dance nonsense, yer gonna land yerself in a snake pit. I swear, my heart canna take much more of . . . Blessed Lord, why are ye lookin' crosseyed? Is it the evil eye come over ye?"

"Shhh! I need to focus if I want to bend my bars so that I can escape."

"The last time ye focused—two days past—it was on the MacNab guards below. Ye said yer spell would cause 'em to run off. Instead, ye gave them a bad case of the running bowels. Not that some of us did not find humor in that mistake. And then there was the other spell what was gonna give the MacNabs flight, right off Campbell lands. Bless the Saints! We had two dozen roosters and hens a-squawkin' and a-flappin' their wings. None of the hens would lay today, by the by."

Maire sniffed. "Sometimes, I don't concentrate hard enough, or I get the spells a little mixed up."

"A little mixed up! Lassie, when ye tried that wind-riding bizness the first day the MacNabs took ye captive, ye promised ye would end up on the other side of the glen come mornin'. The only one ridin' the wind was Grizelle, and I swear she will ne'er forgive ye fer that affair . . . her falling off the parapet like an eagle about to take flight, with her gown blowing in the wind, exposing her bare rump. Good thing that young MacNab lad caught her, though he was laughing so hard they both fell to the ground."

It was true. Maire was not a very competent witch. In truth, she probably wasn't a witch at all, despite having studied with the old crone, Cailleach, when she was a young lass. But Cailleach was long gone now. What choice did she have? There was no one else to rely on. She had to try.

"Either be still, or go away, so that I can concentrate. You're not helping at all. At least I'm trying. What else would you have me do?"

"Pray," Nessa offered with dry humor. She shifted from foot to foot, still not leaving.

"Well, what else did you want to say? I can tell you have something on your mind."

"Aye, that I do. I hate to burden ye with more troubles when yer up ta yer oxters in troubles as 'tis, but there be darkness on the horizon . . . *again*. The Viking is back."

"Let him come," Maire said with a sigh of surrender. She knew, without questioning, which Viking Nessa referred to. That scoundrel, Rurik, had been scouring all of Scotland for her these past few years. Little did he know that the clans, which fought each other over the littlest dispute, stood together when a hated Norseman was involved. They'd been more than willing to hide the location of her Campbell clanstead, *Beinne Breagha*, or Beautiful Mountain, which was located high in the hills. The neighboring clans enjoyed leading the Vikings on a merry chase, in full circles at times. Until recently, that is.

When she'd engaged the wrath of Duncan MacNab—

her brother by marriage and the most evil man who'd ever walked the Highlands—Maire and her clan had developed a whole new set of problems. There was no longer any time for worries about irate Vikings. The very future of *Beinne Breagha* was at stake now.

"Let him come? Let him come?" Nessa practically squealed. "After all these years, we should invite him in like a welcome guest?"

Maire shrugged, then waved a hand at her surroundings. "You ask why I no longer resist meeting the Viking? What can he do to me now?"

Immediately, Nessa's countenance softened. "Och, sorry I am to have raised me voice. Ye be a good girl, despite all that dabblin' in the witchly arts. I don' mean to hurt yer feelings, Maire, but ye are the sorriest witch the Highlands ever saw. Ye are no Cailleach. Mayhap ye really should take up prayer. Have ye e'er considered a nunnery?"

Maire lifted her chin in affront.

"Oh, girl, doona be gettin' yer feathers ruffled jest 'cause ye can't get a spell right. If ye want to be upset, be upset over the sad scrape we are in . . . the worst of all the Campbell bad times. 'Tis not fitting that ye should be the one to suffer most. That Duncan MacNab is Lucifer's brother, I warrant." She was staring woefully at the horrible cage as she spoke. "Who but the devil hisself would do such a wicked thing to a woman?"

"Who indeed?" But wait. Here they were blathering when a more important worry assailed Maire. "How is Wee-Jamie?" she inquired anxiously. Her four-year-old son's well-being was of highest concern. And not just because of her maternal love. If the MacNab got his hands on her boy, she would be forced to give all he demanded. And that would spell doom for what remained of her clan.

Nessa's worried brow relaxed. "The boy is fine. Old John and the others have hidden him well in a cave in the forests. The MacNab willna set his filthy paws on Jamie, even if there be only one Campbell left standing."

Maire nodded.

"I ken you have other dilemmas, dearie, but ye mus' be careful. And doona be discountin' the danger posed by the Viking. He is closer than he's ever been afore," Nessa pointed out. "He'll ne'er give up till he finds ye."

Maire shrugged, though inside she was not so calm as she pretended to be. It wasn't that she didn't feel justified in putting the blue mark on Rurik's face. He'd taken her maidenhead, then spoken blithely of going off the next day to his homeland, as if she had not just given him a woman's most precious possession. But that was not the main reason for her taking such drastic action. She'd asked him to take her with him, foolish wench that she had been. At the time, she'd had good reason to want to be absent from her homeland . . . for a while, at least. But what did the brute do when she'd asked? He'd laughed at her.

Well, she'd gotten the last laugh.

But she was not laughing now.

"Mayhap 'tis time to face the Viking. Mayhap my marking him was the start of all our troubles. Mayhap I need to remove the mark in order to reverse the curse that seems to have struck us Campbells."

"Hmmm," Nessa pondered. "But what if he . . . the Viking . . . hurts ye?" Nessa asked.

"He won't," Maire answered. For some reason, she did not think he would do her physical harm.

Nessa arched her eyebrows skeptically. "He's a Viking."

"Aye."

"Vikings be a bloodthirsty lot."

"I am acquainted with a few Scotsmen who are bloodthirsty, too. Like Duncan MacNab, for instance."

"Duncan resents Kenneth not gaining the land rights from ye through marriage. Duncan means to have ye, Maire. And King Indulf has given his permission. Time is not in yer favor anymore."

"I know," Maire said on a sigh. "'Tis not me he wants, though. It always comes back to the land. Never mind that he is old enough to be my father. Never mind that I've refused his proposals more times than I can count. Never mind that his men stand guard below in my courtyard as we speak and won't leave till I cooperate. Never mind that the MacNab will beat me mightily once he has marriage rights." Maire rubbed her cheek where Duncan had slapped her hard the day before for refusing to accede to his wishes. "In truth, I predict my accidental death within days of my wedding, if I should ever be so foolish as to wed with that bastard." And God only knew what would happen to Wee-Jamie under Duncan's guardianship.

"But how much longer can we hold out?" Nessa wailed, rubbing her hands together anxiously.

"I do not know. I am so tired of fighting this battle alone. If only father were still alive, or Donald, or Angus." Her father, Malcolm Campbell, had died at Brunanburh eighteen years past, along with the son of Constantine, king of the Scots. Her brothers had died in various other battles since then. Her husband of five years, Kenneth MacNab, Duncan's much younger brother, had died mere months ago, but little good he had been to her while alive. 'Twas he who had banished Cailleach from her lands. Only a straggling band of Campbells was left of her clan and only Maire to hold them together against the onslaught of outside forces. It was a heavy load for a woman of only twenty and five years to carry. Unfortunately, there was no one else . . . for now.

"What ye need, me bonnie lass, is a brave knight in shining armor to champion your cause."

"Hah!" Maire scoffed. "All my life I've had only myself to depend on, and that's the way it's always going to be."

"Many women say the same . . . but only till their true love comes along. Yea, what ye need is a true love."

"A true love?" Maire burst out laughing. "I thought you said I needed a knight in shining armor."

"And who be sayin' ye can't have both?" Nessa sliced her a condemning glare. Then, she put a fingertip to her chin, pondering. "Dost think there be any way ye could get the Viking to help in this fight?" Nessa asked tentatively.

"Nay!" Maire exclaimed vehemently. *Blessed Lord! The woman can't possibly be putting Rurik in the category of a brave knight. Or—may the saints rise from their graves—a true love.* "I want no help from the likes of that man. And one thing is certain. He must never, ever, know . . ." Her words trailed off as she bit her bottom lip. ". . . my *secret*."

"Now, now, lassie, ye are not to fear. Old John has come up with a plan."

"A plan?" Maire squeaked out. Old John was the head of her guardsmen, such as they were these days. Even Old John, once a strong fighting man, had only one arm now and was nigh crippled with pain from all his battle injuries over the years. "Why is this the first I'm hearing of a plan? He should discuss his plans with me." The shrillness of her voice rang out, and several of the MacNab sentries glanced her way.

Nessa slanted her a rueful look. "Old John could

hardly come here to talk with ye. There be MacNabs all about the keep." Pulling back from the parapet, Nessa prepared to leave. "Doona be worryin' none. 'Tis in God's hands now . . . and Old John's."

Now Maire was really worried.

CHAPTER TWO

There's nothing like a good fight to whet a Viking's appetite . . .

"Vikings, go home. Ye are not wanted here in the Highlands."

Rurik and his men were on horseback, staring across a wide gully at a dozen Scotsmen, also on horseback, all of them red-haired and florid-faced. Weapons were not drawn on either side, but all of them had their hands on the hilts of their swords, ready to fight if the need arose. Even with six against twelve, Rurik did not doubt that his band would win in an honest fight, but a good soldier fought no unnecessary battles; therefore, he held himself in check.

Like many Scotsmen, these wore the traditional *léine* and *brat* . . . the *léine* being a long, full *shert* down to the knees, resembling an under-tunic, often of a saffron yellow color, and the *brat*, or *pladd*, being a mere blanket of sorts, which was fastened on the shoulder with a brooch, like a mantle, looped under the sword arm and secured at the waist with a leather belt. Their legs were exposed at times, especially when riding a horse. In fact, many Highlanders dropped their *pladds* in battle, fighting naked . . . which was not so unusual; Viking berserkers did the same. The first time Rurik had viewed

Stigand in such nonattire, his eyes had almost bulged out. What a sight that had been!

These men were a scurvy bunch, with crafty eyes, though they rode fine steeds, and their claymores and long-bladed dirks were of the best quality. The man who had spoken, the leader, appeared most sinister of them all. He had seen more than fifty winters, and white strands threaded through the bright red hair that hung down to his shoulders. His mane looked as if it hadn't been washed or combed in a sennight. A full red beard encircled his chin. Most conspicuous about him was his eyebrows . . . or, rather, his eyebrow . . . for the man had only one bushy brow that extended from one hairline to the other, with no break in between at the bridge of the nose. With this single brow the man appeared frowning and ruthless.

Rurik didn't trust him one bit. "And who might you be?" he asked.

"I be Duncan MacNab," the leader replied in a deep Scottish brogue that made his name sound like, "Dooonkin." He was clearly annoyed that Rurik did not recognize who he was. "These are me men . . . MacNabs, all." He waved a hand toward the men who sat astride nervous mounts on either side of him.

"I mean no trouble to you," Rurik offered in a placating tone. "I am looking for the woman called Maire of the Moors. She is of the Campbell clan, I believe."

The Scotsman laughed, a deep-from-the-chest bellow, and his men snickered. "Everyone in the Highlands, and the Lowlands, is aware of yer search for Maire the *Witch*." The leader put particular emphasis on that last word and exchanged smirking glances with his men, as if they knew something Rurik did not. In Rurik's experience, Scotsmen were great ones for smirks . . . when they were not frowning, that was.

"Know you where I might find the witch?" Rurik asked through gritted teeth. He had little liking for being the laughingstock of all Scotland, whether they were laughing at him or some secret jest.

"Aye, I do."

"And you know why I am looking for her?"

Duncan laughed again, a rumbly sound, like a bear growling. "I expect ye want to have that 'tattoo' removed from yer pretty face, *Viking.*" He put emphasis on the word Viking, as if it were a foul substance.

Rurik nodded, grinding his teeth at the villain's continuing laughter and the grins of his men. He saw naught of humor in his face mark. Could it be that he still harbored self-doubts, lingering from his childhood? He had come so far, and not so far, after all, he supposed.

He came out of his musing with a snort of self-disgust and snapped at the MacNab, "Why would you care if I get the mark removed, or not, *Scotsman?*" Mimicking the other man, he put unpleasant emphasis on the word *Scotsman.*

"I doona care one whit if ye be blue, or red, or purple," Duncan retorted. "I'm here t'day to give ye a bit of advice. Leave this land, or ye'll have more than a blue mark to worry on."

"Oh, and what might that additional worry be?" Rurik asked coolly, while at the same time giving his men a surreptitious hand signal to ready themselves for a fight.

"Loss of blood . . . broken bones . . . death," the MacNab answered with equal coolness. "There be naught more a Scotsman enjoys than a Viking bloodbath."

"Is that a threat?" Rurik inquired icily.

"Aye, 'tis a threat. In fact, 'tis a promise, ye bloody barbarian," Duncan replied with equal iciness. Then, without warning, he let loose with a well-known Highland war cry, "*Stuagh ghairm!*"

In the blink of an eyelid, all eighteen men were at arms. Soon the flat-bottomed gully, the width of several longships, rang with the clang of metal hitting metal, the slap of leather from body-to-body contact, the frightened neighing of horses, the whistling of arrows, and the ominous crunching sound made by a hand ax splitting flesh and bones. At that last noise, all eyes turned to Stigand, who was wiping off his broadsword on a clump of heather, the whole time searching the arena for his next victim. His broadsword was aptly named Bone-Cracker . . . boon companion to his battle-ax, Blood-Lover, which was in his other hand. At his feet lay one of the MacNabs, his skull halved from crown to nape.

Several of the MacNab men made retching sounds, then leaped onto their horses and prepared to leave the scene. Rurik wished Beast were with him now. The wolfhound was a great asset after battle, especially talented at rounding up straggling enemy soldiers, like cattle. Quickly scanning the miniature battlefield, Rurik noted that Jostein appeared to have a broken arm and Bolthor had an arrow sticking out of his thigh. He, personally, had been sliced from elbow to wrist by a sharp dirk; it was a shallow gash that could use some stitching in better circumstances. Others in his troop were marked with bruises and bloody noses and cuts, but that was all. On the MacNab side, however, five lay dead, and two men appeared sorely wounded and had to be assisted onto their horses before galloping off.

Among the survivors was the MacNab himself, who bore no visible wounds. When his horse reached the top of a small rise a short distance away, he called out to Rurik, "Begone, Viking! Leave Scotland at once, ye whoreson whelp of a cod-sucking pagan, lest we meet again. And the results will be far different then, that I promise."

"Your promises mean naught," Rurik answered loudly

with a boastful laugh, pointing to the dead MacNabs scattered about. He chose his battles wisely and decided not to react to Duncan's personal insults . . . just yet.

"Doona dare touch the witch," Duncan added, still having the audacity to issue him orders.

Rurik raised his eyebrows at that particular order. "Why?"

"I want the witch."

"Well, isn't that a coincidence? So do I."

The Scotsman shook his head. "Nay, you want her only to remove the cursed mark, whereas I—"

Rurik barely held his temper in check as the vile man let his words hang in the air for long moments. Finally, he prodded, "Whereas, you want what?"

"—whereas I want the bitch as bride."

Why is everybody always picking on me . . . rather, us? . . .

No sooner had Rurik and his men tended their wounds than another band of Scotsmen rode up. And this was the sorriest bunch of fighting men Rurik had ever seen.

At least twenty men came over the hill toward them. They all wore belted *pladds*, but the wide swaths of fabric were worn and faded, unlike those of the more prosperous MacNabs.

An older man of at least forty years appeared to be the chieftain, or leader. He was missing one arm. A somewhat younger man of about thirty was obviously blind in one eye, which stared sightlessly ahead.

One rider had his nose bashed in, was minus one ear, and appeared to have no front teeth. *The world's ugliest warrior?* Rurik wondered wryly. Well, actually, he knew a few Norse warriors who could compete in that contest.

Still another had a nervous twitch that caused his head to jerk incessantly. No doubt he had sustained a blow to the crown in some battle or other. Rurik had seen a similar condition in an old fighting comrade, Asolf the Dim, whose head jerked so much that he looked as if he was motioning someone toward the right all the time. Not a good trait to have in the midst of battle.

Another man was muttering under his breath, but no one was paying any attention to him. Rurik figured that malady was due to a blow to the brain, as well. The sharp rap of a broadsword against the skull could cause such damage.

The only hale and hearty ones in the bunch were the boys, who could be good fighters with the proper training. Several of these boys appeared to be around Jostein's age, but if they fought the way they rode their horses, Jostein could beat them in a trice, and Jostein was not yet an accomplished soldier.

Once again, he was reminded, reluctantly, of his past. This time, it was a mental image of a skinny, underdeveloped halfling. Thank the gods he'd been fortunate enough to have a friend who could teach him those survival skills. Who would instruct these half-men? The one-armed warrior? Or the half-blind one?

Who were these ragtag warriors? What did they want of him?

Ah, well, 'tis none of my concern. He shook his head to rid himself of unwelcome thoughts.

"Are you Rurik the Viking?"

Rurik stood and pulled his sword from its scabbard, just in case. "Yea. Who is it that asks?"

"I be John. Old John," the leader said. "And this be Young John." He motioned with his head toward the half-blind man beside him. "And Murdoc," he added, pointing to the homely one; "Callum," the twitcher; "and Rob," the mutterer.

Oh, good Lord!

"We are of the Campbell clan," Old John said, concluding his introductions.

"Campbells?" Rurik spat out.

"Aye, Lady Maire is our mistress."

He was suddenly alert with interest. "Is this the selfsame person as Maire the Witch?"

Old John's eyes went wide; then he exchanged amused glances with his comrades. Their reaction to his calling Maire a witch was the same as the MacNab's. *Hmmm.* But Rurik had no time to study on the matter more, for Old John was speaking again.

Smiling crookedly, Old John asked, "Wouldst like to locate the witch's lair?"

Now that was a lackwit question . . . after five years of bearing the witch's mark, three years of which had been wasted searching for her. He put one fist on a hip, trying to appear casual. "And if I do?"

"Mayhap we can help ye."

"Why would you help us? We have firsthand knowledge of how much you Scotsmen love us Vikings." Rurik looked pointedly at the bodies that still lay strewn about the gully.

"Might those be MacNabs?" Old John inquired hopefully as he leaned forward to get a better look. Young John squinted his good eye to see better, too. Murdoc scratched his missing ear as he contemplated the question. Callum kept jerking his head toward the dead soldiers. And Rob muttered over and over, something about "dead-as-dung MacNabs."

"Do dragons roar and Saxons stink?" Rurik answered.

Old John smiled widely then. If there was one thing the Scots and Vikings had in common, it was dislike of the Saxons. "Praise God! Ye mus' be the answers to our prayers."

"Me? Me? The answer to someone's prayers?" Rurik was not amused. "I think not."

"Ah, but mayhap you will change your mind. We come to offer you a proposition, Viking."

"A proposition? From a Highlander? Hah! I must inform you that I mistrust Scotsmen mightily."

"Then we are on even ground, because I mistrust Norsemen as well."

Rurik cocked his head to the side in confusion. "Then why would you offer me a . . . what did you call it . . . proposition?"

Old John shrugged. "Desperation."

Rurik had to give the man credit for honesty.

"Lead our clan to victory, Viking. That is all we ask. Deliver us from the pestilence that has overtaken our Campbell lands. If ye will pledge us that, we will deliver ye forthwith to our mistress, Maire of the Moors."

Rurik arched an eyebrow at that unexpected offer. "And might that pestilence bear the name MacNab?"

"It might," Old John admitted.

Rurik frowned with confusion as he recalled the MacNab's last words to him . . . something about wanting to marry Maire. As far as he knew, Maire had been wed these past five years. "Why does Maire's husband not protect her clan?"

"Kenneth MacNab died three months ago."

"MacNab? Maire was married to a MacNab?"

Old John nodded, his face flushing with anger. "Yea, and a miserable cur he was, too. The youngest brother of Duncan . . . younger by fifteen years, I would guess."

Rurik had other questions he'd like to ask, but they could come later. For now, there was one that was foremost in his mind. "Who is your laird, then? Nay, do not tell me it is your mistress, Maire the Witch?" He refused to give her that gentler appellation, Maire of the Moors.

All the Campbell men burst out laughing.

"Females cannot be chieftains of our particular clan," Old John explained, "though Lady Maire has done a fine job of holding all together till the laird can take over."

Rurik was weary of all this vague talk and innuendo. With impatience, he demanded, "Then who in bloody hell *is* laird?"

The Campbell horsemen moved aside, right and left, leaving a path through their group. Riding up on a dappled gray mare was a fat monk with tonsured head and an enormous belly. Sitting in front of him on the horse was a filthy, ill-garbed, barefooted boy of little more than four winters. He was black-haired and green-eyed and soon demonstrated that he had the tongue of a seasoned seaman.

With a compelling bravado for one so young, the child proclaimed in a shrill voice, "I am the *bloody hell* laird."

Bubble, bubble, toil and trouble, for sure . . .

"*Bhroinn, rachadh, gleede, chunnaic.* Nay, that's not it. *Rachadh, gleede, bhroinn, bhroinn.*" Maire exhaled loudly with frustration. "Why, oh, why can't I remember the words of the spell? If only Cailleach were still here! I would have been out of this cage the first day."

For the past two hours, ever since Nessa had left, Maire had been trying one witchly device after another . . . spells, curses, centering, circling, wind riding, visualizing, grounding, even body raising. None of them had worked . . . not even in the backward way they were wont to do sometimes when she got the rituals wrong.

Now she was left with her final alternative. Putting her

palms together, she looked out at the gray skies. "Dearest God, please help me in my dire need."

It was then that Maire saw the six Vikings. They were turning the bend at the bottom of the small mountain she called home, *Beinne Breagha*. Most alarming was the fact that her very own clansmen led the way.

Could this possibly be the answer to her prayer? If so, she was going to give up her witchly attempts and spend lots more time on her knees.

She thought of something else. So, this was Old John's *plan* . . . the one Nessa had referred to. Her mouth thinned with displeasure. Well, she could not be angry with her loyal retainer. Desperate times called for desperate measures, and Old John must have believed there was hope with the Vikings. She had to trust in Old John. What else could she do?

A quick scan of the approaching group showed that her son was not with them . . . nor his monk caretaker. Maire breathed a sigh of relief. Thank the heavens that Old John had exercised the good sense to keep young Jamie hidden in the woods, out of danger, and the Viking's presence.

Even as she noticed the Vikings in the distance, she saw a battered and bloody messenger rush up to the dozen or so MacNab men who'd been left to guard her keep. Almost immediately, the men gathered their weapons and other belongings and, cursing loudly and shaking their fists at her, scattered in the direction of the MacNab lands, like chaff in the wind. Duncan MacNab was a brave man when his opponents were weaker than he. At the least prospect of an equal adversary, however, he would scoot off, waiting for the chance to pounce when a back was turned or chicanery could be practiced.

She was not deceived by their hasty retreat, though. They would return . . . in greater numbers.

But, oh, it grated her pride sorely that it was this man, above all others—Rurik—who came to rescue her from the MacNabs . . . even if only temporarily. The callous brute had beaten her pride to the ground once before. She would not let him do it again . . . despite her ignominious position.

Maire sighed deeply, wondering if her lot would be any better with the Vikings than the MacNabs. She stood and held on to the cage bars, staring out over the Campbell land she loved so much. She tried to imagine seeing her home through the much-traveled Vikings' eyes.

There were Campbells in Scotland who were rich and powerful. Maire's family was of the poorer branch. Though built on stone foundations, her keep, which was referred to as a castle, was little more than a rambling, timber hill-fort perched atop a flattened earthen bank. Two concentric rings of walls and ditches surrounded the fortress, pierced by a single gateway. Beyond the "castle" walls was the village of a hundred wooden huts—wattle and daub with conical thatched roofs. Most of them were unoccupied and in a state of decay, but they bespoke a more prosperous time.

Afternoon was gone and eventide not yet upon them . . . a time referred to as the gloaming, when a mystical aura lay over the land, highlighting the rugged, stone-dotted land with its luxuriant blanket of lavender-colored heather. Visitors to the Scottish Highlands were wont to comment on what they perceived as its harshness but they were blind. There was so much beauty in this stark land it nigh brought tears to Maire's eyes.

That was neither here nor there. She must concentrate on the Viking, and how to handle this new dilemma.

Even from her lofty perch in the cage, she had to admit that these Viking men, expertly guiding their fine horses on the twisted path, were an impressive group. Though several appeared wounded from some recent fight—perhaps with the MacNabs—they all sat tall and proud, never once glancing with fear to the side, where the remnants of her Campbell followers were coming out of hiding, prepared to defend her honor and that of the clan.

But why should the Vikings be fearful? They were men in their prime . . . fierce warriors. Whereas all she had left of her clan were the old and the young, thanks to one war after another these past twenty years. Scotsmen were as bad as Vikings. They loved a good fight, and it mattered not if the enemy were Saxon, Viking, Frank, or fellow Scotsman.

If more women were permitted to be chieftains of the clans, this would not happen, in Maire's opinion. Some clans did allow such, but her particular branch called for the leadership to pass through the males of the family. So all Maire could do was try to hold the clan together till her son could inherit.

What must these Vikings—some of whom she knew were highborn—think of her crumbling wood-and-stone keep? Or her poor guardsmen? Well, Maire refused to bow her head in shame. If her home was not as grand as it once had been, that was not her fault. As to her followers . . . ah, she was proud of them, one and all.

Old John was missing one arm, thanks to a surprise Saxon attack ten years past. Her father, Malcolm, had already been dead by then, but her brothers Donald and Angus had left John in charge whilst they went off fighting in Northumbria. Angus never came home that time and was buried in the cold earth of Northern England. Donald had caused her all kinds of problems since their father's death . . . most importantly, betrothing her to the youngest of the neighboring MacNab clan, Kenneth MacNab. Donald Campbell had died last year, and her husband, Kenneth, just a few months ago. Maire could not regret either of their deaths, though she had thought she loved Kenneth at one time. Neither of her brothers had left any heirs.

Old John was leading the entourage, single file, up the pathway to her keep. His one good arm held a claymore at the ready as he glared at the passing countryside, on the alert for MacNab stragglers.

A short distance behind him rode Young John, who also surveyed the craggy landscape. Young John was only thirty years old, but he was blind in one eye. And he had a problem with dizziness. Often he keeled over without any warning.

A dozen or so others followed behind them. Another dozen of her "guardsmen" and crofters sprang up at various posts along the way. They had sentry duty along the pathway, as if they could stop the Vikings if they wanted to.

Her eyes skimmed over the Norsemen as they came closer, their horses clip-clopping over the wooden drawbridge as they passed through the gateway. She'd met some of them before, when she'd first encountered Rurik on a visit to her cousins in Glennfinnan.

The twins, Toste and Vagn, must be twenty-two now. They'd been a rascally pair of seventeen-year-olds when last she'd seen them in the seaport town. With long blond hair and pale blue eyes and cleft chins, they'd had no trouble attracting women, even then. Now, their bodies had gained a mature musculature. She wondered if they still fooled people by pretending to be each other.

There was that mean-eyed soldier, Stigand the Berserk, with his wild beard and unkempt mane of reddish blond hair. Hard to tell how he really looked under all that hair, but he had a haughty presence about him that was rather appealing. His eyes were deep brown, like a muddy stream, and bespoke some great pain. He was reputed to be a heartless killer.

Maire did not recognize the young man, who could not have seen more than fifteen winters, but he carried himself with the same arrogance as all the others. His blond good looks probably gained him much in female regard, even at his young age.

The huge giant with the black eye patch was no doubt Bolthor the Skald . . . slightly older than Stigand. She'd never met him, but had heard much of his clumsy sagas. They rarely had visitors these days at *Beinne Breagha*; so even the words of a bad poet would be a welcome diversion if circumstances were different.

Lastly came the leader of this Viking retinue . . . the one from whom Maire had the most to fear. Rurik.

By the saints, would you look at that mark? Did I really do that? It certainly is . . . blue.

Oh, he was uncommonly handsome, still. The jagged blue mark down the center of his face did not detract from his appearance at all, in Maire's opinion. In truth, he resembled the untamed, painted Celtic warriors of old.

Five years had passed since she'd seen him last. So, he must have seen twenty-eight winters by now. The years had been kind to the knave.

Though many of the Norsemen had pale hair, Rurik's was midnight black and hung down to his shoulders. The strands were held off his face, on the sides, by thin braids that had been intertwined with gold thread and amber beads. All the men wore slim trews and leather boots, topped by woolen tunics, belted at the waist, and short mantles over their broad shoulders. Rurik's shoulder mantle was of silver fox, held in place by a large golden brooch in the shape of some twisting animal, perchance a dragon. The woaddyed tunic that hugged his frame had strips of appliqued samite along the neckline, short sleeves, and hem, adorned with vividly colored embroidery. His face was clean shaven and well-sculpted, except for a few small scars . . . and the blue mark, of course.

To say he was stunningly virile would be a vast understatement.

The Vikings stopped their horses in the inner courtyard. Only then did they glance up at her, still standing in her dangling cage. In fact, they stared at her with horror. Was it her rundown keep, or was it she herself who aroused such disgust? While Rurik was adorned in finery fit for a Saxon atheling, she wore a simple undyed wool *arisaid*—the female *pladd,* which was little more than a large cloak wrapped artfully about the body and fastened at the center of the chest with a brooch and at the waist with a belt. She had not bathed in days, nor combed her hair. Frankly, she stank, though she misdoubted her body odor would carry down to the courtyard.

Rurik's upraised eyes met hers. Blue, blue eyes . . . hard as icy water in the winter lochs. His expression was a mask of stone, unreadable, except that he appeared to be visibly shaken and very, very angry. His tightly coiled power resonated in the air, though he did not move.

A sudden chill hung in the air, and there was an eerie silence all around. Even the birds had quieted.

Ooh, boy! Now the you-know-what was going to hit the wind . . .

Rurik was stunned by the depravity of this savage land . . . or rather the depravity of a man who could do such to a woman . . . put her in a cage, like an animal. It was unconscionable.

So overcome with fury was he that, for several long moments, he was unable to speak. Fisting his fingers tightly, he slowly brought his temper under control.

Eventually, he met the green eyes of the witch, who was staring at him without trepidation, even though he favored her with his fiercest glower. She no doubt thought his anger was directed at her. Well, it was . . . partly. And she should be fearful, if she had a jot of sense in her body.

She had changed these past five years; he could see that. His upper lip curled at the sight of her straggly red hair. Rurik had a personal aversion to red hair on a woman. Red-headed women tended to be temperamental and fiery-tongued, in his experience. Not worth the trouble. Like his friend Tykir's wife, Alinor. Trouble, trouble, trouble. He had to concede, though, that, despite the wrinkled, blanketlike robe Maire wore, her beauty was apparent . . . a more mature beauty than she had exhibited when she was a mere twenty.

But he refused to be attracted to the witch. Never again!

"Maire the Witch," Rurik shouted suddenly.

Maire lurched. "Magdalene's tears! Are you speaking to me?"

A low, rumbly sound came up from Rurik's chest at her impertinence. "Nay, I'm speaking to that skinny rooster over there."

"You don't have to be testy with me, Viking," she grumbled.

Testy? I will give you testy. "Maire, get your arse down here," he roared.

Chapter Three

He was the rudest Knight in Shining Armor she'd ever met . . .

Dumb, dumb, dumb . . . The man is dumber than a wooly Highland sheep.

"How would you suggest I do that, Viking?" she asked with seeming pleasantry.

"You're a witch. Do you not fly?"

She laughed. She couldn't help herself. The man really was a halfwit. "Not lately."

He scowled at her mirth-making, and she recalled, of a sudden, how prickly his pride had been at one time. Apparently it still was. Men and their stupid vanities! She could not be bothered.

"You cannot be a very *good* witch, if you got yourself in this . . . this"—his eyes went hot with some inner fury as he gazed upon her cage—"this dilemma. A witch should be able to escape."

Well, he was correct there. "Are you going to let me hang here, Viking, or are you going to release me?"

He rested both palms on the horn of his saddle and smiled ferally at her. His eyelids were hooded, like a hawk's. "Hmmm. Methinks there might be great pleasure to be had in keeping you caged . . . but not nearly enough satisfaction for the grief you have caused me these past years."

"Me?" she asked, putting both hands to her chest in mock amazement. She continued in an overstated Scottish brogue, thick with rolling r's, "What could a puir Highland lass like me do to harm a big brave Norseman like you?" She treaded dangerous waters by tweaking the tail of this Viking wolf; she knew that, but could not seem to restrain the impulse.

Rurik shook his head at her foolhardy bravado. Then he threw another jab at her, from another angle. Sniffing in an exaggerated fashion, he remarked, "What is that odor, Maire? Couldst be you are less aromatic than last time we met? As I recall, there was the scent of flowers . . . on certain body parts."

Ooooh, how dare he remind her of her embarrassing surrender to his charms! She could feel her face going crimson with humiliation. As if she did not have a daily reminder of her woman's weakness in the form of one robust little boy with raven-black hair.

Just then, she noticed bits of peat moss clinging to his apparel. For a man who was usually so fastidious about his appearance, it struck an odd note. She smiled in a deliberately gloating manner. "Ah, have you taken a bath in one of our lovely bogs, Viking?"

He snarled some foreign word under his breath. A Norse expletive, no doubt. He recovered rapidly, though, and smiled back at her. "Is that the latest in Scottish fashion, Maire?" He was surveying her poor attire with disdain.

Now it was her turn to snarl.

He smirked at her, satisfied to have provoked a reaction from her.

The maddening arrogance of the Viking infuriated her. She would have liked to wipe that smirk off his face with a bucket of cold water. Instead, she taunted, "And what is that odd mark on your face, Rurik? Couldst be you are less handsome than last time we met?" Instantly, shame overcame her at the unkindness of her comment.

He seemed about to toss back some nasty retort, but they were interrupted. Off on a nearby hillock, she heard Murdoc pick up his bagpipes and begin a plaintive tune. Thanks to all his battle wounds, Murdoc was an unattractive man physically, but, oh, the music he played was rapturous. Tears welled in her eyes, as they always did when she heard the pipes.

Bolthor exclaimed to Rurik, "Is that not the most wondrous sound you have ever heard?"

"Huh?" Rurik said.

The dolt!

Bolthor turned to Old John. "Dost think I could learn how to play the pipes like that?"

"Oh, no! No, no, no!" Rurik was quick to interject.

But Old John ignored Rurik and patted Bolthor on the sleeve with his good hand. "I canna see why not."

Rurik and the remainder of his group groaned. Obviously, they were ignorant men who could not appreciate good music.

Bolthor addressed Rurik, "Can you not see the possibilities, Rurik? Mayhap I could teach Stigand to say the words to my sagas whilst I accompany him with the bagpipes."

"Me? Why me?" Stigand sputtered. "Be damned if I will be caught spouting any bloody poetry."

"Not only will I be a skald, but I will be a bard, as well," Bolthor said with an elated sigh.

"Or one might say, a skaldic bard," Toste offered with a chuckle.

"Or a bardic skald," Vagn added, also chuckling.

"How about a headless skald?" Stigand put in with dry humor. He was not chuckling.

"Now, Bolthor, slow down a bit and think on this,"

Rurik advised. "When have you ever heard of a bag-piping Norseman?"

Bolthor lifted his chin and smiled broadly. "That is the best part. I will be the first."

"This is all your fault," Rurik yelled up at her, surprising her so much that she jumped, causing her cage to sway. Promptly, he added, "Why are you looking cross-eyed?"

"She is no doubt centering herself," Young John answered for her, as if that explained everything. "Perchance her bars will now part of their own volition." He seemed unable to control a snicker. "Then again, perchance not."

Rurik glanced about and realized that, for some reason, he had an amused audience. He turned to Stigand. "Go up to the ramparts and use your ax to chop off that plank that's holding the cage."

Stigand frowned. "But the cage will drop to the ground."

"Yea," Rurik agreed with a sly smile. "That is the point. The witch deserves a good shaking up and the cage is not so high that she will be harmed."

"Nooo!" Maire screamed.

Everyone's head jerked upward, and they all gawked at her as if she'd lost her mind.

"Would you look at what's in that pit down there, you stupid, thickheaded, pompous, jackass Viking?"

"Tsk-tsk! Calling me vile names is no way to endear yourself to your rescuer, Maire." Rurik alighted from his horse and glared up at her, hands on hips. "What pit?"

"Aaarrgh!" she screeched, pointing at the ground below her. "Look, damn you. Look!"

"You have a tart tongue on you, Maire. Best you learn to curb it in my presence, or you will feel my wrath. And it won't be with a tongue-lashing, that I assure you." He sauntered over to the area under her hanging cage, and seemed to notice for the first time the large, circular woven mat. His men followed him.

He lifted up the edge of the mat with the tip of his boot, peeked underneath, and went wide-eyed with shock. "Jesus, Mary, and Joseph!" he cursed loudly. Like many Vikings, Rurik had probably been baptized in the Christian rites, whilst still practicing the old Norse religion. On some occasions, however . . . like now . . . naught sufficed but a good Christian expletive.

"Snakes!" his Norse comrades yelped as one, scurrying back toward their horses and safety. You'd never know they were hardened warriors.

"Someone is going to pay for this atrocity," Rurik vowed, his frosty blue eyes taking in the cage and snake pit in one sweeping glance.

Maire's heart lurched at his fierce promise. Was he actually outraged on her behalf? Despite all her inner warnings to the contrary, Maire couldn't stop herself from remembering Nessa's words: *What you need, me bonnie lass, is a brave knight in shining armor to champion your cause.*

Could Rurik possibly be that knight?

Never tease a Viking . . .

"A knight in shining armor? Me?" Rurik laughed uproariously at Maire, who was sitting at the trestle table next to him, having just finished sewing up the gash in his forearm.

At the far end of the great hall, the maid Nessa was wrapping tight linen strips about Jostein's forearm, which was sprained, but not broken. Bolthor had declined any treatment, other than a washing of the small hole, once Stigand had pulled the arrow from his thigh. A little limp was nothing to the giant skald.

"I did not say precisely that I wanted *you* for a knight

in shining armor," she said defensively, a blush rising on her cheeks and neck.

So, you can still blush, wench? Hmmm. That is a surprise, though now that I think on it, you blushed prettily back then, too . . . the first time I bared your breasts . . . or touched your thigh. Nay, I should not recall nice things about you. 'Tis best to remember you are my hated enemy. "When I wear armor, it is sometimes metal, but just as often, leather. And I would never call myself a knight. 'Tis a Saxon word. I prefer to be named warrior, and—"

"My knight in shining leather, then," Maire suggested with a sad attempt at humor. "Or, my warrior in leather." She pretended to swoon.

But Rurik took her seriously. "I will not be your knight in armor, leather, *pladd*, or any other form."

"Do you deliberately misunderstand my words? I merely said that I am in need of a . . . oh, never mind. You would not understand." She took another stitch to distract him.

He yelped with pain, "Oooww! Did you do that a-purpose?"

"Nay, my needle slipped."

You lie, wench. And you do it with such ease. What other lies do you tell? What secrets do you hide here in your mucky keep? I would have to be a simpleton not to notice the way your clan members shift their gazes whene'er I approach . . . and you, most especially. Any man . . . or woman . . . who will not look a person directly in the eye is hiding something. What could it be?

"I told you to find someone else to mend your wounds, Viking."

"Yea, but you owe me more than any other. I intend to exact my payments one deed at a time. For instance, how soon can you remove this mark?"

"How soon can you rid my lands of the MacNabs?"

He took hold of both her wrists and hauled her forward so that she was nigh nose-to-nose with him. The needle and thread dangled from the skin of his arm, but he did not care. "You will not play your games with me, wench."

Suddenly, he was assailed by the not-unpleasant scent of the hard soap she'd used to bathe her body and wash her hair . . . hair the rich dark red color of an autumn sunset. Green eyes flashed at him through their framework of thick lashes. Her skin was like an ell of ivory silk he'd seen one time in a Birka trading stall, and her face was a perfectly sculpted heart shape. Her clean, but shabby, *arisaid* with its braided belt, hid her figure, but he knew . . . oh, Lord, he *knew* . . . exactly what treasures lay beneath. His memory was perfect in that regard.

And she was looking even better these days.

"Do you threaten me now, Rurik?" she inquired with a wince, and he realized that his hold on her wrists was unnecessarily harsh. He released her and saw that his fingers would leave bruises on her delicate skin. Ah, well, 'twas only just. His mark on her in exchange for her mark on him.

"Are threats necessary, Maire?" He had calmed down somewhat, and his voice did not betray his inner turmoil. "Do not tempt me, for I have many means at my disposal to bend you to my will."

Was there sexual innuendo in his words? He had not meant it so. Or had he? For the love of Odin, the woman really must be a witch. She was ensorcelling him.

Fire leaped in her green eyes, but only momentarily. With a long sigh, she tied a knot in the stitches and carefully put the needle back in its special silver case that hung from the key ring at her waist. "Threats are not necessary. I will do everything I can to remove your mark.

In truth, our situation is so dire that I would sleep with the devil if it would save my people."

He could see by her deepening blush that she immediately regretted her poorly chosen words.

"Sleep with the devil, eh?" He smiled lazily at her. "Now there's an idea I hadn't considered afore." He was only teasing, of course . . . until he heard her barely murmured response.

"To think I hoped for a knight in shining armor! And what do I get . . . a devil in a blue tattoo. As if I would ever want you in my bed again!"

"Maire, Maire, Maire," he chided her. "Didst never hear that it's plain folly to issue a challenge to a Norseman?"

He wouldn't be a Viking if he didn't try . . .

Rurik was not generally a deep-thinking man; he was more a man of action. But he was thinking now. Thinking, thinking, thinking. And the answers to all the puzzling questions that thrummed at his brain were slow in coming.

He wondered idly why he had not seen the boy . . . Maire's son . . . since their return to the castle. Was he off doing little-boy things . . . the sorts of things he'd never experienced as a child? And wasn't it strange, he pondered now, that Maire would entrust her son's well-being to a straggly band of guardsmen who could not manage to keep their own body parts intact, let alone those of a small person?

By the time everyone was settled in and had eaten a cold repast of bannock and sliced mutton, it was well past nightfall. Midnight approached and still Rurik sat by himself in the great hall, thinking, whilst others around him, men and women alike, slept soundly on benches that pulled down from the wall to form sleeping pallets. The soft and loud snores, the snuffling sounds of slumber, and the occasional rustling of clothing were comforting somehow to Rurik. All was peaceful. For now. 'Twas a good feeling.

How odd that he should think that way! For years he had craved excitement. Fighting the battles of one greedy king after another. Visiting far-off, sometimes exotic lands. A-Viking. Trading. Treasure hunting for amber in the Baltics.

Making new conquests in the bed furs.

And now . . . what? Was he developing a longing for peace, of all things? Did he yearn for the tamer life of hearth and family?

'Twas perplexing to Rurik, really, that such strange emotions should assail him. He was filled to overflowing with rage and frustration and dissatisfaction, and at the same time his heart . . . his entire being . . . seemed to swell and ache for some unknown thing.

No doubt, it was the *uisge-beatha* affecting him. He had been sipping for an hour and more at a cup of the potent, amber-hued beverage the Scots called "water of life." Although Rurik preferred plain mead or ale, he decided he could cultivate a taste for this drink.

Rurik stood suddenly and fought light-headedness as he stretched and yawned widely. All of the Campbell castle was abed. 'Twas where he should head now.

Guards from Maire's clan and Rurik's retinue had been posted about the grounds, ensuring the security of *Beinne Breagha*, at least for now. *Beinne Breagha*. 'Twas Gaelic for Beautiful Mountain. Now wasn't that a pretty misname for such a sorry estate? The rampart walls were crumbling down in places for lack of maintenance. Dirty rushes covered the castle floors. The fireplaces had not been cleaned for years and downdrafts of black smoke wafted into the various chambers. The roof surely leaked in a heavy rain; here and there, he could see through to the night sky. The only thing that could be said in *Beinne Breagha*'s defense was that it was, in fact, surrounded by blankets of beautiful flowering plants.

Wearily, he picked up a candle in a soapstone holder, using the hand of his healthy right arm, and climbed the stone steps to the second floor, where there was one bedchamber and a solar . . . testament to some long-ago inhabitants who'd lived a finer life than these present Campbells did. Wincing, he tested his left arm for weakness as he walked, extending it out, then folding it back at the elbow, over and over. It hurt mightily to exercise the arm so, especially since the stitches were still tight and the wound raw, but he hated with a passion any weakness of body.

In the corridor outside Maire's chamber, he came across Toste, who had been assigned guard duty over the witch.

"I'll relieve you now," he told Toste.

Toste nodded. "I'm away to bed then," he said and headed toward the stairway and a waiting pallet in the great hall.

With a loud, jaw-cracking yawn, Rurik opened the heavy oaken door to the left. The master chamber was austere, which suited the dour Scottish personality. Rushes lay thickly over the floor . . . sweeter than those belowstairs, he noted . . . and pegs dotted the walls with clothing hung on them. In one corner was a large, unfinished tapestry on a wooden frame. There were several chests for bed linens and such and one higher chest on which rested a pitcher and bowl and a polished metal in an ivory holder for looking at one's visage.

He set the candle down and picked up the vanity device by its ivory handle. Examining himself closely, he saw a man of mature years—twenty and eight—with a day's growth of beard and stern features. When had he turned so bleak of face? Soon he would be as sour-countenanced as any Scotsman.

And he saw the blue mark, of course. Always the blue mark.

It was vain of him to care so much about the mark, he supposed. But somehow it had come to represent all that he had hated about his youth. Despite everything he had accomplished in his life, the mark had become a humbling symbol to him of how little he really was.

He glanced over at the large, raised bedstead situated in the center of the room, its high head frame set against one wall. The room was dark, except for the flickering candle and the little moonlight that entered the room through the two arrow-slit windows.

With a glare, he surveyed the woman who occupied the bed. Should he shake the witch awake and demand that she cast her removing spells now? Or should he wait till the light of day?

He decided with a sigh of exhaustion to wait. Putting the looking-metal down, he began to remove his garments. With luck, by this time on the morrow, his face would be free of the mark, he thought, as he unpinned his mantle brooch and set it down carefully. It had been a betrothal gift from Theta.

Sitting on the edge of the straw-filled mattress, he toed off his boots, then stood and dropped his braies and small clothes to the floor. Turning, he contemplated the wench. Since it was late summertime, bed furs were unneeded. Maire lay on her side in a thin chemise, hugging a pillow to her chest, like a lover.

He felt a lurch of lust in his loins, which caused him to frown some more. He did not want to desire this traitorous witch.

Walking to the other side of the bed, he slipped down

onto the mattress. For several moments he just lay on his back, his hands behind his back. Then, with a muttered curse of, "Oh, bloody hell, why not?" he rolled to his side, right up against the backside of the witch. Carefully, he arranged his wounded arm on the mattress above her head, but his right arm he wrapped around her waist so that his palm rested on her flat stomach.

As sleep soon began to overcome him, he grinned. There would be sweet dreams this night. And wet, he would warrant.

He couldn't wait.

Lance who? . . .

Maire's body was accustomed to awakening each morning before dawn, and this day was no different.

There was a difference, however.

In her hazy half-asleep state, with her eyes still closed and her senses not yet fully alert, Maire mulled over the events that had transpired the previous day and what she must do on this new day. She was free of her cage and the MacNab . . . *for now* . . . but there were plans to make to ensure their continued safety here at *Beinne Breagha*. First, she wanted to seek out Wee-Jamie and spend some time with him . . . simple but important mother/son activities, like combing his silky black hair, or playing run-run-catch in the heather, or skimming rocks in a favorite trout stream. Jamie was her life, and she missed him desperately.

On her back, she yawned and started to stretch out the nighttime kinks.

That was when she noticed another difference about this morning . . . the most significant difference. There was a man sharing her bed . . . a *naked* man, she realized with a startled yelp. And she wasn't much better, with her thin chemise hiked up practically to her . . . well, hips, and one shoulder strap having slipped down to a bare breast.

It was that horrid Viking . . . Rurik.

Even worse, he was wide awake and staring at her . . . hotly. Well, that wasn't precisely correct. He was staring at her exposed breast as if he were considering whether to lick it or not.

Lick it? Lick it? Where do I get these ideas?

Despite all the reasons she had to hate Rurik, Maire felt an intense ache begin in her breasts, which caused their traitorous nipples to bead for his appreciative scrutiny.

"Maire," he groaned, as if she were deliberately torturing him.

Hah! He wasn't the one being tortured. She was.

He ran the tip of his tongue over his lips, as if they were dry.

They didn't look dry to her. In truth, his generous lips appeared slick and warm and inviting. *Oh, blessed St. Blathmac . . . his lips are not inviting. They are not, not, not,* she insisted to herself. She was losing her mind. In fact, she had to restrain herself from arching her chest upward toward said lips, which would definitely be a brainless thing to do.

And if Maire's day wasn't starting out badly enough, she observed another even worse thing. She realized belatedly that not only did she have a naked Viking in her bed, but she was lying flat on her back whilst he lay on his side, with his left arm resting on the pillow above her head, a hairy leg resting over her thighs, a hand resting possessively on her stomach, and something hard *not* resting at all, but pressing insistently against her hip.

Oh, Maire knew all about men and their morning erections. In truth, it was the only time her husband had been able to bear making love with her. Then, and when he was falling-over drunk from imbibing too much *uisge-beatha.*

She tried to roll over and shove the big brute away, but he was immovable . . . like a stone wall. Besides that, her hair was caught under his arm, and her legs trapped under his thigh.

With a grunt of disgust, she yanked her chemise up to cover her breast.

He chuckled.

"What . . . are . . . you . . . doing . . . in . . . my . . . bed?" she gritted out.

"Best you stop wiggling about, Maire, or Lance will be impaling your sweet target."

She stilled for a second and felt the male appendage pressed into her hip move. It actually moved. Was it growing larger? She didn't dare look. "Lance?"

"My manpart."

"You name your manpart?"

"Nay," he answered and grinned unabashedly, "though many men do."

"Many men are lackwits."

He shrugged. "Mayhap. Where women are concerned, you may be right. In truth, a man's *lance* often has a mind of its own. So, really, women should not blame men for their lackwittedness in that regard."

"Now that's a piece of male ill-logic, if I ever heard it."

"Hush, Maire. You're offending Lance, and he is a very sensitive fellow."

"Well, Lance better get away from me, or risk being broken by a quick chop of my fist."

Rurik winced, but still grinned at her. "I would not mind your fist on me. Not chopping, of course. More like, softly—"

"Aaarrgh! How dare you speak to me so?"

"I dare much, m'lady, and I expect I will dare much, much more before I leave your company."

"I repeat, why are you in my bed?"

"Where else would I be? I am not letting you out of my sight till you remove this blue mark."

If only he knew . . . the blue mark did not detract from his good looks at all. In fact, it brought out the deep blue of his eyes, and made his face appear fierce, like an ancient Celtic warrior. "Aye, I can see why you would want to have it removed. It must interfere with all the women you would like to draw to your bed furs, then abandon."

"Oh, I have no trouble attracting women, even with this mark," he boasted. "Actually, some women like the way . . ." He stopped midsentence and stared at her. "Abandon? Are you implying that I abandon women . . . that I abandoned *you*?"

"What would you call it?" she snarled. She immediately lifted her chin with indifference. "Not that I cared."

He narrowed his eyes at her. "How did I abandon you? You were betrothed to be married, were you not? A love match, I believe you called it at the time."

"Hah! That did not stop you from seducing me. You were relentless, Rurik. You would not leave me alone till I finally succumbed."

"Do not lay all the blame on me, Maire. You were willing, in the end."

"In the end," she emphasized.

He cocked his head to the side. "Were you in love with me, Maire?"

"No!" she practically shouted.

"Then what?"

"I don't want to talk about this any more. Let me up. Or I really will strike a mortal blow to your Lance."

He smiled, not at all intimidated by her threats. "I

will release you for now, witch, but we will finish this conversation afore I leave this cursed land."

She scrambled out of the bed the moment he raised his arm and lifted his leg. Suspecting that he perused her form in the thin chemise, she did not turn, but quickly donned a clean but well-worn *arisaid*, belting it at the waist. Still not turning, out of fear that she might see more of "Lance" than she would prefer, Maire scooted toward the doorway and the chores that awaited her this day.

But Rurik asked a question, just as she put her hand to the door latch, that caused her to stop in her tracks and the blood to run cold in her veins.

"Where is your son, Maire?"

CHAPTER FOUR

Something was fishy in Denmark . . . uh, Scotland . . .

"My . . . my son?" she stammered, dropping her hand from the door latch as she turned back into the bedchamber. "Which son?"

"You have more than one son?" He was half reclining against the headboard, the bed linens drawn up to his waist, his arms folded over the bare skin of his lightly furred chest. His question was asked with seeming casualness, but Maire knew there was nothing casual about his pose or the question.

"Nay, I have only one," she said, walking closer to the bed.

"And that would be James, I presume. The *bloody hell* laird-to-be of Clan Campbell?"

She nodded, though his wording was rather curious . . . offensive, really. " 'Tis true, Wee-Jamie will one day be our clan chieftain . . . if we survive the MacNab threat, that is."

It was his turn to nod with understanding.

"How do you know of Jamie?" The words sounded calm, but inside Maire was tense and wary. Her heart thundered against her rib cage.

"I met him yesterday when Old John came to me with the proposition. And a more foul-mouthed little bugger I have ne'er met."

She gasped. Then, noticing his surprise at her gasp, she took a deep, calming breath. "I did not know that Jamie was with Old John when he met with you . . . I mean, I knew he was with Old John, but I thought they were off in the forests, in hiding. The MacNab would use Jamie against me, you see, if he could lay hands on him. I've had to keep him out of sight for weeks now. As to his foul mouth . . ." She shrugged. "I suppose the lad has picked up bad habits from my men, since I've been unavailable to correct him. And besides that . . ." Her words trailed off as she realized that she was rambling with nervousness and Rurik was watching her intently.

"What kind of mother are you that you entrust your son's well-being to that ragtag guard? By thunder, woman! They have trouble enough holding on to their own bodily appendages, let alone those of a running child."

"I am a good mother," she declared hotly, "and don't you dare say otherwise. You know naught about me, or my son, or my clan. Who are you to be my judge, Viking? Are you an expert on fatherhood now, as well as raping and pillaging?"

His only response was a raised eyebrow.

She decided to steer the conversation away from the dangerous subject of her son. "Exactly what was the nature of the proposition that Old John offered you?"

"You don't know? The offer did not come from you?"

"Old John has the right to speak for me, on occasion. And I was unavailable to speak for myself, as you well know." She shivered inwardly at remembrance of the wooden cage, which she planned to burn this morn in a joyous bonfire of celebration.

He waved a hand as if the details of the proposition were of little import. "I help you build up your defenses against the MacNabs. You remove my blue mark. Those are the essential details . . . all that you need to know *for now*."

She narrowed her eyes at him. "What more could you ask?"

"Oh, lady, you owe me aplenty for what I have suffered these past five years. My time here is short, and my list of grievances is long."

"You can see how poor my clanstead is. We have no coin or treasure to offer you in recompense."

Rurik stroked his upper lip as he regarded her, then smiled—a slow, lazy smile that failed to reach his ice blue eyes. "Ah, then, I will have to take my payment in some other form."

That was what Maire was afraid of.

So, she wants a fight, does she? . . .

A short time later, Rurik was standing at a low chest, splashing water onto his face from a pottery bowl, after having just shaved, when Maire came storming back into the bedchamber without knocking. The force of her entry was such that the heavy oaken door swung back on its hinges and hit the timber wall with a resounding crash. A battle shield, which had no doubt belonged to her father, fell to the floor from its wall hooks. The tapestry in the corner shook on its frame.

"Back already? That anxious to begin your punishment, are you?"

She glared at him. "Did you give an order that I was to be confined inside my own keep?" she demanded. "That huge warhorse of a guard of yours . . . the one with the battle-ax the size of a drawbridge . . . actually laid his hands on me when I attempted to walk through my own gates."

"Laid his hands . . . Who, Stigand?"

"Aye, he's the one. He had the nerve to lift me by the scruff of the neck—with one hand, mind you—and toss me back inside like a . . . like a pestsome dog."

Rurik smiled at that image. Little did she know that she was fortunate to still have her head in place.

"I . . . need . . . to . . . see . . . my son," she said, spacing her words evenly.

"Bring . . . him . . . here," Rurik replied in like fashion.

"Nay," she snapped, with no explanation whatsoever. Then her eyes dropped lower and took in his nakedness. In an instant, a rosy flush spread across her face, down to her neck, and beyond. He could tell that she wanted to bolt, but she stood frozen in place. "Have you no shame? Tsk-tsk. Don some garments, at once." She turned away as if she expected him to comply immediately.

Hah! It will be a sorrowful day in Valhalla when I bend to the orders of a woman, and certainly not a woman who happens to be a witch. Just to annoy her, he took his time drying his face with a linen cloth, ran a carved-bone comb through his long hair, yawned loudly, and stretched widely. Only then did he pull on a pair of braies. "I am decent now," he announced finally.

Her eyes swept over his hip-hugging, low-slung braies, which exposed his flat-ridged abdomen and the beginning of his navel. He had a good body, and felt no shame at her close scrutiny. "You are never decent," she asserted.

He took that as a compliment and tipped his head in thanks.

She made a low, growling sound, which she intended to demonstrate her displeasure, but which he found oddly arousing. When she noticed the effect on him, she repeated the growl in a prolonged fashion, accompanied by the tugging of both hands at the roots of her luxuriant hair.

He surmised that she was getting frustrated.

'Twas always a good sign when women got frustrated, in Rurik's opinion.

"Didst thou barge into my bedchamber for some particular reason?" he inquired sweetly.

"*Your* bedchamber?" she sputtered.

'Twas also a good sign when women sputtered over men's superior actions, Rurik decided.

"I came into *my* bedchamber to inform you that I will not be a prisoner in my own keep. I had enough of that with the MacNabs. I will not abide similar treatment from Vikings . . . whom I gave good welcome into my home, I might remind you, mucklehead."

"I would not exactly describe it as *welcome*," he pointed out as he hitched up his braies, then pulled a brown tunic over his head and gathered it at the waist with a wide leather belt. The tunic was an old one but of the finest wool fabric made by Alinor, his friend Tykir's wife. The embroidered thistle design along the edges in shades of green and yellow was still visible. "Know this, m'lady witch, my guards have been given precise orders to ride your tail like fleas, everywhere you go, even to the garderobe. And that order stands till the blue mark is gone from my face . . . and mayhap even beyond that, for there is still your punishment to be dealt with."

She huffed with disgust and murmured something under her breath that sounded like "We shall see about that."

"I'm ready if you are," he pronounced then, having slipped on a pair of half boots and attached his scabbarded sword to his belt.

"Ready for what?" she choked out.

"To have my blue mark removed. What else?"

"I thought that perchance you might want to break your fast first." Her eyes shifted from side to side as she spoke.

Rurik immediately tensed with suspicion. "You do have the antidote to remove the blue mark . . . do you not?"

"Well, not exactly." She looked everywhere but at him.

"What *exactly* do you mean? How will you remove the mark?"

"I do not know."

Aaarrgh! She does not know. Is the woman demented? What kind of witch is she anyhow? Three long years of searching for her and she tells me she does not know. Through gritted teeth, he asked, "How did you put the mark there?"

"I do not know."

I swear, I am going to kill her . . . and take great pleasure in the act. Does she know how close she is to death? "How do you plan on fulfilling your part of our proposition?"

"I do not know."

Rurik counted to ten inside his head, *Ein, tveir, þrír, fjórir, fimm, sex, sjau, átta, níu, tíu.* Only when he'd regained his calm did he speak. "Well, *I* know something, wench. Best you explain yourself, and quickly, or I am going to hold the world's biggest witch-burning. And guess who will be tied to the stake?"

Maire cringed, but to her credit, she did not cry or beg for mercy, as most women would. "Fanned fires and forced love ne'er do well," she said, instead.

"What in bloody hell does that mean?"

"You cannot force things that come naturally." She must have sensed his rising temper, for she quickly explained, "The answer will come to me when it comes . . . naturally."

"Are you barmy?" Rurik felt like pulling at his own hair, a wee bit barmy himself.

"It's like this . . . ," she began.

Rurik groaned inwardly. Every time a female began with, "It's like this . . ." it was a certainty that her man was not going to like what she was about to say. *Not that I am Maire's man. No, no, no. I am definitely not her man.*

". . . I was angry with you that time that you . . . that we . . . uh . . ."

"Made love?"

"Coupled," she said with a becoming blush.

He grinned at her discomfort, despite the seriousness of their conversation. So much of his life depended on the removal of that damned mark . . . his marriage, his reputation, everything.

"In my anger, I wanted to lash out at you, but I also needed to go away with you, far from the Highlands, for a time, leastways. But as you will recall, you declined my request . . . in a most rude fashion, incidentally."

"Rude fashion?"

"You laughed at me."

"I did? And for that you marked me for life?"

"Nay, you do not understand. My need for escape was more important than my damaged pride. So, whilst you were sleeping, I took a vial from the leather bag Cailleach gave me—"

"Cailleach?"

She frowned in annoyance at his interruption. "Cailleach was the old crone who taught me witchcraft at one time."

Rurik was getting a huge ache in his head from Maire's roundabout explanation, which made no sense at all. "Backtrack here a bit, Maire. You took a vial from the witch's bag. What did you intend to do with it?"

"I was going to slip some of it through your lips

whilst you slept, but I tripped and the liquid in the vial spilled onto your face."

Rurik still did not understand. "What kind of potion was in the vial?"

"Well, I thought it was a . . ." Her words trailed off into an indecipherable murmur at the end, and she picked up with, "but obviously it was something else."

"What did you say? I could not hear you. What kind of potion had you intended to give me?"

"A love potion," she practically shouted. "There! Are you happy now that you know?"

"A love potion? A love potion? Lady, the desire to swive you has ne'er been a problem." He could not stop the grin that crept over his lips.

"Ooooh! Do not dare to laugh at me again, Viking."

"What will you do? Put another mark on me? Slip me a love potion? Turn me into a toad?"

"You *are* a toad," she declared and had the nerve to dump the pottery bowl of wash water over his head before she sailed away, out of the room.

He could not care. He was laughing too hard.

And he did not believe a single word the witch had said. He knew only too well the conspiracies that enemies wove in the course of battle, and there was no doubt in his mind that he and Maire were in a war . . . of wits, if nothing else. The only leverage she had over him was the blue mark, and she would not want to remove it till she had gained all she could from him.

Little did the witch know what a seasoned warrior he was, and how much he relished a good battle. She would never, ever win, whether crossing swords, or wills, with him.

He was sore angry with the witch, and had been for five long years. Still, for now, he could not help delighting in the laughter that rippled through him at her weak machinations.

A love potion? Indeed!

A wise man knows when to slither away . . .

It was late afternoon, and the Campbell clan was celebrating their liberation before a huge bonfire composed of the wooden cage that had held their leader for almost a week.

The number of clan members seemed to be growing by the minute as more and more of them came out of hiding . . . most of them battered or handicapped in some way by war or their harsh lives. Rurik had tried to tell them that it was too soon for celebrating, and that liberation could be a momentary thing, but they would not listen to him. Instead, they gazed at him as if he were a savior sent by the gods . . . or, worse yet, a knight in shining armor called forth by a dim-witted witch.

The only one missing was Maire's son, and Rurik was starting to be sorely annoyed by that fact. He suspected that Maire feared contamination by him . . . as if he might turn the wee-laird into a Viking, of all horrible things.

"What do you think?" Rurik asked Stigand and Bolthor, who had been working with the men all day, attempting to instill some discipline and rigor into their fighting exercises.

"They have heart," Stigand informed him. "Even those who are lathe and weak have the will to fight. That may not seem like much, but it could make the difference."

"And there are those who were fierce warriors and can be again, despite their weaknesses," Bolthor added. "Like Young John with the one eye. Even with just a few lessons this morning, I was able to show him how to better handle himself. In truth, his half-blindness is not near as bad as mine. He can still see blurry shapes with his bad eye. It is a question of balance, and he is an enthusiastic learner."

Rurik nodded. "Toste and Vagn have been assessing the physical defenses." He peered off into the distance where they were assisting some of the younger Campbells, pulling down the rotting timber walls with their crumbling stone foundations with an eye toward rebuilding and remortaring them over the next few days. Of course, there were several Campbell lasses about admiring their work . . . or could it be their good looks? Truly, the twins garnered female admirers no matter what country they were in. "We have much to do to repair the walls," Rurik went on, "but this clanstead is well situated to ward off attacks when guards are positioned strategically."

"It's all a question of time and numbers of fighting men," Bolthor concluded.

"And skill," Stigand added. "*That* the six of us have aplenty, and the others can be taught. In time."

"Jostein," Rurik yelled out to the young man, who was working with his Campbell counterparts on the wall. Hastily, Jostein rushed over to do his bidding. "Dost think you could find your way back to Britain on your own?"

Jostein nodded eagerly, panting from his vigorous activity.

"This is an important mission, Jostein. I would like you to ride out on the morrow. Go to Ravenshire in Northumbria, the estate of Lord Eirik and Lady Eadyth. Explain the situation here, and ask if he has troops to spare that he could send to our aid."

Jostein fair beamed with self-importance over the task he was being assigned. "I could depart right now," he said, overanxious to fulfill Rurik's wishes. "It should be only a three-day trip each way. I could be back within a sennight."

Rurik patted him on the shoulder. "Tomorrow will be soon enough."

Maire walked up to them then. She was still annoyed with him over being confined to the keep, and Bolthor wasn't too happy either. A short time ago, he'd grumbled that he'd never known a woman to visit the privy as often as Maire did. He was even considering the creation of a special saga about it, "The Mystery of What Women Do for So Long in a Privy." He'd immediately quashed that idea when Maire had overheard and whalloped him over the head with a halibut that the cook had just given her to examine for dinner fare.

But now, it appeared that the annoying wench had another matter on her mind. Unfortunately, he was the target of her scowls now. Fortunately, she had no fish in hand, although she was carrying a long stick, which he suspected was her witch's staff. No doubt, she could turn a rake into a fish with one swish of that long wand. Best he keep a safe distance from her.

"Well, now that we've gotten rid of the cage, there's only one thing left to do. Why are you edging away from me like that?"

He inclined his head in question at her first comment, but refused to answer her second. He was no half brain. Leastways, not usually.

"The snakes."

"Huh?" He glanced across the bailey toward the area where her cage had hung. Then he gulped. *The snakes.* He'd forgotten. In the space of that gulp, all his comrades vanished, suddenly called away to the wall rebuilding project. Rurik had a strong distaste for the slimy creatures, probably stemming back to his early days at the farmstead where huge black snakes hung about the sties, seeking the warmth of the pigs' bodies, he supposed. Apparently, his men had a disliking for snakes, as well.

Resolutely, he walked over to the woven mat and flipped it up with the tip of a boot, tossing it to the side. There had to be at least five dozen snakes down in the pit, many of them of enormous size. He had no idea if they were poisonous or not. In truth, it hardly mattered. Bile rose to his throat.

"Shall I go get a shepherd's crook for you to lift the beasties out?" Maire asked.

He jumped, not having realized that she'd followed him and was peering over his shoulder.

"Nay, I do not want a shepherd's crook," he said, mimicking her voice. If she thought he was going to lift each of those disgusting "beasties" out one at a time, she was more demented than he already thought. "Don't you have a witch's curse handy that would strike them dead, or better yet, make them disappear?"

She pondered a moment. "Not handy."

He bared his upper teeth with revulsion. He was a fighting man . . . a strategist. What would he do if he were in the midst of battle? "Methinks I could go to the scullery and get a large kettle of oil from the cook."

Maire inquired of him, sarcastically, "Dost intend to drown them in oil?"

That was exactly what he had been contemplating. He cast her a fulminating glower, which should have made her cower. Instead, she grinned at him.

"Be careful, wench, lest I toss you into the oil pit as well to keep the reptiles company."

"Hah!" she said, but then she added, "Don't worry about it. I'll take care of the snakes myself."

There were some times in life when it was wise for a

warrior to blunder onward, even when he knew the consequences. Other times, 'twas best to retreat. Rurik chose the latter course. "If you insist," he conceded.

She favored him with a glance that was not complimentary.

After several of the Campbell men removed the snakes with long-handled crooks and pronged sticks and carried them off into the distance in covered woven baskets, Rurik breathed a sigh of relief. And he didn't even feel guilty that on this occasion he'd failed to impress Maire by his knight-in-shining-armor talents. He reminded himself that he did not have a chivalrous bone in his body. And he definitely was not a knight.

Still, he was not totally without noble sentiments.

He resolved that mayhap he would impress her next time.

But it would not be with snakes.

Her punishment would be licking? . . .

"Does this appear familiar?" Rurik asked her. He was pointing to a clump of woodbine.

"Umm. I don't think that's it."

Grabbing for the low-hanging limb of an oak tree, he swung back and forth, his feet two boot-lengths off the ground. "How about this?"

"Nay," she said. But what she thought was, *Look at those muscles in his forearms. Holy Saints! I feel warm just looking at him. And who knew that a man could have such wide shoulders and then such a narrow waist. Is it a characteristic of all Vikings, or just him?*

"And this?" He'd dropped to the ground and picked up several acorns. Then some nearby pinecones, followed by the unripened berries on a mulberry bush.

"Nay. Nay. Nay."

After spending the morning and half the afternoon

overseeing the rebuilding of her castle walls and exercising the men in swordplay and hand-to-hand combat, Rurik had hauled her bodily out of the keep and into the hills, demanding that she find the remedy for his blue mark. Somehow he'd gotten the idea that all she would have to do was peruse the various plants growing in the wild and miraculously she would remember the recipe for the potion in the vial she'd spilled on him.

It was not that easy.

"How about this?" He hunkered down to examine some moss growing over the roots of a rowan tree, but all Maire could see was the way his tight trews pulled against the muscles in his thighs and buttocks. He glanced suddenly over his shoulder and made a tsk-ing sound of disgust on noticing the direction of her gaze. "Pay attention, Maire. This is serious. If you can't remember the ingredients in that vial, you will never be able to remove my blue mark. In that case, I will have to kill you. Or something."

His threats did not alarm her . . . leastways, not too much. It was the *something* that caused the fine hairs to stand out on her body. Putting those concerns aside, she pondered the fact that Rurik had not been surprised at her appreciative perusal. He was a man who knew he was comely. That was obvious in the way he groomed and dressed himself. His face was clean-shaven, his fingernails trimmed, his teeth gleamed whitely from a scrubbing with the shredded end of a twig, and even his breath smelled sweetly of mint leaves he'd been chewing. Although the garments he wore today were not new, as evidenced by the fading of colors in the brown wool fabric and fine embroidery, they were still appealing and well cared for. In his long black hair, on the sides only, he had woven thin braids, interspersed with amber beads.

Someone ought to trim the peacock's tailfeathers.

Yea, vanity came easily to him. In truth, she had heard some refer to him as Rurik the Vain. For a man who put so much value on physical appearance, it was understandable, she supposed, that he would find the blue mark so offensive.

Next to him, Maire felt dowdy. At one time, she had been told she was beautiful . . . or had the promise of beauty. In fact, Rurik himself had spoken those words to her when enticing her to his bed furs. But those days were long gone . . . five years ago, when she had been twenty. She could not recall a time, ever, when she'd been carefree, but there had been others to help shoulder the burdens then. Now her hands were chapped and her nails broken from the hard work of trying to maintain her castle. She had no time for scented soaps or hair grooming. Even the red *arisaid* she wore today had been washed so many times, it was now closer to a dull rose. On her feet were thick brogues, suitable for climbing hill and vale, but far from the feminine shoes of silk and brocade that Rurik was probably accustomed to seeing on women.

She shook her head to clear it, as well as to indicate her opinion of the moss Rurik was still handling. He was standing now, a hand on one hip, another hand holding the moss, all the while tapping his foot impatiently while she wool-gathered.

"That is just moss . . . good only for mattress stuffing. Betimes it works for stomach cramps, as well," she informed him.

"I'm getting stomach cramps just walking up and down these hills."

"I could recommend an herbal that—"

"Nay!" he said, much too quickly. "If I am not careful, you may have my head swiveling on my neck with one of your cockeyed potions."

She raised her brows.

"Can you be a little more helpful in trying to locate the herbs that were put in that vial?" he sniped.

"Let's think about what we do know first," she suggested, sinking down to a large, flat boulder. It immediately tipped forward, and she jumped up in panic, then bent over to examine it.

"What in bloody hell is that?" Rurik asked, coming closer. Pressing the edge of the boulder with the toe of his half boot, he caused it to rock back and forth, then side to side.

"It's called a judgment stone. We have many of these throughout Scotland. No one knows for sure if they were hand-hewn to sway in this manner, or if nature honed them thus," she explained. "In any case, long ago the elders of a clan, or perchance the druids, used the stone to determine the guilt or innocence of an accused person. If the stone tipped front to back, he was deemed guilty . . . from side to side, innocent." She paused, putting a forefinger to her chin in thought. "Or mayhap it was the opposite."

"You Scots are a peculiar people, believing in such odd things," Rurik commented with a shake of his head as he went back to leaning against a tree. He picked up a blade of grass, nibbling on the end of it as he studied her.

Shivering a little under his cool regard, she sat back down on the rock, being careful to balance her weight so that it did not teeter. "No more peculiar than the English, or people of other lands, who believed a person's guilt or innocence could be discovered by drowning. You know, if a culprit survived being dunked under water for a lengthy period of time, he was guilty. If he died, he was innocent. And then, what good was that?"

Rurik smiled. "You have a point there."

"Back to the fluid in the vial that I spilled on you . . .

there must have been woad, for the blue color . . . and I recall the scent of lavender . . . so, let's assume crushed lavender, as well. Both would have been mixed in an oil base, to preserve the potency of the ingredients. But I just cannot think what agent would have been in the mixture to give the color permanency. Certainly the woad worn by Celtic warriors, washed off." She shrugged, at a loss as to what the other component might have been.

"Don't you have witch annals somewhere? Written documents that spell out all your . . . well, spells and curses and rituals and such? Like the priests have with their illuminated manuscripts?"

She shook her head. "Mostly the *magick airts,* as they are called, are passed through the generations by word of mouth. Unfortunately, I did not study enough years with old Cailleach before my husband banished her from our lands."

"Your husband did not favor your mentor-witch?"

"Kenneth loathed her."

"Hmmm. What did she do to him? Turn him blue, or"—he chuckled—"turn him into a frog?"

"He was already a frog."

"Like me?"

Worse. Far worse. Unfortunately, I did not know that afore the wedding. Cailleach did, though. If only I'd heeded her warnings. "The selfsame."

Rurik cocked his head to the side, and his mischievous eyes skimmed over her body with a boldness that made Maire squirm uncomfortably on her already shaky perch. "Bolthor contends that witches dance in the forest, naked. Mayhap you should try that, to see if some of your powers come to the fore." The libertine looked as if he would appreciate that spectacle immensely.

She slanted him a condescending scowl. "Not in this lifetime, and certainly not in front of you."

He shrugged, grinning unrepentantly. "Why can't you consult other witches in your . . . uh, coven?"

She glanced up at him where he still stood, leaning back against the trunk of the tree, arms folded over his chest, the blade of grass dangling from his lips. Then she laughed. "I'm not that kind of a witch."

"What kind of witch are you?"

"A solitary."

"Maire, Maire, Maire. You lie through your teeth."

She bristled.

"Methinks you know exactly how to remove the blue mark from my face, but you defy me willfully."

"To what purpose?"

"To gain the advantage in using me and my men against your enemies."

"I do want your services . . . your fighting services," she added quickly when she saw a grin tug at his lips, "but I do not lie when I say that I know not precisely how to remove the mark. To tell you the truth, I *am* a witch, but not a very good one."

He still appeared skeptical.

"For example, if I focused hard enough on that tree on which you lean, I might very well be able to split it in two, right down the center. On the other hand, it's just as likely that I would put a permanent part down the center of your hair."

She saw the moment that enlightenment crossed his handsome face. It was not surprising that he moved away from the tree then, just in case. "Ah! That is why everyone snickers when I mention your witchly arts . . . the MacNabs, your clansmen, even your serving women, and the children hereabouts," he said.

She nodded. "Oh, I am able to practice herbal remedies, and sometimes I even get the witchly spells correct, to everyone's advantage, but I have to admit that there have been some disasters," she told him woefully. "I have failed my people."

"Who says you have to be a witch?"

"There is no one else."

He seemed about to argue with that contention, but changed his mind. Instead, he spat out the piece of grass, straightened himself from his leaning stance, and walked toward her. His walk was lazily seductive, but the expression on his face was suddenly hard and resolute . . . threatening, actually.

When he stood directly in front of her, he gave the stone an abrupt push with his boot, which caused it to rock backward, and she with it. On the forward rock, she was still propped on her elbows, trying to sit up, but he gave the slab another shove.

"What are you trying to do?" she demanded.

But he was leaning over her now, arms braced on the flat stone, on either side of her shoulders . . . so close she could smell the mint on his breath and the male sweat of his skin from a day of strenuous exertions. His left knee was on the boulder, while his right leg still touched the ground and kept the rock moving, front to back, front to back.

Her voice was no longer demanding, but breathy. It wasn't exactly fear. No, it was something else too disconcerting to name. "Rurik? What is it?"

"You. That's what *it* is."

"Me?" she barely squeaked out.

"Yea. I've put you on the judgment stone, and it has pronounced you guilty."

"Ha, ha, ha. That's not how it's done." She tried to get up, but was fenced in by his arms, and could not get her balance with the constant motion of the stone.

He shrugged indifferently. "Whether a stone deems you guilty or not matters not a whit to me. The important thing is that I still have the blue mark. You expect me to put my life and that of my men at risk, whilst you give naught in return. Well, no more. You have put your mark on me. Now I intend to do the same to you."

"What . . . what do you mean?"

"I mean that I intend to have you, witch. My *mark* will be put on you . . . *inside* you . . . in the way that men have been marking women for ages. By the time I leave the Highlands, you will yearn for me like an opium eater for his pipe. That is how I will mark you. In essence, your virtue is forfeit from now on."

"That is so outrageous, it does not merit discussion. You are far too pretty for such as me."

"Pretty, eh?" He laughed, and it was not a pretty sound.

His mirth was not of comfort to Maire, especially since he was staring at her with eyes that could only be described as smoldering. No man's eyes had ever smoldered for Maire before, and she had to stifle the impulse to be pleased.

"Do not attempt to tell me what interests me when it comes to the man-woman arena. In truth, I have been watching you move about all day in that pink blanket-gown you are wearing—"

"It's not a blanket. It's an *arisaid.*"

"Whatever you call it, its pinkish color reminds me of a confection I ate once in the home of an Eastern potentate. It was so sweet, I remember licking the spoon afterward and my fingertips, as well."

Maire was getting truly alarmed, not just by his lecherous words, but by how they made her feel. "My gown is not pink, it is faded red. And I do not understand this licking business. Now let me up."

Of course, he did not obey her order, but kept the stone rocking with a mocking grin upon his face. His eyes were heavy lidded, burning intensely. "Let me explain this *licking business*, then. Never let it be said that Vikings do not make themselves clear. You look good enough to lick, Maire the Fair. All over. Stark naked. Starting with your nipples, which have already hardened with my words and ache for my attentions."

"They do not. . . . They are not." She glanced down, guiltily, before she could catch herself. Of course, there was no way he could see through the thick fabric of her *arisaid*. He had been guessing. The brute.

"You are a perverted man, Rurik."

"Yea," he agreed with a half smile. "That is one of the good things about me. Women love it."

"Never let it be said that you are an excessively modest man." Her upper lip curled back in a snarl. "Well, I am not one of your women, and will not be."

"You were once."

"Never again."

He put up a hand, his eyes sparkling with the love of combat. "Protest all you want, Maire. This is my promise to you. Every day I bear your mark, you will bear mine. On fair days, I will work with your men and mine to build up the defenses of your castle against the MacNabs, but I will devote the long nights to you and you alone in your bedchamber. On rainy days, there will be more time to devote to your marking, and we might just spent day *and* night in bed. I have so much to teach you . . . so many ways to mark you."

She gasped. She could not help herself.

"Somehow, after a few days of this, I think you will remember your dark arts, or find another witch to stir up a remedy for you. Surely, you are not the only witch in all the Highlands."

"You don't scare me, Viking."

"I don't?" The jut of his chin and the determination on his face did not bode well for her. Then, with deliberate insult, he let his gaze move down from her face to her chest. "Speaking of your nipples . . . and licking . . ."

Nobody is speaking of nipples. Please do not bring up that horrid subject again. I can feel that part of my body reacting already.

". . . there is another place I would like to lick on you, sweetling," he said. Before she knew what he was about, he rocked the stone more forcibly, causing her legs to flail, and he landed with deliberate intent between them. His sex pressed intimately against her sex, and it mattered not that there were several layers of cloth betwixt them. His lips were lowering to hers.

To her embarrassment, she heard a panting noise, and it came from her.

But Rurik was equally affected. She could see that in the sensual hazing of his eyes, his half-lowered lids, and the way he stared at her.

Maire knew then, without a doubt, that Rurik did want her in a man-woman way. She also knew that when he was done with her, she would indeed be marked.

Right now, she did not care.

CHAPTER FIVE

He rocked her world . . .

Quickly, Rurik eased himself atop the startled wench who lay like a sacrificial victim, arms and legs akimbo, where she'd landed when he'd rocked the stone. He'd intended only to scare the witch, who would not disclose the remedy for removing his blue mark.

That was what he'd intended.

But, oh, the consequences of a foolish man's warped intentions.

As soon as he'd settled himself betwixt her inadvertently parted thighs, it was as if a thunderbolt struck him. All thoughts of intimidation or revenge fled his head. He should have known that a favorite part of his body would thicken with a will of its own. He wasn't absolutely positive, but Lance appeared to be actually throbbing. Whilst manhood pressed against womanhood, and his senses grew as fuzzy as the moss he'd just been handling, he could not remember why he had hated this woman for five long years, why he needed to have her fearful of him, why it was important that he remain aloof and unmoved by her.

Unfortunately, everything that was male in him moved, of its own accord. Lance—*the bloody lackwit!*—was nigh smiling with anticipation.

I just want to show her who is in charge. I am going

to stop . . . in a moment, he told himself. And he was serious.

"Nay," she whispered.

"Yea," he responded, his arms already reaching out for her.

I am going to stop . . . in a moment.

Really.

She went stiff as he gripped her head with two hands by tunneling his fingers into her hair . . . hair so fine it formed a cobweb of red about her face. Smudges of scarlet bloomed on her cheeks in a most becoming manner, making her seem younger than she was, like a sun-drenched maiden, which he knew too well that she was not. She dropped her green eyes under his steady gaze but not before he admired their misty illumination. Like pale emeralds, they were, shaded by thick lashes of a darker hue, in this light more brown than russet.

"*Ert mjg falleg,*" he told her in a voice he barely recognized for its huskiness. "You are so beautiful."

Her chin shot up at his words, and her eyes locked with his, wide with surprise. "I am no such thing," she protested hotly, but he could tell she was pleased at his compliment.

Women! They are so predictable. He took a deep breath for control, and girded himself with resolve. *I am going to stop . . . in a moment. I swear before all the gods that I will . . . well, some of the gods . . . Loki, perchance. That lighthearted jester of a god is having a good laugh on me now, I would wager.*

It must have been Rurik's long period of self-denial—he could not recall the last time he'd lain with a woman—for Maire was becoming compellingly attractive to him. The consummate woman. All that was feminine and desirable. She made him want her body, but it was more than that; she made him want . . . he felt mysterious yearnings he could not name, which tantalized and terrified him at the same time.

I am going to stop . . . in a moment. I am, I am, I am.

His lips were lowering to hers beginning the mating ritual that came instinctively to all men and women when the sap thickened in their bodies and pooled in certain places. In truth, it was almost as if he could feel the blood flowing, torrid and insistent, from his fingertips, all the way to his toes, and some important places in between.

I am going to stop . . . in a moment, he repeated to himself like a litany, trying to ignore his thundering heart.

But almost immediately, under the assault of a million lustful impulses, he exclaimed to himself, *To hell with stopping!*

"By your leave, my lady witch, be forewarned. I am going to kiss you senseless."

"I do not give you leave," she said on a gasp.

"Oh?" He pondered her protest, but not very seriously, then replied, "More's the pity." With a sigh he set his course to do what he damned well pleased, her wishes notwithstanding. That decided, he settled his mouth over hers. Wanting to be slow and gentle, he entreated and persuaded her into the love play by moving his lips against hers, back and forth, till they slickened and fitted together perfectly. When her lips turned pliant, his senses flamed and he glided the tip of his tongue along the seam.

She obligingly parted for him with a moan.

That moan was his undoing. He made a rough growl deep in his throat and entered her, his tongue lightly touching the roof of her mouth.

Instinctively, she sucked on him, and he almost catapulted off the boulder. Tearing his mouth from hers, he stared down, stunned by the turbulent passions that swirled betwixt them, at just that one kiss. A hunger for her assailed him, so intense he could scarce breathe. He panted, trying to rein in his burgeoning desire.

Her long, sweeping lashes lowered over green eyes that held a glint of wonder. She, too, must be experiencing the selfsame emotions. He should get up now from where he still lay sprawled over her. He had accomplished his goal. He'd scared the spit out of her. But her lips were moist, and, oh, so inviting. He could not resist her allure.

Had she bewitched him with a spell, or one of her love potions?

"You taste like mint," she said in a breathless whisper.

Damn, damn, damn! Did she have to say that? He could not resist her now. "You taste like heaven," he countered. And she did.

Lacing his fingers with hers, he stretched their arms overhead. At the same time, he ground his hips against the heart of her, which lay open to him betwixt her cloth-covered thighs.

"Oh . . . merciful . . . Mary!" she rasped out and arched herself up toward him. "What is happening to me, you wicked man? You are turning me into an inferno."

Her artless admission of arousal stirred all that was masculine in Rurik. And, indeed, a red flush did color her skin . . . skin that was deliciously warm and tempting to touch. He murmured against her parted lips, "I have always wanted to play with fire, m'lady."

When he reclaimed her lips now, there was nothing gentle or slow in his approach. Rapacious and devouring, he pressed his lips and thrust his tongue. Rurik had always prided himself on being an inventive lover who ofttimes followed specific, tried-and-true steps to bring his women to ecstasy. Now, he was barely able to focus through the haze of his excitement. He was a man out of control, and he did not care. Maire—*bless her soul*—gave herself freely to the fervor of his kisses. When he forced her lips open even wider, she made soft sounds of pleasure into his mouth . . . whimpers that spurred his invasion to be even bolder. He could not swear that it was so, but he suspected he might have whimpered back.

Rurik had never known that kissing could be so intimate or so glorious, and he told her so . . . in words that were sinfully explicit. Maire did not seem to mind. Actually, an erotic tremor rippled over her body in response. He even saw goose bumps rise on her bared forearms. In his experience, goose bumps on a woman's flesh during lovemaking were a good thing. Some men disdained all the preliminary exercises and gestures in lovemaking, wanting to get right to the tupping, but there was no doubt in Rurik's opinion that this kiss he and Maire shared was love play of the grandest sort.

But, wait, Maire's hands were fluttering with dismay, and he noticed her eyes darting from side to side. She was starting to think, he would wager, and a thinking female was not a good thing when the male sap was running high.

Swiftly, before she could spout all the reasons why this was not a good idea, Rurik laid a line of nibbling kisses along her jaw, up to her ear, which he exposed by brushing back her hair. At first, he just flicked his tongue against the shell of her ear, wetting its grooves and crevices. When she made a mewling noise, he knew—*he just knew*—that he had hit upon one of Maire's most sensitive spots. All women had them—leastways, those he'd come in contact with did—but they were ofttimes in different places . . . the ears, the back of the knees, the nipples, the sensitive flesh betwixt the woman-folds, the navel, even the arch of a foot. Now that he knew Maire's ears were susceptible to titillation, he launched a full assault. Using the tip of his tongue, he circled her ear, then gently blew it dry. He stabbed and withdrew, then sucked the lobe. All this was accompanied by whispered words of praise and encouragement to her.

Maire grew wild. "I am so ashamed," she cried out at one point. "Look what you do to me. Again."

"Nay, do not say so. Your passion is my pleasure, and there is no shame in that."

She shook her head in denial, even as she reared her neck up with continuing ardor. "I hate you, Rurik."

Rurik knew that. Hell, he hated her himself. Still, the words hurt. "Do you hate my kisses, too?" He could not keep himself from asking that question. *How pitiful I am!*

Her eyes were cloudy with arousal when she met his direct gaze. For a moment, it appeared as if she was going to lie, but then she stopped herself. "Your . . . kisses . . . are . . . sweet . . . agony," she admitted through gritted teeth.

"Ah, well, then we are equal partners, dearling," he confided back to her, "for you make me tremble." And that was the truth. On the other hand, mayhap his knees on the hard stone could be weak due to his landing on those joints so often during combat; they did tend to creak betimes. She did not need to know that, though.

When his lips met hers again, it was, indeed, sweet, sweet agony, for them both. And he was not surprised at the hissing noise he heard. He felt like hissing himself, and purring, and shouting with sheer joy.

But then, he realized that the hissing noise did not come from Maire. *Oh, Holy Thor! Could it be more snakes? Is this the location of the den where the men relocated the snakes from the pit?* His slumberous eyes flew open, and he leaped back off her body and the stone, at once in a crouched battle stance, ready to fight off this new, unknown threat. But, no, it was not snakes in the vicinity. It was a frenzied animal that now hurled itself at his back and began clawing his shoulders. And it was another wild animal, above Maire's head on the rock, that was hissing.

"Don' ye be hurtin' me mother, ye bloody, codsucking Viking," a child's voice shrieked into his ear as small fists pummeled his shoulders and clawed at his neck. At the same time that Rurik recognized it was Maire's son hanging on his back like a miniature berserker, he took in the large black cat perched on the boulder, still hissing, with its back bowed. It was about to launch itself at Rurik's face, he could tell.

"Now, Rose, settle down," Maire said, grabbing for the feline just as it was poised to attack.

"Rose? You named that monster *Rose?* A witch's familiar named Rose?" By now, Rurik had disengaged the foul-mouthed urchin from his back and had him cradled firmly at his side with an arm wrapped around his waist, like a sack of barley. Who knew such a young person could spout so many coarse words? Or could stink so bad?

"Rose is no monster," Wee-Jamie yelled.

"And she's not a familiar, either," Maire declared, shimmying off the boulder to stand facing him with the still hissing cat in her arms. "She's just a sweet pet, given to Wee-Jamie by a passing tinker last year."

Rurik had seen pet harem cats with sleek, silky fur. This cat's mangy hair stood on end, and it was bald in spots. Not a pretty sight. Right now it was staring up at Maire with adoration and docile innocence. But Rose wasn't fooling Rurik one bit. He knew that, given the chance, the cat would put stripes on his ballocks.

Rurik wished his Beast were here now. The wolfhound would make a tasty meal of yon cat.

"You odious wretch! There you are, you rascal," another voice exclaimed. It was the rotund monk, who came rushing out of the trees, his cassock lifted to his hairy calves; Rurik had seen him the first day he'd met the Campbell clan. The panting man almost tripped over a root and had to grab for the boulder to keep from falling over . . . which caused the rock to start rocking again . . . which caused Rurik to recall what he'd been about to do on said rocking rock.

"Father Baldwin!" Maire squealed with embarrassment.

"Were you not told to stay in camp?" Father Baldwin scolded the boy, calling Rurik's lustful thoughts back to the present. "Everyone has been looking for you hither and yon. Dost know the trouble you have caused? Dost know the danger you could be in if one of the MacNabs grabbed you?"

"No one's gonna grab me," the boy boasted, which was ridiculous, considering his position in Rurik's imprisoning embrace.

In a rush of words, Father Baldwin explained how the boy had slipped away from his guardianship and promised that it would not happen again, even if they had to tie the boy and his cat to a tree. At that the child issued an expletive so obscene that everyone gaped at him, and the cat pissed on Rurik's boot. His very expensive skin boots made of cured reindeer hide.

Rurik was too stunned at the cat's audacity to do more than gape . . . and plan his revenge.

"Listen to me, son or no son, you are due for a good mouth-soaping," Maire warned, wagging a forefinger at her whelp, "and do not think I won't do it, either." God, he loved it when Maire was fierce and ill-tempered. She reminded him of a Norse Valkyrie about to go into battle.

"Why do you not bring the boy back to the castle now that the MacNabs have been banished from the grounds? Will he not be safer there under my guardianship?"

The monk's face, right up to his half-bald, tonsured

head, turned nigh purple and Maire looked as if Rurik had suggested that they toss her son into a fiery pit.

"What? What's wrong with my suggestion?" he asked, thoroughly confused.

"Attend me well, Viking. Do not attempt to tell me what is best for my bairn. He is mine, and mine alone."

"Huh? As if I would want him!"

Maire gave him an odd look, then signaled to Father Baldwin, who picked up the cat, which Rurik would swear was smirking, and held out his free hand for the boy. Rurik released him, but not before swatting the youthling on the arse. Wee-Jamie gave him a look over his shoulder so malevolent it would have done Stigand proud. Rurik would be sure to watch his back in the future, though. An attempt at retribution was sure to come from this grimy gremlin.

'Twas odd the way Maire acted concerning her son, as if she feared for his safety in his presence or that of the Vikings who served under him. Rurik shrugged. It was her decision. Besides, he had no particular inclination to have an unpleasant child underfoot.

But then Maire made a soft sound—half plea, half sob. "Jamie," was all she said.

The boy heard, though. Turning, he pulled his hand from the monk's grasp and rushed back into her open arms. Hugging fiercely, the two were giving each other small kisses and speaking of how much they missed each other.

Rurik had never had a mother, and his heart about broke to see these two together. With such a strong bond between them, their willingness to be parted for even a day puzzled him mightily.

In a moment, the boy and the monk were gone.

Suddenly, Rurik and Maire were alone once again, and everything was quiet in the clearing.

He looked at Maire.

Maire looked at him.

He put his hands on his hips.

She did the same.

You'd never know they had been moaning in each other's mouths a short time ago by the expression of contempt on Maire's face . . . a face that was, incidentally, rose-colored from the abrasion of his late-day whiskers. Her lips were still kiss-swollen, and there was a blood mark on the side of her neck from his sucking on her skin like a sex-starved youthling. But her eyes—*for the love of Freyja!*—her eyes were throwing green sparks of fire at him.

If Rurik were a betting man, he would wager now that Maire was not in the mood for resuming their love games.

He understood perfectly. He was having a few reservations himself about what had almost happened betwixt them. Oh, he was not averse to making love with the witch, but he intended to do so on his own terms, not whilst careening dizzily from lack of control. Best he set the record straight, though, afore she launched into him with her usual shrew words.

"I do not much appreciate your ensorcelling me, witch," he informed her haughtily. "Do not do it again."

"Me? Me?" she sputtered. " 'Twas you who put a spell on me. Just like that other time. Do not do it again."

"I know naught of spells. That is your line of work. I am just a simple soldier."

"Hah! There is naught simple about you, Viking."

He chose to take that as a compliment. But before he could reply, Maire was stomping off, back toward her castle.

"Hey! Where are you off to in such a rush?" he asked, hurrying to catch up. "Did I not tell you that you are to go nowhere without me, or one of my guards?"

She said something under her breath that sounded as foul as the offal that spewed from her son's mouth, and kept walking. But then she told him, "I'm going to the kitchens."

"Since when do you work as a scullery maid, or cook's helper? Would you stand still? I can't keep up with you on these sharp rocks. I hope they're not stones from burial cairns. I would hate to think I'm stepping on so many dead people."

Maire ignored his complaints and answered his question. "I work everywhere in my keep. With the shortage of menfolk, I even mucked the stables last month." She held up her work-roughened hand as illustration. "In any case, it's a special meal we are preparing for this evening." Her eyes danced with mischief.

"Why?" he asked suspiciously, then swore as he stubbed his big toe.

"To celebrate the liberation of the snakes, I suppose. Or our liberation from the MacNabs. Or the beauty of a summer day."

"Or mayhap to show hospitality to your Viking savior?" he offered, just to tweak her. He had discovered early on that she was easily tweaked. And Viking men were ever so good at tweaking their women. "Or to thank one particular Viking for teaching you so much about love play?" He waggled his eyebrows at her.

Her only answer was a grunt. Really, the wench had no sense of humor at all.

He knew their situation was dire. The MacNabs could attack at any moment. Maire had done naught to remove his blue mark. If the situation did not alter soon, he might very well have to allow Stigand to lop off her head. And, meanwhile, the wench was turning *his* head and other body parts, with the mere twitch of her hips, or lips.

Still, there was no harm in trying to be a pleasant fellow. So, when he finally matched his pace to hers, he inquired, "And what might this special meal be?"

He should have known better. He really should have.

"Haggis."

The question was who would be the tamed and who the tamer? . . .

Hours later, Rurik walked into the great hall of Maire's keep and surveyed the bustling activity that continued to transform the castle.

While he and all the men and boys had worked on the stone-and-timber walls, many of which were now back to their former condition, Maire had gone indoors to complete some much-needed cleaning. Apparently, recent months had afforded no time to keep up the interior of the castle. More urgent demands . . . like how to withstand the MacNabs . . . had taken precedence. But, no, the condition of the keep bespoke long-standing neglect, not just the past few months since Maire's husband's death. *Hmmm.*

Now old rushes had been raked out, dirt floors swept, and new fragrant rushes laid down. Rusted-out weaponry and shields had been taken down from the walls, and were out in the courtyard, where youthlings were honing and polishing them with sandstone and soft cloths to a glossy shine. Housemaids were scouring the wood trestle tables that had been folded up against the walls during the cleaning operation. And finely woven tapestries were being laundered in a side yard off the kitchen. He wondered who had done the tapestry in Maire's bedchamber and reminded himself to ask her later. Even as he watched, an old woman carried a yoke with two buckets of clean water from the kitchen garden well.

He saw Maire giving orders like a Norse chieftain.

She looked as exhausted as he felt. Pressing the heels of his palms to the small of his back, Rurik arched his shoulders back to remove the kinks of hard labor. There was a strange, immediate sort of satisfaction in working with one's hands, and Rurik suspected that Maire was feeling the same way about the work she'd accomplished this day. He knew he was correct in his assumption when she glanced up and smiled at him . . . before she remembered that he was her enemy, and turned her smile to a frown.

But he'd seen the smile. That was enough. He winked to let her know that he knew.

To his amazement . . . and delight . . . the wench made an obscene gesture at him.

Odin's Blood! He was going to enjoy taming her . . . though not too much. A little taming, that's all he wanted.

"What are you grinning about?" Bolthor asked, coming up to his side.

"A little taming," Rurik disclosed.

Bolthor glanced from him to Maire, then back to him again. "Who will be taming whom?" Bolthor asked.

Rurik glared at his skald. "Did you come here for a reason, or just to provoke me?"

Bolthor smiled lopsidedly at him and scratched his head as if he was not sure. The dolt! But then he revealed, "Yea, I had a reason. The MacNab is waiting in the bailey to speak with you. He is unarmed and alone."

"Well, why did you not say so?" Rurik scolded and rushed outdoors, but not before he heard Bolthor practicing a new saga, which started out with the usual "This is the saga of Rurik the Greater," an introduction that made him cringe every time he heard it.

Rurik was a soldier fierce.
Many an enemy his sword did pierce.

Thus garnered he great self-pride
That none would dare deride.
So armed, the foolish man did boast
From coast to coast to coast
That not only his enemies could he tame
But, as well, a fair dame.
The problem was the dame was no mare,
But a maiden, oh, so fair.
Maire the Fair would not be tamed . . .
Not e'en by a warrior so famed.
In truth, some advised Rurik to take great pains,
Lest he be the one in reins.
But he would not listen,
Though tears of mirth on his friends did glisten
And so it came to pass that Rurik the Vain
became . . .
Rurik the Tame.

Rurik scowled at his skald.

Bolthor merely shrugged and said, "It needs some work."

"It needs scrapping," Rurik muttered and stepped outside into the lowering sunshine. Evening would be approaching soon, and he and his men had not yet bathed or supped.

And there stood Duncan MacNab, cocky as a Sunday rooster, examining the work they'd done to reinforce the collapsing walls of the Campbell castle. If he bent over much farther, and his *pladd* rose much higher on his legs, Rurik was going to get more of a view of the Scotsman's backside than he ever wanted.

Maybe Maire had been correct in keeping her son hidden if her enemy could enter her keep with such ease.

"Does it meet with your approval?" Rurik asked coolly as he stepped up to the man.

Duncan straightened, and being of roughly the same height as Rurik, met his gaze, eye to eye. Rurik made a concerted effort to look away from the single brow that stretched across the other man's forehead and took in, instead, the clean, though unruly, mane of gray-flecked red hair that covered the MacNab's head. He would not have been an unattractive man in his youth, but at fifty and more years, he was way too long in the tooth for Maire, in Rurik's opinion. Not that Maire was actually considering the suit of the MacNab. Far from it.

In fact, he saw her standing in the open doorway of the great hall, staring down the wide steps at the two of them. For once, she had the good sense to hold her tongue and not interfere in men's talk.

"Aye, the work on the wall meets with my approval," Duncan conceded with ill grace. "But why overexert yourself to build up the defenses of this keep when I will be the one to benefit from it eventually?"

Rurik's only answer was a raised eyebrow.

"Listen, man," Duncan said in a more conciliatory manner, turning his back on Maire and the castle. "I can see that you are striving hard to build up the defenses here. And I would have to be blind not to notice all the Campbell vermin who have crawled out of wood and vale to come back home. But you are far outnumbered. You know it, and I know it. And not just in manpower . . . in *whole*-man power, not a lot of limbless, half-blind graybeards."

Rurik bristled, as did some of the Campbell men who overheard the callous remark, including Old John, Young John, Murdoc, Callum, and Rob, whose faces turned red with humiliation. 'Twas unkind of Duncan to demean their manhood so, but then, Duncan was not known for his kindness.

"Your gall passes all bounds, Duncan MacNab. Do not underestimate the power of any man," Rurik said defensively. "If you are half the fighting man you claim to be, surely you know that might is not always measured in weight or height or *wholeness*. Betimes, the difference between victory and defeat is measured in the heart of the warrior. And I can tell you this . . . these men have heart aplenty."

Rurik saw Old John and the others gape at him with surprise. He did not immediately see Bolthor, but he was certain he would be hearing a saga this eve about this very event, making him sound more heroic than was merited. More important, he would warrant that he'd earned points with Maire, who was equally slack-jawed, though that was not why he'd spoken.

Duncan made a snarling sound of anger, but all that issued from his mouth was a profane expletive.

"What brings you here today, Duncan? Medoubts 'tis to make peace."

"Hah! Hardly." Duncan rubbed his mustache with a forefinger, pensively. "I had hoped that we might come to an agreement, soldier to soldier."

"Such as?"

"I could locate the old crone for you." A crafty lift appeared in the center of his lone eyebrow.

Now, that offer surprised Rurik. "The old crone? What would I want with some old crone? Do I look as if I need an aged woman for swiving?"

"You misread me, Viking. I refer to Cailleach . . . the old crone who was mentor to Maire the Witch."

"You would deliver another witch to me? I can scarce wait. Two witches of my very own."

"Not just any witch . . . a powerful witch . . . one who would surely know how to remove your blue mark."

"Are you saying that Maire cannot?"

"I'm not saying she canna, but I notice your mark is still there."

Rurik didn't need any reminders. But something nagged at his memory. "Didn't Kenneth banish the witch from Scotland when he took Maire to wife?"

Duncan threw out his hands as if that fact were neither here nor there.

Rurik frowned. "Speak plainly. Know you where the old crone is?"

"Mayhap I do, and mayhap I do not."

"Aaarrgh! Enough of your games! What is it you want of me?"

"Maire. And her Campbell lands. In return, I give you back your pretty face and safe conduct out of Scotland."

Rurik pondered for several long minutes. It was a tempting offer. Truly it was. Especially since he had a wife-to-be waiting anxiously for him in the Hebrides. A smart-thinking man would jump at this chance.

But Rurik did not always do the smart thing.

And he did not like the MacNab . . . not one bit.

And he did not relish jumping to any man's tune, least of all a scurvy Scot.

And honor was too hard-won for a man to give it up easily.

And the look on the Campbell men's faces when he'd defended them had touched a place deep inside of Rurik.

And he had not yet "punished" Maire with long bouts of bedsport.

Still, Rurik surprised even himself when he declined with a curt, "I am not interested."

CHAPTER SIX

Who ever heard of a Scots Viking? . . .

It was late before supper was served that night. Maire and her women had worked hard to clean the hall—the first time in many, many months, apparently—and she'd insisted that everyone bathe before coming inside to eat. So, the men went to one loch and the women to another, where they made quick work of their ablutions in the icy waters.

Although the Scotsmen did a bit of griping, Rurik and his men didn't mind all that much. Norsemen tended to bathe more often than the average man. Some said that was why women from many lands were attracted to them . . . not because of their wondrous good looks, but because they were less malodorous than their own menfolk. Rurik preferred to think it was both.

He now leaned back in his chair on the dais where the head table was located, sipping at a cup of *uisge-beatha*. The amber-colored liquid went down smoothly, and his gullet was becoming accustomed to its bite, but Rurik was cautious about imbibing too much. He had plans for later that would not be enhanced by his having an alehead. In the meantime, it was rather nice, just sitting in a clean hall, with muscles aching after a day of hard labor, knowing they were safe for a while, and relishing the pleasant scents wafting around them—not just the sweet-scented herbs from the rushes, but the rich aromas of roast meats, soon to come to the table. *I must be getting old, to gain satisfaction from such small things.*

There was another activity bringing enjoyment to Rurik, and that was just watching Maire as she bustled about the hall, ordering maids about in the serving of the meal. She'd changed her *arisaid* after bathing, and this one-piece, belted garment that the Scotswomen arranged so artfully into pleats and gathers was just as faded as the one she'd had on this afternoon. Were they all she had? And her a highborn lady, too. Why hadn't her husband—gone only three months—provided better for her? Oh, Rurik knew the keep was in bad shape, neglected because of other, more dire concerns, but her people raised their own sheep and wove their own cloth.

Hmmm. There was a puzzle here . . . one that Rurik promised himself he would solve later.

Besides, she looked good to him, even in the loose garment. A braided belt called attention to a slim waist and the turn of hips and high breasts. She would hate it if she knew how all her movements pulled the loose fabric this way and that, but mostly taut against her feminine parts, including the sweet, sweet curve of her buttocks. She would also hate it if she knew that she kept touching, reflexively, the love mark he'd put on her neck, and each time she did so, he felt a jolt in his nether regions. Lance—the ridiculous name he was now giving to his manpart, thanks to Maire—was nigh gleesome with anticipation.

Her hair was still damp from her bath and curled about her face since she'd not had time to dry it properly. He remembered suddenly how her luxuriant hair had felt in his fingers that afternoon.

And how her lips had felt under his lips. Oh, Holy

Thor! He would never forget that. No other woman had such a sensual mouth. He should tell Bolthor to concoct a praise-poem to her lips. "Ode To a Woman's Lips." That idea caused his own lips to curl up at the edges in a slight grin. He could only imagine her consternation.

She glanced up suddenly, and her eyes connected with his. In that moment, when time stood still for a mere second, he saw awareness in her gaze. He would wager a king's treasure that she was remembering, too.

A burst of laughter somewhere in the hall caused them both to blink and glance away, as if they'd committed some forbidden act. He forced himself to take several deep breaths and concentrate on other activities.

At the far end of the hall, he caught a fleeting glimpse of Wee-Jamie, followed by Rose, the mangy cat, followed by the huffing and puffing monk, Father Baldwin, who grabbed both boy and feline by the scruffs of their necks and dragged them back outside. The boy appeared to be still filthy and the only one in the entire clan who hadn't taken a bath. If Rurik didn't know better, he would swear the priest was showering the lad with bad words.

Maire noticed the boy, too. He saw the yearning look in her doleful eyes, but she did nothing to call him back. Evidently, Maire still wanted the boy away from the keep, for his own safety. It seemed unfair to deprive a child of the feast, but that was her decision to make, not his.

Old John was there at the high table with him, as well as Bolthor, Stigand, Toste, and Vagn, though the latter two were ogling the sloe-eyed daughter of some sheepherder come down from the hills yestereve. They were all sipping at the potent brew, and, whilst not *drukkinn,* they were all feeling mellow.

Rurik's eyes strayed to Maire once again . . . an involuntary action he could not seem to stop.

Old John coughed when he noticed the direction of Rurik's gaze. "Smitten with our fair Maire, are ye?"

"Huh? Who? Me?" Rurik said halfwittedly.

Old John just smiled and touched his neck, mirroring Maire's gesture. By the holy rood, had everyone noticed the mark on her neck?

Sensing Rurik's discomfort, he said, "Now, now, do not be blustering so. 'Tis a natural thing fer a man to want a woman. The bulls in the fields, the rams in the hills, even the wee fishies in the burns . . . all these are subject to the same urges as we men. Some say it all began with Adam. Aye, methinks 'tis all part of God's plan and you and Maire be no different."

Odin's eyes! Now, I'm being lectured on sex by a one-armed, aging Scotsman! Rurik heard an odd gurgling sound and realized it emanated from himself. "Maire hates me," he pointed out.

"Faint heart ne'er won the fair lady," Old John expounded.

Oh, God!

"Besides, Maire deserves some good treatment from a man," Old John rambled on. "She's had little enough of it in her life thus far."

Now, that was a bit of news he had not heard before. "What mean you? Did her father and brothers not treat her well? Or her husband? Logic says, being the only girl child in the chieftain's family, she would have been spoiled like a pampered pet."

"Spoiled? Hah! Her father died when she was little more than a bairn. Raised by her two brothers she was, but they had no time fer her. Two wives each, Donald and Angus had. All four of them died in the birthing and not a whelp to live from the lot of them. Donald and Angus were not unkind to Maire, precisely . . .

neglectful would be a better word. That be why she spent so much time with the old witch, Cailleach."

Rurik shrugged. Life was hard. Many men from many lands treated their womenfolk so, though Rurik's friends did not, and he considered their homes more pleasant as a result. "How about her husband? Did he not cherish her, as newly wedded grooms are wont to do?"

"Humph! Kenneth was beastly to our Maire. The man had a mean mouth on him, and beat her on occasion, he did."

Rurik bristled with outrage. "Beat? How badly?"

"Not so bad. Many a bruise and blackened eye and cracked lip, of course . . ."

Of course? Of course? There is no natural course in that!

". . . but no broken bones . . . well, except for that one time her arm got broken, but Maire claimed she fell down the stairs. She was no doubt tryin' to protect her husband from her wrathy clansmen, but we had to accept her word."

Rurik clenched and unclenched his fists several times to calm himself. He knew it was not uncommon for a man to beat his wife, especially if provoked, but he felt a wild fury at hearing of Maire's maltreatment. "I thought . . . well, Maire spoke of her upcoming marriage as a love match. Leastways, that is how I recall it, though it has been five years since last we met."

Old John shook his head. "Kenneth was not a bad sort afore the wedding . . . certainly not of the same devilish ilk as his older brother. But he changed. Not just in his attitude toward Maire, but toward the Campbell lands and our whole clan, whose name he'd vowed to take on afore the ceremony. Some people said at the time that his bitterness was caused by . . ." Old John let his words trail off, as if he'd said too much.

"What?" Rurik prodded, then glared at Old John with the silent message that he'd best continue or face the consequences.

Old John took a long swallow from his cup and then disclosed, "Some said another had gone afore him, if you get my meaning, and this Kenneth discovered in the bridal bed. Virginity matters overmuch to men, if you ask me. Rumor was that it was for the lack of a maidenhead that Kenneth turned sour and punished her thereafter, when the foul mood was upon him."

Rurik sucked in a sharp breath. Maire had been abused because of lying with him? In his country, women were more free. Oh, a maidenhead was prized, as it was in other lands, especially in negotiating the bride price, but lack of one was usually not such a huge problem . . . except betimes in uniting noble families. Certainly, it did not warrant beatings.

Now, adultery was another matter. Rurik had traveled to many countries where a husband would be entitled to have his wife's head shorn of all hair for such an offense. In one case, the man had even cut off the tip of his unfaithful wife's nose. But single, unattached women were usually given more leeway.

For the love of Freyja! Why had she not said anything?

But then, he immediately chastised himself as he realized that, in a way, she had. That must be why she'd urged him to take her with him, even if only for a short while. She'd known what the repercussions would be.

And how had he helped her? He'd laughed.

Rurik closed his eyes for a moment as guilt overwhelmed him. All his life, ever since he'd been a small boy, beaten and berated by those bigger and stronger than he,

Rurik had taken great pains not to behave in a like manner to others . . . not weaklings, and certainly not women. And now he had to live with the fact that he'd caused the same pain to be inflicted on another person.

How would he be able to live with that?

How could he make it up to Maire?

He brightened suddenly as an idea came unbidden to him. He owned a prized necklet he'd had made especially by a jeweler in the trading town of Hedeby after a recent amber expedition to the Baltic with his friend, Tykir. He'd intended it as a bride gift for Theta, but he could always find something else for a wedding token. Yea, he reflected, smiling inwardly with satisfaction, he could picture the gold chain and oval, amber pendant lying against Maire's creamy skin. He should probably wait till she was naked before he presented her with the thanks-gift. Definitely. Naked.

"Doona fash yerself over old wounds. Maire survived jest fine," Old John told him with a pat on the forearm. Apparently, Old John had misunderstood Rurik's dismay. He thought Rurik was upset over the abuse of a woman. He didn't know it was much more personal than that. "Besides, we Campbells stick together. We did our best to protect Maire from Kenneth's tempers. 'Tis amazing how many hiding places there are in such a small keep." He grinned at Rurik as he spoke.

So, Maire was beaten only when she was caught unawares, Rurik deducted, much like he himself. Small consolation, that. And she'd had her clan to protect her, when they could, just as he'd had Stigand. He had not realized they had so much in common.

"There is somethin' I been meanin' to tell ye," Old John said then. His face flushed red under his wrinkled cheeks, and that surprised Rurik mightily. Old John did not appear to be a man who embarrassed easily.

Rurik cocked his head to the side with interest.

"What you said about us Campbells today . . . when you was speakin' to the MacNab . . . well, 'twas a mighty fine thing . . . and I speak fer all of us when I say we appreciate it, and we willna forget it, ever."

"It was nothing, I—" Rurik started to say, but Old John put up a halting hand. Now Rurik was the one who felt his face heat up. "I meant what I said, and I don't want anyone's gratitude," he said gruffly. "Let this be the end of it."

Old John shook his head. "I willna speak of it again, but gratitude is a heavy burden . . . fer both parties. Ye must ken what this means, laddie." Old John was beaming at him. "There's only one way we can repay ye fer yer kindness."

The fine hairs stood out on Rurik's body. He knew . . . he just knew . . . he was not going to like what Old John was about to tell him. Still, his wagging tongue took over, "Uhm. What exactly are you referring to?"

Old John puffed out his chest and smiled widely at Rurik.

Rurik braced himself.

"Ye're one of us now, son."

"Nay," he exclaimed with alarm, even though he was unsure what the man was jabbering about. "I am not."

"Aye, ye are a Campbell now."

"Nay, nay, nay!"

"Aye, aye, aye!"

"But I do not even like Scotsmen all that much," he stated with a grunt of disgust.

"What has that to do with anything? We Scotsmen are not overfond of Vikings, either."

He gave Old John his fiercest glare. "I am a Viking, pure and simple."

"That may very well be, but ye are an honorary Campbell now, too. We voted."

"Who voted?" he demanded.

"All the Campbells. That's who. Ye should be proud. It's an old and respected clan we are."

"I don't doubt the honor you do me, but . . ." Rurik rubbed the fingers of one hand across his furrowed brow, trying to find a diplomatic way of extricating himself from this latest mess. "Did Maire vote, too?"

Old John chuckled. "Nay. Only the males of the clan vote on such matters . . . in our clan, leastways."

"I'll bet that rankles her."

"What did ye say?" Old John asked, leaning closer to hear better. It was hard to be heard over the din of hungry Campbells.

"Did that manure-mouthed whelp of hers get to vote?"

Old John nodded, not even needing to ask whom he referred to. "Wee-Jamie voted agin ye, I'm sorry to say," he informed Rurik with a sad face, then brightened, adding, "but luckily, he was outvoted."

"Lucky me," Rurik muttered. This ridiculous notion of the Campbells adopting him had gone far enough. Perchance it was a flummery on someone's part. Still, he did not want to offend unnecessarily. "It's great homage you pay me, but I must respectfully decline. It's a Norse tradition," he lied with sudden inspiration. "We cannot be adopted by any other country."

But it was already too late. Bolthor was standing and clearing his throat, a sure sign he was about to speak.

Rurik braced his elbows on the table and put his face in his hands. God, or the gods, must be punishing him for some misdeed. A big one.

"This is the saga of Rurik the Greater," Bolthor boomed out.

"Greater than what?" Young John could be overhead asking Murdoc at the table just below the dais.

"Damned if I know," Murdoc answered. "The Men of the North be an overblown lot, if ye ask me. They're always thinkin' they be greater than anyone else on God's earth, when everyone knows Scotsmen be the greatest."

He and Young John grinned at each other.

Bolthor did not like to be interrupted when he was performing; so, he started over again. "This is the saga of Rurik the Greater," Bolthor repeated, slicing a scowl of warning at Young John and Murdoc. "Sometimes known as Rurik the Scots Viking."

Hell . . . and . . . Valhalla!

There once was a Viking,
What became a Scotsman,
What learned to love haggis,
And blow on the bagpipes.
Now the Viking wears a pladd,
And the lassies wanna know,
When the wind blows,
Will the arse he shows,
Be Scots . . .
Or Norse?

Rurik would never live this saga down. This was worse than the eel-up-Alinor's-gown escapade, worse than the time Alinor's sheep, followed him and his fellow Vikings across Northumbria, worse even than the time he was caught in a sultan's harem with not one or two, but five of his wives.

Wait till his friends Tykir and Eirik heard about this, along with their respective wives, Alinor and Eadyth.

Wait till his comrades in the Norse court heard about this.

Wait till his bride-to-be heard about this.

Wait till his father-to-be-by-marriage heard about this.

But the worst was not yet to come, it was already at hand, for when Bolthor finished, the hall echoed with a resounding cheer, "Long live Rurik Campbell!"

How could she thank him? Let him count the ways . . .

Maire finally sat down next to Rurik at the high table, at his urging. Well, it wasn't exactly urging . . . more like yanking her by the upper arm and whispering into her ear, "Come with me, wench."

The first thing she did was take a long sip of *uisge-beatha* and murmur with appreciation as she stared into her cup, "Aaah! Just the thing for the end of a long Highland day." Obviously, her body was more accustomed to the burning brew than his, for she did not even wince at the first taste, as he was wont to do.

"What's got your tail in a tangle?" she asked then. "You have such a fiery expression on your face. I nigh expect to see smoke come out of your ears."

"Oooh, your tongue outruns your good sense, m'lady. I'll tell you why my *tail* is in a tangle. I am a Viking. I have been a Viking all my life. I like being a Viking. I will be a Viking on the day I die. Being Viking is a good thing. Viking, Viking, Viking. That's who I am."

"You like being a Viking?" she asked with surprise. Then, "What's your point?"

He made a low, growling noise at her question. "My point," he said, wagging a finger in her face, "is that I refuse to be a bloody Scotsman, adopted or otherwise. Your people had no right to give me the Campbell name without my permission. It's damned humiliating. I'll never live this down."

"Oh, that." She waved a hand dismissively. He'd like

to wave a hand dismissively at her, right across her bottom. Mayhap he would . . . later. "What do you want me to do?"

"Rescind it."

"Me? I cannot do that. Besides, it's an honor . . . not one I would necessarily grant you, but—"

"You are really making me angry, Maire. And, believe me, you do not want to make me angry . . . especially when we have not yet begun your 'punishment.' "

She waggled her hand in that dismissive manner again, as if to say, "Oh, that!" Truly, the woman tempted the devil when she behaved so flippantly. Did she not recognize that her time of reckoning was fast approaching? But then she put a hand on his forearm, her face went soft, and her eyes misted over.

And his anger melted, along with his bones.

"Thank you, Rurik."

He tried to call back his anger, to no avail. "For what?" he grumbled.

"You spoke on behalf of my clansmen. You gave them back their pride. You are a better man than I ever thought . . ."

He arched a brow at her unfinished comment. "Than you ever thought a Viking could be? Or just me?"

She shrugged. "Just know this . . . tomorrow, or in a sennight, or even in an hour, I will probably go back to considering you a Norse toad. But for that one moment, when you stood up to the MacNab in my courtyard and praised my clansmen . . . well, you were a better man then than I have ever known in my life."

"Meekness does not suit you, Maire."

"Cherish it whilst it lasts, Viking," she countered with a decided grin.

Rurik loathed and savored her praise at the same time. Thor's Knees! He could barely speak over the lump in this throat. So, all he said was, "Thank you." But then he relaxed, cast her a deliberately provocative look, and asked, "Does that mean you will be thanking me in other ways later?"

She laughed gaily, a tinkly sound of spontaneous joy, which caused his heart to expand in the most alarming way. "You never give up, do you?"

"Never," he said. "That's the second best thing about a Viking."

She laughed again. "And the first best thing?"

"Aaaah, that you will find out later tonight."

Whiskey and good food soften many a woman's heart . . .

Finally, finally, finally, the feast was about to begin.

Maire couldn't recall the last time they'd had a feast at *Beinne Breagha.* So, even though she personally felt no need to have one now, it was hard to begrudge her people this small pleasure. Their life had been so dire for so long. Even a temporary respite from danger was cause to celebrate.

She could not blame them for wanting to honor the handsome toad at her side, either. No one had been more surprised, or touched, than she today when he'd given her clansmen back their pride with a few words of praise.

Of course, he would be milking that generosity for all it was worth, as evidenced by his insinuations concerning the night to come. He was only jesting, of course.

She hoped.

Or did she hope?

Of course, she hoped.

Aaarrgh!

The man was beguiling her with his sinful skills of seduction. Truly, the rogue could charm the feathers off a goose if he put his mind to it. Maire put a hand to the love mark on her neck and recollected, in detail, how she'd almost succumbed to his charms this afternoon. This feminine weakness had to stop . . . for her son's sake, as well as her own well-being. With a brisk shake of her head, she pulled her thoughts back to the present.

Nessa led the procession of maids from the kitchen into the hall, carrying platters and bowls for the late meal. Taking precedence on the huge wooden trencher in her outstretched arms was the wonderful Scottish delicacy, haggis, which met with applause of appreciation from her clansmen. Foreigners to Scotland were inclined to make mock of haggis, but it truly was delicious, though admittedly an acquired taste. The heart, liver, and lungs of a sheep were ground up and mixed with suet, onion, oats, and seasonings, then stuffed into a bag made of the sheep's stomach, which was boiled slowly for an entire day. It would be sliced and portioned out so that everyone could get a taste of this prized Highland dish.

Maire glanced from side to side and saw that Rurik and all his Viking comrades seated at the high table were gawking at the haggis, a bit green-faced and gap-mouthed. Their bellies, which had been emitting audible growls of hunger just moments ago, suddenly stopped rumbling.

"I've lost my appetite," Rurik declared, and all his friends nodded in agreement.

"That's the biggest haggis I've ever seen," Bolthor said, his one good eye wide with astonishment. He was already muttering something under his breath that indicated he couldn't quite find the right title for his new saga; "For Love of a Haggis," or "Why the Gods Made Haggis, Saxons, Ugly Women, and Other Deplorable Things," or "One Hundred Reasons to Hate a Haggis."

"I'm not eating any of that," Toste declared, his cleft chin raised high, his usually smiling mouth turned southward. Maire had no idea where Vagn had disappeared to . . . probably off to no good with Inghinn, daughter of Fergus the Sheepherder.

"It's only a sausage . . . of sorts," Maire called down the table to Toste.

"Hah!" Toste answered. "A sausage big enough for a giant."

"Mayhap I will give it a try," Stigand said, trying to be polite.

Maire smiled at the big berserker.

"I might not vomit this time," Stigand added.

Maire's smile disappeared.

Fortunately for them, there were other foods being brought forth, too. *Finnan Haddie,* or smoked haddock, herring coated with oats, sheepshead and blood puddings, leg of lamb, a thick Scotch Broth made with mutton stock, barley, and vegetables, a hearty cock-a-leekie soup, and neeps—*Oh, Lord, were there ever neeps!*—boiled, roasted, creamed, and poached. Ever since her incarceration in the cage, Maire had developed a real distaste for that prolific Scottish vegetable, the turnip.

But, wait, here came the tail end of the procession. Four of the young maids were carrying a makeshift tray made out of a small discarded door. On top of it sat what was a rarity in many Scottish homes—a roast suckling pig.

"Aaaaaaahhhhh!" was the communal sigh of pleasure heard round the hall at the sight and smell of this preeminent treat. But suddenly there was a loud roar.

Everybody turned as one to gaze at Stigand, who was staring at the roast pig as if it were one of his children who'd been put into the oven. He was pulling at his hair like a wild man, his eyes were rolling up in his head and a bellow like that of an enraged bear was coming from his wide-open mouth.

"Do not put your beard in a blaze, my friend," Old John cautioned, his forehead furrowed with puzzlement.

Rurik ran up to his comrade and tried to calm him with strange words, "Go easy, my friend. Go easy. 'Tis not Thumb-Biter. Go easy."

But Stigand was not to be placated. With one last glance of agony toward the roast pig, he ran from the great hall and out into the bailey. In the distance, his cries could be heard as one long, continuing wail.

"Shall we go to him?" Bolthor and Toste inquired of Rurik.

He shook his head. "Nay. He must be by himself. His rages are short-lived. Soon, he will return, on his own."

"What was that about?" Maire asked Rurik finally, after everyone had sat back down and started eating.

Rurik wolfed down a good amount of food . . . none of it haggis . . . before he gave her his full attention. He smiled . . . a slow, sex-laden exercise . . . and reached over to finger the ends of her hair that had unfortunately dried into a mass of unfashionable curls. She should have pulled it back into a braid or a knot at her nape while it was still wet. "Like silk, it is," he murmured, pulling one strand straight, then smiling when it coiled right back up.

She swatted his sinful fingers away. "Didst hear me? I asked what's amiss with Stigand?"

His mischievous face went immediately gloomy, and he told her a condensed tale of the childhood he and Stigand had shared on some pigstead in Norway.

"I thought you said . . . or I had heard . . . that you were of noble birth."

He shrugged, and told an equally preposterous story of being abandoned at birth because he had been born weak and undersized.

"You?"

"Me."

A small tic worked in his taut jaw.

"Aha! You made this whole story up to win my sympathy. Well, I am not so easily fooled."

"I take exception to your slander. Think you that I want your pity?" The tic was working even more rapidly now, and his eyes blazed blue ice at her.

"I think you would do anything to get me into your bed, Viking."

He grinned at her. "That I own."

"And keep a rein on your roving hands, or you may lose a finger or two to my dirk." She tugged his palm off her upper thigh, where it had somehow crept, and pointed to the small knife sheathed on her belt.

"Oh, you will be in my bed furs, enticed or not. That is a fact, m'lady. Your pride is great, but my determination is greater."

"Are all Norsemen as deluded as you?"

"No doubt." With that, he tugged on the tasseled end of her belt and pulled her closer to him . . . so close she could smell the soap he'd used to bathe and the sprig of mint he'd chewed. "It's the third best thing about us Vikings. Our delusions." He jiggled his eyebrows at her, as if having delusions were a wonderful attribute.

The man was half-barmy.

"Dost know what your son did to me this eve?"

"What?" Alarm crossed Maire's face . . . too extreme a reaction for his simple remark.

"He put dead tadpoles in my half boots. I discovered them after my bath in the loch."

"The same boots that the cat relieved herself on?"

"Nay, another pair. I threw the soiled boots out in the midden."

"You discarded a perfectly good pair of boots just because . . ." Maire was stunned at the waste, but she decided to keep her thoughts to herself and changed the subject. "Tadpoles, hmmm? Wee-Jamie did that? How do you know 'twas he?"

"Because there was cat fur all about . . . *mangy* black cat fur. Wherever your son goes, that cat is close by."

Instead of making excuses for her boy, or claiming it could have been anyone, Maire promised, "I will make sure there is no repeat."

He nodded. "By the by, where did that suckling pig come from anyhow? I did not see any pigsties about your keep. Plenty of sheep, but no pigs."

"Oh, 'tis a MacNab pig."

Startled, he choked on a piece of bannock. She clapped him hard on the back. Finally, he asked, "You stole from MacNab? With all the animosity that already exists betwixt your clans, you provoked him even more with thievery?"

" 'Twas not thievery," she said, as if he'd dealt her a great insult. "My clansmen were merely reaving, and the MacNabs have forty-eight acorn hogs to spare. All Scotsmen engage in a little reaving now and again. 'Tis a part of our way of life. We expect it of each other."

"Like a Norseman going a-Viking?"

She pursed her lips in disapproval of his comparison.

"I love your lips," he said of a sudden.

She had been nibbling on a piece of haggis and a slice of oat cake when he threw out that bit of seduction. She started to choke and had to take a drink of *uisge-beatha* to stop. "What is there to love about lips? They merely hold the teeth in the mouth and keep the tongue from lolling out." Maire was quite pleased with that saucy rejoinder of hers, but not for long.

"Maire, Maire, Maire," Rurik said in a sinfully husky voice. "The best thing about a woman's mouth . . . about *your* mouth . . . is the way it yields and gives back good kisses to a man, or the way it presses against a lover's ears and whispers erotic encouragements . . ." He mentioned a few that had her sputtering and reaching for her drink again—things so perverted she nigh swooned. "Or the way they skim over that vee of hair from a man's chest down past his navel, or the way they take into their mouth that . . ." What he said then was so far beyond the range of Maire's experience and imagination that she just gaped at him, speechless and slack-jawed.

With a laugh, he put a forefinger under her chin, and closed her mouth for her, but not before pressing a quick kiss there.

"I would *never* do that."

He arched a brow at her. "We shall see."

"Never!"

"We shall see," he repeated. Then, "But as to Stigand, I tell you true, we were raised by a pig herder and his wife, Hervor, the meanest hag this side of *Hel.* Stigand was my only friend, and Thumb-Biter was his only friend . . . till that evil Hervor discovered him playing with the piglet one morning. The next day, we were served Thumb-Biter for our evening meal . . . the first meat we'd had in many a month. After he'd finished retching up the entire contents of his stomach, Stigand ran away, and I ne'er saw him again till three years ago when he joined my troop."

Maire's heart nigh broke at this image of two misfit orphan boys. There was a lot to be mulled over in what Rurik had disclosed to her, and in what he hadn't said as well. She would have to talk to Stigand later to glean more of the missing details. Her heart went out to the little boy that Rurik had been.

Before she could say anything, though, there was a gasp behind her, and she realized that Nessa had been eavesdropping on their conversation. She dropped the dirty trenchers she'd been gathering and exclaimed, "Oh, that poor, poor man. The wee laddie mus' have suffered so." Maire believed she was referring to Rurik and prepared herself for his angry reaction to any sign of pity. But it soon became clear that it was not Rurik, but Stigand, who'd touched Nessa, for she was already making her way across the hall, clucking and tsk-ing, and out into the bailey to comfort the berserker.

Rurik looked at her.

She looked at him.

Then they both burst out laughing.

"God help poor Nessa if she tries to approach Stigand in one of his rages. He's liable to lop off her head. Should I go help her?"

Maire shook her head. The Viking did not know Nessa when her inner sensibilities had been outraged. "God help the berserker."

Chapter Seven

To or-gaz, or not to or-gaz, that is the question . . .

"Did ya know that a pig's orgasm lasts half an hour?" Stigand's question was followed by a loud belch as he grinned at those around him.

Maire was pleased that Nessa had been able to lure Stigand back into the great hall, but his comment now had her wondering how wise that decision had been.

Everyone at the head table burst out laughing at the berserker, who, since he'd returned to the hall, had imbibed a vast amount of ale, after Nessa had cut off his supply of *uisge-beatha*, and that on top of enough food to fill a bear's stomach before winter hibernation. At the urging of Nessa, who hovered about him like a mother hen—or a devoted lover—he'd even eaten some haggis, and he didn't vomit, either.

"*Blindfuller!*" Rurik remarked with a rueful grimace at his friend. "Drunk as a lord!"

But even Rurik could not stop himself from joining in the mirth that burst out around them. Everyone was laughing. Except Maire.

"What's an or-gaz-him?"

As one, every male at the table leaned forward, turning right and left, to stare at Maire. Slow grins crept over all their lips, and their eyes then turned to Rurik to provide the answer.

"You did not or-gaz her?" Stigand asked Rurik incredulously. "But you always gave the impression of being a great lover."

Maire had no idea what or-gaz-ing was, but apparently all of Rurik's men knew that he had lain with her that one time.

"Or-gaz? Or-gaz? What kind of word is that?" Rurik stammered.

"'Tis what *talented* Viking men do to bring their women to orgasm," Toste explained to Rurik as if he were a dimwit. His lips twitched with a suppressed smile as he spoke.

Rurik reached across Bolthor and swatted Toste. The fool just laughed. Then Rurik turned to her. "You did not have an orgasm?" Rurik asked her in a little-boy, wounded voice.

"How would I know? I don't even know what an or-gaz-him is."

Rurik did not seem to hear her as he rubbed the nape of his neck thoughtfully. You'd think she had accused him of some great wrong. "Mayhap I imbibed too much mead that night," he suggested.

Stigand made a snorting sound of disagreement. "On the other hand, mayhap there was a full moon, or a chill in the air."

"Or a dog barking to distract him," Vagn chortled. "Yea, Rurik's dog, Beast, was no doubt barking because he had to go outdoors to piss and Rurik lost his concentration. In essence, a dog's bladder was to blame."

Toste was bent over with belly laughter. "Perchance his braies were too tight. That's as good an excuse as any. I recall one time Olf the Fat claimed his wick went limp due to a too-short haircut."

"Nay, nay, nay! I know what it was. The spell that

marked Rurik's face moved a mite lower," Bolthor offered. "Are you sure your lily's not blue, Rurik?"

Lily? What lily?

The whole time Rurik's friends teased him, the frown on his forehead deepened and deepened.

" 'Twould seem, in some things, Rurik the Greater is not so great," Bolthor remarked with a chuckle.

Rurik reached across Maire and now it was Bolthor that he swatted, but, like Toste, the giant dolt just laughed. Now Rurik's deep frown was accompanied by a continuous growl of irritation.

"Would someone please tell me what an or-gaz-him is?" Maire practically shouted over Rurik's grumbles and his friends' laughter.

"What manner of question is that?" Rurik sputtered, finally seeming to hear her. " 'Tis not a subject for dinner talk, and certainly not for a lady's ears."

"All I asked was . . . what's an or-gaz-him?"

"Uhm, uh, orgasm refers to the ecstasy period during the sex act." Rurik nodded his head as if well satisfied with the reply he'd come up with. When he looked to his companions, they nodded as well. Rurik wiped his brow with a forearm and added, "Whew!"

Well, he might be relieved, but she was still confused. "Ecstasy? What ecstasy? Dost mean like the religious ecstasy when zealots go into a fit and their eyes roll back in their heads?"

"You could say that," Toste said. "Betimes my eyes do tend to roll." His lips twitched with deviltry as he spoke.

"And my limbs have been known to go into tremors," Vagn added, holding his belly to relieve the peals of laughter that emanated from him.

"But there's naught religious about what either of

you do," Bolthor pointed out to the twins. He was also laughing.

"The ecstasy period," Rurik explained to her in a strangled voice, "is the same as peaking."

"Peaking?" She frowned. "Like a mountain peak?"

"Nay, not like a mountain peak." He shook his head with disbelief, as if she were a thickheaded child. "Well, in a way 'tis like climbing a mountain, reaching the peak, then tumbling deliciously over the top and down, down, down."

Each of Rurik's Viking friends, and Old John, too, gave him smart salutes at his presumably brilliant explanation.

"And, to your mind, there is ecstasy in falling off a mountain? And pigs do this falling for half an hour?" She puzzled over that nonsense for only half a second before pronouncing, "Methinks all men must be barmy if they follow this logic."

Bright color started to flood Rurik's face. Although she had lain with Rurik only once, he must be embarrassed that she hadn't experienced this falling-off-a-mountain business with him.

Suddenly, she understood. "Oh, you mean that time when a man grunts and pants and says, 'Sweet Jesus, it's coming, it's coming, it's coming'?"

"That would be the time," Rurik remarked dryly.

"There are times I thank God I'm not a man."

"Women have orgasms, too," Rurik said defensively, in a low voice.

"They . . . never . . . do," she retorted hotly.

"Yea, they do, Maire," he told her, and the smoldering look in his eyes held promise for her future. Maire was almost certain he was giving her a silent pledge—or was it a warning?—that she, too, would be falling off a mountain. And soon. He would be as hell-bent on that task as a knight on a quest.

"This is the saga of Rurik the Greater," Bolthor began.

A communal groaning sounded up and down the high table.

"Its title is 'Viking Men and Randy Pigs.'" He beamed, and everyone went still with interest. Except Rurik.

"Don't you dare compose a saga that attaches my name to pigs and sex," Rurik ordered with a snarl. "Or you may very well find yourself beaten into a pulp of pig slop."

Bolthor did not cower, but, to his credit, he seemed to be contemplating Rurik's warning. Then he started his saga over again, "This is the story of Stigand the Berserk . . ."

With a deep-from-the-belly roar, Stigand stood, picked up Bolthor and raised him high overhead with big hands braced on his chest and groin—not a small feat, considering they were of equal giant size—then tossed him to the rushes below the dais. As Bolthor stood, laughing and unhurt, he adjusted his eye patch and brushed straw off his trews. He barely paid heed to Stigand, who was still storming, "You will not link me with pig sex, either, you lackwit skald. Why don't you speak of wars and such noble enterprises, and leave good men alone?"

After everyone stopped laughing, Maire brought Rurik back to the issue they had been discussing before they'd been interrupted by Bolthor's poetic efforts. "Back to that ecstasy drivel, if you're envisioning me having fits for you, you're more daft than I originally thought."

He smiled at her. "Not only am I going to cause you to have 'fits,' you just might have multiple 'fits.'"

That was an image that would not leave her the rest of the evening.

A rising tide raises all boats, so to speak . . .

Another hour had passed, and the Campbell clan was still celebrating.

Maire yawned widely and wished she could be off to her bed. It had been a long day, topped off most recently with a lute performance by Inghinn, the sheepherder's daughter, a bawdy song rendered by the twins, Vagn and Toste, a playing of the bagpipes by Murdoc that brought tears to the eyes of many in the hall, and two sagas delivered by Bolthor, one about the Battle of Brunanburh, where Maire's father had died years ago, and one a hugely funny story about Rurik and a fake witch who'd put an eel skin up her gown to scare him into believing she had a tail. Had Rurik really made a fortune at one time selling wood crosses and holy water to ward off witches?

Banging on the table with her cup for attention, Maire announced, "'Tis time to end the feast. I know that tomorrow is the Sabbath, and your workload is not so great, but *some* of us are falling asleep on our feet."

"Nay, nay, nay!" the crowd yelled in disagreement. "One more entertainment."

Maire slumped to her seat in surrender. She was outnumbered by a clan that had been too long deprived of merriment. Ah, well! Let them have one more performance then.

People were looking here and there to discover who would provide the next talent exhibition, but no one volunteered. Someone from the back of the hall shouted, "How about one of our lady's witchly feats? A levitation, perchance?"

Maire's shoulders, which had been slumped with exhaustion, went immediately straight. "Nay, I will not be part of your entertainment. That's not what witches do." Actually, levitations were one of the few witchly rituals she *was* able to perform on occasion.

"Ye made Lacklan's bull rise in the air when it kept tryin' ta mate with Fenella's cow, and we were all watchin' then," the same man called out. It was Dougal, the blacksmith.

"Nay! Find someone else. I am too tired."

Rurik stood up beside her and looped an arm over her shoulder, as if in companionship, but there was naught companionable about the twinkling blue eyes of the rogue. She shrugged his arm off, then listened with amazement while he told the crowd, "Have pity on your lady and let her be off to bed. Can you not see that she has been up since dawn and must needs lie down on her bed furs?"

Maire owned no bed furs. The only bed furs on her bed were Rurik's. And, belatedly, she noted that he'd never once mentioned sleep when referring to her going to her bedchamber. She slanted a look at him, and he had the nerve to wink at her.

Her clan members seemed to have pity on her then, and were making tsk-ing sounds of sympathy. Even Dougal had the grace to duck his head shamefacedly.

Maire said a foul word under her breath, one she almost never used unless provoked mightily. She was provoked mightily now. With another expletive, this one directed at the smirking toad at her side, she stomped to the end of the dais and down the short set of stairs. "Bring me that suckling pig," she ordered the cook, who was standing in the kitchen doorway, off to the side of the great hall. And to Stigand, she said, "Don't you dare go berserk on me again. It's not your pet, for the love of heaven."

Soon the platter with the roast pig, which had not yet

been carved, thanks to Stigand's wild overreaction, sat on a small table in front of her. The Vikings had come down off the dais and her clansmen gathered behind her, all of them forming a large circle.

Before she started, she shot Rurik a glare.

He shot her a grin.

The lout!

Maire stood facing east, with her legs slightly apart, just as Cailleach had taught her. Closing her eyes, she inhaled deeply and tried to feel as one with the earth and all its energies. With her eyes still closed, she let all of nature's colors fill her . . . in her head, out to her fingertips, down to her toes. When she felt that her body was centered enough, with her feet firmly planted on the rush-covered floor, she opened her heavy eyelids and raised her staff high above her head in both extended arms. Addressing the suckling pig, she chanted all the ritual words in their original Gaelic, then ordered, "Rise! Rise now!"

Nothing happened.

This time, she repeated the Gaelic chant, then lowered her staff, pointed it at the pig, and ordered, "Rise!"

Again, nothing happened.

Concentration. She needed to concentrate better. After centering herself this time, she strolled three times, deisel or in a sunwise direction, inside the circle of people, holding the staff in both hands over her head as she walked. The Gaelic chant sounded harsh to her ears in the near silence of the great hall. Energy was practically flowing out of the pores of Maire's body when she shouted at the pig this time, "Rise! Damn you! Rise!"

Again, the pig just stared back at her, unmoving, through its watery eyes.

Thoroughly disgusted with herself, Maire turned to the crowd and said, "I'm sorry. It didn't work."

As one, all the men in the room told her, "Aye, it did."

"Huh?"

Maire and the maids and womenfolk glanced around the circle. Cook had a wooden trencher placed strategically in front of his groin. Many of the men had crisscrossed their hands over themselves. Others were hunched over. Some of them were grinning; some were grimacing. All of them were red-faced, with excitement or embarrassment, she could not tell.

Old John was the one to break the silence. "Holy blessed apostles! I didn't know I could still do *that.*" He gazed with astonishment at a tentlike profusion at the joining of his trews.

"I knew an Eastern houri once who could make a man have an erection at twenty paces, just by swishing her hips," Toste said, with equal astonishment. "But she was stone naked. And I ne'er saw her arouse four dozen men at one time."

"Can ye teach me wife to do that?" Dougal asked hopefully, and many other men chimed in with, "Me, too."

It would seem that Maire's levitation experiment had been a success, after all. The only problem was she'd caused the wrong "swine" to rise.

Liar, liar, trews on fire . . .

Maire looked as if she were about to weep.

Rurik had had as good a laugh as anyone over her inept experiment with its ludicrous result, but now he recognized how much her failure affected her. She obviously saw no humor in a hall full of rock-hard cocks with no place to go.

He did.

Bolthor surely did. The dreamy expression on his face bespoke the verse mood taking over.

Hell, the rest of the bloody world would find it hilarious, too.

But he couldn't let her stand there hurting so. Despite all the humiliation she'd caused him, he just couldn't. He knew too well how it felt to be the subject of mockery. There was naught worse in the world than being made to feel small and inadequate.

"Come, Maire," he said, taking her gently by the hand and leading her off to the side. With a jerk of his head, he signaled to Stigand that it was time to break up the crowd.

Stigand just then seemed to notice Maire's distress. His craggy face went soft with compassion, and he immediately began bellowing out orders to disperse. Apparently Maire had won the fierce berserker over. Hah! Soon he would be spouting praise-poems, too.

Rurik dropped her hand and wrapped an arm around her shoulders, tucking her close to his side. With the other hand, he took the staff away from her and set it on the table. He headed toward the stairway where he intended to tuck her into bed, and crawl in after her.

"I am the world's worst witch," Maire wailed. "Cailleach would be so ashamed of me."

"I don't think you are the world's worst witch," he told her soothingly.

"How many witches have you known?" Her voice broke on a stifled sob.

"A few," he said, his eyes shifting from side to side, avoiding direct contact. Truthfully, Maire was the only witch he'd ever met, aside from Alinor, who had turned out not to be a witch, after all. "There was that witch in Baghdad. And two in Cordoba. I cannot count how many witches I knew in Norway; the place is riddled with the old hags . . . not that you're a hag, mind you. And one in Britain, of course . . . a Saxon witch she was . . . the worst kind of all."

Rurik could be facile of tongue, when the occasion warranted. This was not one of those times. He could not seem to stop jabbering.

People who had been exiting the hall, including his own Vikings, halted to hear what utter nonsense he was spewing forth. And half-brain that he was becoming, he continued to spew it forth. "I especially liked the white witch who danced naked in the woods. Her whole coven would join in and, Holy Thor, what a sight that was! Breasts and buttocks twirling all about—"

Maire stopped dead in her tracks and stared at him for a long moment. "You liar," she exclaimed. "You are such a liar."

Bolthor cupped a hand to his mouth and told Rurik in a loud aside, "You went too far with the twirling business, methinks."

Stigand had a different opinion. "Nay, 'twas the dancing naked. Witches like to pretend no one knows of that lewd practice."

Rurik told Bolthor and Stigand to do something vulgar to themselves, then turned to Maire, hooking his thumbs in his belt with deliberate casualness. "Are you calling me a liar?"

Maire looked right and left in an exaggerated manner, then straight at him. "If it looks like a toad and has warts like a toad . . ."

He hitched one hip. Hell, he'd only been trying to make her feel better. How had she turned the tables on him? Well, at least she wasn't weeping anymore.

"I suppose it's a cultural trait amongst you Norsemen since you do it so well," Maire continued.

"Do what so well?" She'd lost him back at the culture thing.

"Lying."

Now, Bolthor, Stigand, Toste, and Vagn stiffened with

affront. "Maire, your words wound deeply. Best you be careful whom you insult. Stigand tends to lop first and think second."

But Maire wasn't paying any attention to him. "You know what they say about Vikings, don't you?" Truly, the woman did push and push. If she were a man, she'd be dead as a herring by now.

Five pairs of fists went white-knuckled at this point.

"Maire, have a caution," he warned.

"Every time a Viking lies, his . . . uh, male part shrinks."

Five male jaws went slack-jawed with disbelief. Indeed, a whole hall full of jaws dropped open. But did Maire know enough to stop then? Nay. She just blathered on.

"Aye, that's what the old proverbs say. The *part* that Viking men prize so much shrinks and shrinks with each lie till eventually it resembles naught more than a wee nub, and eventually falls right off." While she was pontificating, she held her hands an arm's length apart, for demonstration purposes, but the palms moved closer and closer till in the end she clapped her hands together.

Every single man winced. A few might have whimpered.

Now she'd gone too far. He should ignore her, but no man worth his salt could let such an insinuation go unchecked. "Let me see if I understand what you are saying. Every time a Viking lies, his cock falls off?" Rurik demanded of her.

"Eventually."

It was hard for Rurik to tell if that was a sparkle of mischief in her eyes, or some residual tears. In any case, it was the most ridiculous statement he'd ever heard anyone make.

"That's the most ridiculous statement I've ever heard anyone make," he said then. "And why only Viking men?"

"Must have been a witch's curse put on lying Viking men," Maire surmised, waving a hand blithely. And, yes, that was a definite twinkle in her eyes.

"Vikings don't lie any more than Scotsmen."

"Oh, I don't know about that," Maire disagreed. "For example, Vagn . . ."

Vagn jumped about a foot off the floor at being singled out.

". . . when Stigand raised an arm in front of you this afternoon, following your baths, did he not ask you if he smelled? And did you not say, 'Nay'?"

Vagn's face flushed bright red.

Stigand looked at him, saw his guilt, raised his arm and sniffed his armpit, then thwapped him with a big palm on the back of his head, causing Vagn to fall to the rushes. Then, that fool, Vagn, could be seen checking inside his braies, discreetly, for any evidence of shrinkage.

"And Toste . . . ," Maire called out to the rascal, who was trying to sneak out of the hall through the scullery door with the sheepherder's daughter. "Did I not hear you tell Inghinn yestereve that you were in love with her?"

Toste tried to keep walking, but Inghinn stopped. "Well?" she demanded of him in a quivery voice. "Were you lying?"

"I . . . um . . . well . . . not precisely," Toste said. "I was in love with what you were doing with your hands and—"

Inghinn slapped him across the face and stormed away but not before calling over her shoulder, "Now that you mention it, his worm *was* smaller than usual."

" 'Tis not. 'Tis not," Toste protested.

Inghinn's father, Fergus, gave Toste a glower that said this subject of bedding his daughter was not over, but for now he hurried off to placate the sobbing Inghinn.

"She's only teasing us," Rurik tried to tell his comrades. "It's just a jest."

"Oh, really?" Maire said. "Well, I have heard it said just as I have told you, and the only way to reverse the demise of said virility is to correct the lies." Then she addressed the entire crowd. "And, now that I think on it, I'm not so sure it's not true of Scotsmen, as well."

Pandemonium ruled then. All over the great hall, men were checking their braies and spouting out disclaimers to previously told lies.

"Really, Mary, I did not spill that ale. I drank it all meself."

"Calm down, Collum. I will replace the missing bag of barley I charged ye fer."

"Daracha, yer not really as satisfying as I said ye were."

"I'm sorry to be tellin' ye this, sweetheart, but yer buttocks *are* too big."

"When ye eat haggis, yer breath stinks to high heaven."

"Actually, I *don't* like ta do it upside down."

"The hair on yer legs is loathsome."

"I didn't muck out the stables when I said I did."

"Truth be told, that rash on me male parts wasn't really caused by a fall into a prickly bush."

"To be honest, when ye sit on me in the bedsport, I canna breathe."

"Yer nipples are too big."

"Yer nipples are too small."

"Ye have no nipples to speak of."

Rurik put his face in his hands, trying to hide his laughter. This was the most outrageous thing he'd ever experienced in all his life. Maire might not be much of a witch, but when it came to getting even, she was the best. Finally, he swiped the tears of mirth from his eyes, and took her by the hand, pulling her away from the chaos she'd created.

She tilted her head in question.

"We are going to your bedchamber now, dearling," he informed her. "If you are lucky, I might let you check whether I have been telling any lies lately."

CHAPTER EIGHT

Since when did seduction become so hard? . . .

Rurik took Maire by the hand and tugged, hard. He wanted to leave her great hall . . . *now!*

Truth be told, he was randier than a bearded billy goat in a herd of nannies. So strong was the instinct to rut that he feared he might just make a flying leap at Maire—*his very own nanny, for the love of Frey!*—except that he had no cloven hooves to break his fall if he missed his target. And the way his life had been going of late, missing his "target" was a very real possibility.

Maire would no doubt disagree on the cloven hoof part, though, since she was always likening him to a devil's spawn.

Aaarrgh! Who cares if I am a goat or a devil? I must needs plant this rock hardness sprouting from my groin in a place that is hot and moist and welcoming, or die of wanting.

But will Maire be welcoming?

Or hot?

Or moist?

He waggled a hand dismissively at his own internal questions.

I cannot attest to her outward reception, but she will be hot and wet, he promised himself. *After that public challenge to my masculinity regarding orgasms, I will damn well make sure she is burning this time . . . and so sex-slippery we may very well slide off the bed furs. This I do swear . . . a blood oath to myself. My manhood is at stake here. Actually, you could say the reputation of all Viking men is being threatened.*

A niggling thought in his head suggested he might be overreacting. But another niggling thought said there was no such thing as overreacting when it came to a man and his most precious body part.

Rurik attempted to drag Maire from the great hall—and, yes, she was digging in her heels, finding one excuse after another to stop and talk to her people . . . discussing such important things as what time to start the bread dough in the morn, or how much cleaning up from the feast needed to be done yet tonight, or who should shovel out the middens come Monday morn.

"Stop pulling on me. I'm not a child," Maire complained. They were halfway up the stairs that led to the upper floor and her bedchamber.

He stopped abruptly, and she slammed into his back. They both almost toppled over, but he stabilized them by releasing her hand and turning her so that her back was braced against the wall . . . and he was braced against *her.*

A mistake, that.

A pleasure, that.

Too soon, that.

Belatedly recalling her last words, he rubbed himself against her with an agonizing sigh and breathed against her lips, "A child is the last thing I would call you, Maire." Even that slight friction of his arousal against her belly, separated by layers of cloth, provided the most delicious pain . . . so intense he had to close his eyes and catch his breath, lest he embarrass himself . . . and her, too.

"Don't do this, Rurik," she pleaded on a moan, turning her head to the side.

"Do what?" he murmured against the soft curve of her neck, the exact spot where a pulse beat with sensual rhythm.

"Your punishment business."

"Huh?" he said. Then he remembered. "Ah, Maire, I promise you will enjoy my punishment business."

"Oh, what a lot of foolery you men do spout! As if I could enjoy—"

Rurik used a forefinger to tip her face forward and stopped her words with his mouth. From side to side, he moved his lips over hers till they parted. Then he groaned his raging need into her open mouth and deepened the kiss. Like a madman he was then, devouring her with his insatiable hunger. "You . . . taste . . . so . . . damned . . . good."

At first, she tried to push him away with palms pressed against his chest. And then, midway between gentle, whispery kisses and thrusting tongue kisses, she succumbed to the same passion that assailed him. Her arms wrapped about his shoulders and her mons pressed against the cradle of his hips.

"Rurik."

He licked her lips and encouraged her to do the same to him.

"Rurik."

She widened her mouth and allowed him deeper access.

"Rurik."

He nipped her bottom lip in chastisement for her calling his name. Now was not the time for talking, whether it be protests or encouragement.

"It's not me," Maire gasped out.

"Rurik."

Only then did Rurik realize that someone else was saying his name, and it was a male voice.

Inhaling and exhaling deeply to regulate his panting breaths, he pressed his forehead against Maire's.

"Rurik."

Turning to the right, with Maire still in his arms, Rurik noticed Bolthor standing at the bottom of the steps, shifting from foot to foot, as he beckoned.

"This better be urgent," Rurik growled.

"It is," Bolthor said, nodding his head vigorously. Then he tilted his head to the side and inquired, "Didst you or-gaz the lady yet? I hear tell there is a surefire way to spark a woman's ecstasy involving feathers and—"

Rurik growled again.

Discerning that he treaded precarious waters by mentioning Rurik's love skills, or lack thereof, Bolthor rushed quickly to the point. "Fergus, the sheepherder, is beating Vagn to a pulp out in the courtyard. He thinks Vagn is Toste, who was actually the one what poked his daughter, Inghinn. Stigand keeps tryin' to tell Fergus he got the wrong twin, but Fergus is a stubborn Scotsman, and you know how they are . . . thickheaded, when they've made up their minds, unlike us Vikings, what are open-minded and such. I had to hit Stigand over the head with a wooden shovel to keep him from beheadin' Fergus. Broke the shovel, it did. And Nessa is threatenin' to disembowel me whilst I sleep for hurtin' 'her poor wee Stigand.' Can you imagine that? *Poor, wee Stigand!* Meanwhile, Toste is layin' as if dead out in the stables—*drukkinn*, if you ask me—alongside Ian's wife, Coira—she be *drukkinn*, too. If Ian finds out his wife's been opening her thighs to Toste, there's gonna be a war, I tell you. And Coira thinks she's lyin' with Vagn, or so I been told."

Bolthor took a deep breath before adding one last statement, "And every man in the keep is lookin' fer thread to measure his cock."

Rurik stepped away from Maire. "How could so

much have happened in the short time since I left the hall?"

"Well, 'tis not that short a while," Bolthor answered. "Mayhap you've been diddling here on the steps longer than you think."

"Diddling?" Maire choked out.

"Diddling?" Rurik choked out, too. Then, "Take Maire up to her bedchamber," he ordered Bolthor, "and make sure you stand guard outside till I return. I'll take care of Toste and Vagn. Stigand, too."

"I need no guard," Maire protested.

"You need a guard," he assured her, leaning forward to give her one last, brusque kiss. "This night, above all others, I will not allow you to escape."

Maire raised her chin defiantly. "You're trying to scare me with all these 'punishment' threats, but I'm not afraid of you."

"More the fool you," he declared, already heading down the steps.

"You're not as scary as you think you are. There is an old Gaelic proverb you would do well to memorize: 'Great barkers are not biters.' "

God, the woman is daft to push me so. And believe me, I intend to bite her fair body.

Over his shoulder, he heard Bolthor explain, as if an explanation was necessary, "Methinks he intends to orgaz you tonight. Since he hasn't succeeded in the past—with you, that is—well, that *could* be scary."

Rurik wasn't sure if the gurgling sound came from himself or Maire.

How to hide from a Viking with wicked intentions? . . .

Maire was desperate.

Hurriedly, she lit candles all about her bedchamber, preparing to perform a witchly ritual. This afternoon, when Rurik had returned to the keep after talking with Duncan MacNab, Maire had learned for the first time that her old mentor, Cailleach, might still be in Scotland. And tonight, when she'd been attempting a levitation—*Blessed Mary! Have I ever been so humiliated in all my life?*—Maire had recollected some hazy words to a charm for calling forth a witch. So now she wanted to beckon Cailleach, if that was possible. Cailleach would know how to remove Rurik's blue mark, if anyone could. And if that could be done, Rurik would concentrate all his efforts on ridding the Campbell clan of the MacNab threat. Then he would be off to do whatever it was Vikings did . . . raping, pillaging, a-Viking, terrorizing innocent women with "punishments," grooming themselves to be even more handsome than they already were. She would not care if she never saw the irksome man again.

At least, that's what Maire told herself . . . though, to be honest, he did give good kisses. Incredibly good kisses. Kisses so good, in fact, that some weaker-willed lasses might be tempted to sample the "punishments" he doled out . . . or the or-gaz-hims.

"*Trobad, trobad*, Cailleach," she chanted in Gaelic. "Come here, come here." She tossed some herbs onto the dozens of candles burning about the room, causing them to flame higher and brighter. Over and over, she recited various Gaelic words and phrases, hoping that one would be the correct combination. The candle flames began to flicker and dance in an unnatural pattern. Was Cailleach's spirit in the room already?

Going to a small pottery jar, she took a pinch of a powdery substance and placed a portion in each of the four corners of the room. "Eye of a twig, toe of a snake, I summon you, witch, a miracle do make."

There *was* a presence in the room. Maire could feel it.

"*A bheil sibh gam chluinntinn?*" Maire asked softly.

"Do you hear me?" She was a little frightened because one never knew what dark force could be roused when dabbling in the dark arts.

A clap of thunder in the distance was Maire's only answer. Now, it could be an approaching storm, for the air was thick and humid. Or it could be Cailleach's promise to come. Maire chose to believe the latter.

With a smile, she danced about her bedchamber, always on the alert for Rurik's approaching footsteps, reciting all the old charms to cajole a witch to do one's bidding. As she danced, scattering herbs as she twirled and skipped here and there, she began to remove her clothing, down to her linen shift, though she still wore her hose and heavy leather shoes. The room was becoming ungodly hot, and she was so tired.

She had every intention of blowing out all the candles and hiding evidence of her witchly practice before Rurik returned. She also had every intention of putting a lust-killing spell on the room. But first she needed to comb her hair. *Just for a moment.* Or sit down on the edge of the bed. *Just for a moment.* Or lay her head upon the pillow. *Just for a moment.* Or close her eyes. *Just for a moment.*

Unfortunately, all of Maire's best intentions disappeared with the onslaught of an overwhelming weariness.

As she was drifting off to sleep, she heard a voice in her head say, "I'm coming, I'm coming, I'm coming . . ." She thought it might be Cailleach, except that there seemed to be many voices speaking to her. Was Cailleach changing her voice, deliberately, to fool some lurking fairies or trolls?

"Is that you, Cailleach?" she asked with a wide yawn.

The only response was a cackle.

A lot of cackling.

Surely, that was a good sign.

* * *

So much for all his seduction plans! . . .

"Best you be careful, Rurik," Bolthor told him. "There be a hell of a lot of cackling goin' on in there."

Cackling? "Huh?" It had taken Rurik nigh on an hour to break up the fight in the courtyard, to placate Fergus, and to drag Toste out of the stables . . . not to mention waking Stigand and eliciting his promise that he would not lop off any heads during the night. Now, Bolthor spoke to him of . . . *cackling?* "Like chickens?"

"Nay, like witches."

Rurik put his face in one hand and counted to ten for patience. Then he asked, "Did you go in and check?"

Bolthor stepped back and straightened his shoulders indignantly at the question. "Me? Get involved with witches and such? I . . . don't . . . think . . . so! I've already got a shrinking manpart to worry about, and I only have one working eye as it is. I am not daft enough to chance some further spell that might imperil other body parts. Nay, I have performed my duties. I reported to you on the cackling, and that's the end of my involvement. *You* investigate the cackling."

With a grunt of disgust, Rurik waved Bolthor off to his sleeping pallet in the great hall and waited till he was sure the foolish man was gone. A few moments later, from the short distance down the stairway to the hall, he heard the skald say in an overloud whisper, "Stigand, wake up. I need a word that rhymes with *cackling.*"

Stigand sleepily muttered a crude Anglo-Saxon word for fornication.

Even from up the stairs, Rurik could hear the affront in Bolthor's voice as he replied, "That doesn't rhyme, Stigand. Tsk-tsk! Good thing I am the skald, and not you."

Rurik shook his head and smiled as he opened the heavy oaken door to Maire's bedchamber. Instantly, he staggered backward at the intense heat that hit him. There were three dozen candles burning about the room. And the odor! Thor's Toenails, the cloying scent in the air reminded him of a church in Jorvik where they burned incense as part of the services.

Aha! Maire must have been engaged in some ritual or other. Could she have been trying once again to remove his mark? Could it perchance already be gone?

Rushing to the side chest, Rurik picked up her polished brass mirror and checked his face. Immediately, his shoulders slumped with disappointment. The mark remained. Well, either she'd failed once again, or it was another spell she was working on. Hah! If that were the case, no doubt it was a spell to make him disappear.

As he walked about the chamber, blowing out candles to lessen the heat, he glanced toward the bed where Maire slept soundly. Although she wore only a thin shift, he could tell that she must have fallen asleep practically on her feet because she still wore her hose and shoes. In fact, one leg dangled over the edge of the mattress, and there was a brush in her hand. She was snoring softly. Grinning, he made a mental note to remind her of that less-than-feminine habit. He was sure she would appreciate knowing she made sleep sounds not unlike a snuffling piglet.

She'd better not think she was going to escape him by falling asleep. He fully intended to exact his pound of flesh from her this night. He put a hand to his groin as a reminder of what was to come. He continued to be half hard for the wench, despite having been gone from her presence an hour or more. Perchance it was a lingering effect from Maire's levitating demonstration.

After he'd finished with the candles, he sat on the edge of the bed on the same side as Maire, and began to remove her shoes and thin hose. It was not that he was being especially considerate of her comfort, he told himself. Nay, 'twas just that he wanted naked flesh next to his when he brought her to orgasm . . . as he most certainly would, or forever give up his word-fame as a lover. As he began peeling her hose down her legs, which were very long and very well shaped, he imagined where those legs might be when she screamed out her first ecstasy. Wrapped around his waist? Or over his shoulders? Better yet, she could be kneeling on said legs, on all fours, and he could be taking her from behind like a stallion with a mare. That ought to shock the secret of the blue mark from her.

He smiled wickedly to himself at all the possibilities as he resumed undressing her.

He was not touched he told himself, by the numerous darn marks in her stockings, or the blisters at the back of her heels from the heavy, utilitarian brogues that she wore. Leastways, not very much.

With a jaw-cracking yawn, he removed his own boots, then stood to unbuckle his sword belt. As he yawned again, Rurik walked to the other side of the chamber—it was still sweltering—and dropped one item of apparel after another till he was naked as the day he was born. But not as weak and puny as he was as a babe, Rurik reminded himself, gazing down at the work-honed muscles that defined his abdomen and stomach and arms and thighs. He was in perfect physical condition, and he knew it.

Except for the blue mark.

Troubling thoughts swirled within Rurik as he eased down onto the mattress. Was there a sickness inside of him that made physical appearance so important? He didn't judge his friends on how they looked. Far from it. And, although he admired a beautiful woman, he did not consider a flawless form or face to be necessary in a mate.

Consider Tykir's wife, Alinor. She was covered with freckles from head to toe, but in Tykir's eyes, she was a goddess. And Rurik barely noticed her plainness anymore, either. Nay, it was only himself he was so harsh with. And he knew why. It all stemmed back to his childhood and the mockery and brutality inflicted on him because he was not superior in physical attributes. Rurik recognized it was unreasonable to carry over all these old insecurities, but in some ways he had good reason. He was a man with no family name . . . no home . . . though that latter should change soon with his marriage. He had wealth enough, but treasures could be as easily lost as won. Nay, his self-identity was wrapped up in his strength as a warrior and his bodily appeal. In essence, all he had was who he was, physically.

Ah, such deep thoughts when I am so weary. He shifted restlessly on the bed, trying to ease his aching bones. It had been a long, long day, and this was not an overlarge bed. He had to nestle up against Maire, who faced away from him. A real hardship, that. He smiled with pleasure at the way they fitted together. His still painful left arm rested on the pillow, his right hand cupping a deliciously full breast, his erection cradled dead center in the crease of her buttocks. He tried but was unable to stifle another yawn. He was going to awaken Maire in a moment and show her just how well they fitted together . . . in all ways. For now, he was gaining immense satisfaction just holding her and anticipating what was to come. Here in the dark, in this moment frozen in time, it mattered not how he looked, or what he had to prove. He was merely a man . . . with his woman. And it felt so very right.

Just before he floated off to sleep, he heard the oddest sound.

Cackling.

* * *

Was this how the prince awakened Sleeping Beauty? . . .

"Oh, Maaiirre."

Maire came instantly awake at the sound of the male voice crooning hot, breathy words against her ear. In the semidarkness, she sensed it was probably close to dawn, but she knew exactly where she was and who was plastered against her back. With the fingers of one hand playing with her nipple and his "Lance" poking her behind, the toad from Norway was clearly identifiable.

"Oh, Maaiirre."

Perhaps she could pretend to be asleep.

"I know you're not asleep, witchling. When you sleep, you snore, and you're not snoring now."

I do not snore, she wanted to tell the brute, but she was still faking slumber, lying motionless, which was a really hard thing to do when he was rolling her nipple between a thumb and forefinger, causing the most peculiar sensations to ripple through her body. And it hardly seemed possible, but his thick male member was growing thicker. She'd like to whack his wicked fingers and his member. Pretending to be asleep was getting harder and harder.

"Guess what, Maire?"

Guessing games now? She could only imagine what silly amusement he was planning, especially with the deviltry that rang in his voice.

"It's raining," he announced.

It was not at all what Maire had expected him to say. She hoped someone belowstairs had exercised the foresight to place a few strategic buckets about the great hall where the roof leaked.

"In fact, this storm should prove to be a real fjord-filler . . . or loch-filler . . . the kind of incessant, hard-driving summer rain that could go on for . . . oh, let's say, all day, and perhaps even tonight."

Maire's eyelids flew open.

He chuckled. "You do remember, don't you?"

He couldn't possibly mean . . .

"I promised that every day I continued to bear your mark, you would bear mine . . . except mine would be the mark a man makes on a woman in the bed furs. Dost recall my words now, sweetling?"

She did.

"Methinks you do. I can tell by the stiffness of your spine. Here is a reminder anyway, just in case you are a mite dull in the head as most women are wont to be in the face of the superior male intellect."

The man is a dunderhead, pure and simple.

"I told you that on rainy days, there would be more time to devote to your marking, and we might just spent day and night in bed because I have so much to teach you . . . so many ways to mark you."

She shoved aside the hand caressing her breast, sat up, then jumped off the bed. With hands on hips, she glared at him in the dreary half-light. "I have had more than enough of your talk of sex markings and punishments and or-gaz-hims and bed fits and whatnot. If you intend to force me to couple with you, just do the deed and be done. Do not honey-coat it with all these other descriptions."

He just stared at her, with eyes that she could now see were smoldering, like blue fire. He had changed his position on the bed and lay with his arms folded behind his neck on the pillow, his ankles crossed.

"Well, answer me," she demanded, stamping her foot.

"Your nipples are hard," he observed irrelevantly.

She gasped. "They are not."

He arched a brow. "One of them is. Come here, and let me work the other one to equal arousal."

"A-rous-al," she sputtered out and spun on her feet

so he could not see her breasts through the thin shift she wore.

"I can see your buttocks, Maire," he informed her with a laugh. "Very nice, indeed."

She spun back around, about to tell him what she thought of his perverted observations, but a flash of lightning cracked, fully illuminating the chamber, and Maire got her first good look at the Viking reclining in all his naked splendor. The man truly was the embodiment of male masculinity, with perfectly proportioned muscles in all the right places . . . right down to that . . . that . . . *thing* standing at attention betwixt his legs. He certainly had been telling no lies lately, as far as she could see.

She caught herself gaping and snapped her mouth shut. "Have you no shame?"

"Nay."

"Cover yourself."

"Why?"

"Because you look ridiculous, that's why."

"I do not," he said, but there was a twinge of hurt in his voice. The foolish lout was ever sensitive about his appearance, Maire knew that, but this was carrying vanity too far. She noticed that he turned onto his side, as if to hide himself, because of her criticism. He didn't droop, though, as some men might.

She turned away from him and tried to get her emotions under control. Maire couldn't abide the overbearing rogue, but there was a part of him that touched her, too. That was the part she had to protect herself from. She had to.

"Maire," Rurik said, "come here."

"Why?" What a half-brained question that was! Really, it was debatable who was the idiot in this room . . . she or Rurik.

She thought then that he would tell her to come to

him so that he could initiate her punishment, or put his male mark on her, or make her have bed fits. She thought he might smirk, or even laugh out loud at her. But when Maire turned back to the man in her bed, his gaze was stone-cold serious. And he said the worst possible thing to her, considering her vulnerable mood.

"Because," he told her huskily, beckoning with the long fingers of one hand, "I want, with all my heart, to make love with you."

Chapter Nine

She didn't stand a chance . . .

Maire moaned.

It was the softest of sounds, accompanied by a whispery exhalation, but Rurik heard it, and he recognized it for what it was . . . the reluctant arousal of a woman on the edge of surrender. Inwardly, he smiled with satisfaction. He was a master of seduction. The signs were clear. Just the tiniest push and she would be his.

He beckoned her forward with his fingertips in the way of man with woman through the ages. And he gave her his most sultry look as an added incentive . . . the one involving hooded eyes and flared nostrils. 'Twas a favorite ploy that never failed to tempt even the most proper maids.

Unfortunately, Maire was apparently neither proper nor a maid. Instead of doing his bidding, the stubborn wench took a step backward—*backward!*—away from the bed where he still reclined, and said, "Rurik, I do not want to make love with you."

Huh? Had he read the body signals wrong? Was she not interested in sharing the bed furs with him? *Impossible!* He jumped from the bed and stood directly in front of her before she had a chance to blink . . . or run for the door.

He saw a single nervous twitch of her lips, though

she immediately masked it by pressing her lips together and raising her chin bravely. She was obviously agitated by his closeness, which had to be a good omen. He would wager great odds that she was, indeed, interested in love play, despite her words to the contrary.

They were so close he could swear he smelled the feminine musk of her excitement. In truth, she was as skittish as a mare in heat . . . though he did not think she would relish that comparison . . . leastways, not at this stage of their relationship.

He put a hand to her chin and stroked his thumb across her closed lips. The twitch did not recur, but he could sense her tension at his mere touch.

"Explain yourself, m'lady." His voice came out husky and low, betraying his own masculine need. His thumb was continuing its caress of her exceedingly luscious mouth.

"I do not want to make love with you," she repeated.

"Liar!"

She appeared shocked by his accusation, at first. But Maire was at heart an honest woman, and so she amended her statement, "Making love with you is a bad idea."

Bad idea! 'Tis the best idea I've ever had.

He merely arched a brow in question. But while he waited for her response, he moved his hand from her chin down to her neck and curled his fingers around the nape, under her heavy swath of hair, and drew her closer. As she gazed up at him, he felt her breasts under the thin shift press against his bare chest, and his shaft press into her flat stomach. Sexual awareness swirled between them . . . and for just a second an overpowering dizziness assailed him. Surely, she felt it, too.

She licked her lips—a gesture so innocently carnal that his member lurched against her belly.

A rush of scarlet stained her cheeks as she perceived what had happened, and what she'd done to provoke it.

She tried to explain her unwillingness to couple with him. "Rurik, I have lain with only two men in my life . . . you and my husband, Kenneth. Both of you betrayed me in one way or another." She put a halting hand up to his mouth when he would have contradicted her. He nipped at her fingertips, but permitted her to go on. "I have too many responsibilities now to risk such illicit behavior for my own selfish needs. I need my wits about me, and—"

Ah! Illicit behavior? Selfish needs? So, she does want me.

"—groveling in self-pity when I am hurt once again could be the undoing of my clan, which needs my full attention."

"Maire, I misdoubt you have ever groveled a day in your life. And as to being hurt . . . how can you feel great passion unless you risk pain?" That last statement sounded pompous even to his own ears.

"That's just it. I don't want any great passion. I'm content with my life the way it is. And furthermore, have you ever considered what would happen if I were to become pregnant?"

"There are ways to prevent the planting of a male seed in the female womb."

Maire seemed surprised by that. "Ways? What ways?"

"It matters not. Just know that a swollen stomach need not be one of your concerns."

"Did you employ these *ways* the other time we were together?" There was a churlish, disbelieving note to her voice that he did not care for.

"Probably not. I was young then, and more careless."

She pondered his statement for several long moments, then tried a different approach. "Rurik, you do me disrespect in making me your wanton. Give a thought to what my people would say of a mistress who shares a bed with every wayfarer who passes through."

"I am not every wayfarer," he grumbled. God, he was tired of talking. Time for action. Bed action. "Besides, Old John practically offered you to me on a welcome platter, and I daresay he is representative of others in your clan."

"He never did!"

"Yea, he did. As I recall, he compared me to the bulls in the fields, the rams in the hills, even the wee fishies in the burns, and said the urge for mating betwixt you and me was natural. In fact, he even implied that it's all part of God's plan."

Maire clucked her tongue with disgust at words she recognized as coming from the Scotsman's mouth. "He probably thinks you're going to marry me."

Rurik hadn't considered that possibility. But then he shrugged. He would set the old man straight on that question when the time came. A wedding with Maire was the last thing on his mind. A bedding with Maire, on the other hand, was foremost in his thoughts.

"And there are other reasons, as well, why we should not do this . . . thing."

Talk, talk, talk. That's all women do. If women had to go to war, they'd probably try to fight their enemies with words instead of swords or arrows. "Maire, you can cite me a dozen reasons, and it will make no difference."

"Why?" she persisted.

Because I'm so bloody lustful I might just explode. That's why. Because if I don't soon kiss those wonderful, moist lips of yours, I might start drooling. That's why. Because my cock is so hard, it hurts. That's why.

"Stop looking at me like that."

"Like what?"

"Like I'm a pasture of new grass, and you're a hungry sheep."

That's me, for a certainty . . . a randy ol' ram. Best she come here quick afore I start baa-ing . . . or, better yet, ramming her. He chuckled at his own joke.

She glared, not understanding the source of his mirth. "Rurik, the sex act means different things to women than to men."

Here we go. First, Old John lectures me on sex. Now, Maire does, as well. Am I a youthling that I need such education?

"Men have no qualms about spilling their seed in any vessel, willing or not, when lust hits. Women on the other hand . . . leastways, most women . . . give themselves to a man when there are feelings involved."

Rurik groaned to himself. He could guess what was coming. Guilt. Like all women with their feminine wiles, Maire was going to employ guilt in hope of getting her own way.

"When I married Kenneth, I loved him . . . not perhaps as a lover should . . . after all, we'd known each other since we were bairns toddling over the moors together. The Campbells and the MacNabs were not feuding then. But 'twould seem I did not know Kenneth at all." She sighed deeply and paused in memory.

Rurik remembered Old John's words of the beatings Maire had endured from her spouse, and suspected that Maire was conjuring up those dark memories now.

"What has all this to do with me . . . with us?" he asked with a growl of impatience.

"My love was obviously wasted on you, too," she said.

"Me? You loved me?" That was a disconcerting bit of news.

She nodded. She actually nodded. Oh, God, he was in trouble now!

"You must think I was naive to have fallen in love with you . . . a virtual stranger. I realize now what a fool I was to have taken the seductive words of an experienced rogue at face value."

"You thought I was in love with you?" he blurted out, realizing belatedly how insulting his shock must sound.

But she just smiled in a self-deprecating way. Obviously, she blamed herself, not him.

"Do you love me still?" he inquired, horror ringing in his voice. Love was not the emotion he wanted from the wench now. Lust, yes. Love, no.

She laughed. "I loathe you."

He exhaled loudly with relief before he could catch himself.

She laughed again.

In the moment of silence that followed, Rurik pondered all that she had told him. To his shame, he could barely bring to mind details of that time when they had made love five years ago. He had been young, perchance under the influence of *uisge-beatha,* full of his own conceit, and, truth to tell, there had been so many women in his bed furs over the years. No excuse, of course. Another thought came unbidden to him. "Didst think I would marry you because I took your maidenhead?"

"Nay, I was not that lackwitted," she answered.

Whew!

"But I did think you would want more than one night with me. I had my own ego, Rurik. I thought I would be more than a conquest to you . . . soon forgotten. I thought . . . well, that you would take me with you."

He nodded in understanding. "And I laughed when you asked."

"That you did."

"Maire, I was on the Norse king's business then . . . business that could have involved the lives of many men. I could not have taken you with me, even had I wanted to."

She made a moue of her lips, which relayed her skepticism. She knew as well as he that she *had* been just a passing fancy at the time.

"I did not behave honorably toward you," he admitted.

"That is true."

"I will make it up to you." He thought of the amber necklet in his saddlebag and decided that he would definitely give it to her later as a *wergild.* Even though the Anglo-Saxon term *wergild* denoted the value set upon the life of a slain man in accordance with his rank, Rurik felt it applied in this situation, as well. In truth, he had killed Maire's dreams. She deserved just compensation.

Her face brightened. "You will make it up to me by honoring my wishes not to make love?"

"Nay, that is not the reward I will give you. There will be another reward." He made a tsk-ing noise with his tongue. "The die has been cast, witchling. We *will* make love. I thought you accepted that. You have no other option."

He was bigger and stronger. She had to know she could not win this battle. But he did not want her passive . . . he wanted a she-warrior in the bed furs, an enthusiastic participant who would match him stroke for stroke. That was not what he would get, he realized, noticing her shoulders slump with defeat. He thought he saw tears misting in her beautiful green eyes.

He almost gave in then.

Almost.

But he was not a total fool.

"Because you want to punish me?" she berated him.

For the love of Valhalla, the woman never gives up! He shook his head. " 'Tis more than that. You put your mark on me, Maire. You—*a woman*—gave the world reason to make jest of me. And if that wasn't bad enough, you made a public statement this evening, belowstairs, that I failed to pleasure you in the bedsport."

"Just because you did not or-gaz me? Hah! As if I want to be or-gaz-ed!"

Rurik shook his head from side to side. "There is no such word as or-gaz. Bolthor made that up. The word is orgasm, and it refers to . . . oh, never mind. You will know soon enough."

She stamped her foot angrily. "Are you listening to me, you thickheaded lout? I . . . don't . . . want . . . to . . . know." She expressed her sentiment slowly with evenly spaced words, as if he were a . . . well, a thickheaded lout.

He waved a hand to indicate her wants were neither here nor there. "My manhood is at stake now. I need to prove that I am master in this man-woman relationship."

Her upper lip curled with contempt. "And that is what this is all about, then . . . your ego?"

Enough! Whilst they had been talking and Maire had been distracted, he'd been gathering up the fabric of her shift, fistful by fistful. He stepped back now and flipped the hem of the garment up and over her head, then tossed it over his shoulder. She was too stunned at first by his action to attempt to hide her nudity from him.

He was stunned, too. By all the Norse gods and all the saints in the One-God's heaven, she was glorious.

Her red hair hung in waves about her bare shoulders and down her back. Her uplifted breasts were fuller and heavier than he'd expected, considering her slender frame, with dark rose, slightly puffy areolas and pointed nipples that he yearned to explore in more detail. Her waist was small, with flaring hips, which framed a flat stomach and indented navel. Her woman hair was darker and curlier than that on her head, as if hiding some mystery. All this led down to exceedingly long legs and high-arched feet, with toes that curled childlike in the rushes.

He was the one who moaned then as he swept her up into his arms and carried her to the bed. Burying his face in the curve of her neck, he whispered hoarsely, "Nay, my ego or your punishment have naught to do with this crackling in the air betwixt us." He licked wetly at the pulse that beat in her neck and delighted when it jumped in response. "What this is about, m'lady, is one man and one woman. Me and you. And a fire that must be quenched . . . lest we both die of the heat."

"Life is not that simple," she murmured in a last, desperate plea for mercy.

"It is exactly that simple."

In that moment, Rurik realized the truth of his statement. He could not predict what the future held, but his destiny . . . for this moment in time . . . rested right here with this woman. He had not meant to speak his thoughts aloud, but somehow, as he laid her on the bed and came down over her, the words slipped out in an awestruck whisper. "This is our destiny."

The sensual journey had scarce begun when . . . oh, my! . . .

This is our destiny.

Maire replayed Rurik's poetic words over and over in her mind, trying to ignore their poignancy. "Is that what you tell all your wenches afore you tup them?" she asked with decided sarcasm and more coarseness than she usually employed.

If he had chuckled or laughed aloud, she could have forgiven him, but instead he gazed at her through those sky-blue eyes, serious as a clansman at a laird's funeral, and said ever so softly, "Nay, just you."

She moaned then . . . *again.* Oh, she well knew that the far-too-handsome, far-too-confident knave thought she moaned because she was overcome with lust for him. He had an ego the size of the English Channel. Nay, she moaned at his soft-spoken avowal that this act of love they were about to embark upon was their destiny when she understood that they were mere words he spun for his own wicked purposes. The skilled fornicator saw destiny as a temporary event, lasting only till he left her land, or lost his erection.

She, on the other hand, yearned for a destiny with a man who would stay with her for all time. And that man was not and never would be this born-to-swive Viking.

He was good at this seduction business, though. After years of practice, he knew just which words to say to a woman to melt her heart. Good thing Maire was impervious to his charm.

Well, somewhat impervious.

Well, at least she was aware of his devious nature and slick tongue.

She might not be able to fight him off physically, but she must gird herself not to fall prey to his allure.

As he leaned over her where she lay in the bed, he stared unabashedly at her nude body. She gritted her teeth and tried to count the rafters in the ceiling overhead. Anything to keep her mind off what the scoundrel was about to do . . . anything to keep herself uninvolved. The room was dreary and barely light, with rain pounding down on the rooftop. And she knew . . . she just knew . . . it was going to be a very long day.

"You have beautiful skin, Maire . . .'tis like sweet cream." Rurik did not touch her as he spoke. Instead, he lay on his side, propped on one elbow as he continued to examine her naked form. That hard, male part of him that she refused to look at poked her in the hip.

"You have beautiful skin," Maire mimicked him in a deliberately deep voice. "Spare me the insincere compliments, Viking. You know what you want. I know what you want. I'm tired of trying to convince you to be honorable about this, and it's obvious you could overpower me with a flick of your wrist. Let's just get it over with." She grabbed for his member and attempted to pull him atop her.

Rurik let out a howl of anguish and peeled her tight fingertips off of himself, cursing Norse expletives the whole time. He was now kneeling aside her still-reclining form, inspecting himself with a total lack of modesty. When he was satisfied that he would survive, Rurik grumbled at her, "Are you daft, wench? I swear you have left bruises on me. Has no one ever told you to handle a man's part with utmost gentleness?"

"Actually, no." Maire should have experienced at least a twinge of guilt over the obvious pain she'd caused, but she could not summon a speck of remorse. The lecherous brute deserved all she had done and more.

Rurik narrowed his eyes at her, as if he sensed her glee. "Turn over," he ordered.

"What? Why?" It was she who narrowed her eyes at him now. "You're not going to spank me, are you?"

His eyes widened with surprise, then he threw his head back and laughed uproariously. "I hadn't thought of that, but now that you mention it . . . Mayhap later, if you ask me nicely."

"Ask you . . . ask you . . . ?" she sputtered.

But he had already flipped her over so that she was on her stomach, her face pressed into the pillow.

"For now, I have other things in mind," he informed her smoothly.

"Like what?" she demanded, raising herself on extended arms and trying to peer back over her shoulder.

He shoved her back down and put a hand on the middle of her back to hold her there. "Sweetling, I intend to explore every single part of your body . . . back and front. By the time night falls again, I will know *everything* there is to know about you, from scalp to toe and every niche and cavity in between."

Niche? Cavity? Her heart stopped for a second, then began beating again at a more rapid pace. Heat infused her, and not just her face; she suspected that her skin was turning pink all over her body.

"Have you naught to say about that, witch? Have I for once struck you speechless?"

"Why?" was all that came out of her mouth and that in a strangled whisper.

"Because I want to."

She couldn't see him with her cheek pressed to hands folded on the pillow and she couldn't tell by the tone of his voice whether he was serious, or jesting. "Are you grinning?" she asked, unable to control her curiosity.

"Widely."

"This is just a game you play with me . . . a game of torture. Isn't it?"

"Yea, 'tis just that. Sexual torture. The best kind."

Maire should have known he would give a perverted answer like that. She resolved then not to ask any more questions.

He moved her hair aside so that her nape was bare. Then, for a long time, he did not touch her or speak. The only sounds in the room were those of the rain and Rurik's heavy breathing. Or was it hers? She held her breath for a long time, just in case. Eventually she had to release it in a whooshy exhale.

She thought he might have chuckled softly. Leastways, she felt something move against her shoulder blades, like warm air. This waiting was driving her nigh insane, but she would not . . . could not . . . ask the brute to get on with things. That would indicate an eagerness she did not feel.

Finally, she felt the lightest touch . . . probably a forefinger . . . trailing a path from her neck, down her spine, over the crevice at her buttocks, between her thighs and calves, across the back of one knee, then skimming the bottom of first one foot, then the other. The sensation was light as a summer breeze but so intensely erotic that Maire felt as if he'd lit a trail of fire. She had to clench her fists and bite her bottom lip to restrain herself from jerking or crying out.

But that was just the beginning.

Next, he followed the same path, but this time with his tongue, even over her backside—*wicked, wicked man!* He must have sensed her distress over his tasting that part of her anatomy because he nipped with his teeth at the soft flesh there, before moving his tongue down her thighs. When he got to the bottoms of her feet and lapped at the ticklish arches, Maire closed her eyes tightly to fight the urge to squirm . . . or worse yet, giggle.

You'd think he would have been done by then. But, nay, he had barely started. Now he fashioned new paths of survey for his tempting fingers and slick tongue and his palms, which she'd discovered were tantalizingly callused, no doubt from weapon-wielding. Her underarms. The curve of her neck. The sides of her ribs and hips. The small of her back, which she discovered was sinfully susceptible to his expert caresses. When he tried to separate her thighs and stroke her in between, from behind, Maire could take no more. She rolled over on her back and wailed, "Enough!"

That was her biggest mistake thus far. She could tell

even before he spoke, from the gleam in his mischievous eyes and the sensuous parting of his lips, that the rogue had her exactly where he wanted her.

"Nay, witchling, 'tis not nearly enough." He arranged her suddenly boneless arms above her head in a posture that could only be described as wanton. Then he conceded, " 'Tis a good beginning, though."

Their eyes locked, and Marie was riveted in place by the message in his compelling blue eyes. She was not very experienced in bedplay, but she knew without a doubt that this man wanted her . . . badly. Why did he not just take her then? That was what Kenneth had done. None of this teasing aforehand. Usually, he'd been fortified with a goodly amount of *uisge-beatha* first, as if he could not bear to touch her unless he were intoxicated. Not that she had wanted his lovemaking . . . if it could be called that . . . especially after his true, vicious nature became apparent.

But Maire couldn't think about that now. She had to concentrate on the present, lest the Viking catch her unawares . . . lest *she* do something she might later regret.

Rurik did not pounce on her, as she'd expected. No jamming apart of her legs and heavy weight pressing his staff into her tender parts for a quick one-two-three strokes before rolling over into a snoring slumber. Nay, Rurik did things his own way, in his own good time. She should have known.

Now that Maire was exposing new territory for Rurik's exploration, he began another slow, leisurely investigation . . . first with his hot eyes, then his hands and mouth. The man knew things Maire had never dreamed of.

"Are all Vikings like you?" she blurted out once on a panting breath when he was touching her breasts . . . just the undersides, with the pads of his fingertips, when she yearned for something more, like the sharp suckling of his lips.

He glanced up at her through thick, sooty eyelashes . . . and winked. The rascal had the nerve to wink at her! "Nay, just me," he said. "And just with you."

"Liar."

Eyebrows raised, he looked pointedly downward as if to prove that he told the truth, then renewed his "assault" on her. "Is this what you want, sweetling?" he murmured as he began to minister in depth to first one breast, then another. Had she spoken aloud? Did he know what she'd been thinking?

"Nay," she said in a choked voice as her back bowed upward in response to the delicious agony caused by his playing with the areolas and nipples of her breasts. Tracing. Stroking. Fluttering. Squeezing.

"Who's the liar now?" he asked, even as one hand cupped a breast from underneath and pressed upward, creating his very own pleasure mound . . . even as his moist lips closed around one taut nipple . . . even as he began to suck on her with a savage rhythm.

Maire cried out . . . she couldn't help herself . . . and tried to shove him off. Without breaking his sucking cadence, Rurik took both her wrists in one hand and forced her arms back over her head. Each time he drew on her, Maire felt the ache in her breasts intensify, and there was an answering, building throb between her legs, which she held tightly together.

"Watch me," he commanded.

Maire hadn't even realized that she'd squeezed shut her eyes. For some reason, she didn't balk, as she normally would have. Nay, she did as he'd ordered.

Then he did the same to her other breast . . . as she watched. His long hair was clubbed back with a leather thong into a queue at his neck, thus exposing his face for her scrutiny. As he suckled her breast, his cheeks moved in and out with the force of his efforts. Maire did not think there was a more erotic sight in all the world than a stunningly virile man, such as Rurik, paying homage to a woman's breast.

"Did you like that?" he inquired silkily as he adjusted himself to lie atop her body.

She shook her head.

Which was apparently her second mistake of the day . . . or was it the third? She was in such a muddle she could scarce recall her own name at this point.

"Nay? You did not like that? Tsk-tsk! Well, I guess I will have to try harder."

Maire groaned with dismay, but Rurik caught her groan in his open mouth, which was already moving over hers. One of his hands still held her wrists above her head, but the other hand cradled her jaw.

Oh, he was a good kisser. An exquisite kisser. Maire had to credit the Viking with that. She didn't want to think about where he'd learned all those tricks with his lips and teeth and tongue. She was more concerned about how he made her feel. If she wasn't careful, she would be having one of Rurik's famous fits . . . over nothing more than kisses.

He was attacking her ear now, alternating puffs of breath with wet licks of his tongue. Somehow, her hands had come loose, for her arms were wrapped around his wide shoulders, caressing the ropey sinews of his back, and his hands were under her buttocks, lifting her up against his raging erection. Maire realized with astonishment that her legs had parted somewhere along the way, and her knees were cradling his hips.

Maire wanted Rurik inside her. She really did. A strange inner excitement rippled through her and centered in that place where he should surely already be by now.

"Now," she pleaded, and arched her middle up off the mattress in encouragement.

Rurik's head reared back suddenly and he stared at her, gasping, as if trying to swim out of a haze of confusion. She knew just how he felt. But he surprised her by declaring vehemently, "Nay!"

"Nay?" Here she was, as open to this man as any woman could be. The only thing missing was the welcome trumpet.

"Not yet," he explained, giving her a quick kiss before he sat back on his knees between her widespread thighs.

In a rush of embarrassment, Maire tried to cover herself with her hands, but Rurik would have none of that. He pushed her hands aside. Then he did the unthinkable. Before she had a chance to blink or say him nay, the brute grabbed for the pillow and shoved it under her hips, lifting her higher and more open to his perusal. And peruse her, he did. Not to mention other things, which were surely sinful.

No one had ever gazed at her *there*.

No one had ever touched her *there*.

No one had ever told her how she looked *there*.

No one had ever praised her wetness *there*.

No one had ever explained in explicit, sexual detail what he intended to do *there*.

No one had ever prepared her for the feel of a man's tongue *there*.

Everything in Maire centered on him then . . . this man who obviously reveled in a woman's body . . . whose every gesture and touch were attentive and unhurried.

By the time Rurik was done tending to her *there*, Maire

was a mewling, fist-pounding-on-the-mattress, shivering mass of female desire. She felt as if she were . . . well, climbing a mountain. If only she could reach the peak! Only then would this horrible-wonderful throbbing ache be relieved.

And Rurik knew of her distress. She could see it in his admiring eyes. And she saw something else in his eyes, too. Intense, bone-melting desire. He wanted her just as much as she wanted him. And yet he held back. Why?

Before she could ask, he delivered a message to her in a low, masculine growl, "Heed me well, Maire. This is my *mark* on you."

While she observed, his long middle finger flicked back and forth, rapidly, against the slick surface of an oversensitive part of her she hadn't even known existed. Maire keened and bucked, but he would not stop. Inside and outside, she began to spasm with the most incredible sensations. Not pleasure . . . more like the foreshadowing of some great event. But then the pleasure came, too, like a lightning bolt between her legs, and his mouth and tongue were there again, relentless, hurtling her up and out over some great abyss.

Ecstasy, that's what this was. Sheer ecstasy.

Ecstasy? Maire eyes shot wide open at remembrance of that word . . . a word that Rurik had used just that evening. "What . . . was . . . that?"

"That, my dear, was an orgasm."

"Oh. *That* was one of your sex fits?"

"Yea . . . I think so. Did you have tremors?"

She was not certain, but she thought he might be teasing her. Risking his mockery, she nodded.

He cocked his head to the side. "Perchance you did, then. I was too busy rolling my eyes up into my head to notice." Hah! The rogue had noticed every blessed thing. And he *was* teasing her.

Her gaze immediately went to his groin, where a rampant erection still raged up out of a nest of black curls. It was bigger than before, if that were possible. Maire sensed the tightly coiled power that he held in check. "You did not have an or-gaz-him yet?" she asked tentatively, not sure she was using the right term, or in the correct way.

He tried to smile but a choking sound came up from his throat. At the same time, his male member jerked. Just because she was looking?

"I thought it was painful for a man to wait too long."

"'Tis true. 'Tis true. I am definitely in pain." He stretched himself over her then, bracing himself on his extended arms. Adjusting his hips from side to side, he maneuvered his sex into her wet female channel. "Will you be helping to relieve my pain, dearling?" he asked then.

Maire did not have to consider for even a moment before she decided that she, indeed, would . . . because, surprisingly, she was developing a new pain of her own.

CHAPTER TEN

Betimes a man gets skewered on his own petard . . .

Maire must be a true witch, for Rurik was surely under her spell. Had she somehow given him a love potion, or just surrounded him with her enticing aura?

As he stared down at the now willing, most alluring maid, he was more than prepared to join with her in the way of men and women through the ages—*God's pleasure gift to men . . . and women, too.* He knew with a certainty, though, that this time would be different . . . life-changing. And that was frightening to a man who prided himself on self reliance. Had he not told himself from the time he was a boy that he needed no one?

But he needed Maire now . . . desperately.

Would that need be assuaged once the lust-mood had passed? Damn, he hoped so! Never, in all his misbegotten life, had he wanted a woman the way he wanted Maire now. He was a man who loved women and sexplay. He savored both the giving and the taking of passion-joy amongst the bed furs, and it had been especially important to him with Maire to bring her to ecstasy first, which he had done . . . and done well. But it had never been so difficult before for him to forestall his own satisfaction, and he truly feared now that there would be no satisfaction even when he spurted forth his seed.

But he had to try.

With his straightened arms positioned on either side of Maire's head and his hips nestling between her thighs, he reared his head back, the veins standing out tensely on his neck and breath hissing through his clenched teeth. Only then did he begin to enter her tight sheath of hot silk. Slowly, slowly, slowly, he eased his staff one tiny bit at a time, savoring every welcoming clasp of her folds. His head spun with the intensity of his excitement. And he was only in halfway.

Hearing a soft sob, he unshuttered his eyes . . . and saw that Maire was weeping silently.

Nay! he rebelled silently. *Nay, nay, nay! Do not reject me now. 'Tis unfair. I think I am going to die.*

He did not die. Nor did he withdraw. In truth, he was not certain that he could withdraw, so huge was his "Lance." But he did ask, "What is it, sweetling? Am I hurting you?"

She shook her head, though her beautiful green eyes continued to well with crystal-like tears that spilled over and ran down her cheeks.

"What ails you then? Do you . . . do you want me to stop?" Holy Thor! He could not believe he'd asked her *that*. In no way did he want to give her an opportunity to stop such exquisite bed sport.

She shook her head again.

Praise the gods! "What is it then?" he questioned, leaning down to kiss her gently on lips that were moist and parted . . . from crying. Not to mention swollen . . . from his recent kisses. Rurik was still embedded only halfway inside the wench, and he was amazed at his calm in inquiring about her distress when what he wanted to do was tup till his brains fell out.

"You," she answered.

"Me?" *Damn. Damn, damn! What have I done now? Did I unarouse her with some coarse gesture? Or did I say something perverted that frightened her off? Did I—oh, I hope I didn't—mention tupping my brains out?*

"You are so beautiful," she explained.

Ah! So, I'm not as uncouth as I feared.

". . . and this thing you do to me . . . this feeling I get when you couple with me"—she shrugged, unable to come up with the precise words she searched for—"I did not know lovemaking could feel so . . . so glorious."

Glorious? Aha, she likes me . . . she likes me . . . well, leastways, she likes how I look . . . and how I make her feel. That was all Rurik needed to hear. With a roar of masculine exultation, he plunged himself in to the hilt. Pausing briefly to adjust himself from side to side, which caused her inner muscles to shift in accommodation and his erection to elongate, he whispered carnal words against her ear, recognizing that some women liked wicked words in the bed-play. "Your woman folds feel like hot fingers on my sex."

"Your manpart is like soft marble. And it pulses, betimes," she replied.

Some men liked wicked words in the bedplay, too, Rurik had to admit. He was one of them. *Joy, joy, joy!*

"Do you like it . . . not my cock . . . I mean, the way it moves . . . bloody hell, I did not mean to sound so crude," Rurik said with a groan. Blessed Freyja, he was stuttering about like a bumbling lackbrain of no experience.

She smiled softly. "Aye, I do."

Rurik felt himself lurch inside her at that admission . . . one she would perchance hate herself for later; it was exactly what Rurik's male ego wanted to hear.

He began his long strokes then, trying his best to keep them slow, dragging against her delicious friction, but it was not easy, especially when she went wide-eyed with wonder and asked, "Am I going to have another sex fit?"

He laughed, or attempted to, but it came out as sort of a gurgle. "I hope so."

She nodded, which was astonishing, really . . . that she could nod and ask him seemingly casual questions whilst his heart was thundering and his blood nigh steaming. "Will you be having a sex fit, too?"

Questions, questions, questions! he thought. But what he said was, "Most definitely."

He was silent then, and she was, too, as he initiated the serious, pounding rhythm that came instinctively to the male body. Soon Maire caught the idea and raised her buttocks up off the mattress, undulating in counterpoint to his driving strokes. Logical thought was beyond him now. With other women, he might have pondered which was the best method for achieving this or that passion-goal. But not with Maire. Rurik was out of control, lost in a white-hot arousal, and—*Thank you, Odin!*—Maire appeared to be the same.

When Maire began to keen with heightening stimulation, he moaned his own excitement. Soon she was spasming around him . . . a sensation so pleasurable it approached pain . . . and Rurik withdrew, at the last moment, to spill his seed into her woman hair. As much as Rurik yearned to come inside her body, he had promised her no pregnancy. Even so, he reached the height of ecstasy, and sagged down atop her body.

Both sated, they breathed heavily into each other's necks, trying to return to calm and sanity . . . though Rurik was not sure he could ever achieve either again.

She took him by both ears then and raised his head to scrutinize him intently.

"What? What are you looking at?"

Her lips seemed to twitch with some mirth. "I'm just verifying whether your eyes are rolling back in their sockets."

He laughed and took a playful nip at her shoulder before he moved off her and the mattress to stand next to the bed. "They were, for a certainty," he informed her. "And I would wager I engaged in fitlike tremors, too." Then, he ordered, "Stay here."

He went behind a screen in the corner where he washed himself. While there, he checked the mirror to see if his blue mark was still there. It was. He smiled, guessing he would have to endure more love-making with Maire. Still smiling, he brought a pottery bowl of water and a soft cloth back to the bed, where he proceeded to wash her female parts.

He would have thought that Maire might have protested that intimate act, or that she might try to cover herself in modesty, as some women did, now that the lovemaking had ended, but, nay, she reclined back on the pillows, legs slightly spread, and allowed him to tend to her. The wench continually surprised him.

But it might be a good idea if he changed the subject for a bit in order to give his body a chance to renew itself. Glancing about the room, he noticed once again the unfinished tapestry on the wooden frame in the corner. Even in the dismal half-light caused by the rainy weather, the picture was exquisite. Rurik would never claim to be an expert on art, but he knew talent when he saw it. It was not just the brilliant colors, but the different textures of thread and patterns of sewing that gave a dimensional aspect to the scene, which included a man and a woman, seen from the back, holding hands as they watched a young boy playing in the shallow waters at the edge of a loch. The figure of the man was incomplete, as were the white clouds skimming the blue sky, the shredded threads of lavender-hued heather, a red deer peeking out of the forest in the distance.

Something about the scene pulled at Rurik's heart in

a way he could not explain. Not just its beauty. Nay, it was the image it portrayed of a family . . . the kind of family Rurik had dreamed of as a child. A fantasy, really. That's what it was.

"What are you staring at so intently?" Maire inquired, putting a hand on his forearm.

He jerked his head back to look at her. She still reclined on the bed, but she'd drawn the bed linen up and over her breasts in modesty.

"The tapestry," he answered. "Who did it? Your mother?" Someone had told him that the large dusty tapestries in the great hall, which had been taken down the day before to be cleaned, were done years ago by her mother and grandmother. That would explain why this tapestry was unfinished.

Maire laughed softly. "Nay. My mother has been dead for more than twenty years. I did the needlework . . . or rather started it and never got around to completing the design."

Rurik wasn't sure why, but he was shocked. "You?"

"Why are you so incredulous?"

He shrugged with uncertainty. "It's so beautiful."

"And that shocks you? Methinks I should be insulted."

"It's just that . . . I don't know . . . well, why would anyone who could create such beauty do aught else? I mean, why practice inept witchly arts? Or work manually about your keep till your hands turn red and raw? Or waste all the years of your youth trying to hold a hopeless clan together?"

Maire bristled at his assessment of her life.

He rushed to explain himself. "You could become famous for your needlework, Maire. I know kings who would pay you great treasures to create such beauty for them." He paused, then added, "Why did you never finish it?"

"There is ne'er enough time. Other concerns always interfere." It did not seem to matter all that much to her.

He harrumphed with disbelief that anything could be more significant than her talent.

She shook her head sadly at him as if he just did not understand.

He didn't.

"Rurik, there are more important things in life than beauty."

"There are?" His question sounded dimwitted, even to his own ears.

She nodded. "Like honor. And family. And giving of oneself for a greater good."

Rurik did not disagree that those were important values. But this tapestry gave Rurik a new view of Maire that he would like to contemplate more. Later, though. Not now.

Tugging the sheet down to expose her breasts, he told her with a waggle of his eyebrows, "I have talents, too."

Her somber mood lightened immediately. "*That* was ne'er in doubt. Although, I will tell you this, Viking, if your lovemaking had been like this the first time we came together, I would no doubt have trailed after you across the oceans, no matter your desires."

Still sitting beside her on the bed, he glanced up at her through his lashes, without raising his head.

"Oh, do not look so alarmed," she said with a laugh. "I don't intend to chase after you now."

"I was not alarmed," he protested.

"Aye, you were." She laughed some more.

"What's so different now?" he asked, crawling back into the bed and taking her into his arms.

"Now, I am responsible for a child, and a clan. But you *are* a tempting morsel."

Rurik was not sure he liked her speaking thus to him. 'Twas the man's role to tease in the afterglow of love. She was too candid and uninhibited by half.

Nay, he immediately amended to himself with a smile. Her lack of inhibitions was priceless, and to be encouraged, not discouraged.

"You know, Rurik . . ."

What was it about women . . . that they felt the need to prattle on after lovemaking? What was wrong with silence . . . or sleep? "What?"

". . . that really wasn't any punishment."

"Explain yourself, wench," he grumbled, pulling her even tighter against his side, with her face resting on his chest. If she was going to chatter endlessly, he was going to be comfortable.

Twirling his chest hairs about one finger, she remarked, "You have been implying that you would take me to your bed furs as a punishment. But, in truth, it was more like a reward."

Rurik felt both elated and disgruntled by her observation. So he jabbed back, "Ah, but now you bear my man mark, and I swear, by the time this day is over, my mark on you will be indelible."

She seemed to consider his words for a long time, still playing with his chest hairs and throwing one knee over his thigh. It rubbed up and down, and up and down, and up and down. Finally, she peered up and fluttered her thick lashes at him, coyly. "Dost think you could start now?"

Rurik almost bit his own tongue.

Of course he could. Definitely. But 'twas best not to give too much to women in the bedsport lest they think they held the upper hand. So, he said with false indifference, "Perchance."

He saw immediately that he'd miscalculated with Maire. Disappointment shone on her face at his less-than-enthusiastic response, but, even worse, she was proceeding to sit up and get off the bed. "Oh, well, never mind," she said with as much lack of enthusiasm as he had just demonstrated. How dare she! "Mayhap I will go find Nessa and we can put up some honeycombs in pottery containers for the winter months. What else is there to do since the weather is so poor outdoors?"

"Hah!" he exclaimed, immediately regrouping as only a good soldier could. "Nay, nay, nay! You are not escaping my clutches so easily, you slippery wench, you. There will be honey made at *Beinne Breagha* today, I warrant, but not of the bee variety . . . more like the sex-honey variety. And as to what else there is to do, I daresay I have a few ideas."

She paused.

Quickly, he grabbed her by the waist and hauled her back. She landed atop him, thanks to his deft handling. Her hair billowed forward, shrouding her face, and landing in his open mouth. He spat out a few strands, then informed her, "I was only jesting when I said that *perchance* we could resume making love again. What I meant was that we *definitely* would."

She brushed her hair back off her face and behind her ears. Then she raised her head to look at him. To his astonishment, she was smiling. In fact, by the shaking of her body, he would guess that she was barely suppressing outright laughter.

"I knew that," she told him with a saucy grin.

Then, of all things, the witch winked at him. And it became clear as the skies over Oslofjord that she did, indeed, have the upper hand.

Now what?

Maire was new at this game of bold wanton. She'd

just made some outrageously suggestive remarks, but now she was unsure how to follow through.

He stared up at her with those compelling blue eyes of his, waiting for her next move. She had no clue what it would be. Yet.

"Come, Maire," he urged. "What additional things would you like me to do to put my mark on you? Do not go tongue-dead on me."

"I'm thinking," she snapped, not the best way to respond, she supposed, when sprawled atop a naked Northman. But *tongue-dead?* She should just clobber him over his smirking face with the pottery bowl that still sat on a low chest next to the bed. However, the man had uses. *Aye, that's it. I want to use the lecherous lout for my purposes, but how?*

Oh, Rurik was still the same insufferable Viking, but making love with him had been a joyous event, and Maire had experienced little enough joy in her life these past few years. Was it so wrong to gather more while she could?

In truth, the man had surprised the spit out of her with his superb lovemaking skills. Who knew such an earthy exercise could be so . . . ? She couldn't settle on exactly the right word.

Pleasurable? For a certainty.

Shocking? Aye. In a nice way.

Edifying? She had to smile at that one. She was definitely learning *things*, and she definitely wanted to learn more *things*. Besides, she was discovering that she harbored a strong sensual streak. Before it disappeared, she'd like to know more about what had brought it to life, and why.

Harmonious? Strange that this word should pop into Maire's head, but there *had* been this feeling of balance when Rurik was inside her. Not just the oneness, or the wonder of two such disparate bodies fitting together so perfectly, as the Creator had planned. It was more as if . . . *she shuddered to think of the ramifications* . . . their joining had, in fact, been ordained in some way, as Rurik had mentioned earlier. Destiny.

She released a sigh at that whimsical thought and noticed that Rurik was still gazing at her, with his eyebrows arched in question. She also noticed that his manpart had grown hard again and was nudging insistently against her womanpart.

Well, Maire wasn't sure what to do next, but she could always follow Rurik's technique . . . the slow one he had employed at the beginning. Rolling off the top of his body and to her side, she ordered, "Turn over."

Startled, he blinked at her.

She found that she liked being the one in charge.

"Wh-what?" he stammered out.

She also found gratification in making a man—a virile man in her bed—stammer.

"I want to examine your body, as you did mine," she explained, heat suffusing her skin from forehead to toes. Maire was unaccustomed to making such explicit demands of a man, especially a nude one.

His already hardened staff flexed at her words.

And, aye, Maire found that there was gratification to be found in knowing that her mere words could arouse Rurik.

For one long moment, he stared at her, and Maire thought he might refuse, but then he licked his suddenly dry lips, which caused her lips to go suddenly dry. "This had best be good, Maire," he murmured in a husky voice, and flipped over onto his stomach, folding his arms under his face.

At first, Maire's eyes simply swept over Rurik's long form. But even that cursory examination showed him to be a fine, fine specimen of manhood. Broad shoulders. Narrow waist. Slim hips. Firm buttocks. Excessively long legs. And everywhere muscles, muscles, muscles.

She set the long swath of his hair to the side and touched the strong tendons in his neck. He sighed softly with appreciation, which spurred her to sweep her palms across his shoulder blades, then down to the small of his back. Immediately, all the muscles in his upper body bunched with tension.

"Was that bad?"

He made a gurgling noise, midway between a choke and a laugh. "That was good."

She hesitated, and then massaged the two mounds of his backside. Interested in the unusual compactness there . . . much harder than her own . . . she touched him some more, then ran a forefinger down the centerline.

His entire body went stiff.

Was that a mistake? Too brazen? She thought about giving up on this exploration business, but then he coaxed, "Don't stop now, Maire. For the love of Freyja, don't dare stop now."

She smiled at the heady notion that she could affect this seasoned lover so. Resuming her leisurely survey, she moved down to his legs, where she discovered that the backs of his knees and his inner thighs were uncommonly sensitive to touch.

He groaned aloud and rolled over, pulling her halfway atop him . . . her breasts pressed to his chest, her one thigh thrown over both of his. Assailed by a sudden bout of modesty, she tried to adjust herself so that the excited tips of her breasts were not so evident, but he would not allow her to move. Instead, he whispered, pulling her forward, "Kiss me, witch. Before you resume your campaign to drive me daft with your touch, taste me with your lips, and your tongue, and your teeth."

"I'm not a good kisser, like you," she admitted shyly.

At first, his languid eyes went wide with surprise. Then he shook his head as if her inexperience were of no consequence. "Try," he beseeched, "and I will teach you what does not already come instinctively."

Maire did just that, settling her lips over his much fuller ones, then dragging them from side to side for a better fit.

"Open," he murmured against her lips.

She did, and, oh, who knew that just the parting of a woman's lips over a man's could be so erotic? Rurik instructed her in the art of kissing then. Not with words, but with masculine sounds of encouragement, turns of the head, and example. She soon discovered that she was a very quick learner. Rurik considered her an excellent pupil, too, if his ragged breaths were any indication when he finally broke the kiss.

To Maire's immense satisfaction, she saw that his lips were moist and slightly swollen from her kisses. His eyes were luminous with a carnal fire she had ignited. And his manhood pressing urgently against her thigh was thick and hard. She did not want to think how she must look to him. Worse, she was sure. Or better, depending on one's point of view.

Rurik had told her something earlier, in the heat of his lovemaking, which she recalled now. He had said that a woman's passion was a man's greatest pleasure. Well, it went the other way, too, she realized now. A man's passion was a woman's greatest pleasure, as well.

'Twas time to resume her explorations, she decided. Following Rurik's route, she used her tongue and teeth to play with his ears and his flat male nipples. To her delight, he found as much joy in her ministrations as she'd found in his.

At one point, she remarked ruefully, as she studied

his burgeoning member, "By the size of Lance, 'twould seem you have not been telling very many lies, Viking."

" 'Tis no time for teasing, wench," he said huskily, but she could tell her playful words gladdened him. She was not accustomed to such flirting, but found she liked it. Mayhap later she would become more proficient at the gentle art of flirtation . . . if the rogue beneath her fingertips stuck around that long.

By the time she'd splayed her fingers over his stomach and dipped her head to lick the indentation of his navel, Rurik had apparently had enough of her sweet torture. With a masculine roar, he lifted her bodily so that she straddled his stomach.

"Take me," he rasped out.

"Huh?" She tilted her head in question. "Take you where?"

"Inside . . . take me inside of you," he said in a voice so dark and smoky she felt her woman center clench in response.

She was not precisely certain how to do that, but she raised her bottom slightly, and grasping his thick column in her hands, she drew him inside ever so gently. And, by the saints, he felt good.

Rurik's eyes actually rolled back in his head for a moment, and she saw that his teeth were gritted, as if in pain. But she sensed it was a kind of pleasure-pain. When his eyes made contact with hers again, he said, "Lean forward so you can take more of me, sweetling."

More? That was not possible. She did as he instructed and found, to her amazement, that her body was made to accept all of him, as inner muscles shifted and slickened.

"Now sit back."

She did, resting her bottom on his loins, which caused her legs to widen. To her embarrassment, though, she started to spasm around his shaft . . . alternately squeezing and releasing. She tried to lift herself off and turn her face away in shame, but he would have none of that. With hands on her hips, he held her down and pleaded, "Look at me, Maire. I would see you peak."

When she did not immediately meet his gaze, he commenced strumming that bud between her thighs . . . the one now practically pressing against his belly, as insistent in its swelling as his own imbedded erection. "Oh!" she whispered.

"What?" he asked.

She put a hand against herself and confessed, "It feels like butterfly wings here . . . the frantic beating of butterfly wings."

"Ah, Maire. You are truly precious."

A fierce wail erupted from her then as the convulsions began all over again, stronger now. "I need . . . I need . . . ," she cried out, not sure exactly what it was she needed. Perhaps just an end to this throbbing between her legs and the aching in her breasts.

Then, slowly, slowly, slowly, she rocked her hips. So intense was the bliss that she closed her eyes and saw red and white stars behind the lids. When she opened them, it was obvious that he was equally affected. Beads of sweat stood out on his forehead and upper lip, bespeaking great restraint. His eyes were glazed, and panting breaths came from his parted lips. Frustrated at his lack of movement, she grabbed his hands off her hips and placed them over her breasts. "Move, damn you. Move!" she demanded.

He laughed up at her. "With pleasure, my lady." Soft words of guidance and deft hands showed her the rhythm. She figured she must be doing it correctly because at one point he told her, on a groan, "You . . . are . . . incredible."

Maire had peaked so many times since he'd first forced

her to straddle him that she'd lost count. When he whispered into her ear, "You melt like hot honey around me," she felt, indeed, as if her insides were dissolving around him. "Tell me how I feel to you," he implored then.

She thought only an instant and disclosed, "You are the missing part of me, come home." Her words stunned him, she could tell, but it was the truth. He completed her.

Had any other man and woman fit together as well as they did? She had no experience, other than Kenneth, but she decided that she and Rurik must be unique. Adam and Eve, but better. That thought made her smile.

"Do you find mirth in my discomfit?" Rurik asked with a growl, chucking her playfully on the chin.

"*Are* you discomfited?"

"Oh, lady, I am sore discomfited, and you are the cause."

She smiled wider then.

Cupping her buttocks, he rolled them both over so that she was on the bottom. "You like discomfiting me, do you?"

"Immensely."

That was the last word she was able to speak for some time as Rurik began the hard strokes that would bring on his own ecstasy. Maire observed closely as his male explosion approached. Veins stood out on his neck and forehead. His eyes dilated and grew midnight blue. His nostrils flared. And he panted in a fast-paced cadence to match his strokes.

Rurik's ecstasy was a beautiful thing to watch.

At the end, he pulled out and spilled his seed upon the linens between her legs. For an instant, she wished that he could stay within, especially as her insides continued to ripple . . . missing him . . . but she knew that was imprudent.

He collapsed on top of her, his face pressed into the curve of her neck. Maire thought he might have fallen asleep, but he kissed the pulse point in her neck and whispered, "Thank you."

Thank you? What an odd thing to say!

Not so odd, though, she supposed. She was thankful, too, for the pleasure he'd just given her. As his greater weight pressed her to the mattress, not uncomfortably, Maire caressed his silken hair and pondered all that had happened to her that day. It was monumental. Tears brimmed in her eyes as she realized just how monumental.

I still love him.

CHAPTER ELEVEN

The path to love is like a tapestry. All those loose ends . . .

Rurik was frightened.

For a hardened warrior, that was a difficult admission to make. But there it was.

He could handle uneven odds in a battle, he could handle the prospect that he might die without warning, he could handle bloodshed and cruelty. What he could not handle were the overpowering feelings he was developing for Maire.

How could he be so affected in such a short time? Witchcraft? He shuddered at the possibility. There was no denying the fact that when he looked at Maire his insides melted, his heart raced, and he lost his concentration. In essence, he felt rather sick in his stomach. He could not stop touching her, or thinking about her, or smiling. . . . Yea, he'd been doing an inordinate amount of smiling these past hours. Best he be careful, lest he start staggering about like a dreamy-eyed lackbrain.

Truth to tell, Rurik suspected he was falling in love with the witch. Not that he knew from experience how that would feel. But if it was, indeed, true, then he would have to find a way to stop it right now. Falling in love did not fit in with his plans. Nay, not at all.

There were many reasons why he could not allow

himself to love a woman, but three important ones came immediately to mind:

First, he was a warrior, pure and simple. He had no other identity than that. Being arse-over-shoulders in love with a woman—especially one with the talent for turning certain body parts blue and others rock hard—would make him weak and vulnerable . . . something he could not countenance. He'd had love-struck soldiers under his command in the past. They soon lost their focus. Many were brought down swifter than a Saxon arrow, usually by tripping over their own feet.

Second, there was no future in loving a Scottish witch. Rurik hated the land of Alba with a passion and could scarce wait to leave its boundaries. Besides, he was betrothed to a Norse princess, and it had been a pledge made in honor, which must be upheld.

Third, Maire was his foe, and he should not forget that fact. 'Twas she who'd marked his face and subjected him to years of ridicule.

Well, at least he now knew what he must do. He had a new goal to go along with the removal of his blue tattoo. *Do not love Maire.*

It was late afternoon. He and Maire had been making love off and on—mostly on—since dawn, and still he could not get enough of her. Even now, as she slept in his arms, he could not tear himself away, though his belly rumbled with hunger, his body was growing rank from all the sweaty exercise, and the bed linens were uncomfortably damp. So, following his new "Do not love Maire" motto, Rurik called upon his years of discipline to avoid noticing Maire's allure as he carefully disengaged himself from her billowing red hair and clinging limbs.

Actually, he had his eyes scrunched tight. That worked, too.

He was congratulating himself a short time later

when he emerged from the bedchamber without awakening Maire. Closing the door quietly behind him, he nigh jumped out of his skin when the first thing he saw was Toste and Vagn leaning against the facing wall, arms folded over their broad chests and ankles crossed. They were smirking at him.

"What are you two doing here?"

"Guarding the mistress," Toste answered.

"As you ordered," Vagn pointed out.

"I did not ask you to guard her when I was with her," he grumbled. "Besides, why was it necessary for two of you to stand guard?"

"Toste is the guard. I'm just keeping him company," Vagn said.

Both of them were still grinning.

"So, did you or-gaz the wench?" Toste and Vagn both asked him at the same time.

"Would everybody please stop using that ridiculous word? Furthermore, 'tis none of your concern whether I did or did not."

"Well, *you* certainly look as if you've been or-gazed . . . good and proper," Toste said, ducking when Rurik swung a punch at his laughing mouth.

"Yea," Vagn agreed. "Methinks he is still suffering after-tremors, too . . . from his *fit*. Perchance he has or-gaz pains. Mayhap I should go check on the witch's condition."

"You stay away from Maire," Rurik ordered, too quickly and too gruffly.

Both men stared at him with arched eyebrows.

"Uh-oh!" Toste said.

"Uh-oh!" Vagn said.

"I'll give you both reason to say uh-oh if you don't stop flapping your tongues."

Rurik noticed something else. Each of the twins had a

piece of scarlet yarn tied in a bow about his middle finger. "*What* is that?" he asked, pointing at one, then the other adornment.

"A measuring yarn," Toste replied, his face turning bright red. Rurik could not recall a time, ever, when Toste had blushed, even when he'd done some mighty embarrassing things.

"For our cocks," Vagn explained, and his face was red, too. "I mean, for measuring our cocks."

"Holy Thor! Did you two dimwits believe that outrageous tale about Viking lies and shrinking man-parts?"

"We did not *precisely* believe it, but we wanted a measuring standard, just in case," Toste said defensively. "You never know with a sorceress, Rurik. Really, one can't be too careful."

"Not that we are prone to mistruths, mind you. But a wee fib might slip out on occasion." Vagn was blinking his eyes at him with innocence. Vagn glanced at his brother, who nodded enthusiastically in concurrence.

"And what would you do if there was some . . . shrinkage?"

The twins exchanged alarmed looks.

"Mayhap the witch knows a spell for . . . stretchage?" Toste inquired hopefully.

Actually, she does, but I'll be damned if I'll let her work her magic on either of these two.

"Yea, that would do the trick," Vagn said.

"Methinks I have landed in a barmy bin," Rurik concluded, grabbing Toste by the upper arm and pulling him toward the stairwell. "Come with me, and tell me what's been happening. Vagn, you stay and guard Maire."

They had reached the bottom of the stairs and were about to enter the great hall when Toste held him back. "There is some news you should be aware of." When Rurik stopped, Toste informed him of a series of events that had transpired during the night involving three cattle and four sheep. That in itself should have been of no concern. Scotsmen loved reiving, and it was a part of their lifestyle to steal from each other routinely. He told Toste so.

Toste shook his head. "This was different. Not only were the animals killed and their carcasses left to rot, but the creatures had been tortured beforehand and mutilated. Heads lopped off. Eyes gouged out. A ram's testicles stuck in its own mouth."

Rurik tasted bile rising up to his throat. "A warning, then. The MacNabs are leaving a warning . . . not just that they can enter Campbell lands, undeterred, but that they are prepared to inflict torture on innocent parties."

"That is my opinion on the matter, and Stigand's and Bolthor's, too."

"Why didst you not call for me as soon as you heard?"

Toste shrugged. "We only discovered the perfidy within the hour. Actually, that was why I was in the hallway outside your bedchamber. I had just come up to get you."

"I do not like this waiting, like a sitting boar inviting the hunter's lance. Every good soldier knows 'tis better to be on the offense than the defense."

"That is something we need to discuss. Everyone is waiting for you below."

"Is the castle secure for now?"

"Yea, 'tis."

A sudden thought occurred to Rurik, and he gasped. "The boy . . . Maire's son . . . go immediately and bring him into the castle. I care not what his mother says . . .'tis not safe for him out in the forests when the MacNabs can move about so freely. Take one of the Campbell men with you and direct him to tell you where this hidden cave is located."

"I had not considered that possibility, but you are correct. The boy must be brought under the protection of your shield. The MacNabs would not be above torturing a child," Toste said.

"Or the mother, if the child were used for ransom." Rurik's blood ran cold at the prospect of Maire being so endangered. After all, a man who would place a woman in a cage would not be above other unspeakable acts.

"Uh, Rurik, there is one other thing."

Rurik tilted his head in question.

"There's a bite imprint on your neck." Toste's lips twitched with mirth.

Rurik put a hand to the right side of his neck. He did not doubt there was a mark. In truth, he could recall in detail the circumstances under which Maire had cried out in passion and nipped him there. Still, Toste pushed the bounds of friendship by commenting on such.

"Surely you want to be told these things, Rurik," Toste said, noticing his displeasure. "After all, a Viking never lies."

He reached out to swat the laughing rogue aside the head, but Toste danced away out of reach. As they entered the hall, Toste, still laughing, motioned for Young John to come forward. After a brief explanation, the two of them were off and out the front door of the keep. Rurik began to make his way through the hall then, and toward the kitchen. Rain still pounded incessantly on the rooftops; many of Maire's housecarls and cotters were indoors . . . cleaning and honing weapons; weaving and mending. All of them sat in strategic places to avoid the leaks from the roof, which had not yet been repaired.

All eyes turned to Rurik. It was the first the clan had seen of him since the night before. He noticed wariness and questioning looks on the faces of some of Maire's people; not surprising, since he'd been holed up in a bedchamber with their mistress for a full day. But then he caught the eye of Old John, who winked at him. Why were Maire's people not outraged on her behalf, or fretting over their mistress's fate at the lusty hands of her Viking captor? Instead, they seemed to approve. He should be worried about that fact, Rurik decided, but he had enough other worries for now . . . like the MacNabs. He would save that particular worry for later.

He saw Stigand at one of the lower tables, where he was showing Murdoc and several of the boys how to whittle arrows out of a slab of hardwood. The first thing out of Stigand's mouth was, "Did you or-gaz her?"

"Aaarrgh!"

"Do not be grousing at me. You're the one that failed in the bed arts with the maid. 'Twas a logical question, if you ask me. I was only concerned about you, after all." The mirth in Stigand's dancing eyes belied his great concern. "And why are you holding your neck?"

"A cramp?" Rurik mumbled, sitting down.

Stigand's gaze shot to Rurik's crotch as if he expected some instant shrinkage for the lie. "A cramp, eh? Excessive bedsport will do that to a man betimes. One time I got a cramp in my cock. Talk about pain!"

Rurik put his face on the table and groaned.

That was when Bolthor walked up. "Did you or-gaz her?"

Rurik lifted his head and glared at his skald. "If one more person uses that ridiculous word, I am going to cut off said person's tongue. Is that clear?"

Bolthor stared at him for a long moment, as if unsure whether it was clear or not. Then, he pointed out irrelevantly, "Your lips are swollen."

"He's got a cramp in his neck, too," Stigand told Bolthor, as if that had some importance.

Bolthor nodded. "I wondered why he kept his hand there. I thought he might be trying to hide somethin'."

Stigand and Bolthor exchanged looks, then glanced down to check on the condition of his staff. This lying-shriveling nonsense had gone too far.

Rurik was about to swear . . . a famous Norse expletive . . . when he saw that all the males who were gathering about the table, no doubt to discuss the battle plans for the MacNabs, were wearing scarlet bows on their forefingers, including the Scotsmen and boys. Even more ludicrous, the size of the bows on Stigand and Bolthor's fingers would do a dragon proud.

He shook his head at the entire group. Lackwits, all.

The next hour was spent in developing some offensive actions to take against the MacNabs. This was Rurik's area of expertise, and he relished the drawing of maps and discussion of strategies. In the end, they came up with a plan that just might work, utilizing their undermanned troops to the best advantage.

Standing up and stretching, Rurik asked one of the servants to bring a tub and hot water up to Maire's bedchamber, along with toweling cloths and clean bed linens. Then he asked Nessa, who had just approached and was putting a hand familiarly on Stigand's shoulder, if she could prepare a tray for him with a goodly amount of food.

"How much food is *goodly?*" Nessa asked.

Rurik smiled then . . . a slow, lazy smile of anticipation. "Enough to last a *good* long while."

Rurik wasn't smiling for long. As he departed from the hall with his heavily laden tray, following in the footsteps of the servants with buckets of water, he heard Bolthor announce, "This is the saga of Rurik the Greater."

Once there was a Viking
Who lost his knack,
But soon a Scottish witch,
Taught him how to . . .
Get his knack back.
Now, in his bedsport,
There is no longer a lack.

Maire had just donned her chemise and was about to step out from behind the screen when Rurik came through the door.

"Wake up, sleepling," he said cheerily, then observed her in the corner. "Oh, you are already up and about." Then he added in a disappointed, accusatory voice, "You got dressed."

"Of course, I got dressed. Did you expect me to lie about naked for another whole day?"

"I had hoped," he remarked. And he was serious. The dolt! Not that Maire hadn't given him reason to hope. Blessed St. Boniface! Maire hardly knew the wanton who had inhabited her bedchamber this past day. Well, she had regained her senses now. Or, leastways, she hoped she was back to normal.

Just then, she noticed the men standing behind Rurik with buckets of water, all of them grinning. With a little shriek, she jumped back behind the screen. "You could have warned me that you brought others with you. I am not properly attired."

He glanced around, then shrugged sheepishly as he realized his mistake.

Soon, everyone had left, and Maire was soaking in a large copper tub filled with hot, lavender-scented water. While she lay back, basking in this unprecedented luxury, Rurik amazed her even further by lighting candles about the room and remaking the bed with clean linens.

If he had removed all his garments and jumped into the tub with her, flashing his usual grin, she would not have considered it out of the ordinary for his character.

But that was the worst thing about Rurik, or mayhap the best. He was always surprising her.

Instead of attempting further sexual inroads with her, Rurik pulled a low stool over to the side of the tub. With his elbows resting on his knees and his chin bracketed in his palms, Rurik amused her with stories of his past . . . both his childhood spent on a pigstead, the grueling adolescent years learning to be a soldier, a stint with the Varangian Guard in Byzantium, battle stories of fighting under one Norse chieftain or another against the hated Saxons, and poignant tales of his friendship with two brothers, Eirik of Ravenshire in Northumbria, and Tykir of Dragonstead in Norway. All the time, he fed her, and himself, bits of cold smoked venison, hard cheese, oat cake, and bannock, even tart cherries, all washed down with cold ale.

When the water began to cool, Rurik did not insist on helping her wash, as she'd expected, but he did make the strangest request. "Can I lather your hair?"

Who knew that a man's fingers massaging a woman's scalp could be so . . . well, erotic?

If this was part of a plan of seduction, Rurik truly was a master. Maire was finding it harder and harder to maintain the control she had promised herself a short time ago.

When she was done and wearing a clean shift, Rurik placed her on the low stool and combed all the tangles out of her long hair. Long after the snarls were smoothed out of the tresses, which tended to curl if left untended, he braided the strands with an expertise one wouldn't usually expect from a man. But then, Maire recalled that

Rurik was a man prideful of his personal appearance. He must often braid his own hair.

When he was done, he kissed her on the neck and stood back to remove his own garments.

Now it comes, Maire thought. *Now he will take the offense. Now I will have to gird myself against his renewed sexual assaults.*

Once again, Rurik surprised her. Sinking into the now cool water, he said, "Maire, would you do me a favor?"

Her head jerked up with alertness. She had been picking up the wet drying cloths and stacking them near the door with the dirty bed linens. *Uh-oh! What scandalous thing does he want me to do now? Wash his male parts? Get in the tub with him? Dance naked for his entertainment?*

"It would give me great pleasure," he said in a voice smoky with some strong emotion, "if you would work on your tapestry whilst I soak in the tub." He put up a halting hand as she prepared to protest. "Do not tell me it is too dark in here. You can light more candles."

"I cannot afford to waste so many candles . . . or the time. I have other, more important things to do."

He shook his head. "Creating such beauty can never be a waste of time or money. You are going nowhere anyhow . . . not till morning. In the meantime, I will buy you new candles, if that is truly of concern to you."

"Why is it so important to you?"

An astonishing flush bloomed on his cheeks and he confided, "When I was a boy, I always imagined my mother, if she had lived, sitting afore a loom or tapestry, working silently with me at her feet. A fey notion, I know. But there was so much turmoil in my life that the idea of a mother who was serene and gentle in her ladylike pursuits held inordinate appeal."

Maire could not speak over the lump in her throat. There was so much of the little boy still in Rurik, and long-suppressed emotions roiled inside him, though he would never admit to such "weaknesses." She tried to lighten the air of somberness that invaded the room. "So, you think of me like a mother?"

He laughed at that, and his beautiful blue eyes twinkled with sudden merriment. "Hardly that, m'lady. Come here, and I will show you."

She just smiled . . . on the outside. Inside, her heart grew heavy and light at the same time. Heavy, because she felt as if she were standing in a dangerous peat bog, her feet sinking in the mud at the bottom, like quicksand. And light, because she knew there would be such joy in doing something—anything—to please this man. Even if it was just needlework.

How could she refuse him such a simple favor? Rurik was a dolt some of the time. Arrogant all of the time. But she was beginning to see a side of him that was, at times, loveable. So, for the first time in more than a year—mayhap two—Maire sat down before her tapestry frame and began to lay out the threads she would use. Rurik had been right. She should not have ignored this work for so long. It brought a calmness she sorely needed now whilst storms swirled about her. She swept her fingertips over the fabric—a sensuous gesture of appreciation. Truly, the scene . . . this labor of creative love . . . was like an old friend. And old friends should not be neglected too long.

While she sewed, Rurik enjoyed his bath. Then he dried himself off, combed his hair and clubbed it back at the neck with a leather thong, and finally lay naked on her bed with his head propped on one elbow. All the time, he watched her work.

Occasionally, he would ask a question, like, "Do you

create a scene in some sequence? Background first; figures second? Or do you work by color? Or some other method?"

"It varies, usually depending on my mood. Some days I am inclined to work on people or animals. Another day I may have come across an unusual color of dye by experimenting with different plants, and I will be anxious to see how it looks. One time," she related with excitement, recalling an incident she hadn't thought of for years, ". . . one time I was on the moors with Jamie, and I saw a rowan tree. From a distance, its leaves had a shredded, feathery aspect. I experimented and found a way to feather the edges of my yarn on the tapestry to get the same effect. Like this." She pointed to an example in the foreground.

Rurik nodded in understanding, saying nothing more.

"It's odd, really, how you begin to look at things differently as an artist." Maire paused as the realization hit her suddenly that she did, in fact, consider herself an artist. 'Twas strange when she'd thought of herself for such a long time as a witch . . . and an inept one at that. She smiled to herself at the glow of pride that swept through her. *I am an artist. A good artist.* But then she continued her discussion with Rurik. "Sometimes appearances can be deceptive. What appears to be one thing from a distance is something else altogether up close. These sheep, for example. From where you view my tapestry, they are clearly wooly-haired sheep, I warrant, but from my vantage point, they are just clumps of undyed yarn."

Rurik chuckled at her enthusiasm over her craft, then waved a hand for her to resume her work when she stopped to glare at him.

Another time, he commented, "Is that unfinished male figure your husband?"

"No. The people in this tapestry don't represent anyone in particular," Maire lied.

Rurik thought for a moment and said, "Make the man's hair black then . . . black as a raven's wing. And be certain to use silk thread to denote its silky texture." He waggled his eyebrows at her as he touched his own hair.

Maire's heart raced at his words, but then she realized that he was just teasing . . . He did not suspect that the man really was supposed to be him . . . that the woman was she . . . and the boy, their son, Jamie. That was probably why she'd never been able to complete the tapestry . . . because it was not real. She would have been better off picking fantasy characters.

"In fact," he continued, "when I am old and no longer so comely . . . or when I am dead, it would please me immensely to know that I have left something of beauty behind. Well, leastways, that I contributed in some small way to the creation of a more permanent form of splendor. A legacy of beauty."

Oh, Rurik, if you only knew, you create beauty in your own way . . . not just in how you look. And your greatest legacy is a boy with hair black as a raven's wing and silken to the touch.

Still another time, Rurik remarked, "You seem happy when you sew. Nay, happy is not the correct word. You seem *peaceful*."

"Hmmm. I suppose I do feel peaceful."

"Methinks I will carry this image into future battles with me. In the midst of all the blood and carnage, I will call up a mind-picture to soothe me—'Maire at Peace.' "

Maire's heart skipped a beat at the prospect of Rurik being at war, surrounded by imminent peril, possibly injured or killed. It was silly of her to mind so. After all, it was Rurik's occupation to be a fighting man. And yet Maire hated to think of him endangered.

Mostly, there were silences while she sewed on her tapestry . . . easy, comfortable silences. Once, Maire looked up to see Rurik just staring at her. Their eyes connected, and he smiled, softly. She smiled back. It was such a precious moment that tears welled in her eyes, and she had to resume her work quickly before Rurik could notice and think her a foolish, smitten maid.

Then Maire became absorbed in her work, pausing only when she heard a commotion coming from below-stairs and realized that her people were making for bed. She must have been working for many hours.

Glancing over to the bed, she saw that Rurik had fallen asleep. She set aside her threads and placed the precious needles in their special silver case, which had been passed down through generations of Campbell women. Walking over to the bed, she looked down at the insufferable rogue. At rest, he was handsome in an altogether different way. His black lashes lay against his skin like fans. His mouth was full and sensual, but not in a threatening way. The blue mark stood out, of course, but, truth to tell, Maire liked it. Without it, his features were too perfect.

With a sigh, Maire slipped her chemise over her head and eased herself into the bed. Resting her face against his warm chest, she felt the steady beat of his heart.

Still sleeping, Rurik wrapped one arm around Maire's bare shoulder and tucked her more tightly against his form.

During the night Rurik awakened her in the best possible way—making sweet love to her. It was a silent, gentle loving . . . as powerful and bone-melting as his more aggressive, blood-pounding bedplay had been earlier.

Words were not necessary.

They both knew they were falling in love.

And they both knew how utterly impossible such a love would be.

Sometimes destiny was not all the bards claimed it to be. Sometimes fate dealt the harshest blows by planting love where there was no chance for the seedlings to grow. Sometimes love was like an unfinished tapestry, never to be. Sometimes Maire wished she really were a witch so that she could make wishes come true with a mere swish of her magic staff.

CHAPTER TWELVE

Betimes a boy needs a father's touch . . .

"Ahoooommm! Ahoooommm! Waaaraaaa!"

"*What* was that?" Rurik asked as he bolted upright in bed, awakened from a sound sleep mere minutes past dawn.

"Ahoooommm! Ahoooommm! Waaaraaaa!"

"Holy Thor! It sounds like a herd of elephants farting."

Maire sat up beside him, rubbing her eyes sleepily with one hand, and holding on to a sheet tucked about her breasts with the other. "I know you have traveled a great amount, Rurik, but have you actually encountered a herd of elephants . . . breaking wind?" she inquired incredulously.

"Nay. Not precisely."

"Tsk-tsk!" she chided playfully. "Best you watch your lying, Rurik. You know what they say about Vikings that misstate the truth."

"Well, I have seen elephants, but not . . ." He stopped abruptly. "That is not the issue. What *is* that ungodly racket?"

"Murdoc is probably teaching Bolthor how to play the bagpipes."

"At dawn."

"They will be busy with more crucial duties the rest of the day. This would be the only time."

Rurik put his face in his hands. "I have survived a childhood of abuse in a pigstead. I have survived near-mortal wounds in battle. I have survived five years of ridicule over my blue face mark. But I doubt that I can survive both Bolthor's sagas *and* his playing the pipes." All the time he spoke, the most ungodly noise was rising up from the courtyard below their windows . . . rather like a lusty mead fart, or the blowing sound of mockery made by children with outthrust tongues, except that this sound was louder. Much louder.

"Ahoooommm! Ahoooommm! Waaaraaaa!"

"Mayhap we should send Bolthor and a set of bagpipes onto the MacNab lands. That would be enough to make them surrender, methinks."

Maire put fingertips to her lips to stifle a giggle.

"Ahoooommm! Ahoooommm! Waaaraaaa!"

He jumped out of bed and began to don his braies. "I will put a stop to this nonsense, that I swear." Even though he was in a rush, after he was fully dressed he took the time to comb his hair and put a narrow braid on either side of his face, interlaced with colored beads. And he shaved, as well. Old habits died hard.

Maire was still watching him with a bemused expression on her face when he was done.

"Well? Are you going to stay abed all day? I ne'er took you for a slug-a-bed." He walked over to the bedstead and couldn't help smiling at the alluring picture she made. The bed linen still covered her bare form, but it revealed as much as it concealed. With her slumber-mussed hair and sex-flushed cheeks and kiss-pouty mouth, the witch looked like naught more than a wench who had been well tupped, but to Rurik she resembled a goddess. He would be a fool to attempt to discount as mere lust all that had passed between him and Maire this past day and night.

"A slug-a-bed?" Maire exclaimed with mock affront. "Does that mean I am to be released from my bed prison . . . finally?"

He shrugged. "For now."

Disappointment passed over her face, which she immediately replaced with a look of intense relief. Quicker than he could say, "The Saxons are coming!" she was up and about, her bed linen draped about her modestly, like a Roman senator in his toga, already searching for daytime apparel.

"Ahoooommm! Ahoooommm! Waaaraaaa!"

"Oh," he said, suddenly remembering something he'd intended yestereve. He went over to his leather saddlebag, which sat in one corner. He finally found what he was searching for . . . an object wrapped in soft black velvet. Handing it to her, he said gruffly, "This is for you."

She'd already pulled on a clean, well-worn chemise while his back was turned. For some reason, the condition of her chemise tugged at his conscience. He had noticed on more than one occasion that his garments were of much finer quality than hers, even though her station in society was higher.

Her eyes went wide with surprise that he would offer her a gift, and Rurik found immense pleasure then, not only in the gifting—a practice all Norsemen enjoyed—but in the anticipation of her delight. "You have a gift for me? No one has ever given me a gift that I can recall."

No one has ever given her a gift? How can that be? Rurik's blood boiled with rage at all the men in her life who had so neglected this woman . . . her father, her brothers, her husband.

"Ahoooommm! Ahoooommm! Waaaraaaa!"

I swear, I am going to kill Bolthor. This latest endeavor

pushes the bounds of friendship. Hell, it would push a foe to the brink, as well.

Sitting on the edge of the mattress, Maire began to unravel the cloth, uncovering the oval gemstone pendant suspended from a delicate gold chain. Although the jewel resembled a hazy emerald, it was actually a rare green amber he'd discovered last year when amber hunting with Tykir in the Baltics. One of Tykir's jewelry makers in the trading town of Birka had set the stone for him.

But, wait, Maire did not appear pleased. In fact, a small sob escaped her lips, and she began to weep, but not before attempting to hand the jewelry back to him.

"What? You do not like it? Look, Maire, it matches your eyes exactly. Truly, this pendant was meant for you. Let me help you put it on."

She shook her head. "Oh, Rurik, how could you?"

"What? How could I *what?*"

"Pay me . . . for services rendered . . . that's what. Just because I behaved as a . . . a harlot does not mean I deserve to be treated as one."

At first, her words didn't penetrate his puzzled brain, overwhelmed as it was by the cacophony of sound coming from Bolthor's unmusical mouth. When they did, he felt a sense of outrage that she would think such of him.

But her pain outweighed any insult he suffered. Dropping to one knee beside her, he pressed the pendant back into her hand. "Maire, I give you this gift in payment, but not for bedplay. When Old John told me how you suffered for having lost your maidenhead, I knew it was my fault. I treated you shamefully, and for that I am sorry. It was after my conversation with Old John that I decided to make reparation to you in some small way, and then I recalled this pendant that I'd actually discovered myself in the sandy shores off the Baltic seas. Most amber is the shade of tree sap or yellowish gold. Almost never is it green. The same day, Tykir found a hunk of golden amber the size of a man's head. So, it was a lucky day for both of us." Rurik realized that he was rambling with nervousness. Never had he expected her to decline his gift.

"Old John told you about . . . Kenneth?" Her body tensed, almost as if in fear.

"Just that he mistreated you after the wedding, and that some speculated the reason might have been that his bride was no longer a virgin. I assume that is why you asked to go with me, for protection."

"'Twould seem my faithful retainer has a loose tongue." She shook her head sadly.

"No doubt," Rurik agreed, "but he has your best interests at heart. He was not gossip-mongering."

She accepted his explanation. Unfolding her clenched fist, she gazed, longingly, at the necklet that had been grasped in her palm.

"Here, let me put it on you," Rurik suggested.

She stood and allowed him to do so. The ornament looked beautiful on her, even in the dowdy undergarment. The jewel itself hung low, just above the swell of her breasts.

Turning her head to glance back at him over her shoulder, she said, "Thank you."

"'Twas my pleasure, m'lady." He had just leaned down to press a gentle kiss to her lips when they heard a commotion out in the hall.

"Lemme go, you cod-suckin' Viking bastard!"

"Ouch! Kick me again, you smelly whelp, and your backside's gonna wear a blister the size of my hand."

"Jamie," Maire said.

"Toste," Rurik said.

They both rushed to the door, and, to their amazement, they found the little boy lying flat on his back on the corridor floor, practically spitting fire. Sitting on the boy's stomach, panting heavily, was Toste, who had a bruise above his right eye, scratch marks on his face, and a rip in his tunic.

Off to the side was the scraggly pet cat, Rose, whose back was arched, its teeth bared as it hissed its displeasure. The animal's fur was caked with mud and bits of grass and twigs. In some places, there were bald or thinning spots on its pelt.

"Go back to whate'er you were doing," Toste suggested with a grin. "I have the situation under control."

The "situation" said a word so foul Rurik blanched and Maire gasped.

"Nice amber," Toste commented irrelevantly, his gaze snagged on the gift Rurik had just given Maire.

Maire squealed with embarrassment and placed crossed palms over the exposed skin above her chemise bodice.

"I thought it was supposed to be a bride gift," Toste added with a grin at Rurik.

Rurik felt his face heat up at Toste's carelessly tossed remark. It had been a gift he'd planned to give to his betrothed on the morning after their wedding, to show his pleasure in her, but a man could change his mind. Couldn't he?

Quickly, he glanced at Maire to see if she'd heard Toste's words. Her face was bright red, but that might still be the result of Toste ogling her breasts. He hoped so.

"What are you doing up and about so early?" Rurik inquired of Toste and Jamie, wanting—nay, needing—to change the subject.

Toste sliced him a disbelieving scowl. "Are you daft,

man? Everyone from here to Northumbria is awake from all that caterwauling Bolthor is producing."

Rurik had to grin at that.

But Maire was not grinning. Forgetting momentarily that she wore only her chemise, she placed a hand on each hip and demanded, "What are you doing in the keep, Jamie? And don't think you are going to escape punishment for that word I just heard come from your mouth."

"He made me come here," Jamie spat out. The boy, still flat on his back, imprisoned by Toste's greater weight, looked directly at Rurik as he spoke.

"You?" Maire inquired of him, incredulously.

"Aye, the bloody damn Viking what's been swivin' me own mother, that's who," Jamie answered for him.

"Jamie, stop it! Halt that midden talk right now!" Maire told her son. Then she directed her attention back to Rurik. "How could you, Rurik? I told you how important it was to keep Jamie hidden away, protected from the MacNabs."

"Yea, you did, but some things happened yesterday, whilst we were otherwise occupied. I made a decision, as chieftains are often called upon to do, that will better protect the boy." His chin rose in defiance, daring her to disagree with his expertise.

"What things? What have the MacNabs done now? And why was I not told afore this?" Her green eyes grew cloudy with anger, and her cheeks flushed with the strong emotion roiling through her. Despite all that, the only thing Rurik could focus on was her heaving chest, highlighted by the amber pendant.

"See, mother, he's just a bloody Viking. See how he gawks at your tits like a lackwit calf."

"That's it," Rurik declared with an exclamation of disgust. Shoving Toste aside, he picked up the now squirming and squealing Jamie and tossed him over his shoulder.

"This boy has been begging for a battle with me since first we met. So be it."

"Nay!" Maire shrieked with alarm. "Jamie is my son, and mine to correct when he has done wrong."

"You're wrong, Maire. This is between me and the boy. I think the first thing we will start with is a bath. You stink to high Asgard, boy."

"Doona be callin' me 'boy.' I am James, High Laird of the Campbell Clan." The boy sounded pathetic, his head bobbing against Rurik's back as he spoke upside down.

"Hah! Right now you are more like the High Laird of Stench. Methinks Bolthor should create a saga about you."

As if on cue, Bolthor, somewhere in the distance, let loose with another, "Ahoooommm! Ahoooommm! Waaaraaaa!"

Still addressing the boy, Rurik sniffed in an exaggerated fashion and asked, "Have you been rolling in a sheep pen?" When Jamie merely gurgled in response, he added, "Yea, first a bath, then we will have a man-to-man talk and set some terms."

"Rurik . . . please . . . ," Maire begged, genuine alarm ringing in her voice. Really, she protected the child overmuch if she thought contact with a Norseman would contaminate him in any way, but that was precisely how she acted. "We need to talk." This last was said in a weaker voice of surrender.

"Yea, we do, when I get back." Rurik was already stomping off toward the stairs, intending to dump the flailing child into the nearest loch. "Send Toste after me with clean garments for the whelp, along with soap, drying cloths, a comb, and scissors. And tell Toste to bring that damn cat with him, too. Rose is not smelling much like a rose these days and needs a good dunking, too, I be thinking."

"Me? Touch that bloody cat? Have you seen the size of the monster's claws?" Toste retorted. Rurik had forgotten he was still there.

But Maire homed in on something else. "Scissors?" she asked in puzzlement.

"Scissors?" The boy paled with dismay. "You dare cut me up, and me clansmen will cut you to pieces."

Rurik laughed. "You misread me, boy. I intend to trim your grimy hair. A man who neglects his hair is a poor man, indeed."

Rurik would bet that Maire and Toste were both gaping at his bit of absurd wisdom. Well, 'twas true. If a man did not care for his hair and his teeth, he might as well be a barbarian, in Rurik's opinion.

"You're a toad," Jamie spat out with childish venom.

Rurik grinned. "It takes a frog to know a toad, little one."

"I am *not* little," Jamie proclaimed.

"Have some food prepared for our return, Maire," Rurik requested over his shoulder, ignoring Jamie's ludicrous statement. "I daresay that by the time this wee *giant* and I get back to the castle, Jamie and I will be famished."

"I should take a bite outta yer arse," Jamie snarled.

"Try it and we'll have 'Campbell Laird Haggis' for dinner tonight. Or 'Wee-Laird Stew.' "

"You don' even know me; so, doona be sayin' laird this or laird that," Jamie huffed.

"Oh, I daresay we will get to know each other very well by the time I'm finished." There was a deliberate, ominous ring to his words. "You might get to know me better than your own father."

Even from the great hall, Rurik could hear Maire in the upper corridor moaning over and over, "Oh, my God! Oh, my God! Oh, my God!"

It was only a question of when *the ax would fall . . .*

"Oh, my God!" Maire said as Rurik and Jamie returned to the great hall a full two hours later.

"Oh, my God!" Old John said, as well, gawking with amazement. "I shoulda known. I shoulda known."

"Oh, my God!" Young John said, squinting through his one good eye as he spoke. Bolthor had fashioned an eye patch for him over his wounded one.

Murdoc lowered his bagpipes, Callum muttered, Rob twitched, Nessa set down a trencher of bannocks on the head table, but they all concurred with an, "Oh, my God!"

Even Stigand, Bolthor, Toste, and Vagn were incredulous. They exclaimed as one, "Bloody hell!"

Rurik had just walked into the hall from the courtyard door and was heading toward Maire and the high dais, where everyone was about to break fast with the morning meal. He was holding the hand of the surprisingly docile child next to him . . . a child whose hair had not been cut after all, but instead had two narrow braids on either side of his face intertwined with colored beads. Jamie's face and body had been scrubbed clean and he glowed, both from the scrubbing and good health and from the sudden adulation he seemed to have developed for the huge Viking at his side, whom he kept gazing up at for approval. Above a pair of trews, her son wore a miniature *pladd,* fastened at one shoulder with a brass brooch in the form of intertwining wolves, which Rurik must have given or loaned to him.

Rurik looked as if he must have bathed again, too . . . if his wet hair was any indication. Or more likely he had fallen in the loch during the initial bathing confrontation with Jamie.

And—*Blessed Saints!*—was that Rose trailing behind them, almost presentable with her newly washed and brushed fur. Had Rurik really bathed a cat? Did he not know that felines did not favor dunking in a loch? They much preferred tongue lavings.

Tongue lavings? Now, those words brought to mind one of Rurik's tantalizing areas of expertise. *How can I think about such inconsequential exercises in the midst of this latest disaster?*

Maire heard Bolthor mutter in a low voice, as if preparing the words to a saga he would develop later. "This is the saga of Rurik the Greater," he began.

Onct was a Viking warrior,
Blind as a bat was he.
Not in the eye,
But in his mind,
For the one thing he could not see—

Maire interrupted the skald's verse-making with a sharp jab of her elbow into his ribs. "Don't . . . you . . . dare!" she warned.

Bolthor ducked his head and rubbed his side . . . not that she'd done the giant block of flesh any real damage.

The closer Rurik and Jamie got to the high table, the more apparent it became to everyone that they were father and son, so remarkable was the resemblance. Everyone, that is, except Rurik, who was beginning to notice the gaping stares of astonishment.

"What? Has no one e'er seen a clean boy afore? Or is it just Wee-Jamie that has ne'er been viewed in all his glory?" Rurik turned his attention to the child at his side, who was gritting his teeth at what he perceived to be an insult. Maire noticed that his grip on Jamie's hand tightened to make sure he did not bolt and do something foolish, like go roll in a puddle of mud to be contrary. "Jamie and I *both* decided that a young laird must take better care of his personal appearance if he is to set an example in all ways for his clan. Is that not so, Jamie?"

Rurik and Jamie exchanged a long, meaningful look in which Rurik silently conveyed the message, "You promised, boy. Now, do your duty," and Jamie silently conveyed, "Don't push me too far, Viking."

Finally, Jamie nodded, and everyone breathed a sigh of relief.

Meanwhile, Maire's heart had practically stopped beating. This was it . . . the crucial moment. Who would be the person to tell Rurik he had a son? As the minutes ticked by and no one spoke up . . . not her people, nor Rurik's retainers . . . she realized that they were leaving it up to her. It was her responsibility and no one else's to inform the father of his paternity.

She let loose a sigh of relief, but her heart was still heavy. She knew it was a temporary reprieve.

It was only then that Maire felt free to examine Rurik in detail. After all that had passed between them the day and night before, this was the first time they'd come together outside the bedchamber. It was still hard to believe that this beautiful man had done so many wicked things to her, and that she'd done such wicked things to him in return. She was the one who allegedly practiced witchly arts, but truly Rurik must have put a spell on her. How else could she explain her behavior?

Was Rurik affected at all? Or was what she perceived as extraordinary lovemaking just routine to him?

His eyes connected with hers then, and instantly

turned smoldering. He was remembering, too. And, aye, he was equally affected, Maire exulted to herself.

And had Toste really mentioned something about the amber pendant being a bride gift? Maire was shocked and thrilled at the same time, to think Rurik might be contemplating marriage . . . if, in fact, that was what Toste had meant. With deep emotion, she touched the spot on her chest where the special necklet rested under her *arisaid*. No one else could see it, but she knew it was there. For some reason, she wanted to hear from Rurik's lips the significance of the gift. Mayhap she'd misheard or misunderstood. Until she knew for certain, the gift would be for her eyes only.

Maire looked at the Viking knight who approached and he looked back at her, causing a thrill of excitement to ripple over her body. All he had to do was look at her now, and she melted. Rurik gave her a wink to show he understood that sizzling magical thing that ricocheted between them. Maire felt her lower stomach lurch and her breasts tighten at that mere movement of his eyelid. Such a simple gesture, and yet, everything Rurik did now would have erotic undertones to her. The sight of his slender fingers touching the hilt of a sword would remind her of *other* things those fingers had done. The sight of his lips breaking into a lazy grin would remind her of the kisses he'd laid on her with such expertise. The shift of his hips as he walked would remind her of—

"We're starved," Rurik said, jarring her from her wanton reverie. "Aren't we, boy?"

"Aye," Jamie agreed. "Can I sit with me friends?" He pointed toward a group of boys of a similar age at one of the lower tables.

Rurik looked to Maire for her opinion. She nodded, but not before adding, "As long as you stay inside the keep, or within eyesight. I mean this, Jamie. It's important that you do not stray."

"I ken what ye say, mother," Jamie said in an uncharacteristically meek voice. "Rurik 'splained it to me. The bloody MacNabs, and all."

Maire was about to correct him for his foul language, but decided to wait till later. "Come here first and give your mother a hug," she encouraged. "I have missed your hugs these many days we have been separated."

"Mo-ther!" Jamie protested, glancing toward his friends to see if they were watching. Still, when Rurik released his hand, he jumped forward and gave Maire a sloppy kiss on her cheek and an exuberant child hug with his arms wrapped tightly around her shoulders.

Into his neck, Maire whispered, "Are you all right, sweetling?"

"Aye," Jamie whispered in an overloud voice directly into her ear. "But I still think Rurik is a bloody hell Viking."

"That he is," Maire found herself concurring in an undertone.

As her son rushed off to be with his friends, Maire smiled and wiped away a tear.

Rurik was watching her closely. "You coddle the boy overmuch," he said, but Maire could also see something else in his blue eyes . . . eyes that marked the only difference between him and his son. Jamie's were green, like hers. Well, that, and the blue mark. Rurik must have yearned at one time for the kind of maternal affection he'd just witnessed between her and her son.

So, instead of reacting adversely to his "coddling" remark, she said, "You and I have much to talk about."

To her surprise, he conceded, "Yea, after we eat, we will sit down and discuss all that must be done about the MacNabs."

Rurik had misunderstood. She had meant to tell him, at long last, about his son . . . before someone else did. But now she realized there were issues that had greater priority.

At first, the meal passed in silence. An awkward silence, to her, because people's heads kept pivoting from her to Rurik to Jamie, as if expecting some explosion. But Rurik seemed unaware of the looks. He was wolfing down his food to assuage the great hunger he'd alluded to earlier. He paused at one point and commented, "Kenneth must have been a handsome man."

Maire choked on her ale.

He clapped her heartily on the back.

"Why do you say that?" She tried to make her voice as casual as possible as she picked at an oat cake.

"Well, Jamie shows promise of great size and uncommonly good looks. Since the boy does not resemble you, except for the eyes, I assume he got these traits from his father."

The others at the table began to make strangled sounds and kept their eyes averted, just waiting to see what Maire would do next.

What she did was nothing, coward that she was. "Kenneth was passable in appearance," Maire replied. *Talk about evasion and half-truths!*

Rurik seemed satisfied with that explanation and resumed eating.

If a Viking's you-know-what falls off, eventually, for telling a lie, I wonder what happens to a Scotswoman who fails to tell the truth for five long years. Maire knew—she just knew—she was going to pay someday for her lack of honesty, and perchance this was her punishment . . . never knowing precisely when the ax was going to fall.

Even more alarming, there was absolutely no doubt

in Maire's mind that the "ax" would be in Rurik's hands.

Men and their plans! . . .

Rurik found it difficult to justify his actions to a woman, but Maire deserved to be kept abreast of the happenings on her clanstead . . . especially since she was, for all purposes, the clan chieftain, till her son reached his majority. He'd already outlined the essentials for her, involving Toste and Vagn slipping inside the MacNab ranks, but he could tell by the bullish expression on her fair face that she remained unconvinced.

"But it's a dangerous plan," Maire said, wringing her hands with dismay as they walked along the parapet of her keep.

Yea, she was unconvinced . . . even though Rurik had just explained to her the new dangers posed by the MacNabs, why he'd needed to bring her son into the safety of her keep, and the bare bones of the scheme they'd concocted.

What he didn't explain to her was this new feeling of protectiveness he felt toward her. Originally, he'd agreed to provide his shield and manpower, limited as it was, in return for her removing the blue mark, but now he could not hide the fact that he would stay till she was safe, blue mark or not. And it was not just honor that bound him, either. What it was, exactly, he suspected, but would not name aloud for fear of the power it would wield over him.

"Yea, 'tis dangerous," he agreed, pausing and reaching out to brush his knuckles across her cheek. "But, really, any plan would be at this point."

To his amazement, instead of slapping his hand away as would have been her wont just days ago, she leaned into his caress, much like a cat purring out its pleasure at a petting. Of course that prompted him to recall how she had purred for him the night before . . . on more than one occasion. It would be an understatement to say that he and Maire suited well . . . in the bed furs, leastways . . . and in the petting.

Too bad he was otherwise betrothed.

Too bad Maire was a witch and lived in god-awful Scotland.

Too bad he had not recognized her worth five years ago and taken her with him, as she'd requested.

Too bad he still carried the ignominious blue mark.

Too bad he had become such a maudlin Viking, weeping in his mead, so to speak. One should not argue with fate, whether it be dealt by the Christian One-God, or the Norns, the wise old women whom the Norse fables held responsible for the destinies of all men.

Clearing his suddenly tight throat, he persevered in his attempt to convince her to accept his plan. "We are seriously outmanned. Even if all the males here were of prime age and whole of body, we would still be outmanned. We need to outmaneuver them. Many a time a war is won with wit, rather than weaponry."

"But sending Toste and Vagn inside the MacNab stronghold! Dost really think that is the best course of action?"

He shrugged. "'Tis worth a try. It's only been three days since Jostein left for Northumbria, and we cannot be sure that he will even reach his destination, let alone bring help in time. I sense the MacNabs feel some need to gain a resolution, or an advantage, in your dispute."

"Hmmm. You may be correct in your thinking," Maire said. "I wonder if it might be related to King Indulf's scheduled trip to the Highlands this autumn. Long have I suspected that Duncan has fed Indulf and his advisors a false tale of the situation here. Mayhap he wants the entire business resolved afore then."

Rurik nodded solemnly. "And that resolution would involve his marriage to you and taking over the Campbell lands in guardianship till Jamie is of age."

"Aye, it makes sense now that I think on it. I had predicted to Nessa just days ago that Duncan would have me killed within days of the wedding, if I should be so faint-minded as to agree . . . and Jamie would be killed, as well . . . eventually. But now I am leaning toward another idea . . . that he would wait till after the royal entourage has left the area. What he wants is a united front, giving the appearance of peace betwixt our clans. After they leave, however, 'twould be a different story altogether." She made a slicing motion with a forefinger across her throat.

The fine hairs stood out on Rurik's nape at her calmly pronounced death sentence. "It will not happen," Rurik declared.

Maire's chin shot up with surprise at the forcefulness of his pledge. "You may not be able to prevent it."

"It will not happen," he repeated with deadly calm. "Even if I die in the effort, there will be others after me to fulfill my promise of protection."

She tilted her head in question.

"The brothers, Eirik and Tykir, would come forthwith if they heard of my passage to Valhalla. Or their father's old friend and mine, Selik, who resides in Jorvik. Or my good friend, Adam, who is in the Arab lands just now, studying medicine."

She raised her eyebrows. "You would save me with a healer?" she teased, no doubt trying to lighten their mood. "Is he a monk? Would your monk-healer pray over our situation as he prepares his medicinal cures? Oh, that would be such a picture! A witch and a doctor trying to save a clan with spells and herbs!"

"Adam is as strong a soldier as he is a healer," he declared defensively, chucking her under the chin. "And, nay, Adam is hardly a religious sort." He grinned at that last thought. *"Hardly."*

"So," Maire said, whisking her hands together resolutely, "your plan involves Toste and Vagn infiltrating the MacNab keep. To what purpose? And what makes you think they would be able to do so?"

"Maire, Maire, Maire. Have you learned naught of those twins in the time they've been here? Those two rogues have been slipping in and out of the beds and keeps of women of many lands since they were mere youthlings. Believe me, they can scale a wall, tread soft as a kitten, and make themselves nigh invisible when it is warranted."

She let out a breathy exhale, but did not contradict his assertions. "Once there, presuming they are successful, what in the name of Mary could they do that would save my clan? The two of them could not fight the entire MacNab clan, could they? Would they be opening the gates for us Campbells to enter? Explain to me how that could occur, undetected. Besides, the MacNabs would have an advantage, fighting inside their own grounds, wouldn't they?"

Rurik smiled at Maire's brisk interrogation. She had become accustomed to taking charge and apparently did not know when to relinquish some of that leadership. Taking her hands in both of his, he kissed the fingertips . . . and her pouting lips . . . ignoring her tsk-ing reprimand. Before he continued in that enticing vein, he laced the fingers of one hand with one of hers and drew her forward to continue their walk about the parapet. While they strolled, Rurik explained, "Actually, you will play a part in the plan, indirectly."

"Me?" she squealed, and tried to halt in her tracks.

God, I love how I can make her squeal. "Yea, you, dearling. You and your witchly arts," he replied, forcing her to keep pace with him, despite her digging in her heels. "I will go to the MacNab stronghold this evening, unarmed, under a truce flag. Whilst there, I will outline your grievances, including the senseless slaughter of sheep and cattle, the placing of a high-ranked lady in a cage—that would be you—and a long list of other complaints that Old John gave to me, going back to the time of Kenneth's death. As recompense, I will demand that they immediately desist in their harassment of the Campbells, pay a *danegeld* of gold coins, and sign a peace pact with your clan."

When Maire dug in her heels this time, he was unable to make her budge; so, he stopped with her. He still held her fingers laced with his, though, and he could feel her rapid pulse.

"Have you gone daft, Rurik?"

Perchance. Daft over you. "Trust me, Maire. I know what I am doing." *Leastways, I think I do.*

"What makes you think Duncan would agree to any such thing? He will laugh in your face."

"Yea, he will," Rurik replied with calm indifference. He let his words hang in the air for several long moments, while she tapped one foot impatiently. He wasn't sure why he tormented her so, except that she looked so tempting with her flushed cheeks and jutting chin and heaving breasts . . . especially her heaving breasts.

"Stop leering at my breasts, you . . . you libertine."

Caught in the act . . . of being a libertine. "I was not," he lied. "I was just thinking and my eyes may have drifted."

She made a harrumphing sound of disgust. "Get to

the point, Viking. What threat can you levy that would force compliance?"

"A spell," he announced brightly. "A magic spell."

"Witchcraft," she said in a dull, disappointed voice. "You would use me thus, even knowing that sometimes I fail?"

Sometimes? The way I hear it told, most times you are less than successful. But he rolled his shoulders as if her complaint were of little consequence.

"Word of my ineptness has spread as far as the MacNab lands, I am sure. Threats of my inflicting a spell on them will have no effect at all, unless they laugh themselves to death."

"Sad, but true."

"Not that I am in accord with your plans . . . but I should go with you."

"Nay!"

"Why?"

"Too dangerous. Duncan might take you captive. Then he'd have you exactly where he wanted from the start."

"How about you? Is it not dangerous for you, too? Could he not take you captive?"

"He could, but he would not enjoy wedding and bedding me nearly as much . . . nor gain the same land wealth."

"Notice that I am not amused by your poor attempt at mirth."

He shrugged.

"Rurik, this is my battle. I should be involved. This is a Campbell feud."

"Uh-uh-uh, Maire, do you misremember already? I was voted a Campbell by your very clan. Rurik Campbell, that's what Old John called me." *God, did I really give credit to that ridiculous notion?*

Her small groan indicated that she had, indeed, forgotten. "You are no more Rurik Campbell than I am Maire . . ." She paused and examined his face closely, as if searching for answers. "What is your other name?"

"I have none."

"You must. Do you Vikings not take on the name of your father . . . as in Thork Ericsson, which would be Thork, son of Eric?"

He pressed his lips together tightly and refused to answer.

"You do know your father's name?" she asked tentatively, sensing that she opened the gate to a path he would not walk.

"Yea, I know my father's name," he snarled. "But he denied me at birth, and I would not give him the respect of using his name now."

She gasped and reached out a hand, as if to comfort him.

He stepped back, being long past the stage of wanting or needing pity for his family's ill treatment. "Back to our plan," he said. "In my travel bags, I have ten ells of sheer fabric that I obtained in the Eastern lands, where the *houri* wear them whilst dancing for their sultan masters." He waited for that information to sink in, as indicated by the blooming blush on Maire's cheeks. "Eirik's wife, Eadyth, is a beekeeper, and she commissioned me to purchase the cloth, which she uses to make head-to-toe garments to avoid being stung by her bees. I figure that Toste and Vagn can drape themselves with lengths of this ethereal fabric and thus, in a dim light, resemble—"

"—ghosts," Maire finished for him.

He smiled. "Yea. The most lustful ghosts this side of the Skelljefjord. But let me explain further. At first, I will warn Duncan and his chiefs that, unless they comply with my demands, you will inflict a grievous spell on their land that involves the ghosts of their misdeeds . . . which they will of course scoff at . . . till they see Toste and Vagn in all their spiritual glory. Because they are twins, they will be able to confuse their victims into believing they can float about from one place to another. They will be seen in multiple places at the same time. The next part of the plan will be ingenious, really, stemming from something you started."

"Me?"

He nodded. "Yea, I will tell them that not only will their keep be infested with ghosts, but a curse will be placed on them whereby . . ." He waggled his eyebrows at her.

"Go on," she prodded, already suspicious.

". . . whereby their man parts will shrink, and they will be unable to perform in the bed furs."

She laughed then, despite her obvious inclination to frown at him. "Hit them where it hurts the most, you mean."

"Precisely. But the whole point is that eventually we want to lead them to *Ailt Olc.*"

"*Ailt Olc?* Devil's Gorge?"

He nodded. "That narrow valley that separates your land and theirs on the north side. There we will attack them till they are all dead or have surrendered."

"But, Rurik, even if you are able to accomplish all that, you fail to consider two things. One, that is an exposed area, visible from all sides, with few hiding places. Second, we Campbells are still severely outnumbered by the enemy."

He smiled widely. "That is the best part of our plan. Look below and see our plan in operation." Maire directed her gaze to where he pointed off in the distance to the military exercise fields beyond the castle walls.

There, she noticed something she hadn't seen before. All the young boys, even Jamie under the watchful eye of Stigand, were target practicing with slingshots, of all things, and some of them were very, very good. It took only a moment for understanding to dawn. "Like David and Goliath, from the Bible."

"Yea. Am I not brilliant?"

The wench did not respond to his self-compliment. Instead, she glared at him. "You would use children to fight? You would place children in that kind of danger?"

"Nay, you misunderstand. The young ones would only be used in the background where it is safe."

She seemed to accept his explanation without argument . . . for now. "And those sheep moving along the periphery of the field . . . what are they doing there?"

Rurik chuckled. "Look closer, m'lady. I got the idea from your tapestry. Remember how you said that things are not always what they appear from a distance."

"Rurik!" she exclaimed as she narrowed her eyes and peered more closely. "Those are not sheep. Those are men hiding under those sheepskins."

He couldn't resist then. It had been much too long since he'd held her in his arms . . . at least two hours. So, Rurik picked her up by the waist and swung her into a hearty embrace. Breathing deeply of her scent, he placed a kiss at the curve of neck where it met her shoulder and whispered, "The plan could work. Dost agree?"

When she gave a tentative nod, he announced in a husky voice, "I have another plan, as well."

Maire moaned . . . especially since he'd already turned around and walked her, with her legs dangling off the ground, to the back wall of the parapet, beyond view of those below. Her garment was already halfway up her thighs, and his erection was already pressed against her woman place, and his lips were already nibbling at her parted mouth, when Maire registered his words.

"Aaah, Rurik, I must tell you, some of your plans are questionable. Some are bad, regardless of what you may think. Some are good." Then she did the unthinkable. The saucy wench placed a palm on each of his buttocks and squeezed, adding in a seductive purr, "And some are spectacular."

Rurik would have smiled, but he'd forgotten how.

CHAPTER THIRTEEN

The highs and lows of love . . .

For the rest of that day, Maire's great hall was so a-bustle with activity, she scarce recognized it or her people. Whatever else Rurik might, or might not, accomplish that day, he'd already succeeded in renewing the self-confidence and hopes of her battered clan. For that, she would be forever thankful to him.

All of the women were working industriously on disguising garments for the children to wear while they plied their slingshots from the trees. Little more than hooded robes, the costumes were made of quickly basted woolen scraps of brown, black, green, and beige that should blend in with the foliage. The more mature boys who would be positioned closer, behind boulders, would wear cloaks of iron gray or sheep pelts, complete with heads.

Rurik, Stigand, and Bolthor were out in the exercise yard training, as much as possible in this short time, the men and older boys who were capable of wielding weapons. To Maire's delight, he'd reported during the noon meal that some of them were extremely proficient with sword and lance and bow and arrow, despite their physical impairments or age. These skills, combined with the advantage of surprise and location, might just be enough to triumph over the MacNabs.

Just to be sure, Maire was praying . . . a lot. Too bad

the monk, Father Baldwin, had gone off to a neighboring district to perform a funeral. She could use a few priestly prayers at this point.

She had asked Rurik earlier if he wanted her to attempt a good luck spell, but he'd declined with touching gentleness, fearing her charm might backfire. Under other circumstances, she might have been offended, but the fate of her clan was at stake now. She could not let her ego stand in the way. Truth to tell, she was not a very good witch.

Whatever the outcome of this fight, which should take place the following morning if tonight's ghostly scheme worked, Maire had to be thankful for the pride Rurik was giving back to her people. She had forgotten how much a man's dignity was influenced by his feeling that he could protect his family or his clan.

"Whoo-whoo!" Toste and Vagn said as one, coming up to the table where the sewing was taking place. Waving their hands in the air eerily, they were modeling the gossamer-thin fabric made into shroudlike garments, which would help them pass for spirits.

" 'Tis not bad," Maire said, pressing a forefinger to her lips as she studied them pensively. "Tell me true, Nessa. What think you?"

"I think they are enjoying this game overmuch," Nessa concluded while the women watched the twins prance about in front of them, swirling the voluminous folds of their garments, the whole time making what were supposed to be ghostly sounds. "Their foolery will be the death of them if they are not careful."

"Oh, we will be very careful, Nessa. Fear not," Toste said, coming up behind Maire's maid in a whirlwind of transparent cloth to press a quick kiss to the exposed nape of her neck. Then he pinched one of her buttocks.

"Oooh, you go too far," Nessa squealed, rubbing her

backside as though he had hurt her, which he obviously had not.

"Best ye exercise caution, Toste," warned Fenella, a young farm girl from the village, "lest Stigand see you fondling his lady love. He is said to have a tendency to lop off heads first and ask questions later."

"That was not a fondle," Toste contended. "Believe me, I am noted for my fondles, and that was not a fondle."

" 'Twould seem you are noted for many things," Maire commented dryly.

"I am not Stigand's lady love," Nessa protested, but it was clear from the roses blooming on her fair skin that something was going on between her and the berserker. Maire could not recall a time when she'd seen Nessa blush . . . not even when her husband, Neils, was still alive, and Neils had been an outrageous teaser. "Furthermore, Stigand has not lopped off any heads in a long while."

Everyone just gaped at Nessa's defense of the burly Viking, who surely did not need to hide behind the skirts of a wench.

"Back to me," Vagn interjected with a saucy grin. "Well, back to the subject of me and my brother," he amended. "Our disguise will be perfect this evening when it is dark—no moon is expected, thank the gods!—and when our apparel is donned *properly.*" He and Toste exchanged meaningful smirks on that last word.

"Am I supposed to rise to that bait?" Maire tried to keep her expression stern, but it was difficult when these two rogues were around.

"What bait?" they both asked with mock innocence, batting incredibly long eyelashes, and putting hands on hips that were enticingly narrow. By the rood, Maire could see why maids swooned in their paths. These two braw laddies were nigh irresistible when they employed their abundant charms.

"Tsk-tsk-tsk-tsk-tsk," was all that Maire could come up with. Nessa was shaking her head at their antics. And some of the younger women giggled.

"Well, if you insist, we will tell you about the *proper* attire for a ghost," Toste said with a long sigh, as if the women had been pestering him for an answer. "When we dress this evening before we enter the MacNab castle, we will be"—he paused dramatically—"*naked.*"

"I don't believe you!" Maire exclaimed. She looked to all her maids for corroboration, but they were staring at the two men. 'Twas plain as a wart on a witch's nose that they believed . . . and would like to be there for the unveiling.

"Hah! Would we dare lie?" Toste grumbled. Both he and Vagn held up middle fingers, which sported scarlet bows of yarn.

Those stupid measuring yarns . . . nay, my stupid tale of lies and shrinking manparts! Do men really care so much about the size of their appendages? Maire wondered.

Absolutely, she answered herself with a grin.

Women are by far the superior species, she decided. *Do we spend excessive time worrying over the size of our female parts?*

Of course not . . . well, except for our backsides, which sometimes tend to grow overnight, or worse yet, sag.

"Dost care for a demonstration of how these garments would look over the naked form?" Vagn asked and lifted the hem of his scandalous robe, reaching for his belt.

"*No!*" Maire practically shouted, even though she

could see that some of the women wouldn't have minded such a display.

Vagn dropped the robe with an exhale of disappointment.

"Nude ghosts!" Nessa whooped. She was still gape-mouthed at the astounding mind-picture. "Where will you keep your sword?"

Almost immediately, Nessa realized her mistake. Her blush deepened even before Toste and Vagn glanced downward and answered as one, "Which sword?"

"Are you jesting? I cannot imagine Rurik approving of such a plan," Maire said.

" 'Twas *his* idea," Toste informed her with a rascally wink. "Now that Rurik has got his knack back, he no doubt likes the idea of naked flesh. He *has* got his knack back, hasn't he?"

"Tell the truth now, m'lady, did he or did he not orgaz you?" Vagn added.

Maire just groaned. At the same time, all her ladies were asking, "Or-gaz? Or-gaz?"

"What idea?" Rurik inquired behind her. "What idea came from me?"

Maire pivoted on her bench and saw him and all the other men and boys coming into the great hall. Not only had they finished their exercises, but apparently they had visited the loch for a quick bath, or swim, if their wet hair was any indication.

As Rurik swaggered toward her, she noticed the most heart-wrenching thing. Jamie was following in his wake like a faithful puppy, and his youthful swagger mimicked Rurik's. Her son had long demonstrated a talent for aping the characteristics of others, and apparently Rurik had become his idol of the moment. She also noticed that Jamie carried a crudely made, miniature wooden sword in his belt, just like Rurik. Stigand, who had a talent for whittling, must have made it for him, but the way Jamie wore it, low on his left hip, was identical to Rurik's practice. If all that wasn't bad enough, Jamie still wore the thin braids on either side of his face.

An odd silence followed as others noticed the same things she did. They waited for her to say something, or for Rurik to finally understand what they all saw so clearly.

"What idea?" Rurik repeated, calling Maire's thoughts back to the present. He slid onto the bench next to her, way too close, and grinned at her apparent discomfort at his intimacy in front of so many people.

"That Toste and Vagn would dress as naked ghosts," she answered and slid away slightly from the heated pressure of Rurik's hip against hers.

He just sidled his buttocks along the seat so that now he was even closer. Then he waggled his eyebrows at her, daring her to proceed in this game of evasion. When she remained in place, he told her, "How else would ghosts be, but naked? Besides, Toste and Vagn work best in that state of nonattire, or so I have been told. And they may very well have to enter the castle via a wench's pallet."

Maire laughed softly at the prospect. "A wench inviting a naked ghost into her bed? Dost really think any female in her right mind would be so foolhardy?"

Silence prevailed while a kitchen maid set pitchers of cool ale and wooden goblets in front of them.

"Anything is possible with these two," Rurik declared after taking a long draught of the beverage. "Believe you me, nothing that happens to them comes as a surprise to me anymore. I recall a time in Cordoba when the two of them had to be rescued from a brothel where they were being held captive by the smitten harlots." In the meantime, while he had been talking, he had somehow turned slightly so that a part of his body she'd become particularly familiar with . . . and, aye, fond of, too . . . began to prod her hip.

Shocked, Maire scolded Rurik, "You lecherous lout, you! Best you keep Lance under control in public places lest some bird fly by and mistake it for a perch."

"Maaaiirre!" Rurik responded with equal shock, though a smile twitched at the edges of his lips. "Shhhh," he quickly added, not wanting others to overhear.

But it was too late.

"Lance? What lance?" Toste wanted to know.

"That is Rurik's name for his manpart," Maire blurted out before she had a chance to curb her tongue.

Toste and Vagn burst out laughing, and all the women perked up with interest at this new, beguiling subject.

"Lots of men name their manparts," Maire said defensively, repeating Rurik's lackwit words to her. She could feel her cheeks flame with embarrassment at her runaway blathering.

Rurik groaned and rolled his eyes with disgust, apparently knowing what was to come.

" 'Tis true. 'Tis true," Toste agreed. "I call mine Bliss . . . as in 'Here comes Bliss.' "

Several of the younger maids puts palms to their lips to stifle giggles. Several of the men who'd just come up, including Bolthor and Stigand, snorted with disbelief.

"I favor simplicity," Vagn stated with a wide grin. "I just call mine Big."

"You are such a liar," Rurik declared.

"I call mine Big, too," Stigand declared.

No one snorted at him . . . or called him a liar. And Nessa, bless her heart, was nodding her concurrence.

For the love of Mary! These Vikings certainly are earthy people . . . to speak of such matters so openly.

"*Mjollnir,*" Bolthor announced of a sudden. Everyone turned to him. He raised his chin and explained, as if daring anyone to laugh, "I named mine after Thor's hammer. Betimes, I refer to it as Hammer."

No one laughed.

"This is the saga of Rurik the Greater," Bolthor began. "And the Great Norse Practice of Cock-Naming."

"Hey," Rurik protested, amidst the barely suppressed snickers around him. "I'm not the one who brought up this subject. So, don't be associating me with *that*."

"What's this about a *Norse* practice?" Old John asked. Maire hadn't even noticed that he'd approached with some of her clansmen. "Scotsmen name their parts, too."

All the women gaped at Old John, then exclaimed as one, "They do?"

Old John nodded vigorously. "In my day, I called mine the Tickler." Every female jaw dropped even lower. "And I knew a man from Glenmoor, Angus the Bull, who named his The One-Eyed Dragon. Well, he did." The last was added on seeing the looks of incredulity around him.

Bolthor launched into his skaldic verse then:

Man is a peculiar lot,
Believe me, like it or not,
When it comes to his manpart,
He cannot be brain-smart,
Instead he gains fame
By giving it a name,
Be it Sword or Lance,
Even Last-Chance,
Or Pleasure-giver,
Not to mention Sex-Burr.
How about Log-of-Life,
or Gift-to-Wife,
Dancing Hog, Prancing Dog,
Third Leg, Make-Her-Beg,

Big John, Small Tom,
Bad Bart, Good George,
Pleasure Flute, Manroot,
Woman-Luck, Son-of-a-Duck,
Fancy Swiver, Nest Diver?
Ah, yes, man is a peculiar lot.

There was a stunned silence in their section of the hall before Maire regained the use of her tongue. "For shame, you men!" she choked out, mustering as much consternation as she could. "Not just you, Bolthor, but all you men. Speaking of such crude things amidst ladies!"

All the men glanced about self-consciously, as if they'd just noticed they were in mixed company. The groups began to disband and move about the hall to resume their tasks amidst much sniggering and outright laughter.

That was when Maire realized that while all this lewd conversation was going on, Rurik had somehow managed to snake his hand under the table, where his fingers had linked with hers and his thumb was drawing seductive circles on her palm. The message that his clear blue eyes transmitted to her was, "I want you." She would guarantee that her traitorous eyes sent the same message back to him.

She averted her face, not wanting him to know how easily stimulated she was by him. She could not believe that she had allowed the man to take her against a wall this morning, in full daylight, on an open parapet. And she could not believe she had enjoyed it so much. Rurik had been forced to muffle her cries with his mouth.

"I know what you're thinking," Rurik whispered against her ear.

How had he gotten so close to her? She swung her face around so quickly that she almost met him, lip to lip. He chuckled and drew away slightly.

"You . . . do . . . not!" she stated firmly. "Know what I am thinking, I mean."

"Yea, I do, Maire." He was back to circling her palm with his thumb, and she felt the caress all the way to the tips of her breasts and in her woman's center.

She groaned softly.

He smiled softly.

"Dost think yourself a mind reader now, as well as a warrior?"

He shook his head, and licked his lips.

Belatedly, she realized that he was copying her very own gestures. Instinctively, her mouth had gone dry, just staring at the luscious lout, and she had darted a wet tongue over her lips. She hated that her emotions were so close to the surface and so easily read by him. Therefore, she could not explain why she knowingly stepped into his trap by asking, "What exactly do you think I am thinking?"

He gave her a smoldering look that translated to, *Ah, Maire! I thought you'd never ask*. But what he said was, "Your body carries my 'mark' in all the ways I promised that it would. When your gaze snags on my mouth, you recall the pleasure of my kisses. When I take my cup in hand, you see fingers that have played erotic songs on every part of your body. When I stand and my lower half becomes visible to you, you remember in vivid detail how it feels when I fill you." He took a deep breath, then continued, "That, m'lady, is what you were thinking."

"Your conceit knows no bounds, Viking," she sputtered out. "And as to your 'mark' on me, is that what all of yesterday and last night was about . . . revenge? I know 'twas what you promised, but somehow I thought . . . I thought . . ." Maire couldn't believe how hurt she was that she had been the only one so affected by their lovemaking. She averted her face so he could not witness her humiliation.

Rurik put a forefinger to her chin and turned her back to him. "Nay, that is not the way of it, witch. It may have started out thus, but somewhere betwixt the kissing and the tupping, other forces took over." He put up a halting hand. "Do not think to ask me what those forces are because I truly do not know. Perchance, sorcery?"

Maire wanted to believe him, but . . .

"Sweetling, can you not comprehend that everything I said of you is true of me, as well, in reverse?"

She frowned in confusion.

He leaned forward and brushed his lips against hers . . . a feathery light kiss that felt like heaven.

Her eyes darted right to left to see if anyone had noticed the kiss; she was still uncomfortable allowing her people to observe the Viking's familiarity with her. But those few people who had noticed apparently approved, for they were grinning.

"Do you want me to explain?" he asked in a low, masculine voice that was as potent as a long swig of *uisge-beatha*.

Oh, God, yes! "Nay!" she said quickly.

But not quickly enough. He was already revealing his very own secrets. "When you lick your lips, as you are right now, I remember the wanton things I taught you to do with your mouth . . . or mayhap you are Eve to my Adam, and that type of sensuality comes instinctively to you."

Maire's lips tingled just hearing Rurik's praise, even though she could hardly credit its truth. She was not a sensual woman . . . leastways, she never had been before.

"And when you twist your body away from me, trying to avoid eye contact, all you do is call attention to the outline of your breasts and your nipples, which I fantasize are turgid with desire for me . . ."

Turgid? Oh, my! If they had not been before, they were now.

". . . and I recall the taste of suckling them. Surely nectar of the gods!"

Maire could swear she actually felt the rhythm of his lips pulling at her.

"And when you walk away from me, buttocks moving ever so slightly, I remember how well they fit into my hands when I lift you for my entry. And then . . . for the love of Freyja . . . how that woman part of you clasps my manpart in joyous welcome."

"God's Teeth!" Maire exclaimed then. "Ne'er have I heard of lovemaking without one speck of bare flesh touching another."

"Word sex. 'Tis one of my many talents." He chuckled, and squeezed her hand.

"I never know when you are teasing me, or telling the truth."

"Do you like word sex, Maire?"

"Are my eyes rolling back in my head?" she said with a snort of disgust at herself.

"You are priceless," he hooted. "Nay, your eyes . . . your beautiful, emerald eyes . . . are straight. But how about mine? Are they staring at the back of my skull yet?"

She had to smile at that, even as she shook her head. There was satisfaction in knowing Rurik shared her bodily distress.

"I do feel a bit of a tremor coming on, though," she told him in a saucy tone, her eyelids half-lowered. Heavenly hosts! Where and when had she developed a talent for flirting?

"Me, too," he said, but his voice and expression were stone-cold serious.

"Oh, Rurik," she breathed, unable to say more.

"Precisely," he breathed back, understanding perfectly . . . so sensitive was this thread that was developing between them, fiber by emotional fiber.

Fortunately, or unfortunately, their attention was diverted then. At the far end of the hall, a group of her clansmen were laughing at the antics of her son and a few of his friends.

Callum had just passed through the hall, ahead of them, his head twitching to the right as was its wont ever since he'd suffered a head blow at the Battle of Dunellen. He was the same age as her brother Donald, who'd been his boon companion, and was once a fine soldier—in fact, an expert archer—but his marksmanship was no longer dependable because of the incessant jerking of his head. Bolthor had been working with him on methods to regain his center of balance and compensate for the twitch; to Maire's amazement, it worked sometimes. Eventually he might regain many of his old abilities.

Now, Jamie was leading his pack of rascals, imitating Callum—strutting and jerking their heads at the same time. Really, she was going to have to sit her son down and have a long talk with him. His wild behavior had grown out of control these past weeks since he'd been living in the forest cave with the men.

But Maire had no more time to dwell on improving her son's manners, for Rurik had dropped her hand and risen in his seat with a loud roar of outrage. His face grew red and his fists were clenched as he stared wide-eyed at something. At first, she couldn't fathom what had evoked such fury in him. Her eyes scanned the hall, but she could see naught but her son and . . .

Oh, my God! It was Jamie that had flamed his anger. And Rurik was already strides ahead of her before she'd risen from the bench and hurried after him. "Rurik, wait . . ."

Rurik had already reached the laughing boys and grabbed Jamie by the scruff of his neck, mid-twitch. His legs dangled far off the rush-covered floor. Before the startled child could blink up at him, Rurik delivered a smart slap to his buttocks and growled, "That will be enough of that, boy."

Now, Maire was outraged. How dare he take a hand to her son! How dare he!

By the time she reached the chaotic scene, clansmen were lined up as spectators, little boys were scrambling to run away before Rurik inflicted a similar punishment on them, and Jamie was rubbing his bottom with one hand and using the other to wipe tear-filled eyes as he howled loud enough to raise the rafters. You'd think he'd had a broadax laid against his backside, instead of a callused hand.

Jamie was standing now and Rurik was hunkered down in front of him, one hand on each shoulder. "I thought we'd come to an understanding, Jamie. You are to be laird here one day. Is this any kind of example for you to set—making mockery of another?"

Jamie shook his head, but said nothing, probably too frightened of another blow to his bottom.

"A real man does not need to make himself bigger by reducing the value of another . . . especially one who is smaller, or suffers some bodily disadvantage."

"But I was only playin'," Jamie blubbered defensively.

" 'Tis no excuse. Know this, a bully as a boy grows up to be a bully as a man, and that is not a noble goal to set for yourself. Do you understand what I'm saying?"

The boy nodded and, seeing an opportunity for escape, ducked under Rurik's arm and bolted for the courtyard door. A small smile curving his lips, Rurik let him go, motioning to Stigand to follow him and keep guard over the wayward child.

Rurik turned then and noticed Maire standing behind him. He smiled, as if expecting her to congratulate him on the way he'd *handled* her son.

Ha! Fuming, Maire tried to speak in an undertone, but her words came out harsh and loud. "You had no right, Viking. Who gave you permission to reprimand my child?"

Rurik's body stiffened, and he inclined his head in surprise. "I thought to do you a favor. You have no husband. The boy needed to be shown now, whilst the misdeed was fresh, that derision is a bad trait for a boy to develop. Dost disagree with that sentiment?"

"You abused my son!"

"I never did!"

"You struck him in anger."

"I gave him a light tap on the arse with the palm of my hand. He barely felt it."

"Well . . . well . . . who gave you permission to lay a hand on him?"

"I need no permission to do what is right."

"Begone, Viking! He's not your son." The minute the words left her mouth Maire knew she'd made a mistake. Rurik's head jerked back as if she'd slapped him, and his nostrils flared with barely controlled anger.

Even worse, her clansmen inhaled in one communal gasp. It was one thing to neglect telling a man he had a son, horrible as that might be. It was quite another to actually lie about the fact. How would she ever be able to backtrack from that blatant misstatement?

"I mean . . . he's my son. You should have let me manage my own son."

Rurik's gaze connected with hers, and she saw both disappointment and fury there. "You're doing a poor job of it, Maire, if his foul tongue, ofttimes filthy appearance, and now meanness are any indication."

Oh, Rurik's words were cruel, cruel daggers to Maire's soul. And unfair . . . well, partially unfair. But she could see by the proud jut of his jaw that he would take them back no more than she would hers.

"And I'll *'begone'* soon enough, m'lady. That, you can be sure of."

Maire put her face in her hands and tried to think how best to retract her harsh words. When she glanced up, though, Rurik was gone. And all of her people were looking at her with disapproval. One by one they turned away. Except for Bolthor.

Chortling at some inner mirth, the skald began, "This is the saga of Maire of the Moors."

Once there was a maiden
Who told a great lie.
Thought she that the truth
No one would e'er buy.
But, alas and alack,
The worst thing about lies,
Is the weaver is oft
Caught in her own alibis.

Then, as an afterthought, Bolthor added some more to his saga:

. . . And good thing she is not
A Viking man caught in a falsehood,

Because then there would be
Even bigger trouble . . .
Well, actually, smaller.

Bolthor's poem was so awful that she should have been laughing out loud. Instead, she was crying inside.

From the mouths of babes . . .

For the rest of the afternoon, Rurik avoided Maire. He was so angry—and, yea, hurt—that he feared what he might do or say in her presence.

Her protectiveness regarding her son was excessive. If Old John had taken the same action as Rurik had done, he doubted Maire would have been so furious. There was a puzzle here . . . why she feared his contact with the boy. . . . that he could not solve. Apparently, she had come to the conclusion that he was a fit bed partner, but unfit company for her son. Why?

"Yer frownin' agin. Am I the winner?" Jamie asked him.

They were playing the Viking board game, *hnefatafl*, which Rurik had just taught the boy. Before that, following a short man-to-man—or rather, man-to-not-quite-man—talk about the spanking incident, Jamie had taught Rurik how to use a slingshot. Rurik, in turn, had agreed to show him the Norse game, at which the youthling was already gaining proficiency. He was a very bright lad, Rurik thought with uncalled-for pride on his part.

"Nay, you are not the winner," he snapped.

"Then ye mus' be frownin' 'cause yer still mad at me mother. Doona be. She likes you."

"And how would you be knowing that?"

"Sheesh! Everyone kens *that*." Jamie gave him an incredulous stare, as if his head must be very thick. "Every time she looks at you, her eyes go all big and cowlike."

He demonstrated in a way Maire would find quite unflattering. "I 'spect any time now she'll start mooin'."

Rurik choked on the cup of *uisge-beatha* he'd just put to his mouth. "I hardly think your mother would like you speaking of her in such a manner."

"Why? Is there aught wrong with being smitten?"

Smitten? She didn't act smitten when she berated me in front of one and all. Rurik shook his head at the child's ridiculous question. He never knew what the rascal was going to say next and tried to remember whether he had been the same at that age. But of course he had not; he'd been too busy trying to find his next meal.

"Can I have a drink of that?" Jamie asked, reaching for the cup of powerful Scottish brew.

"Nay, you cannot!" he exclaimed and pulled his cup out of the way.

"Why?"

"Because I said so."

"That's no answer. It's what me mother allus says."

"It's a good answer," Rurik declared. *Holy Thor! I sound like a bloody damn father.*

"Ha! Will you teach me to use a broadax?"

"You couldn't even lift a broadax."

"Well, a lance then?"

"Nay!"

"Why?"

"You know why."

"'Because I said so,'" he mimicked.

"Precisely."

The whole time they were talking, the game continued, and the boy talked, and talked, and talked . . . when he was not petting his cat.

"I like cats."

"That's obvious." The feline was sitting at Jamie's feet licking its mangy fur . . . well, not quite so mangy now since Rurik had given it a good scrubbing in the loch. And, hell and Valhalla, hadn't that been a sight . . . him with gauntlets on his hands and a frontispieced helmet to protect his face, handling the screeching, scratching, misnamed Rose. "I much prefer dogs," he pronounced, "like my wolfhound, Beast. Now there is an animal! Man's best friend, that's what a dog is."

"Rose is my best friend," Jamie said in a wounded voice.

"Humpfh!" was Rurik's doubtful rejoinder.

"She likes you," Jamie told him accusingly.

Uh-oh! Here comes the guilt maneuver. Women and children . . . that's the route they always follow with men. Try to make a man feel guilty for the least little thing. "I rather doubt that," he answered. Rose, meanwhile, continued to glare at him with her usual attitude of superiority. She kept her distance, though, still not having forgiven him for the bath.

Without a pause for transition, the blathering boy moved on to a new subject. "Betcha I would make a good Viking."

"I doubt that."

"All that rapin' and pillagin' and stuff. Betcha I'd be the best damn raper and pillager in the world."

Rurik had to laugh, not only at the boy's imagination, but his continuing foul tongue, as well. "Do you even know what raping and pillaging are?"

"Well, nay, but they sound fun."

"I hardly think your clan will want you to go off a-Viking. Best you stay here in the Highlands and do your clan things . . . like reaving and feuding."

"I could go a-Viking with you during the seasons when I'm not reavin' and feudin'."

"Do you never stop talking?"

"That's what my mother says all the time."

"Wise woman," Rurik muttered under his breath.

But Jamie heard and yelped with glee. "See? Yer smitten, too."

They continued playing the game for several blessedly silent moments, but Rurik should have known it wouldn't last.

"Tell me 'bout swiving."

"I beg your pardon."

"Swiving . . . what's it feel like?"

Rurik grinned. "Good."

"How good? Do ye mean plum pudding good, or horse racing good, or hard swimming good, or catchin' a big trout good?"

"All of those."

"Does your dinky have to be bigger than your little finger to swive?"

Dinky? Oh, for the love of a Valkyrie! A dinky! Rurik's eyes almost bugged out of his head at the sight of the imp waggling his littlest finger at him. "Yea, it does," he answered with as straight a face as he could manage.

"How much bigger?"

Aaarrgh! Rurik clenched his fists and reminded himself that he probably would have liked some older man to explain these things to him when he'd been a boy. "Much."

"How big is yours?"

Rurik was beginning to pick up the rhythm of the halfling's chatter and found himself chuckling. "Immense," he replied, and hoped no one was eavesdropping on this boy-man talk.

"Can I see?"

"Nay, you cannot see, whelp." Enough was enough. Rurik folded up the board game, declaring himself the winner, and stood.

He stretched his arms out widely and yawned. It was

the time of day between daylight and dusk . . . that odd period that the Scots referred to as the gloaming. Soon Rurik would be off to the MacNabs, and their plan would sink or swim.

Although Rurik was reasonably confidant that they would succeed, one never knew when going into battle. Therefore, his men were completing last-minute personal tasks, in case they did not return on the morrow. For instance, Stigand was off somewhere with Nessa, swiving her silly, he suspected. Bolthor was banished to the outer, outer courtyard for a last—it would be the last—bagpipe lesson from Murdoc. He had been playing the instrument in the great hall till a short time ago, when everyone protested, lest their hearing be impaired forever.

Rurik should talk with Maire one last time. This might be his only opportunity. He did not want to leave this world without telling her . . . he knew not what. On the other hand, mayhap it was best that no words were spoken, after all.

As if reading his mind, Jamie asked him in his small-boy voice, "Are ye gonna die tonight?"

"I hope not, son," Rurik said, starting to walk away. *Son?* He had no idea where that endearment had come from. It had just slipped out.

But the boy surprised him by saying, "I hope you don't die, either . . ."

Rurik's step faltered but he did not stop.

Then Jamie added the clincher, ". . . 'cause I have somethin' important to tell ye."

CHAPTER FOURTEEN

Some good-byes are best said without words . . .

Dusk would be settling soon over the Highlands, and it was time for Rurik and his men, as well as a handful of Campbell clansmen, to make their way to the MacNab lands. They were gathering in the courtyard, preparing to depart . . . everyone except Rurik, that is. He was still inside, making some final preparations.

Maire found him in her bedchamber, where he was tying the laces on a fine-mesh metal shirt that he would wear under his tunic. All of his weaponry was laid out on the bed. His war braids were in place. His blue zig-zag mark stood out like the tattoos of Celtic warriors of old. In effect, he resembled a grim-faced soldier about to go into battle . . . which, in a way, she supposed he was.

She entered, without knocking, and closed the door after herself.

He glanced up but briefly, then said coolly, repeating her own words, "Begone, Maire." He turned his back to her as he stood and drew his tunic over his head, then belted it at the waist.

Maire winced at his terse words and stiff demeanor, but she was determined to talk with him. In truth, there were some important things he needed to know before he put his life on the line for her clan.

"I apologize."

He was attaching a brooch to his shoulder mantle and would not meet her gaze. After a long pause, he asked, "For what?"

"For speaking to you so harshly, especially in front of others. But you have to understand that Jamie has been my sole responsibility for a long time, and it is hard for me to give up any of that control." She was babbling . . . saying too much. But she was beyond nervous. She was petrified.

He shrugged. Now he was fiddling with his belt buckle. "How about your husband? He has only been gone three months. Did he not ever reprimand the boy?"

Now would be a good time for Maire to tell him the truth about Jamie, but somehow she could not do so when he stood rigid with anger and not even facing her. "Kenneth had no interest in Jamie."

She could tell by the reflexive tilt of his head that he was surprised that a father could have no feelings for his only son. Fortunately, he did not pursue the subject.

"Rurik, why won't you look at me?"

He released a long breath. "Because I'm so bloody furious with you, I would be tempted to raise my hand to you." Then, he laughed softly, and revealed, "Or take you in hand."

"That latter has a certain appeal," she said softly.

He did turn then. "Is that why you're here, m'lady? For a good-bye swiving?"

Maire gasped at his crudity. She did not protest, though, because the cold, lifeless expression on his face held her transfixed. Was this how he appeared before battle? Or had her actions caused him to lose all feeling for her?

She raised her chin haughtily and, blushing furiously, declared, "Aye, a good-bye swiving is what I want . . . if it is the only way to break through that ice wall you have erected around yourself."

He shook his head. "Go away, Maire. You apologized. I accept. 'Tis over." Then he turned away again and began to gather his weapons.

'Tis over. 'Tis over. Oh, surely, he did not mean that everything was over. Maire's heart hammered against her ribs as panic settled in. She had to do something, quickly . . . but how could she get his attention . . . really get his attention?

Unbidden, an idea came to her.

But, oh, do I dare do such?

Do I have a choice?

In a rush, while Rurik was rummaging through his saddlebag on the bed, searching for some last-minute object, Maire began to peel off her garments. Every single one of them, including her hose and shoes. When she was done, and Rurik was about to put his sword in its scabbard at his hip, he asked churlishly, "Are you still here?"

"Aye."

"Why?"

"Because . . . because I haven't thanked you for the amber necklet you gave me," she said in a rush of words.

"I thought you had."

"Not properly."

He sighed. And still he would not make eye contact with her. God, the man was stubborn as a Saxon mule.

"Would you like to see how it looks?"

"Why? I already know how it looks."

"Nay. You don't." She could be as stubborn as he if the occasion warranted . . . and this one did.

"Enough of your games, Maire! In your anger belowstairs you divulged your true sentiments, and mayhap that's for the best because I will soon depart from these lands and—"

Rurik's words trailed off as he pivoted and got his first good view of her amber necklet . . . framed as it was by her nude body. Eyes wide with astonishment, he muttered something under his breath that sounded like, "Odin help me!"

His attention seemed particularly fixed on her breasts. No surprise there! Actually, there was a surprise there. When Maire peeked downward, just for a second, she saw that her nipples were distended with arousal. Oh, how mortifying! This must be how men felt when their staffs had a will of their own, waving in the wind at the least little provocation.

"Well, how do you like the necklet now?" she demanded as if that were the question paramount in her mind. It was becoming increasingly obvious who the lackbrain was in this chamber, and it wasn't the one in battle gear. It was the one with hands placed brazenly on hips, tapping a bare foot with impatience.

Maire noticed the instant a transformation began in Rurik. Just before he drawled, "I like the necklet fine," his posture relaxed and a slow smile emerged on his lips, which twitched with the effort to remain stern and unmoved. But he couldn't fool her. He was moved. Maire could tell . . . even without examining that part of him which she knew to be highly movable.

Not giving herself, or him, a chance to think, Maire launched herself at him like a rock in a catapult, exclaiming in a long moan, "Ruuuur-iiiick!"

He had no choice but to catch her by opening his arms, then holding her up by the buttocks till she wrapped her legs around his waist.

"Why are you doing this, Maire?" he rasped out, already backing up and sitting on the bed, with her straddling his lap.

Now he wants to talk? Is he demented? I cannot answer logical questions when my blood is nigh boiling and every fine hair on my body is practically dancing. Still, she mustered the strength of will to tell him, "Because there are things I need to talk about with you, and you kept ignoring me."

Rurik was already undoing the waist laces of his trews and clumsily shoving the garment down his thighs, even though she had not moved from his lap. When he'd gotten them as far as his knees, he looked at her and smiled. *Blessed Bones of St. Bartholomew! He has a fine, fine smile.* "I could develop a fondness for your method of talking," he drawled.

Who knew a drawl could be so . . . sexual? Was it a Viking trick, or did all men have this knack for twisting a woman into sensual knots with a mere lowering of the voice? "You wouldn't pay attention to me," she complained.

"I'm paying attention now." The drawl was more pronounced than before. Without any preliminaries, he lifted her bottom up, then down, till she was filled with his rampant erection.

Aye, he was paying attention.

Maire closed her lids briefly, just in case her eyes were rolling. When she opened them, she saw that his teeth were gritted and cords were standing out in his neck. The man couldn't drawl now if he tried, Maire would bet.

Sure enough, he finally grated out, "Do . . . not . . . dare . . . move." He anchored her hips to make sure she complied. That created an overwhelming compulsion in Maire to do just the opposite of his bidding. In fact, if she did not move soon, she was certain the butterflies fluttering beneath her woman hair were going to burst free. So she tightened the inner walls of her body to hold them in.

Rurik's member lurched, and he groaned, but he still held her firmly in her place. "So," he said, once he appeared to be more in control, "talk."

"Now?" she squealed.

"You said you came here to talk," he reminded her.

"Are you demented? I can't talk now."

"Why?"

"Why? Why? I'll tell you why. Because I feel as if I'm sitting on a flagpole. That's why. Mayhap you can do various things at one time, but simple woman that I am, I can concentrate on only one thing at a time."

He was smiling. The lout! "And that would be?"

"The fact that you're not moving." She tried to squirm in place but he would not allow even that small motion. "Move, damn you, move!"

"Not yet," he replied.

Is he trying to punish me? She eyed him suspiciously, then entreated, "Make love to me, Rurik."

He held her eyes and answered, "Convince me."

Aye, it's punishment he's after. But no rack or whipping post for this rogue. Nay, he has a more devious torture in mind. "I am not experienced in the love arts . . . you know that. How would I convince you?"

"Use your imagination." He let go of her hips and leaned back on his elbows. The brute was going to make her initiate all the moves, when she didn't even know what the moves were.

"Rurik, we don't have much time."

He shrugged. "Then you'd best think quick."

She tried clenching her inner muscles again, and holding them taut. That was an exercise he'd seemed to like before.

Rurik bit his bottom lip as if stifling a cry.

Aha! A small victory, I spy. She repeated the maneuver, this time engaging a rhythmic hold-release, hold-release pattern. "How was that?" she asked.

"A start," he choked out.

A start? Just a start? Hah! I'll show you, Viking. She spread her legs wider and glanced down to where black curls blended with red, both glistening with her woman dew. When she looked back up, she saw that Rurik had been staring at the same spot . . . and he liked what he saw . . . oh, yes, he did! His face might remain impassive, but a part of him he could not control flexed and swelled, filling her even more.

Even so, the man still did nothing to initiate the undulations that her body craved. What could she do that would knock the complacency out of him?

Her gaze fixed on the chain shirt that came to a vee in the front under his tunic. Some soldiers pulled the mail all the way down and between the legs, with padding underneath, to protect the genitals. His lay open. That gave her an idea . . . a wicked idea.

Did she dare?

Did she dare not?

She pulled back slightly so that Rurik was still embedded in her but the base of his staff was exposed. Then she spread her legs even wider so that nub of woman pleasure Rurik had introduced her to was clearly visible to him.

She was too embarrassed to let her gaze connect with his. She thought she heard a hitch in Rurik's breathing, though, which she took for a good sign.

Then, garnering every bit of nerve she had, Maire took the flexible mail by its pointed front tail and ever so lightly stroked the base of Rurik's column, back and forth, side to side.

"For the love of Frigg!" Rurik roared.

There was no doubt in Maire's mind now. She was on the right route. Still, she asked, pretending uncertainty, "Dost want me to stop?"

"Bloody damn . . . bloody damn . . . whffffffff."

"Oh," she said coyly, stroking him again with the cool metal. "Does that mean you like it?"

"Yea, I like it."

"How much?" she teased with the metal poised a hairbreadth away.

"Immensely."

"I wonder if you would like it more or less if I did the same with my tongue."

He let loose with a strangled laugh. "Unless you are as double-jointed as Ivar the Boneless was said to be, I would say that is an impossibility in your present position. Perchance you could save that sex feat for another time."

Would there be another time? Would Rurik come back, alive and whole? Would he then mention the "bride gift"? Would he stay in the Highlands? Nay, Maire could not think of those questions now.

"But, yea, witchling, I would enjoy having your mouth on me there," Rurik continued in a low, husky voice. "More than you could ever imagine."

While she was pondering what to do next, the V edge brushed across her woman hair . . . just a feathery pass, but the fiery sensation it ignited was exquisite. Tentatively, she let the metal edge make a return pass . . . this time just barely touching the distended bud that held such prominence there. 'Twas like lightning striking her most sensitive body part. Or warm honey spreading out to all her intimate folds.

Maire was utterly shocked at the wantonness of her act, and the pleasure she took from it. Though her hand still held the supple metal fabric, she jerked it away, lest she be tempted to repeat the sweet torture.

Rurik grabbed her by the wrist and gently placed her hand back at the joining of her thighs. In a voice thick as the warm honey she'd imagined, he urged, "Do it again."

Sacred Saints, she did, and almost swooned at the intensity of searing heat that pooled there.

"Again," he prodded.

She had no choice but to comply, so far gone in arousal was she now. And the point of this whole exercise had been to arouse Rurik! This time, the warm honey and searing heat sensations were joined by an interior spasming . . . one, two, three sharp clasps of the thick spear on which she sat.

Rurik groaned . . . a long, lust-ridden, male sound. Even so, he pleaded, "One last time, sweetling. Come to the edge . . . just the edge of your peak for me . . . just a little higher."

"I can't."

"Do it, Maire . . . one last time." His command brooked no argument.

Maire stared down at herself and Rurik where they were joined. As if she were a puppet and Rurik were pulling her strings, she held the pointed fabric slightly above them. Then she let it swing from side to side like a rapid pendulum, creating a vibration against the ridge of her femininity.

She was keening almost continuously now, tears streaming down her face, as wave after wave of escalating excitement hit her. "Oh . . . oh . . . oh . . . oh . . . oh . . ." She must have swooned into unconsciousness for a brief moment, because the next thing she was aware of was being on her back and Rurik attempting to reassure her with soft crooning words, "Hush, now, pretty. You did good. Very, very good. There is naught to be ashamed of." His soothing words were contrary to what he was doing . . . creating new waves and new spasms with long, slow strokes of his hard staff. As his strokes became shorter, he hammered against her, driving her body from one side of the mattress to the other. And the only sounds were those of Rurik's panting and their slick parts hitting one another. Then, finally, the explosion of every nerve ending in Maire's body as Rurik pounded into her one last time with a delicious male shout of triumph.

Then silence.

Bad news can always wait . . .

"I have to leave, dearling," Rurik said a short time later, kissing the top of Maire's head.

"I know," she murmured, but made no effort to move from where she lay cradled at his side, her face resting on his chest, which had finally subsided from its passionate heaving.

And he was no better. His braies were still draped about his knees in a tangle. Holy Thor! The last time he'd been so anxious to have a female that he'd taken her with his braies about his boots he'd been an untried boy, not an experienced man. But that was how Maire affected him.

He looked down at his lady—and, yea, that was how he regarded her . . . *his* lady—and ran a hand over the mass of hair that was spread out over his chest, down to his waist, and over his upper arms. Like a massive skein of blazing silk, it was. "Amazing how I've developed a taste for red hair," he commented idly as he rubbed several strands between his thumb and forefinger. "I always thought I misliked flame hair on a woman."

"You do not like red hair?" she inquired, lifting her head to regard his face.

"I never did afore. I recall the first time I saw Tykir's wife, Alinor. I could not understand how my friend saw beauty when I considered her nigh homely."

"Because she had red hair?"

"Well, because she was covered with freckles from head to toe, as well."

"And now?"

He shrugged as if only mildly interested. "Now, I concede Alinor has a certain attraction."

He kissed Maire lightly on the lips and made to rise. "I really must go. If I do not, we may find a troop of Vikings and Campbell clansmen barging through yon door."

"Give me one more moment," she said, pressing him back down.

I'd like to give you more than a moment, witch. I'd like to give you some memories that would sizzle the hair off your skin and put a permanent blush on that pretty face. "That is what you said a short time ago, afore you bent me to your will and seduced me to your bed." He chucked her under the chin playfully to show he had not been all that upset over the way things had turned out.

Her face turned bright red with embarrassment. How a woman could retain a speck of modesty after what she'd just done was beyond Rurik, but then, who could understand the workings of a woman's mind?

"The seduction was not all one-sided," she protested.

"It was at first."

"I beg to differ, not when . . . but that's neither here nor there. There is something I need to tell you . . . something important."

He tilted his head in question. "Let me dress whilst you talk, then. I really do need to go soon. I would like to arrive at the MacNabs afore it is full dark."

She nodded and moved aside so that he could rise. Almost immediately, she covered a good part of her body with the bed linen. Still visible above the cloth were her bare shoulders and the amber necklet, which suited her so well. How could he have ever thought of giving it to anyone but her?

While he drew on his garments, Maire tried several

times to tell him something that was apparently bothering her, if her wringing hands and stammered speech were any sign.

"I should have told you long ago . . . ," she began and halted. Then she tried another route, "I hope you will control your temper till I get to the last because . . ." She abandoned that pathway as well. "It's about Jamie, you see, and how . . ."

"Jamie! All this nervousness is about Jamie! What has he done now?"

"It's not what he has done. It's what I . . ."

"I know . . . you found out about him watching through a peephole in the scullery as Dora took a bath."

Maire's jaw dropped open. "He did *that?* Oooh, I do not need you to warm his bottom. I will do it myself."

Hmmm. If it wasn't that incident, what could it be? "Oh. Surely you're not this distressed because he and his friends spread honey on the garderobe seat?"

He could tell by the angry glint in her green eyes that she hadn't been aware of that misdeed either. Jamie's arse was going to be hot, not warm, Rurik would warrant

"I am not the one who brought up the subject of his dinky," he asserted, refusing to take the blame for that foolishness.

"His . . . his *dinky?*" Maire sputtered.

So, it was not that either. "Well, the only other thing I can think of that might have you this upset is his asking me if he could go a-Viking with me."

The anger quickly disappeared from her expressive eyes and was replaced with hurt. *Why hurt?* "My Wee-Jamie asked to go away with you?" Her voice was barely a whisper and carried myriad emotions, mostly pain.

"Yea, he did . . . the rascal . . . but, of course, I told him it was out of the question."

She breathed a visible sigh of relief, which struck

Rurik as rather odd. Why would she think he'd even consider taking her young son away from his homeland and his mother?

Maire inhaled and exhaled several times, as if to calm herself. "Rurik, you might not come back from this mission tomorrow. I cannot let you go into danger without telling you . . . something. You *need* to know."

He was already fully garbed and putting his sword in its scabbard. "Is this news something that will upset me?"

"Possibly."

"Cause me to lose my concentration?"

"Probably."

"Change my life in any way?"

"Undoubtedly."

Rurik couldn't imagine anything involving her son that would affect him so. The scamp must have done a deed that was really, really bad for his mother to be so distressed.

She was about to say more, but Rurik put up a halting hand. "Nay, save it till I get back. Bad news going into battle means bad news coming back."

"But—"

"Nay, Maire. Leave be, for now." He leaned down to give her a good-bye kiss. When he was done, he murmured against her mouth, "When I come back, I promise to reciprocate for you the events of today. Mayhap I will demonstrate what *I* can do with a piece of chain mail."

She nodded, not really hearing his words, he could tell. He made for the door, opened it, and was about to leave her chamber when she called out, "Rurik, there is one thought I would have you take with you . . . something I never would have believed just a few days ago. I don't think this will upset you." She paused briefly, then said, ever so softly, "I love you."

He just nodded at her words, and left. Oh, he knew

she'd wanted him to say the same phrase back to her. He could not.

Maire was wrong about the effect her declaration would have on him. Rurik *was* upset.

How had his life become so complicated?

How was he ever going to explain to Maire that, once his mission here was completed, he had another mission to accomplish?

His wedding.

When first we practice to deceive . . .

Rurik was in the lead, riding his horse down the narrow path from Maire's mountainside castle. When they got to the bottom, they rode in a tight vee-formation, with Stigand and Toste on one side, and Bolthor and Vagn on the other. A half dozen of the Campbells fell in behind them. Although these ten accompanied him, Rurik would be entering the MacNab clanstead on his own, unarmed, while Toste and Vagn snuck in wherever they could. The others would stand watch outside.

"We're running late," Toste pointed out, as if that weren't obvious from the darkening sky. "Did you have to or-gaz her *again?*"

"Who says I did?" Rurik replied. That was the trouble with Norsemen. When they were not a-Viking or a-battling, they were meddling in other men's business.

Stigand untied the red yarn from his middle finger, ripped it in half, then handed a piece to Rurik. "Best you commence measurin' yerself if yer gonna be lyin'."

Rurik started to tell his berserker that he hadn't precisely said that he hadn't or-gaz-ed Maire. *Damn, I can't believe I'm using that ridiculous word now, too.* But he was too dumbfounded by Stigand's cutting his yarn in half.

He had no time to chastise Stigand because Vagn

launched into him. " 'Tis obvious you or-gaz-ed yourself boneless. In truth, we could probably fold you up and put you in a saddlebag. I doubt there's a drop of man seed left in your body. If the lady didn't share in the pleasurin', then shame on you." Vagn grinned mischievously. Good thing he was two horse widths away, or Rurik would have swatted him aside the head.

"There's an odd gleam in his eye . . . have you noticed?" Toste asked his brother. "Rather like incredulity. What do you suppose the witch did to him in the bed furs to cause incredulity?"

Everyone looked at Rurik.

Rurik pressed his lips shut and stared straight ahead. He was saying nothing. He could feel his ears turn red, though.

"Your ears are turnin' red," Stigand accused Rurik with a hoot of laughter.

"Uh-oh," Toste and Vagn remarked. "That good, huh?"

"I've been thinking," Bolthor said.

Everyone groaned.

"This is the story of Rurik the Greater . . . ," Bolthor began.

"Who is getting greater by the moment, if his red ears are any indication," Stigand added, ducking to avoid the swing of Rurik's fist. "And, by the by, why is your chain mail sticking out from under your tunic? Did you forget to lace the ties?"

Rurik glanced down at his groin and, sure enough, the vee end of his chain mail was sticking out. Now, his face and neck were no doubt turning red, as well as his ears. "Why must you men always be poking into my personal affairs? I am a single Viking, unattached by wedlock to any woman . . . as of yet . . . so what is wrong with me or-gaz-ing my brains out, if that is what I want to do?"

Everyone grinned, knowing they'd provoked a reaction

from him, which had obviously been their objective from the start. He turned away with a snort of disgust . . . mostly at himself.

"Methinks I have a good title for this saga," Bolthor announced enthusiastically. "Sex and the Single Viking."

The Viking man
Had much conceit.
Especially in the bed furs,
Excessive charm he did secrete.
But came a lady witch
With a complaint she did bleat.
Turns out the Viking's skills
Left her incomplete.
But do not issue a challenge
To a Norseman's male meat,
As this lady soon learned her lesson
Beneath the bed sheet.
The Viking man
Will ne'er retreat.
So much or-gaz-ing
Did he to her mete
That now the fair lady admits defeat,
And says her female parts
Are beat, beat, beat.
Thus the Norseman
Proves once again
That he is all man.

CHAPTER FIFTEEN

The things some men will swallow! . . .

The events of the night went surprisingly well. Rurik was permitted to enter the MacNab keep, alone and unarmed, while Toste and Vagn somehow entered in a clandestine manner.

The castle and grounds were prosperous compared to the Campbell holdings, which prompted Rurik to wonder why some men in their greed never had enough. On the other hand, he noted in the background another MacNab brother, Graham, and his wife and numerous grandchildren; so, 'twas likely that the ever-growing extended family felt the need to sprawl out and swallow up its neighbors. Rurik had also been told that Duncan entertained a convoluted notion that he was entitled to the Campbell lands through his dead brother's marriage.

At first, Rurik outlined the demands of the Campbells with the threat that, unless the MacNabs immediately ceased their threats upon the Campbells in deed and word, spirits would overtake their land.

Duncan and his men could scarce prevent themselves from falling over into the rushes with laughter. It was the expected initial reaction.

Rurik was invited to join them for a cup of ale before he departed . . . although he wasn't entirely certain that the unscrupulous Duncan would allow him to leave.

He was a despicable man, Duncan was. A *nithing* . . . totally devoid of honor. Rurik swore an oath to himself to make the man pay one day, not just for the continuing threat against the Campbells, but especially for putting Maire in a cage and attempting to force her into a marriage that everyone knew would lead to her eventual death.

The MacNabs continued to laugh and make jests over Rurik's threat of spirits overtaking their keep if they did not desist in their threats against the Campbells.

They weren't laughing for long. Soon, terrified soldiers who manned the ramparts and courtyard began to rush in with reports of dozens of ghosts flying about the MacNab castle.

Dozens? Rurik thought. *God Bless Toste and Vagn, and their ingenuity.*

Duncan and his men laughed about the ghost sightings, as well, till the numbers grew alarming, and the spirits' warning of an evil spell placed on all MacNab men started to ring true.

"What kind of spell?" Duncan demanded of Rurik, ice in his voice and his one hand on the hilt of a dagger that had been lying on the table.

Rurik shrugged and tried to appear casual as he replied, "Oh, something to do with . . . let me see, how did Maire word the spell . . . 'Every time a MacNab man harms a Campbell, in word or deed, his cock shall shrink . . . till his manhood is no more . . . and the MacNab line dies out.' "

Duncan made a grunting sound of disbelief. Still, he glanced down at the joining of his thighs, as did every other male in the great hall.

Maire had been right when she'd advised him not to offer threats . . . that men, including the MacNabs, would go into battle without a thought when their lives were in the balance, but when it was their precious male parts, that was another story altogether. That's why his men and hers had been so willing to accept the lies-linked-with-shriveling-cocks nonsense.

"I cannot credit Maire using the word *cock* in one of her ludicrous spells," Duncan replied. "Despite her claims of being a witch, she is a high-born lady. *Cock* is a man-word . . . crude and unseemly for a woman of her station to use."

Rurik made a moue with his mouth that translated to, "Who can say what women will do?" Then he added, aloud, accompanied by a waggle of his eyebrows, "Mayhap the lady has changed."

"What kind of game do ye play here, Viking?" Duncan yelled, standing with bull-like rage. "Maire Campbell is a notoriously inept witch. None of her spells ever worked, according to my brother, Kenneth. Why should we believe ye now?"

As if to belie Duncan's protests, more men, and several women, ran into the hall complaining of new ghostly visits. One of the ghosts had been waving what resembled a penis and testicles, which the ghost claimed had fallen off a MacNab villein stationed at the edge of Campbell lands.

Rurik, who remained sitting, sipping a cup of ale, stifled a grin. Old John had been responsible for that last-minute inspiration, handing Toste a dead ram's male parts, wrapped in a cloth. Good thing Duncan's man hadn't looked too closely at the hideous thing. He didn't know about Scotsmen, but Viking male parts were much more beauteous than that.

"Where is she?" Duncan bellowed. "How do we get her to remove the spell?" Rurik suspected that Duncan didn't really believe, but he was fearful of taking chances.

Rurik shrugged. "I cannot be certain where she is at

the moment . . . ofttimes she flies off during the night, no doubt to visit with her coven or gather more familiars. Those black cats are hard to keep about . . . the animal sacrifices, you know." Maire would kill him if she heard him speak of covens or familiars, and especially sacrificial rites. "Or mayhap she is dancing naked in the woods with her sister witches." Yea, Maire would swat him good if she heard of this.

Duncan made a growling sound of impatience and drew his one-brow low over his eyes. "Get to it, man."

"Well, I do know that she goes to the witch's cairn in Devil's Gorge every morn, just after dawn."

"Devil's Gorge?" he snorted.

Rurik nodded. "Yea, that narrow valley between *Beinne Breagha* and *Beinne Gorm*, which is so named because of its treacherous landscape in the wintertime. Maire goes there daily . . . something to do with renewing her powers and balancing herself . . . the kind of foolishness she is always spouting. But methinks 'twould be a bad idea for you to go there . . ." He let his words trail off deliberately, as if he'd revealed something he ought not to . . . like the fact that Maire would be alone, in a vulnerable spot. "Yea, 'twould be much better if you approach Maire in her own keep. I'm sure she would be willing to accept an offer of peace from you there."

Duncan said nothing, and Rurik knew he had no intention of making any concessions. Rurik would bet a king's treasure that the MacNabs would be going to Devil's Gorge, and they would be there, down in that valley, long before dawn.

Just as he had planned.

Miracles come in all forms . . .

Late the next morning, Devil's Gorge . . .

Rurik and his men, with what was left of the Campbell clan, withdrew for a short respite. 'Twas time to assess their losses and prospects.

The prognosis was not good.

Swiping a forearm across his sweaty brow, with chest heaving for breath, Rurik glanced over at Stigand, whose skin remained as dry as old leather and whose breathing was normal, though he'd worked twice as hard as Rurik. "How bad?" he inquired.

"Not so many deaths . . . just Young John, Rob the Mutterer, one of the shepherds, and the stable lad. But injuries aplenty." Scanning the "battlefield," he pointed to the larger number of MacNab deaths and casualties. "They have lost fifteen men, or more, and they have a like number of seriously wounded."

Their plan had fallen into place as if ordained by the gods. Once the MacNabs were far into the gorge, the boys had done their work with the sling shots to distract the men. Then the archers had gone into play, followed by hand-to-hand combat with sword and lance . . . not to mention Stigand's famous battle-ax, Blood-Lover.

Even the deadly snakes had been brought forth again to scare the nervous war horses. Rurik didn't want to think about where such a large number of vipers were kept hidden in this misbegotten land. Vagn had been heard commenting to Toste, on first seeing Old John bring the snakes forward, that he was never again going to sit on a privy seat with ease, of take a stroll in a dark wood, let alone make love with a wanton maid on a grassy moor. Bolthor had promised to develop a saga about it . . . if they survived.

But alas, all their efforts, successful as they'd been, had not been enough.

"Despite it all, we did good, didn't we?" Rurik asked Stigand now, though he already knew the answer.

"Yea, we did. These Scots are a tough breed, I'll give them that."

"It was a good plan, Rurik," Bolthor interjected from Rurik's other side. "Everyone worked together, even the young ones with slingshots in the trees. But the numbers were against us from the start."

"Well, it appears as if all of us will be drinking mead this day in Valhalla," Rurik told his comrades, who nodded. Not a tear was there in any of their eyes. Death was a fate every Viking expected because of his violent life. All of the men joined their right hands together in one communal fist and raised it high in the air, shouting "To Thor!"

Rurik's men went off to give directions to the Campbell clansmen who remained . . . directions for the final segment of this battle. No doubt, most of them would be going to their deaths this day, but they would be going down with dignity . . . and they would be taking a considerable number of MacNabs with them.

Off in the distance, the MacNabs, red hair shining in the sunlight, could already be seen assembling for the final clash, which would settle the fate of the Campbells once and for all. Rurik sighed audibly. He was only sorry that he had been unable to be the champion Maire sought . . . her knight in shining armor.

Well, Rurik had one last task before he entered the fray. Turning, he motioned Maire forth. She had been standing far back, up behind some boulders, where he had ordered her to stay. He would have much preferred that she remain in the keep, but she had refused, knowing her son was out here.

"Is there no hope then?" she asked worriedly, rushing into his arms. He tried to hold her at arm's length, not wanting to soil her with the blood that stained his garments, but she would have none of that.

He drew off his leather helmet with its nose guard and kissed her softly, probably for the last time. "Not unless there is a miracle, and I see no sign of that."

"What will happen now?"

"I want you to gather all the children and young boys. Go back to your castle and assemble only the essentials. Waste no time, Maire . . . do you hear me? It's important that you not be there when Duncan arrives."

"When . . . when Duncan arrives?" she stammered, terror in her green eyes.

The implications of this lost battle had still not seeped into Maire's brain. Perhaps that was for the best. But she must obey his orders nonetheless.

"Take every horse, mule, or means of transport and leave the Highlands immediately. Head toward the borders. With luck, you will run into Jostein and Eirik and his troops along the way. But, if you do not, head directly for Ravenshire in Northumbria. You will be given refuge there."

Tears were streaming down Maire's face. But Rurik hardened himself not to notice. It was critical that she obey him immediately.

"Is there naught that could save the day?" she asked on a sob.

He shook his head. "Only the sight of a hundred or so warriors on the horizon, riding fierce destriers, swords aready, under the raven banner."

Wistfully, they both turned to the south where a long plateau was visible above the ravine. Then they both gasped.

"Holy Thor!"

"Holy Mother of God!"

It was not a troop of soldiers.

There were no war horses, or weapons glinting in the sun.

And there was no sign of the raven . . . though there did seem to be crows . . . lots of crows.

"What . . . is . . . that?" she asked breathlessly.

"Have you been praying?"

"Of course I've been praying," she snapped. "Why?"

"Well, it appears as if a plague of crows has come to overtake the battlefield. Like in your Christian Bible."

"I hardly think crows are the same as locusts," she replied dryly. "And you hardly resemble Moses . . . or how I imagine Moses would look."

"Those aren't crows," Toste said, hurrying up to join them. "They're witches."

"Witches!" they all exclaimed. Bolthor, Stigand, Vagn, Old John, Murdoc, Callum, and several others had joined their incredulous group.

Narrowing their eyes, they peered at the horizon as the figures got larger and larger. Sure enough, they *were* witches . . . in every shape and size. All in black. Straggly gray hair predominated, but there were younger witches, as well . . . some of them were even comely. Toste and Vagn were already taking note of those, he could tell. Crystal amulets glinted in the sun. Many carried gnarled staffs to perform their magic; some held brooms in their hands . . . whether to fly away, or whisk clean the battlefield, Rurik couldn't begin to guess. And there was a herd of black cats, as well.

"St. Columba's Chin! I do not know for sure, but I swear those are all the witches in Scotland," Old John declared with amazement.

Everyone turned to Maire.

"Wh-what? Why is everyone gawking at me? It's not my doing."

"Did you cast a spell for this?" Rurik asked, his eyes narrowed suspiciously.

"Well, not exactly," she replied. "I did perform a ritual several nights ago . . . remember all the candles?"

He nodded.

"But I did not ask for *this,*" she said, sweeping an arm out to encompass the horde of witches. "All I asked was that Cailleach come back. One witch. That's all."

Rurik groaned. Another of Maire's spells gone awry. But he could not be angry with her now. Mayhap she had inadvertently handed them the means to victory.

"Cailleach?" Stigand inquired. And what a comical picture he made, standing with a bloody long-handled ax in one hand, a bloody sword in the other, war braids sticking out in disarray, and a dumbfounded look on his face.

"That's Maire's mentor witch."

"Which one would that be?" Bolthor wanted to know, scanning the advancing crowd of screeching witches.

"How the hell would I know?" Rurik snapped.

Everyone glanced at Maire again.

She shrugged sheepishly. "I don't know. They all look the same from here."

Rurik could already see the dreamy verse-mood expression passing over Bolthor's face. It said, silently, though loud and clear just the same, "Saga coming."

If Rurik and his men were staring, gape-mouthed with astonishment, the MacNabs were frozen in place, no doubt wetting their braies with fright. Then they attempted to flee for their lives.

At a quick signal from Rurik, he and his men moved forward in an aggressive assault. In a matter of minutes, the MacNabs were pinned in by Vikings and Campbells on one side and witches on the other. With much cursing and some struggling, but only one more death, the MacNab clan soon surrendered.

Maire looked at Rurik then.

And he looked at her.

They both smiled.

He had told her just a short time ago that the only thing that could save the day was a miracle.

It was a miracle.

Mission accomplished . . .

It was over.

Finally.

All of it.

And no one was happier than Rurik, who sat alone an hour later on a boulder contemplating the empty, blood-stained battlefield, which had earned its name this day . . . Devil's Gorge. Well, empty except for the lone body of the MacNab, which he'd ordered left behind, exposed to the vultures and animals of prey to feed on . . . a most appropriate end for the vermin he had been. Soon Rurik would travel to the loch on the other side of the knoll and wash off the red weapon-dew soaking his tunic and braies. And he would clean his sword, which still carried the life fluids of his prime enemy of the day—Duncan MacNab.

Duncan was by now prowling the depths of the earth on his nine-day journey to the lowest level of all the nine worlds, Niflheim, Land of the Dead. Ruled by Hel, Queen of the Dead, Niflheim was said to be a gloomy place of ice, snow, and eternal darkness. Surely a perfect place for the evil Duncan to pay for all his misdeeds.

Or perchance he was strolling through the fires of the Christian hell, with Satan's pitchfork poking his seared skin.

Rurik shrugged with indifference. Either way Duncan was now paying for his mortal sins . . . just as the miscreant had paid with his life under Rurik's wrath.

And pay Duncan had . . . with his life, in the heat of

battle, engaged in one-on-one combat with Rurik . . . which was as it should have been.

Rurik had known Duncan was a *nithing*, a less-than-nothing of a man, when he had first viewed Maire hanging in a cage above her ramparts. True men did not attack women in such a way. His opinion had been reinforced when he'd learned how Duncan intended to force Maire into marriage and a presumed early death after that. Even his needless torture and killing of dumb animals had been an indication of Duncan's tainted personality.

So, from the beginning, Rurik had decided that he himself would inflict punishment on the evil villain. When Old John had tentatively broached the possibility of mercy for the old laird, Rurik hadn't hesitated in his refusal. That kind of man would never give up. He would come back with a vengeance greater than before.

Therefore it had been Rurik who stepped forward to challenge the MacNab in that final battle, and they'd both known it was a fight to the death. Thank the gods, Rurik had been the victor.

To Duncan's credit, he had not pleaded for mercy or screamed in agony when the Raven came to take him to the Other Side. A groan at the final thrust of Rurik's blade and the clenching of his fists had been his only concession to what he had to have known was impending doom, then a stiffening of his body before the final death tremors had overtaken him.

Punishment to the remaining MacNabs had followed soon after. Two dozen of the fiercest soldiers, all red-haired, had been dispatched to a secure holding barn on Maire's estate. On the morrow, they would be escorted on the long trek to Jorvik in Britain, where they would be sent as slave gifts on longships to King Olaf of Norway. 'Twas not the worst fate. If these men were good workers, they could secure their freedom in time, and even return to the Highlands, if that was their choice, though many slaves grew to like the Viking way of life, and took blond-haired Norse women to wife.

Finally, Rurik had made a tentative pact with Douglas MacNab, a twenty-year-old nephew of Duncan . . . already the father of three young daughters. Douglas was also red-haired, and something about all this red hair was starting to trouble Rurik, though he could not fathom why. He'd put that puzzle aside for the time being. The final terms would have to be decided by Maire, but Douglas appeared willing to live in peace with the Campbells and make reparations for years of abuse.

So, all is settled, Rurik thought now as he pondered the empty battlefield. *My mission here is done.*

His blue mark could be removed, even as soon as tonight, with the help of the other witches. Surely, one of them would know how.

What then?

Ah, that was the question, and also the reason why Rurik sat staring dolefully at the scene that should be filling him with triumph. He should be off celebrating, filled with glee. Instead, a crushing weight pressed down on him. And deep down, he sensed the reason why.

Now that his work was completed here in Scotland, he had a wedding to attend.

And it was not to Maire.

Not that he wanted to marry Maire.

Really.

Even if he wanted to, he couldn't.

And he didn't want to.

Really.

Why, then, did it feel as if a fist had reached inside his chest and was squeezing his heart?

Why, then, did he keep recalling her words to him yestereve, "I love you"?

Why, then, did he wonder what news Wee-Jamie wanted to disclose to him when he'd said, "I have somethin' important to tell ye"?

Why, then, did fear overwhelm him . . . fear that he was about to lose the most important thing in his life?

Chapter Sixteen

Vikings and Scotsmen share one thing. They love to party . . .

Eight hours later . . .

Chaos reigned at *Beinne Breigha.*

But it was chaos of the best, most marvelous kind, in Maire's opinion. She stood in the doorway of her great hall, which gave her an equal view of activities both inside and outside the keep.

Bagpipe music had been blaring sweetly for some time now. Well, some of it was sweet, when it came from the expert mouth and fingers of Murdoc. And some was not so sweet, when it came from Murdoc's apprentice-in-training, Bolthor.

Everywhere could be heard sounds of levity. Giggles. Chuckles. Belly laughs. There was so much joy that Maire could scarce contain her own gaiety. In fact, she suspected she wore a continual, silly grin on her face.

Females, young and old, garbed in their best *arisaids*, danced at will and occasionally burst into Highland songs as they helped set the trestle tables for the largest celebratory feast ever seen by her Campbell clan. "Is there aught more beauteous than a comely lass with a smile on her face?" Old John was heard to remark on more than one occasion.

Even in the worst of times, *Beinne Breagha* boasted an abundance of nature's blessings, whether from land or water. If ever they'd appeared to be poor of victuals, it was not for lack of food, but more for lack of time or people to prepare fine fare. Already the boards groaned with fishes of a dozen different varieties . . . baked, boiled, jellied, pickled, minced, and smoked. A mass of eels still slithered in their scullery barrel awaiting the perfect moment to be boiled and added to the leek and curdled cream sauce. And not to be ignored at this special event was the Scottish favorite, smoked *craigellache,* or salmon.

Even the standard fare seemed uncommon today: tupney pies; cock-a-leekie soup; blood sausages or black pudding; potted headcheese made of boiled shin meat and marrow bone; vegetables, including the infernal neeps; and of course, haggis.

To satisfy the sweet cravings of young and old, there were preserved fruits; cook's famous currant and hazelnut pudding; *uisge-beatha*-laden cream custard, known as *crannachan;* and Scotch shortbread. Honey still in the combs sat on high shelves in the kitchen, away from sticky-fingered children, to be slathered on oat cakes or bannocks in the course of the feast.

Males, young and old, dressed in their best *pladds,* stole kisses and made assignations for later as they passed to and fro from the great hall to the courtyard where a huge red deer stag was being roasted on a spit, rotated by children who took turns at the honored task. To supplement the red meat and fish were hams fresh from the smoke huts and chickens stuffed with chestnuts and boiled eggs. Later in the evening, once the wee 'uns had fallen asleep on their mothers' laps from pure exhaustion, the scullery maids would carry out a silver bowl, passed from generation to generation, containing the Campbell flummery. The base of the frothy concoction was soaked cereal, the liquid of which set to a clear jelly, flavored with rosewater and topped with cream and honey and its own distinctive ingredient . . . *uisge-beatha.* Definitely an adult drink.

The most chaotic thing about this whole chaotic scene was that there were witches here, witches there, witches essentially everywhere. Ugly witches. Beautiful witches. Dour and sweet. Although there were a few young witches, most of them seemed ancient. Some of these were white of hair, toothless, and hairy-warted, with dried-apple faces, but others were softly aged with wise, all-knowing eyes. Though they varied in physical appearance, they all had one thing in common . . . cackling. Even the prettiest of them let loose with a decided cackle now and again. Mayhap that was why Maire had never become a very good witch; she'd never been able to cackle.

The way Cailleach was cackling right now.

"Ye've made a fine mess of things this time," her mentor proclaimed as she opened her arms for Maire's enthusiastic embrace. "Tsk-tsk-tsk!"

"I didn't mean to call up *all* the witches in Scotland," Maire replied defensively. She pulled back to get a better look at her beloved teacher. It was alarming to see how much Cailleach had aged in the past five years. Or had the witch always resembled an old hag?

Cailleach waved a bony hand dismissively. "'Tis not *that* mess I be referrin' to, dearie." She pointed to the exercise yards where Rurik was helping some men set up targets and other equipment for the games to be held on the morrow . . . archery, wheel throwing, wrestling, triple jumping, and horse racing. Although Rurik had already been to the loch to bathe with the other men, and his hair was fancy-braided on the sides with amber beads, he had stripped off his tunic and was working bare-chested now, with his black braies hanging low on his hips.

Maire's heart lurched and her blood thickened with desire at just the image of Rurik's ridged abdomen and the thin mat of hair that ran down in an enticing vee toward his . . .

Her thoughts broke off at that juncture on hearing yet another cackle.

"*That* be the mess I am referring to, girl."

"Rurik?" she asked with surprise.

"If Rurik be the name of the too-pretty Viking with the wicked eyes glancing this way, then, aye, that be the selfsame mess I see ye embroiled in."

Maire looked toward the exercise yards again. Sure enough, Rurik's *wicked* eyes were directed toward her. And she could swear, though the distance was considerable, that he winked a sensual promise her way.

Maire felt her face heat up under Cailleach's all-discerning scrutiny.

"So, that's the way the wind be blowing," Cailleach said with another cackle. " 'Twould seem the mess is even worse than I thought. A Viking, though. I canna fash where yer good sense has gone."

"What's wrong with a Viking?"

"Not a thing. Not a thing . . . if all ye want from him is a strong fighting arm . . . or a virile bed partner. But methinks ye want much more."

"And if I do?" She raised her chin defiantly.

"If ye do," Cailleach repeated her words back at her, "then I foresee teardrops ahead. Dinna know that Norsemen are rovers? They mislike settling in one spot fer long."

"Mayhap this one is different," Maire argued, as much to counter Cailleach's contentions as to assuage her own doubts.

"Mayhap. Mayhap," Cailleach acquiesced. But then

she asked the question that had been niggling at Maire's conscience all afternoon, "What will the Viking do when he discovers he has a son?"

If she cackled at him one more time! . . .

"So, yer the one?"

Rurik just about jumped out of his skin at the crotchety-voiced inquiry, which was accompanied by a high cackle.

Spinning about, he saw Maire's old mentor witch, Cailleach, sitting on a pile of wooden shields, watching him. He was the last one on the exercise field, where he'd just donned his tunic and was buckling his belt. The old crone must have come up behind him. He shouldn't have been startled by her presence. There were witches everywhere. In fact, many people were complaining about them . . . except Toste and Vagn, who claimed to have tupped a few of them already, though Rurik could hardly credit the truth of their boasts, especially when they claimed to have been ensorcelled into performing some perverted acts. Those two wouldn't have had to be ensorcelled into doing anything of a sexual nature, perverted or not. On the other hand, they had been avoiding lies of late, like every other man within miles of *Beinne Breagha,* Viking or Scots, because of Maire's outlandish tale connecting falsehoods and shrinking man parts. So, mayhap they were telling the truth.

"The one what?" Rurik finally managed to answer.

"The one Maire has gone weak-kneed over?"

Rurik's lips turned up with pleasure. "Maire is weak-kneed over me?"

"Aye, and well ye know it, too. A rogue like you specializes in such nonsense. Truly, if women knew what men were thinking half the time, they would be slapping their faces right and left." She chuckled . . . rather cackled . . . at her own joke, then continued, "Ye delight in turning a lass's fancy just for the fun of it."

"You don't know me well enough to determine my motives."

"Oh, I know ye, boy. I know ye better than you think."

"Boy? I am no boy. What do you here anyway?" Rurik snapped at Cailleach. "Other than offer insults."

The old biddy cackled a few more times before submitting, "I know ye like my Maire well enough to bed her, but I wonder . . ." She let her words trail off and narrowed her rheumy eyes at him, studying him as if he were a piece of meat for sale at market.

"Well, spit it out, witch, what is it that you wonder?"

"I wonder . . . do ye love her?"

That question stopped Rurik cold. "You overstep yourself. What business is it of yours how I feel about Maire?"

" 'Tis very much me business. Maire has suffered these past years. I do not want her to suffer more."

Rurik stiffened with affront. "I mean her no harm."

Cailleach shook her head sadly at him. "That may not be your intent, but I suspect it is inevitable."

Rurik was uncomfortable with this conversation and started to walk away.

"You did not answer my question, Viking. Do ye love her?"

Rurik turned slowly and eyed the pestsome witch. "Nay, I do not." He raised a hand to halt her next words. "But I care about her. I do. Methinks I am incapable of love. That capacity, if I ever had it, was burned out of me as a child."

Cailleach nodded knowingly. "In the Northlands . . . Kaupang. Aye, I ken how that might be."

Rurik's head jerked up. How did she know where he'd spent his youth? Fine hairs stood up all over his alert body. Truly, the witch gave him a creepy feeling; she knew too much. But he would turn the tables on her. "Can you remove this blue mark?" he asked, touching his forehand and running a forefinger down his nose and through the center of his chin.

The witch laughed. She had the nerve to laugh at him. Then she shrugged. "Mayhap I can. And mayhap I cannot."

Rurik clenched his fists to keep from reaching for the witch's scrawny neck.

"Getting rid of that mark is important to you, isn't it?" Cailleach inquired amidst a few more cackles.

"What manner of question is that? Yea, I want the mark gone. Is there aught wrong with that?"

"Not if ye do not make it more important than everything else. Some say the peacock must lose its feathers afore it can truly sing."

"Are you daft, old lady? Stop speaking in riddles."

"Aye, I will speak plainly to ye, lad, and make sure ye listen well. Yer life is about to be turned upside down. We shall see what kind of man ye are when ye finally land on yer feet. We shall see if ye deserve Maire. Or if that bloody mark is all ye care about in this world."

Oh, that was unfair . . . to lay the blame on him. Why was it such a bad thing that he wanted his face restored to its former appearance? Who said it was the *only* thing he cared about? He was not *that* vain and self-centered. Just because he could not love, that did not mean he could not care.

Rurik closed his eyes to calm his roiling temper. When he opened them, the witch was gone . . . though he thought he heard the sound of cackling laughter in the distance.

Little did the witch know. His life was already turned upside down.

* * *

Yep, lies always come back to bite you in the butt . . .

"Can we go celebrate now?"

Rurik's warm breath whispered into her ear, causing incredibly sensual currents to ripple through her body. For a moment, Maire paused and relished the exquisite sensations that caused her breasts to peak and heat to pool between her legs.

Finally, inhaling sharply for composure—a futile exercise—she turned in her seat at the high table and addressed the rogue, "I thought we were already celebrating . . . for two hours, to be precise. What else do you call these massive amounts of food and ale, not to mention lute and bagpipe playing, singing, juggling, and more of Bolthor's sagas than any sane person should be required to hear?"

Even Rurik, who was not an overly modest man, had said, "Enough!" when Bolthor had told not one, or two, or three, but four different sagas about Rurik's heroic deeds during today's battle. And Toste and Vagn had yelled, "More than enough!" when Bolthor had attempted, instead, to tell a saga entitled "A Tale of Witch Swiving," immediately after "Ghostly Seductions."

Rurik laughed, his mouth still way too close to her ear. "I had in mind more of an intimate celebration."

She knew what he meant, and, truth to tell, her thoughts had been wandering in that direction all day. But she had things to tell him first. Taking one of his hands in hers, she twined their fingers together, marveling at how small her hand—which was not all that small—looked in his much larger one. At the same time, she delighted in the pressure of his callused palm against hers, and the beat of his pulse where their wrists met. Maire feared she was a lost cause where this man was concerned. Bracing herself, she started what had to be one of the most difficult conversations of her life. "I have wanted to thank you. You saved my clan, and for that I will be forever grateful."

"You are welcome, m'lady," he said graciously, then waggled his eyebrows at her, adding, "Perchance you would like to thank me in a more private place. Methinks a little chain mail exercise would not be amiss."

Maire's face flamed at his reminder of her outrageous conduct of yestereve. "Rurik, I must know. What are your plans now?" She couldn't believe she'd asked that question. She'd promised herself that she would not, even though it had been foremost in her mind all day.

"I don't know," he answered honestly. "Well, actually, I do know, but must we discuss this tonight?"

Her heart sank at the seriousness of his tone. But he was right. This was a night for celebration. She could learn of his plans later.

There was a critical matter to be discussed, however.

"About Jamie . . . ," she began.

Rurik groaned.

"I told you afore you left for the MacNabs that there was something important I had to tell you. Well, this is the time—"

"Speak of the little devil," Rurik said, chuckling.

Jamie and his little band of urchins were swaggering across the cleared area in the middle of the great hall where some ring dancing had just ended. The rascals . . . six in all . . . were wearing miniature tunics, like the Vikings wore, and each had their hair braided clumsily on the sides of their faces. But they'd added a new touch this evening . . . blue, jagged lines down the center of their faces . . . probably made with blueberry juice, Maire guessed.

She felt Rurik stiffen beside her. Alarmed, she looked at him and quickly advised, "Now, don't be getting your whiskers in a twist again. They're not mimicking you. They're emulating you. You're their hero of the day."

But Rurik wasn't angry this time. She could see that. Instead, his head was tilted to the side and a puzzled expression caused his forehead to furrow. "I'm not upset . . . precisely," he murmured distractedly. "It's just . . . his black hair."

"Hair? Jamie's?" *Oh, God! Oh, no, not now! Not this way!*

"Something's been nagging at me for days, especially today after the battle," he explained, turning to stare at her. "All of the MacNabs had red hair. Every single one of them."

Maire tried to pull her hand out of Rurik's grasp, but he would not release her. Maire felt a desperate need to run from the great hall, even if Rurik followed after her. "Rurik, not now. Let's go outside and discuss this. Not here."

It was as if he didn't hear her. "And you have red hair, too," he pointed out, as if speaking his thoughts aloud unconsciously. "So, how is it possible, Maire, that . . ."

Her heart thumped madly in her chest.

". . . that your son has black hair?"

He looked at Jamie, playing a running tag game with his friends, then back at Maire, then at some of the curious faces of people in the hall, including his own Viking comrades, who were noticing his distress. Everyone's actions seemed to have slowed down. A sudden chill hung in the air, and Rurik's face filled with understanding, and then horror.

He pulled his hand out of her clasp and put his face in both hands. For several long moments, he stayed thus, and Maire's heart sank with dread. "Please, Rurik, let us go outside and discuss this in private."

Finally, he lifted his head, and he gazed at her with contempt. "Tell me," he demanded in an icy voice.

"Aye, I will tell you," she agreed on a long sigh. She barely stifled a sob as she admitted the long-withheld news, "Jamie is your son."

The bratling is mine? . . .

A son? I have a son?

For four long years I have had a son and never knew!

How many people know? Am I the only one in ignorance?

Oh, God! That foul-mouthed, arrogant, precocious, filthy—in essence, adorable—Scots-child is mine. Mine!

How could she? How could she keep this from me?

Rurik was so angry he feared what he might do. But even in the midst of the red haze that nigh blinded him, Rurik realized that his loss of temper could ruin the celebratory feast for all of the Campbell clan, and that he did not want on his conscience.

He grabbed Maire by the wrist and led her forcefully away from the guests, smiling right and left as he passed through the crowd toward the stairway leading to the upper bedchamber. Only he knew how brittle was his tight-lipped smile, and only Maire knew how painfully his fingers dug into the flesh of her wrist.

Once out of view of her clan and his Viking friends, Rurik practically dragged her up the stairway, down the corridor, and through the oaken door to her bedchamber, which he slammed after them. He shoved her away, fearing he might do her bodily harm, and only then did Rurik relax his tense muscles and press his forehead against the door.

Tears filled his eyes—tears, for the love of Freyja!—but he could not say if they were signs of hurt over Maire's betrayal, or signs of happiness over his instant paternity. So many emotions overwhelmed him, one after another, that he could scarce keep track.

"Rurik, I'm sorry . . . I can explain," she offered, placing a hand on his shoulder.

He shrugged her off and turned so abruptly, she almost fell backward. "Explain? Explain?" he shouted. "How can you explain not telling a man he is a father?"

"You weren't here," she pointed out with infuriating logic. "As you must recall, you left Scotland afore I could have known I was quickening. Then I married Kenneth, and it seemed more expedient to just let him be father to Jamie."

"Expedient? Expedient?" he sputtered angrily. " 'Tis obvious that the man knew Jamie was not of his seed." An alarming thought occurred to Rurik then. "Did he mistreat the boy?" Oh, he would never forgive her that negligence. Never!

She shook her head vehemently. "I would never have allowed that. He just ignored him most times, even in the beginning when he had no reason to doubt his fatherhood. 'Twas only later that Jamie's appearance made it obvious he was no MacNab. Nay, Rurik, you must believe me. Kenneth never struck Jamie. He only . . ."

Rurik divined her unspoken words. Kenneth had only struck *her.* He closed his eyes and inhaled and exhaled several times for calm. Because his seed had taken root in a woman's body, she had been subjected to physical punishment from another man. Did she not know how he would feel knowing that? But, nay, he refused to take the blame for her sins.

"So, you did not tell me in the beginning because I was far away, and because you had a new husband to appease," he said in a surprisingly calm voice as he opened his eyes and speared her with a glower. "What is your excuse for not telling me these past days I have been here in Scotland?"

"Fear."

Well, that made sense, he supposed. "Fear of what?"

"You."

That made sense, too. "I do not make a habit of beating women, even when I am sore angered."

" 'Twas not fear of physical pain that locked my tongue. 'Twas fear that you would take Jamie away from me."

His head jerked up at that unexpected admission. "Why would I do that?"

She shrugged. "Revenge."

He cocked his head as he continued to study her. "You do not think much of me, do you?"

"Men have this thing about carrying on their line. I feared you would develop an instant attachment to your son, and be unable to separate yourself from him. Since you have made your opinions of Scotland clear on many an occasion, 'twas obvious you would not be staying here. So, really, any sane-minded woman would harbor the same fears."

Sane-minded? Huh! Devious, seductive, secretive . . . yea. But sane-minded? I have my doubts. "Who else knows?"

"Well, I do not think the MacNabs ever knew for sure, though Kenneth probably discussed his suspicions with his brothers at one time or another. Certainly, they never made a connection with you." She took a deep breath, then went on, "But on the Campbell estates, everyone knows."

"*Everyone?*" he shouted.

"Well, forgive me for pointing this out, Rurik, but you and Jamie are identical in appearance, except for the difference in years. They could not help but note the similarity."

"Your sarcasm knows no bounds, m'lady. Truly, you tug the wolf by the tail when you risk my wrath thus." But her words remained imbedded in his brain. What a sightless fool he must be . . . not to have seen what everyone else did. Had they been snickering behind his back every time he passed by? Was he once more, as he'd been as a child, a pitiful subject for mockery?

"Rurik, I've told you that I'm sorry. You have to admit that I tried on several occasions to broach the subject. What else could I have done?"

"Thor's Blood! You could have told me."

She stared at him, chin raised with more bravado than she had a right to display. "What will you do now?"

He glowered at her, his chin raised also, unable to express his bone-melting fury. "I do not know," he said, opening the door behind him. "I just know that I cannot bear to be in your presence now. You revolt me."

She flinched, as if he'd struck her, and tears immediately welled in her green eyes, but he steeled himself not to care.

"One thing I do know," he said in a scathing tone before he exited the chamber, "you will pay for this perfidy. You *will* pay."

Does somebody need a hug? . . .

"I tol' ye I had somethin' important to tell ye," Jamie said matter-of-factly as he plopped down on the ground beside Rurik.

So, the boy had known, too . . . or suspected. The situation got worse and worse. For the past hour, Rurik had been sitting at the edge of the loch, staring out over the nighttime waters, thinking . . . thinking . . . thinking. And not a solution in sight.

"Shouldn't you be abed?" he asked the boy.

"Me mother sent me to find ye. She said ye might need me?"

Damn, but that witch was going to drive him barmy. Could she not leave him be till he'd settled his thoughts?

"Do ye?"

"Do I what?"

"Need me."

Rurik's shoulders slumped. How did he answer a question like that? "What I need is to be alone for a bit."

"To settle yer temper?"

He shook his head at the boy, and tried to see him more clearly in the moonlight. Did he really resemble him? Was there a miniature version of himself walking the earth? Why did his heart swell with pride at such a prospect?

"Are ye gonna beat me mother?" the impudent lad inquired. "If that's what's on yer mind, I gotta tell ye . . . I won't allow it."

Rurik chuckled. The boy did have ballocks . . . even if they were small ones. "And how would you be stopping me?"

Jamie made some punching motions in the air. "I'd beat ye to a pulp with me bare hands, and kick ye in the shins, like I used to do with me fath . . . I mean, Kenneth . . . and put slugs in yer ale."

A sadness swept over Rurik and squeezed at his heart that his son had witnessed his own mother's abuse. Had he learned early on to dodge his fath . . . Kenneth's fists, just as Rurik had developed survival skills as a child? If so, Rurik felt new anger boil up in him. He had always sworn that no child of his would go through what he had. 'Twould seem the choice had been taken from his hands.

"I do not beat women," Rurik told the boy flatly.

Jamie let out an exaggerated sigh of relief. "Guess I'll be goin' a-Viking with ye after all, then."

Rurik had to laugh at that. "What would make you think so? That is the last thing on my mind."

The child blinked at him several times before blurting out shakily, "Don't ye . . . don't ye want me?"

Rurik put his face in one hand and rubbed his fingertips across his creased forehead. When he looked up, the boy was gazing at him as if he'd asked the most important question in the world. "Of course I want you." And, to Rurik's amazement, he realized the truth of his statement.

"Well, then?" Jamie asked, putting his hands on his tiny hips with impatience . . . just as his mother was wont to do on occasion.

"Well, then, *what?*" Rurik asked.

"Don't ye want to hug me? That's what me mother always does when she gets teary-eyed."

Before Rurik could register the fact that the rascal was accusing him of weeping, or that he'd asked him for a fatherly embrace, he was standing and his son was hurling himself high into his arms.

With the child's face nestled in the crook of Rurik's neck, and his skinny arms wrapped around his neck like a vise, Rurik hugged his son for the first time. And it was a glorious, glorious feeling.

His life would never be the same again.

And Cailleach had been right . . . his life was turning upside down.

Fate's toe was big, for sure . . .

It was after midnight and Rurik was making his way through the trestle tables in the great hall, which still bore the remnants of the night's feast. There would be much cleanup work to do on the morrow.

Well, that was none of his concern. Rurik had more important things on his mind. Like his son, whom he'd just tucked into a pallet in an alcove off the great hall with promises that he would be there when the boy awakened. There were a hundred things Jamie wanted of him. Lessons in archery and swordplay. Trout fishing. A walk to his favorite mountain peak. Horseback riding. An exploration of the cave where Jamie had been hiding for weeks on end. And talk, talk, talk about every subject that would be of interest to a small boy, and some things that should not be of interest to a small boy.

How was Rurik going to do all this . . . deal with Maire . . . have the blue mark removed . . . and leave for the Hebrides and his wedding?

"Are you all right?" a male voice asked out of the darkness.

Rurik had just stepped from the hall doors into the courtyard, and he jumped with surprise. It was not one male, but four of them. Bolthor, Stigand, Toste, and Vagn. All waiting to accost him. All with worried frowns marring their faces.

"Nay, I am not all right," he grumbled, sinking down to the stone steps.

They sank down beside him.

"How long have all of you known?" he demanded of them.

After a short bout of silence, Bolthor spoke for the group. "Several days . . . from when the scamp first got a bath and wore braids similar to yours."

Rurik snorted with disgust.

"We figured that you must know, deep down, or that you would soon discover the truth," Toste revealed. "After all, Jamie is a mirror reflection of yourself."

Rurik turned on Stigand. "You above all others knew how I would react. You saw firsthand, when we were children, how I hated being the subject of mockery. How could you have withheld the news from me?"

Stigand shrugged. "I did not think you would care."

Rurik's head reared back with affront.

"You always said bringing children into a world of pain and degradation was not to your taste. I thought you would not want the child."

"You are a fool to think such," he declared hotly. "As much a fool as I for not seeing the truth."

Anyone else who proffered such an insult to Stigand would be holding his severed head in his hands by now, but his old friend just shook his head sadly.

"Ah, but now that you know," Vagn opined, "is it not a grand feeling to have a son? Leastways, I always imagined that it would be the highest accomplishment for a man."

"Yea, it is a proud feeling," Rurik admitted, "and at the same time humbling."

"I could be his foster father," Stigand suggested hopefully.

Rurik gaped at him. Who would have thought the burly berserker could blush, or that he would entertain such a thought?

"Nay, I will be Jamie's foster father," Bolthor countered.

"Nay, me," Toste said.

"Nay, me," Vagn piped in.

Rurik put two hands in the air, as if in surrender. And he laughed for the first time in hours. "You can all be the boy's foster fathers," he conceded.

There was some grumbling, but finally agreement.

"This is the saga of Rurik the Greater," Bolthor began.

"Do not think of starting on me now, skald."

But Bolthor just spoke over him, and for once, truer words were never spoken.

Betimes a man goes all through life,
Happy without family or wife,

But fate sticks out her big toe,
And down does the man go.
Then the man learns that being alone
Is not the place for a man grown,
Especially if his seed takes root,
And into this world comes a precious offshoot.
When that babe is a boy,
Oh, the wonderous joy!
For then discovers the man
What it is to be a real man . . .
A father.

They all nodded, deep in thought, probably wondering what Rurik would do now.

If only he knew!

He actually ate the witches brew . . .

Rurik awakened about dawn in the stables on a bundle of straw he'd raked together. To his surprise, he'd actually slept, despite the turmoil of the night before . . . perchance in reaction to a long, eventful day that had begun in battle. How could so much have happened in one day?

But something had awakened him, he realized, even before he opened his eyes. There was someone in the stable beside him.

Was it Maire?

Was he ready to face the wily witch and all the problems aswirl betwixt them?

Should he shoo her away?

Or forgive her monumental transgression?

Was he ready to face all this so soon?

Slowly, he opened one eye, then shut it quickly on a groan. It was a witch, all right, but not Maire the Witch.

"What do you want?" he asked Cailleach. With eyes

still scrunched tight, he rolled over onto his stomach and buried his face in his folded arms.

"Time's a wasting, Viking. Get up and start to set your world aright," she advised.

Really, the old hag had a death wish, ordering him about so.

Then the witch did the unthinkable. She whacked him across the buttocks with her broom and cackled several times with relish at her act.

He was half-reclining on his back within seconds, casting killing glares at the outrageous old crone. He refused to budge beyond that.

"Did ye hear me, ye lazy lump of Norse flesh? Rise and shine . . . though I doubt ye'll do much shinin' today. Yer skin looks a mite green. Exactly how much *uisge-beatha* did ye suck up las' night?"

"Not enough, apparently."

"Ooooh, ye are a foolish lad, maligning a witch so. I have powers, ye know."

"Really? Well, what say you to waving your magic wand and getting rid of this bloody blue mark on my face?"

"Is that all ye care about?"

"I'm getting mighty tired of answering that question."

"Well, yer gonna be lots more tired by the end of the day. Ye have much to do this day, Viking. Company's coming."

"Huh?" Rurik said. "What company? We have no need of more people here . . . not with every bloody witch in Scotland roosting in every free space."

"Watch yer tongue, boy, or ye may find this witch roosting on a body part that canna bear the weight."

"Don't push me too far, witch. I cannot guarantee the consequences." Suddenly, he sniffed . . . and sniffed . . . and sniffed. "What's that smell?"

"Yer breakfast."

Oh . . . Good . . . Lord! Rurik's gaze had moved sideways to where a huge cauldron was boiling over an open fire—*an open fire in a stable!* The witch was already ladling out a wooden bowl of some grayish liquid with pieces of something floating in it. She shoved the bowl into his lap and handed him a wooden spoon, then ordered, "Eat!"

"Why?"

"Ye need yer strength today."

He was alert of a sudden. "Is there to be another battle?"

"Ye could say that."

Rurik's eyes darted to his sword, which lay to the side.

"Not that kind of battle," Cailleach said with a few cackles.

"What other kind is there?" he asked.

She pointed to the bowl with the silent message that he was to get to it.

"What's in it? Eye of a newt? Toe of a snake?" he jested.

She just waited.

He took a tentative bite. It was thin porridge, with chunks of apple. Leastways, he thought it was apples. It didn't taste too bad. In fact, it tasted good.

"Why are you being nice to me?"

Cailleach laughed outright then, with more enjoyment than his question merited, in Rurik's opinion.

"What's so amusing?"

"Ye won't think I'm so nice by the end of the day, Viking."

Chapter Seventeen

The blues were spreading . . . blue eyes, blue fists, blue balls, whatever! . . .

By noon, the witch situation was totally out of control.

Despite her heavy heart over the strained relationship between herself and Rurik—he refused to speak to her at all—and despite her concern over Jamie's reaction to his new father—he was ecstatic—Maire had other, more pressing matters to attend to. She stormed out into the courtyard and screeched, "Cailleach? Come here! Right now!" She might not be proficient at the art of cackling, but she certainly could screech.

Cailleach was in the courtyard before her, engaged in some kind of dance with five other witches . . . something involving jumping up and down and swaying from side to side, with hands joined and lots of cackling. Supposedly, they were doing a thanksgiving rite related to the defeat of the MacNabs, though it looked more like a bunch of old women engaged in fits. Several of her servants, some of whom had already threatened to run away, were white of face, as if they were viewing ghosts . . . though witches were probably in the same category as ghosts when it came to scaring people.

Maire's screech apparently carried as far as the exercise yards, where the games were already in progress, and some of the men and women glanced her way, including

Rurik, who immediately turned away. That hurt. But she could not dwell on that misery now. She had a more compelling problem.

"You have to get rid of all these witches," Maire whispered urgently to Cailleach, who had come at her bidding.

"Why? Ye're the one who called for them."

"I . . . did . . . not," she protested, as she had numerous times already. "I called for one witch . . . *you* . . . not fifty witches."

Cailleach shrugged with unconcern. "What difference does another witch or two make?"

"Wh-what difference?" Maire sputtered. "I'll tell you what difference. One witch showed the dairy maid how to milk a cow without touching the teats; now, Bessie is giving milk nonstop; we cannot supply enough buckets for all the milk. Furthermore, the milk has drawn all the cat-familiars who are hanging about the keep, which has caused the castle staff to turn skittish. Five of those cats were pregnant and gave birth, right in the rushes, and don't think that didn't cause a stink."

"Is that all?"

"Nay, that is not all," Maire snarled. "Effa, that witch from Skye, is searching high and low for the knucklebone of a virgin. She claims there are none to be found."

"I been meanin' to tell ye that ye must rein in the doings of some of yer young people. Do not fash yerself, though; have ye considered that perchance no one will admit to virginity when it means givin' up a body part?"

Maire snarled once again. "Toste and Vagn have been taking turns in the bed furs with that young witch from Inverness, and I swear, if the stories are true, she is teaching them some *really* perverted things."

"Naught wrong with that," Cailleach opined, examining her overlong fingernails with unconcern. "A man can never learn enough things about the sex arts . . . a woman, either, for that matter," she added, staring pointedly at Maire.

By the faith! Is she really advising me to learn sexual perversions?

"At least ten witches have offered to supply me with a love potion to lure Rurik back to my bed," she complained.

"And that is a bad thing?" Cailleach's gray eyebrows lifted. "Seems to me ye need all the help ye can get, lassie."

"Old John claims that a love elixir was put in the barrel of *uisge-beatha* last night, which caused the men to be more virile and the women more passionate."

"Surely, no one is complaining about that."

"Some of the witches have gone into business . . . selling the men antidotes for lying and shrinking man-parts. 'Tis a sham, and you surely cannot condone such chicanery."

"Ye can't blame a witch fer tryin' to make a livin'. Times are tough fer witches, ye know. And who's to say the concoctions don't work?"

"There are rowan ashes on all the windowsills."

" 'Tis the best remedy for warding off the evil eye."

Maire took a deep breath for patience. "Cook is practically steaming from the ears over all the cauldrons missing from his kitchen, and he says *you* have been roasting what resembles a dog in his fireplace. The place reeks."

"Me?" Cailleach demurred, all innocence and batting eyelashes . . . or what few eyelashes she had left. Then she laughed . . . or rather cackled. "It's a small roe deer I'm roasting. I needed the heart and liver fer one of my special remedies, not to mention the hooves, ears, and testicles."

Maire's jaw dropped open.

"Yer problem, dearie, is not witches," Cailleach said, patting her hand lovingly. "It's frustration, pure and simple."

"Frus-frustration?" Maire was so flummoxed by Cailleach's need for animal testicles that she could scarce speak about this new contention of hers.

"Aye, 'tis a well-known fact that men get frustrated when they canna get enough . . . you know, loveplay. Actually, in some of them, the frustration builds and builds till they are nigh blue in their manparts." She scrutinized Maire, who was shocked into temporary silence, before adding, "Have you checked your female parts lately?"

"For . . . for what?" Almost immediately, Maire regretted her question.

"Blueness."

"Aaarrgh!" was Maire's only response as she rushed away from the courtyard and toward the exercise fields, where it appeared as if her son . . . *her little boy* . . . was about to participate in the archery contest. Blessed Virgin! With his inexperience, he was more likely to miss the target and shoot his cat.

And Rurik, fire in his blue eyes, was staring at her as if he'd like to make her the target.

Of what? That was the question.

Revenge?

Lust?

Love?

Maire was so tense and upset over all the happenings of the past day that her entire body was rigid. She glanced down at her clenched fists . . . then winced.

She was squeezing so tight they were blue.

* * *

Blue on blue, heartache on heartache . . .

Bolthor was standing next to Rurik as they both watched Maire come sailing toward them.

"I know what your problem is, if you ask me," Bolthor offered.

"Who asked you?"

"Frustration."

"Huh?" He turned on his friend with disbelief. His life was falling apart. The woman he'd cared about and trusted had betrayed him. He had a son he'd never been aware of. There were witches everywhere. He couldn't hit a target today, for the life of him. And Bolthor spoke of frustration.

"Yea." Bolthor nodded his head vigorously. "What you need to do is bed the wench. That is the best method for solving problems betwixt men and women. Otherwise, all these frustrations build up inside a man and make him miserable."

Rurik gaped at Bolthor, then shook his head as if he were a hopeless case . . . which he was, of course. "Go away."

Instead of going away, Bolthor had the affrontery to suggest, "Methinks I have the perfect name for my next poem. 'Rurik the Greater: Saga of the Blue-Balled Viking.' I could describe how yer blue balls match yer blue face and how there must be some significance to that happenstance. What think you—"

Rurik did not think. In fact, without thinking, he reached out and punched his skald in the nose. Bolthor swerved at the last moment, and the punch glanced off his jaw, instead. Still, he was knocked to the ground, where he rolled about, laughing like an idiot. It was Rurik then who went away . . . right toward Maire . . . whom he had been avoiding all day.

Could life get any worse than this?

* * *

He was breaking her heart . . . again . . .

"You!" she said in the steeliest voice she could manage, pointing to Jamie and the bow and arrow in his tiny hands. She motioned with her forefinger that he was to put the weapons down instantly and move off the game area.

Jamie grumbled under his breath but did as he was told, dragging the bow, which was as tall as he was, in the dirt after him.

Then she turned on Rurik. "You!" she said, also in a steely voice, and motioned with her crooked finger for him to follow her. She didn't look back to see if he obeyed her orders, as Jamie had done. She hoped, though. Fervently.

Maire had had more than enough of her wildly ricocheting emotions. Here, there, everywhere. He loves me, he loves me not. I love him, I love him not . . . well, that latter hadn't entered her field of emotions yet, but it probably would. He's angry with me; he's hurt. He wants my body; he wants revenge. I want his body; I want deeper affections. I want him gone; I want him to stay. At any one moment, she had no idea how either of them was feeling.

Mayhap it was time for Rurik to leave *Beinne Breagha,* just as it was time for the witches to leave. As heartsick as Maire felt over that prospect, she was more distraught over the upheaval in her life, and that of her son. Now that the MacNab threat was over—and, aye, she was thankful to Rurik for that—the Campbell clan needed to set a new course, with her as acting laird till Jamie came of age.

But how would Rurik fit into that picture? That was what Maire needed to know from Rurik. That was why she had ordered him to follow her to a private place.

He soon caught up and walked side by side with her, in silence. It was not an uncomfortable silence. In truth, they both needed the solitude of their own thoughts to formulate what they would say to each other.

To Maire's surprise, they had unconsciously walked to the judgment stone . . . that rocking boulder where she'd had such a memorable physical encounter with Rurik. She glanced at him. He glanced at her. And they both glanced away quickly, lest their true sentiments be revealed.

Giving the flat boulder a quick shove with his booted foot, he watched it rock back and forth, staring pensively. Was he thinking about placing her on the rock, and letting it judge her? Could the rock be any more unfair than his current assessment of her transgressions?

He walked away from the boulder then and leaned against a tree, legs crossed at the ankles—a lazy posture that was belied by the tense set of his jaw and the thin line of his pressed lips. He waited for her to speak.

"I'm sorry," she said simply.

"You said that afore."

"It needed saying again."

"If you say so."

"What are your plans?"

"For what?"

For me. For us, her heart cried out. But what she said was, "For Jamie."

He shrugged.

"Are you happy about being a father?"

He didn't answer immediately. When he did, she could tell that he was trying to hold some strong emotion in check. "Yea, I am happy to be father to Jamie. He's a fine boy, despite . . . well, he's a fine boy. But I am not happy to have lost four years of his life."

"Oh, Rurik! How could it have been any different?

Even if I'd informed you, I was married by then. I had never actually told Kenneth about how Jamie was conceived. Be honest. I was nothing to you. A bairn would have been an inconvenience."

He shook his head. "I would have wanted to know. Even if I could not have taken an active part in his life, I had a right to know. I would have looked out for his welfare . . . even if only from afar."

Maire could understand that sentiment. "What will you do now?"

"About what?"

Me? What about me? What about us? "Will you stay in the Highlands?"

"I cannot. I must go to the Hebrides to . . . well, suffice it to say, I have a . . . uh, job to do there."

A lump the size of the rocking boulder formed in her throat. "You will allow yourself no time to become acquainted with your son?" she choked out.

"Mayhap . . . mayhap I could take him with me."

Before his words were out, Maire cried, "*No!*"

"Not forever," he offered in a voice that was soft and conciliatory. "Just for a short time."

"No!" she repeated adamantly, then added quickly, "I could not leave Scotland with him, even for a short time."

Rurik's face pinkened with embarrassment.

Maire tilted her head in question, then realized her mistake. Rurik hadn't invited her. Just his son.

"You are not taking my son from me," she declared firmly. "Do not even think I would allow you to do that."

"Not even if it's for Jamie's own good?"

"What good could there be in taking a child from his mother?"

"Young boys are sent away to foster all the time."

"Not my boy!"

"Perchance this is a decision best left to the boy. Ask him, Maire. Ask him what he wants."

"This is my decision to make, and mine only."

"Nay, you are wrong. 'Tis my decision, too. I am his father."

"You told Cailleach that you are incapable of love."

"Cailleach has a big mouth."

"That is neither here nor there. Jamie is only four years old. He needs love."

"He has it," Rurik said flatly.

"You love him? Already?" Oh, this was worse than Maire had envisioned. If Rurik loved him so soon, he would never abandon the boy to her sole care. Never. "Rurik," she pleaded, "it would kill me to lose my son."

He pushed away from the tree and brushed past her as he returned to the path leading back to the keep. Over his shoulder, he informed her in a voice so muted she could scarce hear, "Just as you are killing me."

Who better to get love advice from than a witch? . . .

"Seduce him."

"Wh-what?" Maire shrieked, jumping with fright. Cailleach had come up behind her where she stood on a small knoll overlooking an inlet on the loch behind the keep at *Beinne Breagha*. Rurik was alone, swimming . . . swimming hard . . . the kind of energetic exercise a person engaged in when he had a demon riding on his back . . . or a witch.

"Ye heard me. Seduce the Viking. It won't be the first time."

Maire's face warmed with embarrassment at the idea that Cailleach might be aware of exactly what she'd done to seduce Rurik the last time they'd been together. But she couldn't know that. Could she? "What good would that do? It will take a lot more than a bout of lovemaking to solve our problems."

Cailleach rolled her eyes. "For a witch, betimes ye are mighty dumb. It might open the door a crack, girlie, and that's all ye need. A crack can be as great an opening as a wide-open door in some circumstances."

Maire knew Cailleach had only her best interests at heart, but could she really seduce Rurik again? That business with the chain mail had been an inspiration. She had no more tricks up her sleeve.

"You need no tricks, Maire," Cailleach said, as if reading her mind. "Just you."

Maire was about to question her old friend some more, but the witch was gone in a whirl of dust. So, Maire turned back to her study of the loch, and the swimming Rurik, and already she was walking downward, murmuring to herself, "I . . . can't . . . believe . . . I'm . . . going . . . to . . . do . . . this. I . . . can't . . . believe . . . I'm . . . going . . . to . . . do . . . this. I . . . can't . . . believe . . ."

Female seduction: the highest flattery to men . . .

Rurik couldn't believe his eyes.

Maire was walking gingerly into the lapping waters of the loch . . . naked as the day she was born . . . except for the amber necklet. Her hair was plaited off her face into a single braid down her back. She shivered, then dove into the cool water. When she came up out of the water, like a red-haired sea nymph, she didn't even glance at him. She just began swimming toward him with firm overhead strokes that propelled her swiftly to his side.

If Rurik could have run, or swum away, he would have. But there was nowhere to go, except toward the shore . . . and her. He stood his ground in abdomen-high water and waited. She arrived moments later, splashing water around her like a puppy just learning to swim.

He was not going to be amused.

"What are you doing here, Maire?" he growled.

She stood wobbily and brushed some loose strands of wet, red hair off her face. As she panted for breath, her breasts heaved where they were barely covered by the blue water. Droplets of water rolled down in a mesmerizing path from the amber pendant toward the enticing cleavage between her breasts.

He was not going to be mesmerized by her breasts.

"I came to seduce you," she informed him, finally answering his question . . . not that he recalled precisely what his question had been.

He was not going to be seduced.

"Why?" he asked, and his question sounded lack-witted even to himself.

She blinked at him, the wet clumps of her lashes oddly endearing. Her lips quivered slightly, as if she were unsure what to reply. And the water continued to lap about her breasts.

Really, he was not going to like her clumpy eyelashes, or her trembling mouth . . . even if it did look moist and kiss-some . . . and he most definitely was not going to notice those bobbing breasts.

"Because I want to," she said boldly, ". . . to seduce you, that is. Because it seems to be the only way to break through that wall you've erected around yourself. Because I'm so sorry, and I want to make it up to you. Because it's not right for the parents of a little boy to be so at odds with each other. Because I'm afraid you'll leave suddenly, and this might be my last chance."

He was not going to . . . oh, to hell with the inner protests!

He didn't know what to say, being drawn in two different directions as he was. Anger and the need for revenge were powerful emotions, even when offset by a soul-deep yearning to surrender to her seduction . . . not to mention an erection, luckily hidden underwater, strong enough to float a longboat.

Tears welled in Maire's green eyes as he waited too long to respond, and she spun around, proceeding back to shore with steady, proud steps.

"Oh, all right," he called after her. Rurik didn't know where those words came from. They just emerged, and he had to admit, they felt good . . . as if he'd just shrugged off a huge weight.

She stopped in her tracks, and waited.

He couldn't find the right utterance to please her; so he decided to act, instead. Diving underwater, he came up quickly behind her. Wrapping his arms around her knees, he dragged her underwater with him, hearing her squeal of surprise through a watery filter.

They rolled around together, underwater, as each tried to wrest control from the other. Legs entwined, arms around each other's shoulders, they pressed their lips together, then let the waters float them to the top.

For a minute, they stood, just staring into each other's eyes, afraid to speak, not wanting all their problems to intrude. Maire's hands were still on his shoulders, his were at her waist. Her breasts ebbed and flowed against his chest hairs, and he could see that the nipples were turgid from the cool water.

He was about to tell himself that he was not going to be aroused by that erotic sight, but that would be a lie. And Rurik was not about to risk the fate of a lying Viking . . . especially not at this instant.

"Wrap your legs around my hips," he urged in a sex-husky voice.

Without speaking, she did as he asked.

He took her buttocks in each of his palms and eased himself into her sheath. "You are so incredibly tight . . . and welcoming," he whispered against her exposed ear, as he adjusted himself inside her.

"You are hot marble," she whispered back. "How can you be so hot when the water is cold?"

"You heat me, heartling." Rurik had no idea where that endearment came from when moments ago he had been hating her . . . or thought he'd been hating her. But he could tell that the endearment pleased Maire because she moaned softly and repeated the endearment back to him. He had to admit, he liked the sound of it on her lips.

Then he showed her how to move on him. And, Holy Thor, she was a fast learner. By the time he lowered his mouth to hers, he was voracious in his appetite. His hands were everywhere at once. His lips were alternately pressing and gentling her, his tongue plundering, then licking. As his peak fast approached, he wanted to end his torment, and he wanted this agonizing pleasure to last forever.

"Aaaaaahhhhhhh!" he cried out, his head reared back over his arched neck as his orgasm arrived in deep waves that seemed to suck the very life out of him. And Maire's insides continued to clench and unclench him as she arrived at her own peak and shattered with little sobs of, "Oh . . . oh . . . oh . . . oh!"

He stood stock still in the water, her face buried in his neck, his arms wrapped tightly about her lower back as he kissed the top of her hair. What had just happened?

He'd been seduced, good and proper, and in a humiliatingly short period of time, that's what.

He should have been angry, he supposed.

Instead, he smiled.

"Uhmmmm, Rurik," she inquired, leaning back slightly, which caused his "Lance" to take new interest in her shifting channel, "you did not pull out before the end. Do you suppose that spilling your man seed inside my body while we are in a loch will prevent me from conceiving? Will the water wash it away?" Her face was flame-red as she asked her question, but it was an important one . . . one he'd obviously not thought of.

"I have no idea," he answered truthfully. "Later, I will probably be alarmed by that fact, but for now I cannot care. I am more interested in what 'Lance' is up to." He waggled his eyebrows at her and flexed himself inside her body.

She laughed . . . a most frivolous, joyful sound. "*Up* being the most important word, I presume," she replied impudently.

"Precisely." He was about to show her just how far *up* he could go, when he heard an odd sound. Close by. And it sounded like . . . a dog.

Swirling about, with Maire still in his arms, and Lance still in his element, Rurik almost fell over with astonishment. It was a dog, all right, who was swimming rapidly toward him, his tongue lolling out with excitement.

" 'Tis Beast. My pet wolfhound," he informed Maire.

"But how can that be? Isn't he in Northumbria with . . ."

They both looked toward the shore, and groaned simultaneously. Standing and sitting astride horses were a vast array of finely dressed folk: Tykir, Eirik, Selik, and their wives, Alinor, Eadyth, and Rain, not to mention a large number of children. And witches were swooping forward, too. And a slew of Scotsmen. And his comrades-in-arms, Bolthor, Stigand, Vagn, and Toste, including Jostein.

Lance immediately drooped and slipped out of his

safe harbor. Maire drooped and slipped down into the water till it covered her up to the chin.

"Do something," she ordered him, as if this were all his fault.

He did the only thing he could think of.

He waved.

Rurik the Greater wasn't feeling so great . . .

Rurik was sitting at one end of the great hall, sipping *uisge-beatha* with Tykir, Eirik, and Selik, who declared the beverage a gift from the gods, and determined to carry barrels of it back with them to their estates in Northumbria and Norway. All five of his Viking comrades were there in the background, indulging equally, even Jostein, who was full of himself for actually succeeding in bringing Rurik's three friends back with him, along with a troop of fifty men, even if their services were no longer needed. The soldiers were camped outside on the hillside of *Beinne Breagha*, none the worse for wear, especially since they'd been given rations of *uisge-beatha*, as well.

Eadyth was off examining some natural beehives with Nessa. Eirik's wife was an expert in raising bees and selling their products in the markets of Jorvik, including what she called the world's best mead. It was.

Alinor, Tykir's freckle-faced, red-haired wife and the most pestsome woman this side of *Niflheim*, had one of Maire's weavers in hand and had trotted off to an outbuilding, where she was examining the looms. Already she had mentioned a new pattern they might not be familiar with. No doubt, she would be inspecting the sheep, too. Alinor thought she knew every bloody thing in the world about the wooly-headed animals and their products. She probably did.

Rain, a noted healer and wife to Selik, was in the

kitchen, where a line of patients had already formed for her medical diagnoses. Everything from ringworm to the lung cough.

Beast, the traitor, was off trailing after Rose, of all things. Eirik had told him with disgust that Beast was too fastidious by far and had declined to breed with his bitch wolfhound, Rachel. Fastidious, hah! Not when he'd developed an affection for an ugly cat!

And Maire was an even worse traitor. She'd left him to face all his friends alone. In fact, she was probably hiding somewhere, hoping she wouldn't have to come out till everyone was gone, which was not bloody likely. He'd been the one who'd had to walk out of the loch bare-arsed naked, to the laughter of one and all. He'd been the one to carry her garments out into the water so she could cover herself. He'd been the one to shoo everyone away so she could emerge in dignity. And how did she thank him? By running away and leaving him to face the jests of his old friends. And that was just what they'd been doing for the past hour . . . making mock of him.

The most persistent teasing related to the witches.

"Ne'er have I seen so many witches in one place in all my life," Eirik proclaimed as he watched through the open door, wide-eyed and gape-mouthed, as a half dozen of the old hags practically flew by in the courtyard, chasing after a herd of black cats, which were chasing after Beast, who was chasing after Rose. "Not that I have ever really witnessed witchery in the past." Eirik sank back down into his chair and directed a gaze of astonishment at Rurik.

"Do they all live here . . . born and bred?" Selik inquired with equal amazement. "Are they *your* witches, Rurik? Or do you have a habit of drawing witches to your person . . . like the one who marked you?"

"Nay, they are not my personal witches. They're here

because of Maire," he explained with a frown on his face.

"Maire called up this vast array of witches?" 'Twas Tykir who spoke now, and his tone implied that Maire must be daft.

Now, Rurik had considered Maire daft on more than one occasion, but he did not like others suggesting the same thing. So he defended her by saying, "It was an accident. She only wanted one witch . . . Cailleach, her old mentor . . . to come, but her spell went awry . . . and all the witches in Scotland somehow arrived." The explanation sounded rather daft, even to Rurik's ears.

Rurik hoped his explanation, daft as it was, would satisfy Tykir, who was the most persistent fellow when he got a bug lodged in his . . . well, body cavities.

"A spell? Gone awry? Is Maire really a witch, then?"

He should have known Tykir would not just drop the subject.

"Yea, she is a witch. Nay, she is not a very good witch. And, afore you ask, yea, I have made love with the witch again. And, nay, she has not turned other body parts blue."

Everyone raised his eyebrows at the excessive explanation.

"I see you still have the blue mark," Eirik remarked, not even trying to hold back the smile that twitched at his lips.

Rurik's only response was a growl of displeasure.

"But Rurik *Campbell?*" Tykir asked with that infernal grin on his face. And, really, Tykir had the most irksome grin in the whole wide world. Besides, what the Campbell name had to do with his blue mark, he had no idea. He suspected his old friends were jumping from one distasteful subject to another, just to throw him off balance. 'Twas a tactic he'd employed with them on more than one occasion. "How could you . . . a fierce Viking warrior . . . become a Scotsman?"

"I told you," Rurik hissed. "It was a misunderstanding. I did not become a Scotsman."

"I suppose you will be eating haggis now," Tykir commented with an exaggerated sigh, "and playing the bagpipes."

"Nay, I have not developed a taste for haggis, and Bolthor is the one who has taken on bagpipes as his weapon of choice."

"Odin's Balls! Do not tell me," Tykir said in an aside to Rurik, so as not to offend the skald. "Bolthor is playing the bagpipes . . . *and* reciting poetry?"

Rurik nodded and plastered an evil grin on his own face. "And I can guarantee you, he will be doing both *for you* back at Dragonstead this winter."

Tykir looked as if he'd been poleaxed.

"But you have a son," Eirik pointed out, still belaboring the Campbell appellation that Rurik had been given by Maire's clan, "who will one day be a Scottish laird."

"Yea, but being father to a Scots-boy does not make me a Scotsman. Oh, what's the use! You men will believe what you want anyhow."

"Rurik is right." It was Bolthor coming to his defense, to Rurik's surprise. "He did not become Rurik Campbell because of Wee-Jamie. He became a Campbell because he is their hero."

Rurik groaned aloud. He could just predict what Bolthor would say next, and apparently so could everyone else, because they were grinning from ear to ear.

"This is the saga of Rurik the Greater," Bolthor began.

"Hey," Tykir protested.

"If you knew what was good for you, you would stop right there," Rurik advised Tykir in an undertone.

But Tykir blundered on, "I thought I was supposed to

be the great one. Remember, Bolthor, you always used to say, 'This is the saga of Tykir the Great'?"

Rurik shoved his cup to the side and pressed his face to the table. He wished he could just fall asleep and waken when this whole nightmare was over.

"Ah, you are correct in that, Tykir," Bolthor explained, "but Rurik reminded me that 'Great' was your title; so, we changed his title to 'Greater.' "

"Except when he lost his knack," Toste interjected with a chuckle. "Hoo-eee! He was not so much greater then."

"His knack?" Tykir, Eirik, and Selik all inquired.

Rurik moaned against the tabletop, where his forehead still rested.

"Yea, he forgot how to or-gaz a woman in the bed furs, but not to fear," Toste blathered on, "he got his knack back eventually."

Tykir put his lips near Rurik's ear and whispered, "Does or-gaz mean what I think it means?"

"It does. And I swear, Tykir, if you do not take your skald home with you to the Northlands, I am going to take away *your* ability to or-gaz."

Tykir and everyone else at the table were laughing hysterically.

Bolthor was already launching into his latest saga, to Rurik's mortification. Good thing no one could see his telling blush . . . for certainly then they would be teasing him about being a blushing Viking, and Bolthor would be telling a poem about it for all posterity to recall.

Once was a Viking warrior
Who loved the glory of war,
But came he to Scotland
Where folks came to understand
That here was a figure

Who was more than soldier.
He was a hero,
Through and through.
That is why he is now called
Rurik, the Scots Viking.

A stunned silence followed Bolthor's saga, which was the usual response. Finally, Tykir cleared his throat, then remarked, "You have refined your rhyming skills, Bolthor."

Forsaking modesty, Bolthor nodded in agreement. "I must tell you, though, Tykir, Rurik has given me much more fodder for sagas than you ever did. There is: 'Rurik the Vain,' 'The Viking Who Lost His Knack,' 'Rurik the Blind Viking,' 'Rurik the Scots Viking,' 'Sex and the Single Viking,' 'Vikings Who Name Their Cocks,' 'The Blue-Balled Viking,' and ever so many others."

Rurik turned his face so his cheek was resting on the table top. Then he cracked open one eye. Sure enough, everyone was staring at him, openmouthed with incredulity. It took a lot to turn a Viking warrior incredulous. But he had. And it was no great achievement.

"Of course, I am thinking that Toste and Vagn might be good topics for some of my upcoming sagas," Bolthor continued.

Toste and Vagn could not have appeared more horrified if he'd suggested they cut off their manparts.

"Yea, I can see all the *twin* possibilities. 'Sex With Two Witches.' 'Vikings With Extra-Ordinary Endowments.' 'What Twin Vikings Can Do In the Bed Furs and Others Cannot.'"

It was Rurik's turn to grin widely. Mayhap there was hope for him yet. Mayhap Bolthor would decide to latch on to the twins and devote his poetic life to their escapades.

But then Selik tilted his head to the side and asked, "Why do all the men here have yarn bows tied on their middle fingers?"

"Well, actually, I can answer that," offered Stigand, who had been quiet thus far.

Rurik stood abruptly, not even waiting for the lengthy reply that Stigand was sure to give . . . one which would somehow make him look even more foolish.

"Where are you off to?" Eirik asked with a knowing smile.

"The garderobe."

But what he was thinking was he'd like to find Maire's hiding place and hole up with her there for a day or so . . . or a sennight.

When rogues become fathers . . .

Tykir was waiting for him in the corridor outside the garderobe. Not a good sigh. Nor was it a good sign that Tykir wore a serious expression on his usually mischievous face.

"I am worried about you, Rurik," Tykir said right off.

"Why?"

"You are not yourself."

Hah! That is an understatement! "It will take some getting accustomed to fatherhood, that is all."

Tykir smiled. " 'Tis a wondrous thing, is it not . . . being a father?"

Rurik smiled back. "Yea, 'tis. I ne'er thought to be a father . . . I am not sure why. Nor did I crave the passing of my blood on to another. But I find myself grinning in the most ridiculous fashion whene'er I gaze upon the child."

Tykir nodded in understanding. Then he brought up the topic that Rurik had been avoiding. "About Maire?"

"What about Maire?"

"Do you love her?"

Rurik refused to answer. He was not being deliberately rude. In truth, he did not know the answer.

To his dismay, Tykir began to laugh uproariously.

"I cannot imagine why it should be so funny that I might conceivably be in love with a Scottish witch." He looked at his friend, who was so much like him, then admitted, "Well, all right, 'tis rather funny. A joke on me. In fact, the supreme joke from the gods in a lifetime of jests at my expense."

Tykir shook his head at him, tears of mirth rimming his eyes, "On the other hand, perchance it is a *gift* from the gods."

Now there was a thought.

CHAPTER EIGHTEEN

He carried male cluelessness to new heights . . .

It was evening, and they were celebrating another feast . . . this time in honor of their guests. Good thing there was lots of food left over from the night before.

Rurik sat beside Maire, dressed in richly embroidered garments that would do a prince proud. She had managed to drag out an old *arisaid* of the softest emerald green wool with gold braiding that predated her wedding . . . a perfectly suitable garment . . . but she hated the fact that Rurik was more beauteous than she was, both in form and apparel. Her hair was a mass of red curls since she'd been unable to dress it properly after her impromptu bath in the loch.

Tykir, Rurik's friend from the Northlands, had taken the liberty a short time ago of tugging on a lock of Maire's hair and watching with a bemused expression on his face as it sprang back into a tight coil. He'd glanced at his wife's red hair, then back to her, before he'd commented to Rurik, "Another flame-haired goddess!"

Rurik—the oaf—had muttered something under his breath that sounded like, "Redheaded women . . . God's plague on man."

She'd elbowed Rurik in the ribs, hard, at that insult, but it had barely fazed him. Not only was he thickheaded, but he was apparently thick-skinned as well.

Rurik's friends had seemed to find her actions vastly amusing.

She would like to wring Rurik's neck . . . not just for forcing her out of seclusion but for sitting at the high table with her now as if everything between them was just fine and jolly, when he knew as well as she did that everything was a shambles. Oh, she'd managed to seduce him in the loch, but look how that had turned out. And, truly, she didn't think she had many more seductions under her belt . . . so to speak.

Under ordinary circumstances, she would have enjoyed herself. A person couldn't help but like Rurik's friends. They were attractive and charming and full of teasing mirth.

Even the older couple, Selik and Rain, who had to have seen close to fifty winters, were surprisingly fit and pleasing to the eye. Rain, who was allegedly a famous healer in Britain, equaled her husband in great height, and their blond hair matched as well, even to the sprinkling of gray strands. They'd brought four of their eight natural children with them, between the ages of ten and seventeen. They'd left behind the other four, plus many foster children, in an orphanage they operated outside the trading city of Jorvik in Northumbria, under the care of a young woman named Adela and an elderly man named Ubbi.

Already Rain had taken Maire aside and asked whether there might be a place here at *Beinne Breagha* for some of the young people searching for trades. Maire had readily agreed, especially since so many men and boys had lost their lives the past few years to wars or feuds with the MacNabs. They had a need for new blood in the Campbell clan.

Then there was the darkly handsome Eirik, Lord of Ravenshire in Northumbria, who must have seen close to forty winters. Not as handsome as Rurik, of course, but then no one was that handsome. The half-Viking, half-Saxon man brought with him his wife Eadyth, who had to be the most beautiful woman Maire had ever seen, with silver blond hair and violet eyes. Over a silk headrail, she wore the Norse *kransen,* a gilt circlet with embossed lilies on it. Though in her mid-thirties, Eadyth's creamy skin showed no sign of aging. This couple had brought with them Eadyth's illegitimate son, John, a sixteen-year-old boy who was already causing Scottish lasses from miles around to swoon. He had been adopted by Eirik, of course, as had Eirik's two illegitimate daughters, seventeen-year-old Larise and fifteen-year-old Emma. John and Jostein had apparently become great friends, and both of them had eyes on two of Selik and Rain's daughters. In addition to those three children, Eirik and Eadyth had also brought four they had had together, all boys, and all full of rambunctiousness.

Jamie was having the time of his life with all this young company. Beast and Rose were enjoying themselves, too, if all the yipping and meowing were any indication.

Maire was amazed that this noble couple openly acknowledged the illegitimacy of some of their children, but she was equally amazed when she was told that Eadyth was an accomplished businesswoman who sold the products of her beehives in the markets of Jorvik—mead, honeycombs, and timekeeping candles.

Finally, there was Tykir, Eirik's half brother and Rurik's best friend in all the world. Oh, what a wicked-eyed, mischievous fellow was Tykir, despite being of middle years . . . about thirty-five or so. As vain as Rurik, he had his hair plaited on one side only, where a thunderbolt earring dangled from his ear.

He was constantly fondling his red-haired, freckle-faced wife, who was less than thirty, or gazing at her with open adoration . . . when he wasn't pinching her buttocks, that is . . . or she wasn't pinching his. Alinor had their squirming two-year-old son, Thork, sitting on her lap right now, and she was breeding again . . . due to drop that winter.

Rurik's three friends had taken to wearing red bows of a largish size on their middle fingers. When Alinor had inquired about their purpose, Tykir had told her, in blunt terms. She'd swatted him on the shoulders, and chided, "What lies have you been telling, fool?"

"Just a precaution, wife," he'd chortled.

Eadyth had grinned at her husband's bow and remarked, "A bit of an embellishment, wouldn't you say?"

"Not big enough," Eirik had disagreed.

Alinor addressed Rurik now. "Will you be leaving with us two days hence? Tykir and I plan to spend several sennights at Greycote and then Ravenshire, afore returning to the Norselands for the winter. We would love your company."

"More like you would love having me to tease, Alinor. I swear, 'tis your greatest pasttime," Rurik countered dryly.

Alinor stuck her tongue out at Rurik, which Maire thought was a most scandalous thing for a fine lady to do. Rurik and Tykir laughed at her antics, though, and her son, Thork, thought it was a great trick, and did it repeatedly himself.

"But, nay," Rurik replied, "I will not be leaving Scotland . . . not that soon, leastways."

Maire's heart skipped a beat. What did he mean? Was he staying longer because of Jamie? Or had her seduction managed to melt the wall of unforgiveness that had surrounded him? Did they have a future? Or was this a temporary reprieve?

Leaning forward, she tried to get a better look at

Rurik's face. That was when the amber pendant slipped forward, out of the confines of her gown.

Alinor's eyes immediately latched on to the necklet. "Oh, my goodness! The bride gift!" With a chuckle, she turned on Rurik and berated him with a wagging forefinger, "Why, you rogue, you! You did not tell us that this precious piece you selected for a bride gift was intended for your Scottish witch."

Rurik made a choked, gurgling sound deep in his throat, and his skin paled. "Alinor, lock thy tongue!"

It was Tykir who spoke next. "But I thought the necklet was intended for Theta . . . as a bride gift . . . once you have the blue mark removed and she has wed with you . . . in the Hebrides . . . where you purchased land and . . ." Tykir's words came out slow and halting, then stopped suddenly as he realized their import.

Maire came to the same realization, just moments later. Her skin went instantly clammy, and her throat closed as she speared Rurik with a wounded expression.

The knave looked guilty as sin. "Maire, I can explain . . ."

Explain? What is there to explain? Rurik is betrothed to another woman. He gave me a necklet intended for his bride. I am the most foolish, pathetic woman in all Scotland . . . nay, in the entire world.

"Oh, my God!" Alinor said. "You didn't, Rurik? Tell me that you didn't do such a lackwitted thing."

But shock yielded to fury and Maire was already standing, unclasping the necklet. Throwing it to the table in front of Rurik, she declared in an icy voice, "I expect you to be gone afore morn."

"Now, just wait a minute," Rurik protested.

"I hate you," she seethed, throwing the words at him like stones.

"You can't hate me. You told me that you loved me."

All the women at the table exclaimed, "She did?" as if it were of great import.

Maire bared her teeth in a snarl. "I take it back."

"You can't take it back. Uh-uh. Especially not in two days. You love me, and that's that."

"You are the most infuriating, insensitive, lecherous, traitorous, half-brained, two-legged animal ever to walk the earth."

"What's your point?"

"Oooooh! I'll show you my point, you clodpole." She took a huge cup of *uisge-beatha* and tossed it into his stunned face.

Then she walked proudly from the now silent hall. Once she reached her bedchamber, though, she sank to her knees and cried fiercely for all she had lost that day.

If all else fails, beg . . .

All that evening, and all the next morning, Rurik pounded on Maire's door, but she refused to respond. He could hear her crying, though, and that nigh broke his heart and brought tears to his own eyes.

"I can explain. Really," he'd said at first.

Then, "Alinor and Eadyth and Rain have convinced me . . . I am a loathsome, lackwitted lout."

Another time, "I want you to have the necklet, Maire. It was meant for you . . . I mean, I think that deep down I always intended it for you, not Theta.

"About Theta . . . ," he'd tried to explain, "I never loved her, or anything like that. 'Twas just that all my friends had settled down happily and it seemed the right thing to do. I was already regretting my decision long afore I entered Scotland.

"I've sent all the witches away," he apprised her by midmorning. "At great risk to myself, I might add. Several of them cast worrisome spells on me, but I told them

I had my own personal witch to remove the spells. That would be you . . . not Cailleach, who refuses to depart, by the by. She won't stop laughing at me, or cackling. Why do you suppose that is? I think she gave me the evil eye. Either that, or her one eye has developed a twitch.

"Jamie has taken to kicking my shins. And he put slugs in my morning ale. Best you come out and reprimand him, Maire. Actually, it was milk, not ale. Ugh! The dairy cow still won't stop giving milk, and some of the cats look as if they are going to explode. Who ever heard of a Viking drinking milk? Bolthor has already created a saga about it.

"I'm hungry. Cook won't give me anything to break my fast," he said at noon. "Aren't you hungry, Maire? You will wither away to nothing, and then where will you be? I may have to resort to eating the leftover haggis. Ha, ha, ha."

Over and over, he kept coming back to repeat his different pleas.

"I'm lonely. No one will speak to me, not even Stigand, or Bolthor, or Toste, or Vagn, or Jostein. Bolthor made up a new saga, in addition to the milk one. 'Tis called 'Rurik the Dumb-Arse Viking.' What think you of that?

"Guess what? Someone has finally spoken to me. Stigand. And you would not believe it if you saw him. He is clean-shaven and his hair trimmed. I swear, he is actually handsome . . . not as handsome as me, of course, but more than passable. That is not the most unbelievable part. Stigand is in love. With Nessa. They are going to marry and settle here in the Highlands. Do you think you will be coming out by then?"

Another time, "Answer me, witchling, or I am going to order Bolthor to come play bagpipes outside your door."

Then, "Lance misses you.

"If you don't come out soon, I'm going to go play with my chain mail . . . alone.

"I'm bored. If you're not coming out, I may have to go find a war to fight.

"You'll be sorry."

Over and over, Rurik trekked up and down the stairwell and down the corridor to Maire's door, to no avail. He was developing some really fine muscles in his calves and thighs from all that climbing . . . not that they weren't already fine.

Old John remarked in passing him one time, "The cracked bell needs no mending." When Rurik just frowned at him, he translated, "Some things cannot be fixed."

Rurik refused to believe that, even when Nessa added her opinion, "All yer talkin' shakes no barley."

Finally, Alinor took pity on him and took him aside. She was the most meddlesome person, but she was a woman. She must know things . . . things that he, a lowly man, did not. Not that he would ever refer to himself as lowly in her presence. "I have the answer," she announced without preamble. "Tell her that you love her."

"That's it? That's your great advice? Pfff! Incidentally, I think you have grown more freckles whilst I've been gone from Dragonstead. Devil's Spittle, that is what I always heard them called. Has Satan been spitting on you of late? Ouch! Why did you hit me?"

"Do it," she ordered. Hands on hips, her belly sticking out as if she'd swallowed a small boulder, she resembled a pregnant virago . . . which she was.

"What is it with you and Tykir and your insinuations that I must love Maire?"

"Tykir told you that you are in love?" Her red eyebrows arched in astonishment. Then she smiled widely. "Well, that settles it then. You must be in love."

"On, nay, that is not what I said . . . what he said . . .

what it meant. Oh, Good Lord, where are you going now?"

"Eadyth! Rain! Come quickly!" Alinor was shouting as she waddled down the corridor. "I just found out. Rurik is in love. We have a wedding to plan. Tell Cook to whip up a haggis. Tell the men to go shoot a boar. Tell Bolthor to prepare a nuptial saga. Tell that witch, Cailleach, to cast a spell on that bloody bedchamber door and make it melt away."

Rurik pressed his forehead against the door and pleaded, "Maire, you have to come out. Things are getting really, really bad."

The ladies had her back . . . and were pushing . . .

It was midafternoon, and the pounding started again.

Maire glanced up from the tapestry, which she'd been working at diligently all day, and wondered what outlandish idea Rurik would come up with this time to convince her that she should let him in.

But it wasn't Rurik this time.

"Maire, let us in, please. It's Alinor."

"And Eadyth."

"And Rain."

Did she really want to be badgered by more people who thought they knew what was best for her? On the other hand, did she want to offend her guests?

"Come in," she called out.

The three ladies swept into her bedchamber with eyebrows lifted . . . no doubt because the door hadn't been locked.

"I unlocked it this morning when I went to visit the garderobe and filch some food from the scullery."

Alinor grinned. "You didn't inform Rurik of that fact?"

"Of course not."

"Ooooh! I think I am going to like her," Alinor told the other ladies. "She is going to be soooo good for Rurik."

Eadyth and Rain nodded, also grinning.

"I must tell you, right off, if you are here to plead Rurik's case, forget it."

"Would we do that?" The three put palms to their chests to indicate their innocence. "The dolt does not deserve you," their spokesperson, Alinor, said.

Well, that was correct. Rurik didn't deserve her, but she wasn't sure she liked Alinor stating that fact . . . or calling him a dolt. "I want naught to do with the man."

"I can understand that," Eadyth said. "How could he be so insensitive?"

"Or cruel?" Rain added.

"Or thickheaded?" Alinor further added.

The ladies circled behind her to examine her tapestry.

"Oh, Maire, it is exquisite!" Rain declared and touched the cloth lovingly.

"I wish I had such a skill with needles," Eadyth agreed on a sigh. "Alas, my talents lie more with bees . . . not so fine or feminine a talent."

Maire started to protest because she had heard of the marvelous honey and mead Eadyth produced and sold, not to mention her unusual timekeeping candles, but before the words could leave her tongue, Rain was speaking. "I am a good doctor . . . there is no denying that . . . but so much of my life is involved with sadness and death. I have always wished I could create beauty." She inhaled and exhaled loudly with regret, then asked, "Is that you and Jamie and Rurik? What a lovely family you will make!"

Maire was almost done with the tapestry, and it was true . . . there was no hiding the fact that the male figure was Rurik. She couldn't have done it any other way. But a family? Nay, that would never be. For some reason, she had felt a need to complete the work, though, like a rite she must perform to put an end to her fantasy. Thereafter, it would be a reminder to her of foolish woman notions that could never be.

"You must come to Dragonstead sometime . . . in the spring or summer when it is loveliest . . . and make a tapestry for me of Tykir's beloved home," Alinor urged.

"Oh, really, I cannot foresee any time when I—"

"Alinor! Must you always think so fast? My brain cannot react so quickly. I would like Maire to do a tapestry of Eirik and me at Ravenshire with our entire family. Would that be too many figures for you, Maire?" Without waiting for Maire to answer, Eadyth tapped her chin pensively. "Mayhap she could go to Dragonstead in the springtime, then come to Ravenshire in the fall." She turned to Maire, who was dumbfounded by these requests. Did they not understand that once they left Scotland, she would have no connection with them, because Rurik would have no connection to her . . . other than through Jamie?

Blessed Mary, she was getting a pain in the head. "Oh, I couldn't," Maire said. "I have too much work to do here at *Beinne Breagha*. And, besides, the tapestry is just idle work. I have more important things to engage in than such frivolity."

"Frivolity!" the three ladies exclaimed as one.

Rain patted her on the shoulder. "There is naught frivolous about creating beauty."

"That's what Rurik said."

"He did?" Alinor cocked her head as if pondering a great puzzle. "Perchance the dolt has promise, after all . . . deep down."

"I have the perfect answer," Rain announced.

Maire hadn't realized there was a question to be answered.

"Rurik and Maire will want to winter together alone, here in the Highlands, after their wedding—"

Maire gasped. "There is not going to be a wedding . . . leastways not betwixt me and Rurik."

"—but come spring, they can take a wedding trip to the Norselands, and—"

"There is not going to be a wedding."

"—come summer, they will arrive at Ravenshire, still on the wedding journey, and then—"

"There is not going to be a wedding."

"—in the autumn, she will be in Jorvik to do my tapestry, before taking the tail end of her wedding trip back to Scotland."

"There is not going to be a wedding."

All three ladies clapped their hands together, as if they'd just settled Maire's fate. She couldn't allow that. Standing abruptly, she almost toppled her stool. Folding her arms over her chest, she asserted in as firm a voice as she could muster, "There is not going to be a wedding. I would not marry the loathsome lout now if he were the last man on earth. And that is final!"

"Really?" Eadyth inquired. "Well, I can understand that. He is a loathsome lout."

"But then, all men are loathsome louts at one time or another," Rain pointed out.

" 'Tis true. 'Tis true," Alinor concurred. "I recall the time Tykir thought he could win me over with feathers."

"Feathers?" Maire choked out.

Alinor rolled her eyes. "Yea. In the bed furs."

Maire almost swallowed her tongue at that mind picture.

"Of course, that was after the lackwit kidnapped me and delivered me to the king of Norway, just because he thought I was a witch and had put a curse on the king's manpart, causing it to take a right turn." She grinned after delivering that long-winded description of one of her husband's doltish acts.

Aye, Maire was going to swallow her tongue, for sure.

Eadyth laughed in a way that implied she knew more of these stories and they were mirthsome, indeed. " 'Tis no worse than my Eirik. He would not bed me the first few weeks we were wed because he mistakenly thought I was an aged crone. Talk about doltish! Can you imagine that?"

Maire could not.

A wistful expression came over Rain's face, as if she were lost in memory. "I am not so old that I cannot recall the time Selik established an orphanage for me to win me back. The dolt! Did he ever ask if I wanted to adopt dozens of homeless children? Nay. He just blundered ahead."

Maire narrowed her eyes, suddenly realizing that these three ladies . . . these three *devious* ladies . . . were attempting to manipulate her.

"I am not going to marry Rurik," she asserted.

"Absolutely not," the three ladies said. Meanwhile, each pulled out lengths of yarn and began to measure her shoulders and bodice and waist and hips and shanks and arms.

"Wh-what are you doing?"

Each glanced at the other, guilty as sin, and said, "Nothing." But she heard Alinor whisper to the others, "Same size as me, except for a little more in the bodice."

Then, they all gazed at her with complete innocence.

"There is not going to be a wedding," she repeated again.

Alinor waved a hand airily.

They all sailed away then, leaving Maire with much to think on, after she locked the door behind them. Did she really hate Rurik? Did she consider his crimes unforgiveable? Hadn't she sinned against him, as well, by keeping Jamie's birth a secret for so long? Had Rurik forgiven her for that crime? Was she any less forgiving?

She straightened with resignation. All these questions were wasted exercises because, after all, the man was betrothed to another woman.

The witch offered him a proposition he couldn't refuse. Could he? . . .

"I have a deal for you. Heh, heh, heh."

Rurik had been sipping at the same cup of *uisge-beatha* for the past hour and was in no mood for more abuse from the old witch, Cailleach, but since she was the only one in the whole bloody keep willing to speak with him, he said, "What the hell!" Then he motioned for her to sit down on the bench opposite him at the table.

The witch, who was looking especially old and haggard today—she must have been imbibing one of her own ghastly brews—waved aside his offer of a drink. Instead, she sank down on the bench and got right to the point.

"I have cast the rune stones and come to the conclusion that you are no good for Maire."

"Hah! You and every other person in creation! What else is new?"

"Your sarcasm will gain you naught, boy." She studied him in the most disarming way, causing Rurik to shift uneasily. "If it's a new bairn taking seed that has ye worried, forget about that. Don' let another child be a reason fer stickin' aroun'."

"Wh-what?"

"The seed ye spilled inside Maire when makin' love in the loch . . . it did not take. Ye are free of that burden."

So, Maire was not pregnant. He didn't even bother to ask how Cailleach would know such a thing and so soon.

Lackwit that he was becoming, though, he accepted that the old witch had such talents. Rurik should have been relieved that Maire was not increasing, but, oddly, he was not.

"Go away, Cailleach. I am not in the mood for your witchly games."

"Are you in the mood for having the blue mark removed?"

That got his attention. He sat up straighter. "Can you remove the mark?"

"I can . . . if I want to."

"And what would make you want to?" Rurik suspected that he was not going to like the answer.

"A deal. You agree to leave Scotland, alone, and I will remove the blue mark."

He'd been right. He didn't like the answer. "You dislike me that much?"

"I do not dislike you at all. In truth, I rather like you. But you would not be a good man for Maire."

Rurik was insulted. He wasn't so sure he would make a good mate, either, but it was not for an old hag to tell him so.

"Oh, do not be gettin' yer bowels in an uproar," Cailleach advised. "Maire needs a stable person in her life. Someone who will stay put . . . be there for her and the boy, not only in a crisis, but for the everyday. Not a very exciting life, is it? Not like *a-Viking*, leastways."

Rurik wasn't so sure about that. Adventuring did not hold the great appeal it once had. And he had enjoyed the everyday humdrum of living at *Beinne Breagha* the short time he'd been here. Would it wax dull after a while? But, nay, thinking back on Maire's tapestry and how he'd felt viewing the scene, he suspected that boredom would not be a problem.

"And a man who is incapable of love . . . well, what kind of relationship would that be for Maire?"

"Love, love, love! I am sick to my gizzard of folks telling me that I must be in love with Maire."

Cailleach's grizzled gray eyebrows went up at his vehement response. "Who has been telling you *that?*"

"Tykir . . . Alinor . . . Eirik . . . Selik . . . Jamie . . . everyone!"

Cailleach smiled widely at him then, as if he'd given the right answer, and Rurik didn't even know what the question was.

"Down to the bone here, laddie," Cailleach said then, reaching out to shake his hand in their potential agreement. "How much do ye hate the blue mark?"

"Immensely."

"Will ye be leaving Scotland . . . in return for removal of the blue mark?"

He didn't even hesitate before pulling his hand from her bony grip. "Nay!"

"Nay?"

"Nay!" Rurik had no idea what his answer meant. He just knew that he was not trading Maire for a perfect face, and that was what Cailleach's offer meant. He didn't think he would actually stay at *Beinne Breagha*, but in the future he wanted no one to say he'd sold his integrity for the price of vanity.

The witch rose from her seat then with a secretive smile, not as unhappy as Rurik would have expected. "I hope you know what this all means. You've just given yourself the key to unlock your dilemma."

Huh? What key? What dilemma? He mulled over in his mind what the witch had been hinting at, and then he brightened with understanding. How could he have overlooked such a simple fact?

He gazed at Cailleach, who nodded at him, and murmured as she walked out, "Not as dumb as I thought he was . . . fer a Viking, that is."

A gesture to melt any woman's heart . . .

In the end, Rurik decided to resolve the impasse in the way of all Viking men. By brute force.

Maire had implied at one time that she'd like a knight in shining armor. Well, she was bloody well going to get one. The only difficulty was, the plated suit of armor he'd found in the castle guard room was not all that shiny; in fact, it was a mite rusty in spots.

But, damn, he felt good for the first time in what seemed an eternity . . . though it had only been less than a day. As a soldier, he was accustomed to aggressive action, not sitting back waiting for something to happen. Furthermore, he did not much like the mewling, pleading creature he'd become.

Yea, brute force was the best strategy. Actually, men throughout time had been resolving their dilemmas with women in much the same way. Hell, Adam had probably had to take Eve in hand a time or two also, before she got them kicked out of the Garden of Eden. Wasn't that just like a woman, by the by?

Rurik was striding from the courtyard, through the great hall, with Stigand's battle-ax over his shoulder. Who knew the damn thing was so heavy! Best he be careful of slipping or he might very well be minus a limb.

Hot springs of hell! but he was in a fine mood now that he'd resolved to settle this silly squabble with Maire. He didn't even mind that people were stopping right and left to gape at him as he clanked and creaked on his way.

Jamie halted him in his path, however, looking weepy-eyed and little boyish.

He hunkered down to the boy's level, almost whacking himself aside the head with the flat blade of the ax.

Hunkering in a suit of armor was not very easy, he discovered, and he almost fell over. Adjusting the weapon to stand like a brace on the floor, he put one hand to Jamie's drooping chin and lifted it. "What is it, son?"

"Are ye . . . are ye gonna chop off me mother's head?"

Rurik almost laughed aloud at that, except that he could tell that the boy was serious. "Of course not. I would ne'er harm yer mother . . . I told you that afore."

"Yer not?" Jamie blinked at him hopefully.

"Nay," Rurik said, straightening and patting the boy, "I'm just going to chop down her door."

Three words . . . three simple words . . .

Maire had just completed the tapestry and was putting away the needles and spare threads when she heard a loud—very loud—cracking noise at her locked door, followed immediately by another. In her surprise, she almost knocked over the entire tapestry frame.

There was a third cracking noise, which caused the door to shake on its hinges. She glanced over and saw the tip of a metal blade sticking through the wood, which immediately disappeared . . . on the backswing, she presumed.

Rurik is chopping down my door, was her first thought. Her second was, *The man is losing his mind.*

"Rurik, are you losing your mind?" she screamed over the racket.

There was blessed silence for a moment.

"Are you talking to me, Maire?" Rurik asked, followed by a muttered "Praise be to the gods!"

"Aye, I'm talking to you, dunderhead," she said, unlocking and flinging open the door before he had a chance to swing the ax again. And it was a mighty big battle-ax, she noted.

But that wasn't the most astonishing thing.

Rurik was standing before her in an old suit of armor that must have belonged to her father or one of her grandsires . . . booty stolen from some raid on Saxon or Norman lands, because Scots soldiers did not wear metal armor. He smiled at her tentatively, as if testing the waters. The visor on his metal helmet kept slipping down, though. Finally, he flipped the helmet off with exasperation and tossed it out into the corridor, where she heard it roll, then bang down the stone stairway.

She returned his smile with a frown.

Which immediately caused his smile to turn to a frown, too. "What? You don't like knights in shining armor now? Well, how was I to know that? I'm coming in."

"You'd better, unless you want an audience for your stupidity." She pointed to the corridor and stairwell, where dozens of people were crammed, trying to get a firsthand glimpse of the Viking idiot in action.

He tossed the battle-ax in their direction and everyone scampered out of the way. Then he stepped through the broken door and locked it behind him. He didn't just walk in, though. He lumbered in . . . creakily.

"There is no need to lock the door," she said.

"Yea, there is," he said, advancing on her. He stopped when he was a hairbreadth away. To her dismay . . . or perhaps not to her dismay . . . she noted the sensual flicker in his stormy blue eyes. " 'Tis past time for us to end this silly squabble." He was already beginning to peel off the armor, starting with the arm pieces.

"Silly squabble? Silly squabble?" she squeaked out, shoving his immovable metal chest. He didn't budge one speck. "This 'silly squabble' involves your betrothal to another woman . . . and your giving me the bride gift that was intended for her."

"I already told you that the amber necklet must have been intended for you. It would not have suited Theta, at all. Her eyes are brown, not green, and she much prefers crystal stones, as I recall." He stopped talking when he realized he was not helping his cause. So, he began to remove more of his armor.

Maire was disconcerted to see that he wore the flexible chain mail underneath. "Even if I accepted your explanation regarding the necklet," she said, "there is still the matter of your betrothal." She hated the fact that tears rose in her eyes; she had thought the well had run dry with all her sobbing.

He waved a hand airily. "The betrothal is no longer an issue. I have decided that the best course is for you and me to wed." Rurik appeared dumbfounded at his own words, as if they had just slipped out of their own accord.

She stared at him, insulted by his halfhearted proposal. "Bigamy now? You would practice bigamy?"

"Bigamy?" he repeated dumbly. "Oh, you mean the *more danico*. Nay, I will not indulge in that Norse practice of multiple wives."

"Speak plainly, Viking." She narrowed her eyes at him.

"Theta agreed to wed with me only if I would have the blue mark removed. Since that is no longer an option, the betrothal is invalid. I will inform Theta of that fact by courier . . . Jostein and John, to be specific."

"Why is removal of the blue mark no longer an option?" She was beginning to feel as thickheaded as the doublespeaking Norseman standing before her.

He gave her a look that said she should already know the answer. "Because Cailleach offered me a deal. She would remove the blue mark if I would give you up and leave Scotland forever. And I said nay."

"You said *nay?*" She backed up and hit her shoulders against the bedpost, overcome with amazement. Rurik had chosen her, over his own renowned vanity? How could that be?

"Of course. What else did you think I would say?" he asked, affronted. He had all the armor off now. "There is another thing, Maire. Cailleach told me that you are not carrying my child . . . you know, from our mating in the loch. I'm sorry. I mean, I'm sorry if you're sorry."

He's not leaving Scotland?

He's choosing me over his vanity?

He's sorry that I'm not pregnant?

Just then, Rurik noticed that her tapestry was finished. He walked over to examine it more closely. For a second, Maire could have sworn she saw an expression of intense yearning in his eyes as he touched the cloth, reverently. "Maire, dost think that the fantasy could become reality?"

She put a hand to her mouth, afraid to believe what he was saying, afraid not to believe, as well. "Rurik, stop speaking in riddles. What is it you are trying to say?"

He mumbled something under his breath, and Maire could scarce breathe for what she thought she heard. His face was flushed and he seemed unable to meet her questioning gaze, even as he walked back to her.

"Wh-what did you say?"

He raised his head and made direct eye contact with her. He looked so bleak and unsure of himself. *Rurik? Unsure of himself?* That, in itself, was an amazing happenstance.

"I love you."

Three simple words. That's all. But they were everything to Maire, who began to weep in earnest now.

"You're crying? I knew it! I knew it! They were the wrong words to say."

"Oh, Rurik . . ." She put her face in her hands and sobbed uncontrollably. "They were the right words to say. The perfect words."

"But you are weeping," he protested, coming up and putting his hands on her shoulders, drawing her into his embrace. And, oh, it felt so good to be in his arms once again.

"Happiness," she blubbered out.

"Aaaahh," he said dubiously. "Tears of happiness."

"Do you think you could say it again?" she asked, drawing back to stare up at his face.

"Well, I don't know." He pretended to consider. "They were a long time in coming, and I do not know if I can manage them twice."

She smacked him on the shoulder with an open palm.

He winced, though he probably didn't even feel her smack. "If you insist," he said, and his face went suddenly serious. "I love you, dearling. Witch of my heart. Sweet Maire of the Moors."

Maire nigh swooned at his charmingly expressed sentiments.

"Dost think you could say the words back to me?" he inquired in an oddly vulnerable voice. He looked so adorable as he made the request.

"I love you, heartling. Viking of my dreams. Fierce Rurik of the Beloved Blue Mark."

Her words must have pleased him, too, because Rurik kissed her then, and it was a kiss like no other . . . a kiss for all time.

Later, after they'd sealed their love in other ways amidst Rurik's bed furs, he mentioned something about bringing out the chain mail. But Maire had other ideas. She asked him, softly, as she nuzzled against his chest,

"Ah, Rurik, I don't suppose you know where to get an array of . . . uhm . . . feathers?"

And that is the story of how Rurik the Vain became known as Rurik the Scots Viking. In fact, to no one's surprise, Bolthor composed a saga about it, which he recited to one and all at the wild Viking/Scottish wedding held at *Beinne Breagha* a few short days later:

Love is a fiercesome weapon,
Stronger than lance or bow,
It can bring a man low,
And raise him on high,
All in a single blow.
Rurik was the strongest warrior,
Feared and lauded by all,
But when it came to it,
A mere Scottish witch
Was his downfall.
The gods have a sense of humor,
On that everyone is agreed,
Why else would they have created
Man's love of woman
Save that they needed a joke on high?

READER LETTER

Dear Reader:

There is nothing more compelling than a Viking . . . unless it's a Scottish Viking. And, yes, there were Vikings in Scotland as early as the tenth century.

The first Norsemen came to Scotland before the ninth century . . . at first, as plunderers, later as settlers, seeking new lands to cultivate since their native Scandinavia was becoming overcrowded and rife with politics. The primary sites they homed in on were the Hebrides, and the Orkney and Shetland islands, because they could be easily reached by sea from their homeland. When they settled on the mainland, it was primarily in narrow coastal areas, unlike the broad regions they terrorized and settled in Britain.

Although I have written many Viking novels, this is my only venture into Scotland. If I thought writing early medieval novels about Vikings in Britain or Norway was difficult, I was stunned by all the complications that cropped up in this Highlands setting. I love Scottish novels, but, believe me, Scotland has a totally different language, culture, geography, and people, despite being next-door neighbor to Britain.

With that in mind, and for the sake of my modern readers, I have taken some literary and historical licenses and provide these disclaimers:

(1) **Scotland.** There is disagreement as to when Scotland first took on that name, rather than Pictland. I have sided with those historians who claim the kingdom began to be called Scotland by the end of the term of Constantine, who died in 952.

(2) **Campbells.** In Gaelic, Clan Campbell followers were called Claim ua Duibhne, after Duncan mac Duibhne, and the name did not actually change to Campbell till the thirteenth century. Campbells generally settled in Argyll in western Scotland. I have placed this small fictional subgroup of the Campbell clan earlier in history and in another geographical area.

(3) **Language.** Just as modern readers would be unable to understand the Medieval English spoken in Britain at that time, they would be equally unable to understand Gaelic, which was the primary language of Scotland during the tenth century, not the Scots language, which is really a lowland form of twelfth-century English—actually several regional dialects evolving out of twelfth-century English.

(4) **Clans.** Clan names, per se, were not used in the tenth century. There were groups of people similar to clans, and the word *clan/clann* was used during this period, and earlier, since it means child or children, but it wasn't used as part of a proper name. Actually, if I were going to be strictly correct (which I choose not to be) the "mac" should be dropped as being redundant; therefore, a person would not say Clan MacGregor or Clan MacNab, but instead Clan Gregor or Clan Nab.

(5) **Names.** In Gaelic oral tradition, a man was better known by his father's and grandfather's name than by his place of origin or other descriptions. Modern readers would get a headache with these often

lengthy, hard-to-pronounce Gaelic designations, which changed with each generation and with women who often took on their husband's name. For example, Alasdair MacIain MhicCaluim was Alexander, son of John, grandson of Calum. ("The Evolution of the Clans": <http://www.highlandnet.com/info/misc/clans.html>)

In Scotland, as in many other countries of that time, people were just given a single descriptive name, such as John Black-teeth, Robert of Red-hair, Rurik the Warrior, Mary the Dairymaid, or Kenneth the Blacksmith. You can see how cumbersome this could become in a novel, especially if there were more than one John or Robert or Rurik or Mary or Kenneth.

Also a man's name might be different depending on whom he was addressing. For example, the same person might be John Duncanson to Scots, and Eroin mac Donnchaidh in the isles, or Johannes filius when speaking or writing Latin.

Confused enough yet?

It goes against my journalistic background to have to provide these disclaimers. Historical accuracy is extremely important to me in my work. But then I have to remind myself, these are romance novels. In all my Viking novels, I have created a fantasy Norse world against a historical backdrop, and in each of them the most important elements are the romance, the humor, and the sizzle (in that order).

In essence, *The Blue Viking* represents the way I imagine history could have been lived, not necessarily the way that it was.

A special thanks goes out to fellow author Melanie Jackson, who was gracious in helping me with some of the Gaelic and Scottish history.

As always, I am interested in knowing what you readers think of my Vikings. I can be reached at:

Sandra Hill
PO Box 604
State College, PA 16804
shill733@aol.com
www.sandrahill.net

GLOSSARY

Arisaid—a large length of wool, the female version of a pladd (see below) which was little more than a large cloak which wrapped artfully about the body, down to the heels. It was fastened at the center of the chest with a brooch and at the waist with a belt.

Bairn—a child.

Bannock—a flat cake made of oatmeal, barley, or other grains, often baked on a griddle.

Berserker—an ancient Norse warrior who fought in a frenzied rage during battle.

Blindfuller—drunk as a lord.

Braies—slim pants worn by men, breeches.

Brogues—durable, comfortable, low-heeled leather shoes; or a strong regional accent.

Burns—brooks or rivulets.

Danegeld—in medieval times, especially in Britain, a tribute or tax paid to Vikings; in other words, you pay or we plunder.

Dirk—a dagger.

Druids—a pre-Christian religious order among the ancient Celts.

Drukkinn (various spellings)—drunk, in Old Norse.

Ell—a measure, usually of cloth, equaling 45 inches.

Haggis—a pudding made of the minced heart, liver, and other organs of a sheep or calf, minced with suet, oatmeal, onions, and seasonings, then boiled in the stomach of the slaughtered animal.

Hnefatafl—a board game played by the Vikings.

Housecarls—troops assigned to a king's or lord's household on a longtime, sometimes permanent basis.

Jorvik—Viking word for Viking-Age York, known by the Saxons and Romans as Eoforic.

Léine—a long, full shirt down to the knees, resembling an undertunic, often of a saffron yellow color.

Loch—a lake, an arm of the sea similar to a fjord.

Midden—a refuse dump.

Mjollnir—the name of Thor's hammer.

Neeps—turnips.

Nithing—a person of no worth, less than nothing.

Norns of Fate—three wise old women who destined everybody's Fate.

Northumbria—one of the Anglo-Saxon kingdoms, bordered by the English kingdoms to the south and in the north and northwest by the Scots, Cumbrians, and Strathclyde Welsh.

Pladd (or brat)—a large length of fabric like a sort of blanket, which was fastened on the shoulder with a brooch, like a mantle, looped under the sword arm for better maneuverability, and secured at the waist with a leather belt. Men usually wore it over the léine or long shirt which left the legs exposed.

Reaving—robbing, raiding for plunder, usually cattle or sheep.

Sennight—one week.

Skald—a poet.

Soapstone—also called steatite, a soft rock composed primarily of talc, often used for hearths, tabletops, carved ornaments, etc.

Tinker—an itinerant mender of pots and pans.

Trews—close-fitting trousers, often tartan.

Uisge-beatha—Water of Life, early name for Scotch whiskey.

Valkyries—Odin's female warriors who led valiant fighting men after their death in battle to Valhalla, the hall of the slain.

Wergild (various spellings)—a man's worth, paid in reparation for a death or some crime.

Can't get enough of *USA Today* and
New York Times bestselling
author Sandra Hill?
Turn the page for glimpses of her amazing books. From cowboys to Vikings, Navy SEALs to Southern bad boys, every one of Sandra's books has her unique blend of passion, creativity, and unparalled wit.

Welcome to the World of Sandra Hill!

The Viking Takes a Knight

For John of Hawk's Lair, the unexpected appearance of a beautiful woman at his door is always welcome. Yet the arrival of this alluring Viking woman, Ingrith Sigrundottir—with her enchanting smile and inviting curves—is different . . . for she comes accompanied by a herd of unruly orphans. And Ingrith needs more than the legendary knight's hospitality; she needs protection. For among her charges is a small boy with a claim to the throne—a dangerous distinction when murderous King Edgar is out hunting for Viking blood.

A man of passion, John will keep them safe—but in exchange, he wants something very dear indeed: Ingrith's heart, to be taken with the very first meeting of their lips . . .

Viking in Love

Caedmon of Larkspur was the most loathsome lout Breanne had ever encountered. When she arrived at his castle with her sisters, they were greeted by an estate gone wild, while Caedmon laid abed after a night of ale. But Breanne must endure, as they are desperately in need of protection . . . and he is quite handsome.

After nine long months in the king's service, all Caedmon wanted was peace, not five Viking princesses running about his keep. And the fiery redhead who burst into his chamber was the worst of them all. He should kick her out, but he has a far better plan for Breanne of Stoneheim—one that will leave her a Viking in lust.

The Reluctant Viking

The self-motivation tape was supposed to help Ruby Jordan solve her problems, not create new ones. Instead, she was lulled into an era of hard-bodied warriors and fair maidens. But the world ten centuries in the past didn't prove to be all mead and mirth. Even as Ruby tried to update medieval times, she had to deal with a Norseman whose view of women was stuck in the Dark Ages. And what was worse, brawny Thork had her husband's face, habits, and desire to avoid Ruby. Determined not to lose the same man twice, Ruby planned a bold seduction that would conquer the reluctant Viking—and make him an eager captive of her love.

The Outlaw Viking

As tall and striking as the Valkyries of legend, Dr. Rain Jordan was proud of her Norse ancestors despite their warlike ways. But she can't believe it when she finds herself on a nightmarish battlefield, forced to save the barbarian of her dreams.

He was a wild-eyed warrior whose deadly sword could slay a dozen Saxons with a single swing, yet Selik couldn't control the saucy wench from the future. If Selik wasn't careful, the stunning siren was sure to capture his heart and make a warrior of love out of **The Outlaw Viking**.

The Tarnished Lady

Banished from polite society, Lady Eadyth of Hawk's Lair spent her days hidden under a voluminous veil, tending her bees. But when her lands are threatened, Lady Eadyth sought a husband to offer her the protection of his name.

Notorious for loving—and leaving—the most beautiful damsels in the land, Eirik of Ravenshire was England's most virile bachelor. Yet when the mysterious lady offered him a vow of chaste matrimony in exchange for revenge against his most hated enemy, Eirik couldn't refuse. But the lusty knight's plans went awry when he succumbed to the sweet sting of the tarnished lady's love.

The Bewitched Viking

Even fierce Norse warriors have bad days. 'Twas enough to drive a sane Viking mad, the things Tykir Thorksson was forced to do—capturing a red-headed virago, putting up with the flock of sheep that follows her everywhere, chasing off her bumbling brothers. But what could a man expect from the sorceress who had put a kink in the King of Norway's most precious body part? If that wasn't bad enough, Tykir was beginning to realize he wasn't at all immune to the enchantment of brash red hair and freckles. Perhaps he could reverse the spell and hold her captive, not with his mighty sword, but with a Viking man's greatest magic: a wink and smile.

The Blue Viking

For Rurik the Viking, life has not been worth living since he left Maire of the Moors. Oh, it's not that he misses her fiery red tresses or kissable lips. Nay, it's the embarrassing blue zigzag tattoo she put on his face after their one wild night of loving. For a fierce warrior who prides himself on his immense height, his expertise in bedsport, and his well-toned muscles, this blue streak is the last straw. In the end, he'll bring the witch to heel, or die trying. Mayhap he'll even beg her to wed . . . so long as she can promise he'll no longer be . . . **The Blue Viking.**

The Viking's Captive

(originally titled MY FAIR VIKING)

Tyra, Warrior Princess. She is too tall, too loud, too fierce to be a good catch. But her ailing father has decreed that her four younger sisters—delicate, mild-mannered, and beautiful—cannot be wed 'til Tyra consents to take a husband. And then a journey to save her father's life brings Tyra face to face with Adam the Healer. A god in human form, he's tall, muscled, perfectly proportioned. Too bad Adam refuses to fall in with her plans—so what's a lady to do but truss him up, toss him over her shoulder, and sail off into the sunset to live happily ever after.

A Tale of Two Vikings

Toste and Vagn Ivarsson are identical Viking twins, about to face Valhalla together, following a tragic battle, or maybe something even more tragic: being separated for the first time in their thirty and one years. Alas, even the bravest Viking must eventually leave his best buddy behind and do battle with that most fearsome of all opponents—the love of his life. And what if that love was Helga the Homely, or Lady Esme, the world's oldest novice nun?

A Tale of Two Vikings will give you twice the tears, twice the sizzle, and twice the laughter . . . and make you wish for your very own Viking.

The Last Viking

He was six feet, four inches of pure, unadulterated male. He wore nothing but a leather tunic, and he was standing in Professor Meredith Foster's living room. The medieval historian told herself he was part of a practical joke, but with his wide gold belt, ancient language, and callused hands, the brawny stranger seemed so . . . authentic. And as he helped her fulfill her grandfather's dream of re-creating a Viking ship, he awakened her to dreams of her own. Until she wondered if the hand of fate had thrust her into the loving arms of . . . **The Last Viking**.

Truly, Madly Viking

A *Viking named Joe? Jorund Ericsson is a tenth-*century Viking warrior who lands in a modern mental hospital. Maggie McBride is the lucky psychologist who gets to "treat" the gorgeous Norseman, whom she mistakenly calls Joe.

You've heard of *One Flew Over the Cuckoo's Nest*. But how about *A Viking Flew Over the Cuckoo's Nest*? The question is: Who's the cuckoo in this nest? And why is everyone laughing?

The Very Virile Viking

Magnus Ericsson is a simple man. He loves the smell of fresh-turned dirt after springtime plowing. He loves the feel of a soft woman under him in the bed furs. He loves the heft of a good sword in his fighting arm.

But, Holy Thor, what he does not relish is the bothersome brood of children he's been saddled with. Or the mysterious happenstance that strands him in a strange new land—the kingdom of *Holly Wood*. Here is a place where the folks think he is an *act-whore* (whatever that is), and the woman of his dreams—a winemaker of all things—fails to accept that he is her soul mate . . . a man of exceptional talents, not to mention . . . **A Very Virile Viking.**

Wet & Wild

What do you get when you cross a Viking with a Navy SEAL? A warrior with the fierce instincts of the past and the rigorous training of America's most elite fighting corps? A totally buff hero-in-the-making who hasn't had a woman in roughly a thousand years? A dyed-in-the-wool romantic with a hopeless crush? Whatever you get, women everywhere can't wait to meet him, and his story is guaranteed to be . . . **Wet & Wild**.

Hot & Heavy

In and out, that's the goal as Lt. Ian MacLean prepares for his special ops mission. He leads a team of highly trained Navy SEALs, the toughest, buffest fighting men in the world and he has nothing to lose. Madrene comes from a time a thousand years before he was born, and she has no idea she's landed in the future. After tying him up, the beautiful shrew gives him a tongue-lashing that makes a drill sergeant sound like a kindergarten teacher. Then she lets him know she has her own special way of dealing with over-confident males, and things get . . . **Hot & Heavy**.

Frankly, My Dear . . .

Lost in the Bayou . . . Selene had three great passions: men, food, and *Gone with the Wind*. But the glamorous model always found herself starving—for both nourishment and affection. Weary of the petty world of high fashion, she headed to New Orleans for one last job before she began a new life. Little did she know that her new life would include a brand-new time—about 150 years ago! Selene can't get her fill of the food—or an alarmingly handsome man. Dark and brooding, James Baptiste was the only lover she gave a damn about. And with God as her witness, she vowed never to go without the man she loved again.

Sweeter Savage Love

The stroke of surprisingly gentle hands, the flash of fathomless blue eyes, the scorch of white-hot kisses . . . Once again, Dr. Harriet Ginoza was swept away into rapturous fantasy. The modern psychologist knew the object of her desire was all she should despise, yet time after time, she lost herself in visions of a dangerously handsome rogue straight out of a historical romance. Harriet never believed that her dream lover would cause her any trouble, but then a twist of fate cast her back to the Old South and she met him in the flesh. To her disappointment, Etienne Baptiste refused to fulfill any of her secret wishes. If Harriet had any hope of making her amorous dreams become passionate reality, she'd have to seduce this charmer with a sweeter savage love than she'd imagined possible . . . and savor every minute of it.

The Love Potion

Fame and fortune are surely only a swallow away when Dr. Sylvie Fontaine discovers a chemical formula guaranteed to attract the opposite sex. Though her own love life is purely hypothetical, the shy chemist's professional future is assured . . . as soon as she can find a human guinea pig. But bad boy Lucien LeDeux—best known as the Swamp Lawyer—is more than she can handle even before he accidentally swallowed a love potion disguised in a jelly bean. When the dust settles, Luc and Sylvie have the answers to some burning questions—can a man die of testosterone overload? Can a straight-laced female lose every single one of her inhibitions?—and they learn that old-fashioned romance is still the best catalyst for love.

Love Me Tender

Once upon a time, in a magic kingdom, there lived a handsome prince. Prince Charming, he was called by one and all. And to this land came a gentle princess. You could say she was Cinderella . . . Wall Street Cinderella. Okay, if you're going to be a stickler for accuracy, in this fairy tale the kingdom is Manhattan. But there's magic in the Big Apple, isn't there? And maybe he can be Prince Not-So-Charming at times, and "gentle" isn't the first word that comes to mind when thinking of this princess. But they're looking for happily ever after just the same—and they're going to get it.

Desperado

Mistaken for a notorious bandit and his infamously scandalous mistress, L.A. lawyer Rafe Santiago and Major Helen Prescott found themselves on the wrong side of the law. In a time and place where rules had no meaning, Helen found Rafe's hard, bronzed body strangely comforting, and his piercing blue eyes left her all too willing to share his bedroll. His teasing remarks made her feel all woman, and she was ready to throw caution to the wind if she could spend every night in the arms of her very own . . . **Desperado**.

NEW YORK TIMES BESTSELLING AUTHOR

SANDRA HILL

Viking in Love

978-0-06-167249-8

Viking princess Breanne and her four sisters are forced to flee to the castle of Caedmon of Larkspur. The Viking warrior is a distant relative and his home is very much in need of a feminine hand, but Breanne never expected he would try to lure her into his bed.

The Viking Takes a Knight

978-0-06-167350-4

All Ingrith wants is refuge for herself and a group of orphans from a vicious Saxon commander. John of Hawk's Lair longs for peace and quiet, not a nagging wife and noisy children. But despite their differences, an uncontrollable attraction sparks between him and Ingrith.

The Viking's Captive

978-0-06-201908-0

A journey to save her father's life brings Tyra face to face with Adam the healer. He's tall, muscled, and perfectly proportioned. Here's the physician who could cure her father, and the lover who could finally seduce her to his bed furs.

At Avon Books, we know your passion for romance—once you finish one of our novels, you find yourself wanting more.

May we tempt you with . . .

- **Excerpts** from our upcoming releases.
- Entertaining **extras**, including authors' personal photo albums and book lists.
- Behind-the-scenes **scoop** on your favorite characters and series.
- **Sweepstakes** for the chance to win free books, romantic getaways, and other fun prizes.
- Writing **tips** from our authors and editors.
- **Blog** with our authors and find out why they love to write romance.
- **Exclusive content** that's not contained within the pages of our novels.

Join us at
www.avonbooks.com